The Body by the Shore

The Body by the Shore

Tabish Khair

HarperCollins *Publishers* India

First published in India by HarperCollins *Publishers* 2022
4th Floor, Tower A, Building No. 10, Phase II, DLF Cyber City,
Gurugram, Haryana – 122002
www.harpercollins.co.in

2 4 6 8 10 9 7 5 3 1

PISBN: 978-93-5629-285-7
EISBN: 978-93-5629-290-1

Typeset in 11/14.5 Arno Pro at
Manipal Technologies Limited, Manipal

Printed and bound at
Thomson Press (India) Ltd

For

Seb Doubinsky,

and the shared endeavor of staying alive in "Viborg City".

Statutory Warning: This is not news or fake news; it is a work of fiction.

The Competitive Exclusion Principle: "Complete competitors cannot exist".

Contents

Part I:

MACROBIA

1
Merezhkovsky

It is less than three months ago that we arrived and were installed in a room of our own. Kurt led me in, as he had into that five-star hotel in London. My head was still swimming with London. The shops, the restaurants, our suite. What were you imagining, gal, I ask myself now: a honeymoon? But this was not London. This was an oil rig in the middle of nowhere. I remember, I looked around from the helicopter as it was landing and exclaimed: God, Kurt, it's nowhere. "Snowhere," Kurt corrected me. He likes punning. I realized later that despite the cold, there would be no snow on the rig. Ice sometimes, on the metal outside, but no snow. I would have preferred snow. I had often imagined it.

We are in what I call the guest corridor or the luxury corridor. Below us there lie the company men's rooms, the sealed sections, some open space where the dismantled derrick had once stood, and, of course, the galley. There are floors under the galley too, going all the way down to what Kurt calls the module deck and the drill floor. But they are closed; the doors locked or welded shut. Much of the rig is shut. You wouldn't want to go to the levels below, Kurt had replied when I asked on my first day here. That is where they did all the real work, the drill floor and the module deck. The place is smeared with dangerous chemicals, he had laughed. It is only now that I wonder how he knew so much about this oil rig when he claimed, the night he talked me into this, to be coming here for the first time? A new job, he said. Someone at the party. Great salary, Sugar.

But I never ask questions anymore. I often talk to myself, like now, silently. Sometimes I say things to Maman. In my head, though. Kurt says I mumble under my breath. He jokes that it is the first sign of insanity on the rigs. But questions, no, never, or nothing significant in any case. I have seen and heard things that make me keep my questions to myself. I do not even enter anything significant in the diary I had bought in London. It has thick creamy paper and came with a pen and inkstand, fitted into a papier mache box with Victorian illustrations on it. I had bought it for the pen, as I had never held anything other than ballpoints and felt pens in my life. It is mostly empty. There are detailed entries for two days in London and the first three days here. After that? After that, the entries get guarded, scant, and then the personal remarks disappear. The last observation is about how the blue of the sky vanishes into the milky white of the horizon, and that is from my sixth or seventh afternoon here. After that, I have seen other colors in the sky, sometimes incandescent conflagrations, as if the sky was alive; I have seen pure light seeping out like molten silver through cracks in gray clouds. This is the North. But I have not jotted them down. Instead, my diary has become a housekeeping account: what to order, what might be missing in the pantry that is my charge. Look at the entry for today: "Salt running out, max a week's supply left. Order minced meat, parsley, ginger. Green vegetables, if possible. Maybe stuff for some Caribbean dish, just for a break? Check the wine in the bar and cabinet. Note: Guest wanted a chardonnay yesterday and there wasn't any. He would not try the Riesling: too sweet, he said."

The very next day after our arrival there was the chopping of helicopters again, deafening if you are outside in the cold, the churning of the water around the rig, and the "guests" were here. You can hear the chopper coming from a distance; their noise is so different from the breaking of the waves, the cries of gulls and the rush of the wind that we get here. You get used to all those natural sounds, deafening though they are when you arrive, and after a night or two, there is almost a kind of loud silence. But the alien, mechanical noise of helicopters or powerboats cuts through this loud silence. Now I know that the guests always come and leave in twos and threes by helicopters, landing on one of the two helidecks, each flat like a pancake, in the upraised North and South corners of this giant metal box in the sea. They use only one of the decks. It seems to me that the other, on the abandoned half of the rig, is not in operation. On occasion, we have powerboats docking too, bringing the supplies, some ordered by me; other things too, company men, whatever, but never the guests, the experts. Sometimes a boat docks at night and Kurt goes out, but I am told to stay in the room. I don't know what those night boats bring or remove, but once, two months ago, I heard shouts. They stopped abruptly.

There is one man in charge of all this. His name is Vyachislav Mikhailov. Kurt calls him Michael. What is his job? I asked Kurt ages ago. He is the tool pusher, Kurt had laughed in answer. What is that? The drilling manager on a rig, he replied. Those days, I still asked him questions and he answered. But, I observed, they are not drilling on this rig anymore, are they? Kurt had told me it was an abandoned rig, turned into an adventure resort by a company, and they were employing us—him and me—to cater to the guests. Of course, they cannot drill here, Sugar, he replied. Do you see any derricks or booms anywhere? I just call him that because he once worked on active rigs. He used to be a drilling manager. Well, I said, his voice does drill into my ears. I don't know why I said that. It is a low voice, actually, almost syrupy. But it gives me the creeps: perhaps because it is the voice of a politician in the body of a soldier.

How did Kurt know so much about Mr. Watch, I wonder now? I mean, if this is his first trip too? What do you really know about Kurt, gal, I ask myself, as I chop and clean in the plush kitchen. What do you know except what he has told you? Maman's daughter, you, gal, I scoff at myself. Unexpectedly, I start laughing until tears stream down my cheeks. I look around. One of the men is there on their side of the galley, now looking at me through the glass partition. I hold up an onion, and laugh a bit more, wiping my eyes. He shrugs, makes a wry face and turns away. I can hear him think: women!

I was finishing high school and working all the time for my cooking lessons and elocution classes—I knew I would get nowhere in the real world with a Caribbean accent—when I met Kurt. It feels like years ago, but how much time has passed? Six, seven months? I thought he owned the beachside villa in which he lived. It was not just the clothes he wore; it was the ease with which he lounged, it was his aura of privilege. I had cleaned villas; I had come to recognize that aura. I thought he was a rich American, living in St. Martin for part of the year. It was only after I started going to bed with him that I realized he was only the caretaker! Though, maybe, even that was a lie. Onions, I think.

All those billionaire villas—with their swimming pools and security cameras—had caretakers. The owners had too many houses all over the world. No amount of wealth can alter the fact that you may be only in one place at one time. It might come, but they haven't managed to do that yet. Hence, they hired someone, usually a man, sometimes a couple (but never with children), to live in the villas for the nine, ten, maybe eleven months that they could not vacation there. And to organize their stays and parties when they were there. But Kurt was not like the caretakers I had met; he was like the owners.

I met Kurt by the sea on the Dutch side of St. Martin. St. Maarten, I should say. I was visiting the sea. I remember that phrase "visiting the sea" from a poem we had in school, where the poet, it was a woman, goes out for a walk by the sea with her dog and mermaids come out to look at her. I always loved reading; it took me out of my little island.

No, I didn't have a dog, not unless you count the strays that tagged after you at the beach and had to be kept at an arm's distance, because they could have rabies. I was out jogging. Early morning, before school. Jogging on the sand is the best thing for you; it shapes your calf and thigh muscles better than jogging on solid ground. You need to jog less for better results, and it is more pleasant too. I must have been lost in thoughts and run too close to a stray because suddenly there was this big mongrel growling at me. I say mongrel, but it looked well-fed and groomed, almost like an Alsatian. I froze. The worst you can do is run. And I had not noticed it early enough to pick up a stone or a branch. There was nothing within reach. The dog moved towards me, one paw at a time, head down, like a wolf stalking its prey. Very theatrically, a dog acting its part. I inched away to a spot further back where half-burnt branches and stones had been left behind from a barbeque, but the mongrel snarled and jumped. I managed to dodge and kick it away, but it did not run. I wished I was not wearing soft canvas shoes; I have strong legs, and a hard-shod shoe would have taught the cur a lesson. Instead, it circled me, wary but aggressive. That is when Kurt came into my life. Wielding a large stick, he interposed himself between me and the stray, and gave the beast a dramatic whack that was more sound than effect.

As the dog yelped, jumped almost as if it was doing a circus loop backwards, and then slunk away from the beach, I turned to Kurt to thank him, but Kurt spoke first. He always does. Words come easily to him, at least in speech, because he seems to find it impossible to write the novels that he is always planning. Or was until we came to this rig. Here he always seems to be talking to Mr. Watch and his cronies, serious talk I can never fully overhear, very little alcohol, no drugs at all. Come to think of it, I have never seen him read a book. That would have assured your new boyfriend, Maman. He hated me for reading books. Among other things.

"M'lady," Kurt said on that first meeting, "Not a word against canis lupus familiaris. Had it not been for its lupine intervention, I would have languished on this lovely beach, watching you jog past, as I have many mornings until today, wondering what Venus was doing by the waves, but unable to approach, alas, unable to approach for I am a mere mortal, entirely lacking the brawn of Aries or the beauty of Adonis." That is the way Kurt speaks at times. But he does it with a gleam in his sky-blue eyes and a half-smile that make it seem more than the junk it is, as if he was composing a poem for you on the spot. There was a time I used to find it impressive. It sounded like book-learning to me, something I had struggled to obtain all my life, against the inclinations of my family and my island, where books are considered foreign luxuries. I had struggled even against my own self, for I had always been the kind of girl who was good at sports, winning races without even trying and, what is worse, looking good, many said gorgeous, while doing so.

I knew the villas on that part of the beach, as I had worked part-time as a cleaning woman in villas in the neighbourhood for at least two years. One of my odd jobs. It was the only way I could keep studying and earn money for the lessons that I was taking on the side. The lessons that would take me out of the island! Both you, Maman, and your current boyfriend—one of those no good beach bums you always fall for, who demand "respeck" from me—were against me studying further. Get a regular job, Maman told me, as if her having a regular job in a local fish factory all her life had made any difference. They laid her off during the pandemic, no pay for nine or ten months: "I work for dem all mi life," she went about saying, shaking her head in disbelief. It made me miss a whole year of schooling. And then they called her back when they needed her again, employing her on a lower salary! And you went, Maman, grateful to have the job back! What difference did a regular job, as you call it, make? To you, that is; your men have lived off you.

All except your father, Maman would concede; but I never met my father, and I doubt that he could have been any different. What kind of man would have Nancy as his surname? Yes, that is my surname, for Maman has faithfully given her children the surnames of their fathers, so that not one of us shares the same surname! The fathers have been good at coming and going. Maman's partly to blame. She sends out the wrong vibes. It attracts grifters from miles around, that and her dark golden skin, which she passed on to me. We would look like sisters if she did not straighten her hair, something I refuse to do. Her features are like mine: given the angle, they reveal a glimpse of everything that has been on those islands—Indian, Chinese, African, European—so that she attracts loafers from all these communities and many in-between. Stop dreaming, drop your fancy ideas, Missy, quit high school, Maman would tell me, get a reg'lar job. Her new boyfriend recommended marriage. "Get married, gal, you wan go all overripe an' rotten like a forgotten mango?" That is the only thing men ever wanted me to do: get married. Fuck'ry!

I had seen Kurt that season lounging around outside his villa, mostly alone but sometimes with others like him. He was new to the island. So were the guests at the villa. I had not seen them before. They were mostly white, but even the occasional black guests were like Kurt, clad in the same trendy beachwear, negligently handling the same expensive electronic stuff. I am sure all of them had got that expensive gene-vac that, they say, makes you immune to all kinds of flus forever. And he would be at home with them, one of them, which is why I assumed that he owned the villa. So, when he suggested it, I agreed to go into the villa—it was a magnificent place, a vaulted living room, five bedrooms, each with a view and a bathroom, a covered patio with space for dining, a marbled swimming pool surrounded by the usual tropical plants. This is what he said: "If M'lady would care for refreshments to becalm her nerves, this humble villa offers her a choice of a bar and a well-stocked kitchen." I later discovered that Kurt was a past master in concoctions to becalm the nerves, though he himself adopted the simpler option of a sleeping pill on many nights.

Five days later, we were in the master bedroom, making love on silk sheets. I had never allowed a boy to get me so soon. But Kurt was not a boy. The skin on his face was stretched and taut, networked with fine, almost-erased wrinkles: it is a skin rich people can afford in middle age, even old age. His nose and lips were beautifully sculpted, and I was not certain all of it was genetic. But it did not matter. Then. My mother's boyfriend would have been happy to know that I never had anything against marriage, provided it was with someone who would never need to live off my earnings. I did not want to be you, Maman.

Kurt was about two decades older than me; he had grown up in the USA, mostly New York, he claimed. He had more money than I had ever seen, money he spent on buying me a pearl necklace that I slept in for a week. He had mannerisms and mystique, like wearing only certain brands, using only Apple or Dell devices, opening doors and pulling back chairs for women, including a chit of a girl like me, drinking only French wines or Belgian monastery beers, taking sleeping pills before going to bed. He took me to the best restaurants on the island, places I had only seen from the outside, or where I only knew people who served the Dutch and American tourists. Above all, not only could he speak like a book, he was even writing one! As he told me that very morning when I revealed my love for literature to him, he was actually a writer.

He is the world come to your narrow doorsteps, gal, I told myself. How could I have resisted him? No, I'll be honest: why should I have resisted him?

Even Maman liked him, once he hinted at his intention—yet to materialize—to marry me. She did not trust him, perhaps, but she liked him. He made it possible for her to feel reassured about my future; she has three other children, all younger than me, each from a separate man. Separate surnames too: did I mention that? I stopped going to school a month later and started living with Kurt in his grand villa. It was a business deal, ostensibly: he fixed me up as the housekeeper, the salary being double what my mother was earning after decades at her precious fish-packing factory, and Kurt even paid for me to complete my cooking classes. It was a few weeks later that I discovered Kurt was not the owner of the villa. And this oil rig came up soon after that. It came up as an offer, for three months, triple the pay I was already getting, lucrative, temporary, a chance to run my own catering show … And now?

Now I even wonder if any of the things Kurt told me about himself are true. Now I know it will be longer than three months. There are moments I am sure that it will be forever. This rig will be the last thing I will see. Something strange is going on here, and Kurt is not what he seemed to be. Nothing is.

~

Born into a large and aristocratic Russian family in 1866, Dmitry Sergeyevich Merezhkovsky came close to winning the Nobel Prize at least a dozen times, considered himself a messiah-like figure, moved away from his forced tolerance of Bolshevik communism and into fascism, particularly as an admirer of Mussolini (whom he lobbied to attack Russia in 1937) and Hitler (whom he compared to Joan of Arc), and is remembered today as a significant modernist writer.

But there was another Merezhkovsky who has also survived into history: Konstantin Sergeyevich, an older brother, a biologist-botanist.

There is only one record of a meeting between the two brothers after both had made a name. Konstantin died twenty years before the younger, Dmitry, who passed away in 1941, even as the full devastation of Nazism was being unleashed on the world. In 1902, Konstantin had become curator of zoology at Kazan University, Tatarstan, and was then promoted to a lecturer in 1904. That is where he started researching the symbiotic origins of complex cells. But in 1914, he was dismissed from the university, after being prosecuted for raping twenty-six girls, including one who had been his student from the age of six. He had also actively assisted a right-wing organization, the Kazan Department of the Union of Russian People, in hunting down Jews and "anti-nationals". Anti-semitism was common to both the brothers. Escaping first to France, in 1918, Konstantin moved to the Conservatoire Botanique in Geneva, where he developed his ideas by working on lichens. Obsessed with anti-Semitic eugenics, and short of money, on 9 January 1921, he was found dead in his hotel room, having tied himself up in his bed and inhaling an asphyxiating gas from a metal container.

It was in Geneva that in 1919 or 1920, Dmitry, then in Paris on his second exile from USSR, came to see him, according to the memoir of Devorah Abadi, who was then working as a secretary at the conservatory, and who joined the brothers with some other colleagues at a café in Vielle Ville. Devorah Abadi's book is a kind of confessional memoir, in which she largely struggles with her own choice to move to Geneva and then to the USA, in contrast to many branches of her East-European family who could not escape the anti-Semitism brewing in Europe. Two of her siblings disappeared in concentration camps, as did a large number of other relatives and friends. As such, the memoir does not contain too many dates, and it is difficult to ascertain if Konstantin and Dmitry met in the winter of 1919 or early 1920. Moreover, the meeting also comes up as an observation on changing times; Devorah narrates it as one of the earliest occasions when she realized that, perhaps, she needed to get out of Europe. This is how she puts it, as translated from French:

> "It was a café in one of those old arcaded streets of Vielle Ville, and there were eight of us, perhaps nine. All of them knew the Merezhkovsky Brothers, I think, though only two others were Russian. I was one of two women, the other being the younger Merezhkovsky's wife, also a writer, I think. Maybe I had been invited to give her company. I had been taken there by Charles, whom I later married, and with whom I finally left for the USA. Charles had just met Konstantin—their research areas overlapped—and I am certain when they invited him, and asked him to bring his fiancé, they had no idea I was a Jew. But they were cultured men, and they evaded my existence as much as they could. Despite that, there was a moment when the two brothers conducted a discussion that was, to my Semitic ears, a prelude to the war drums to come. It started with Dmitry's reference to how he had finally read a collection of stories, *Earthly Paradise, or a Winter Night's Dream*, that his older scientist sibling had published many years ago. As far as I could tell, it was about eugenically designed boys, perfect of course, who were killed by law at the age of thirty-five, as life after that age was not worth living. Now, younger Dmitry had no problems with all that: designing boys, killing them,

dismissing the life of everyone over thirty-five, though both the brothers were well over that age. All that was fine and intellectual enough to Dmitry. His difference with his brother had to do with the role of sex as religion, what he called the "battle of two abysses"—the Pre-Christian abyss of the Flesh and the Christian abyss of the Spirit—which he resolved, for someone who abhorred the Bolsheviks, in the strangely Marxist terms of thesis and anti-thesis. I gathered that thinking about sex did not play much of a part in the older brother's designing of boys! I could see Charles squirming uneasily next to me, as Dmitry thundered, probably quoting from one of his books, which were quite popular in those years. I remember the line verbatim: "Being aware of myself in my body, I'm at the root of personality. Being aware of myself in the other person's body, I'm at the root of sex. Being aware of myself in all human bodies, I'm unity." The older Konstantin spoke a little about his research—which used to fascinate Charles—but mostly that was the kind of thing they discussed, both the brothers, and most of the men. It was all about "I" and "unity" and the "pure" future, and though I had not heard what was happening elsewhere, or actually I had heard and ignored it, when, a few years later, I started hearing similar talk—less intellectual, less literary, more effective—from political and other pulpits. I looked at our young children, and said to Charles: we need to get further away from people who want so much purity, for our children can never be purified. I had just read about what they were doing in Germany with *rheinlandbastarde*. But why my dear,

Charles asked me, in his gentle, scholarly manner. That is when I recalled to him this incident from the past—Konstantin had committed suicide many years ago—and Charles understood. He didn't fully agree, but he understood, and he shared my fears for our children, despite this being, as he noted softly, Switzerland. He also said, 'You know, my dear, I never understood how Dr Merezhkovsky could reconcile his utopian ideas with his actual research. The younger brother, Dmitry, I can understand: he was a writer and writers can imagine anything, good or bad. That is both their strength and their weakness. But Dr. Merezhkovsky was a scientist, and a good one, believe me, and all his research pointed away from this talk about purity, unity, oneness. I am partly convinced by his theory of symbiogenesis—that all complex cells (Dr. Chatton has proposed to call them eukaryotes, dear) evolved from the symbiotic relationship between less complex ones, essentially microbes. It will grow bigger in the future. There is something there. Basically, if true, and I believe it is essentially true, what it suggests is that all multicellular organisms are neither pure, nor singular, nor exclusive; that finally all forms of life—even the minutest—are part of a complex whole, and have always been. There cannot be two more opposed vision of life on earth. No, of life in the universe, my dear.' But having given me that gentle lecture, he agreed with me. That is when we started exploring ways of moving to America. It was just in time."

~

I remember when the oil rig first came up.

The party had lasted until two in the morning. But then the guests had gone away, and the people staying in our villa retired to their rooms. I would not call them couples: the men were in their forties, the women in their twenties, more sexy and stylish than models, totally devoted to the men, and, I told myself, if these were couples, gal, then the coupling could not last very long. Kurt and I were still outside on the beach, picking up the abandoned plates, glasses and bottles, folding away and stacking the deckchairs that had been put out for the party. Our chores, though the way Kurt went about it, you would wonder if he had actually done such work before. He lingered. He sat down and waited. Then he put in a burst of activity. And sat down again to sip from his can of beer. Finally, only one deckchair was left, far out near the dark lapping waves. Kurt and I sprinted for it at the same time, but I was faster, and I reached the chair first, flopping down in it. Kurt came up and sat on me, straddling my thighs. Then we started kissing, and slipped from the chair to the sand.

It was a clear night, moonless, and you could see the stars so clearly that you felt they were looking at you, as if there was a vast intelligence out there, and it was not oblivious to something as insignificant as you. Unlike many, I have never felt lost under the night sky, with the waves surging. Small definitely, insignificant perhaps, but never lost. The sea sucked in and sucked out the waves, a rhythmical sound that I often felt as a physical sensation, having grown up with it near me, as if it was the breathing of the earth, sometimes relaxed, sometimes labored, but always there.

We lay on the cool sand and I shivered a bit, for the night can get chilly, so Kurt removed his Burberry cotton trench coat and covered us with it like a blanket. He would still do things like that in those days; we had been together for just a few weeks. He lit a cigarette—Kurt smokes only during parties—and offered it to me, though he knew I do not smoke. I wrinkled my nose in disgust. It was then that he brought it up.

"Michelle-M'lady," he said in a false hoarse voice, an impersonation of some leader or film character I did not recognize, "We have been made an offer we cannot refuse." Then he explained it to me.

It seemed that some friends of some friends of his (I had by then understood that in Kurt's circles everything had to do with friends of friends; the villa we were housekeeping also belonged to friends of friends) had started a brilliant new project. Those were his words: a brilliant new project. They had turned an abandoned oil rig in the North Sea into a resort for the rich and the idle. They were looking for a housekeeper and manager for the guests—just what Kurt and I did at the villa—and were willing to pay a minor fortune. I was taken aback by the sum he mentioned and I questioned it.

Have you ever lived on an out-shore rig, Saccharum Officinarum? he asked me.

It would be isolated, with maybe only one monthly trip, by chopper, to a nearby Russian city, a dump with bars. Even on functioning rigs, workers never stay for more than three months in most cases, he said. I had never even imagined that people lived on rigs. I had not given rigs much thought, though there was oil in and around some of our islands, and if I imagined them, I suppose I saw them more like tubewells, a motor pulling up the oil and pumping it through pipes to some refinery on the coast.

But oil rigs were far from my world then. The conversation stopped. A fish jumped in the water, large enough to make a splash that we heard over the waves. The lights of some cruise ship appeared near the horizon, at first like a cluster of stars, then larger and gaudier. Kurt and I lay there on the sand, the water less than ten feet from us.

"Let's get blankets," said Kurt, and ran back to the villa. He came back with five, two of which we spread on the sand, further away from the water, and the others we wrapped around us. Kurt let his expensive trench coat lie on the sand—he is careless with clothes, despite always buying only the best stuff—but of course, I could not allow that. Just using such an elegant coat as a blanket had been close to sacrilege to me. I got up, dusted his coat, folded it neatly, and put it on the solitary deck chair. When I turned back to Kurt, he had hogged all the blankets, so we tussled over them, and I pulled all of his blankets away, one by one. He lay there and shivered dramatically. I tossed him one blanket. Then I snuggled into him and we shared them.

After a while in silence, with just the sea breathing, I asked him, "Why me?"

He did not understand. I elaborated: "They know you as a friend, Kurt, but why dem wan pay me fi work pon dis rig?"

Kurt smiled. Perhaps it amused him that in my exasperation or bewilderment I had slipped into language that I usually reserved for family members. Then he pointed at the folded coat on the deck chair. Because of that, he said.

"Because of what?" I asked, enunciating carefully this time.

"Your housekeeping. Your cooking, this party. They were impressed by what they saw," he said. And he wriggled his eyebrows suggestively at my body, "But seriously, Lady Sugar, they need someone like you up there. They cannot afford to hire a five-star cook, and you are just as good, they said. Better, I told them. Also, no strings attached. Can stay away for three months without issues. And then I am going to work for them. So why not come along?"

Looking back, one is always amazed at one's innocence: I suppose that is the way with mere mortals. For if you looked back and wondered at your venality, you would be a reformed saint, wouldn't you? I look back and wonder at my innocence. I believed everything Kurt told me. Just as you start off by believing everything *your* men tell you, Maman. Also things about me. I am beginning to understand you a bit now: how there are lies we women prefer not to hear. Because, surely, that was a whopping lie: "They cannot afford to hire a five-star cook." But then, I had not been to the rig yet, and I had no idea what they could afford. Now I know, and that is what makes me careful: they could have afforded a five-star cook, but they hired me, an insignificant young girl from a little island. A girl—and Kurt had spoken the truth there—with no strings attached. A girl who could disappear—and would be forgotten.

But I was once innocent—most of us are—so I asked Kurt: Why should anyone want to go to a rig for a vacation?

Why does anyone climb the Everest or trek the Sahara? Was his reply, as he pulled me on top of him.

2

The Photo

HER mother would have said: You are letting yourself go again, Jens Erik.

She will say: Far, are you going to the gym these days? Or are you only hitting the bars with your police chums? The words would be the essentially the same, except that his daughter would call him "Far", Dad, and not by name. But the same tone, that faint, and, to his mind, relentless disapproval.

Jens Erik sucked in his belly at the thought, as he pulled on a crisply ironed cotton shirt. Ex-police chums, he corrected her mentally.

He looked down at his belly. It was not a bad belly for a man of fifty-seven, but neither mother nor daughter would ever concede that. Both of them had men in their lives who apparently subsisted on dried rice cakes.

That reminded Jens Erik: he should stop at the *pølsevogn*, sausage-wagon, outside the station when he goes into town to meet his daughter later in the week. Pernille will take him out to some fancy café. One of those crowded places where the distance between tables was even smaller than the portions served. That much was certain, he thought, as he put on his brown suede jacket.

It was time for his daily walk.

What happened to all the old cavernous bodegas, with their stretches of bare, beer-sticky wooden tables, he asked himself? Shouldn't they have returned at least after the pandemic? Even during the crisis, they had social distancing everywhere except in these fashionable cafés! They were either closed or crowded.

The pølsevogn would be a good precaution. He could fortify himself with a hotdog and exchange a word with Hanif, the Bangladeshi *pølsemand* who served the pork his religion forbade him from eating—weird religion that got worked up about pigs—and had become, in the years he worked as a police informer, almost like a friend to Jens Erik.

Not that Pernille would accept that Jens Erik thought of Hanif, whom he had met two years before Pernille was even born, as a friend.

Far, I know you, she had said when he once brought up his friendship with Hanif during one of their arguments, as an example of his openness to "foreigners". Far, I know you. You cannot think of anyone from outside Jutland as a friend. Do you even know anything about Islam or, say, Hinduism?

The first lot does not eat pork and the other lot does not eat beef, Jens Erik had observed, neutrally. He had not meant it as a joke.

There you go! Pernille had thrown up her hands: I am sure you will vote for the Danish People's Party next time, Far.

Jens Erik had not replied to that because he could not imagine voting for any party other than the Social Democrats—why, his father and grandfather had voted for them! Though he did feel that the Danish People's Party had a valid point or two about the threats posed to Danish culture.

Jens Erik frowned at the memory of this conversation. It was like so many others between him and his daughter. His middle age—fifty-seven was nowhere near old age, not any longer, humpf!—expanse did not bother him much. It was still more muscle than lard, but meetings with Pernille did. Or rather the turn their conversations could take, because, despite swearing to himself that he would not do it again, almost every time they met, daughter and father ended up arguing.

Pernille would bring up either her boyfriend, another of those emaciated rice-cake eaters, or some complicated political problem in a godforsaken part of the world where they killed each other for eating or not eating pork, beef, chicken, and frog. Jens Erik could not make up his mind what was the greater minefield, her vegan boyfriend or some mutually cannibalizing country in Asia, Africa, South America!

It had not always been like that.

Until the age of eleven or twelve, Pernille was closer to him than to his wife. She was his little girl. He carried her around everywhere in his spare hours. He taught her to identify berries and mushrooms, which ones could be plucked and eaten, which ones had to be avoided.

Those days he was still married to her mother. He blamed the rift between him and his daughter neither on the growing friction between him and his wife and their eventual divorce, seven years later, when Pernille left high school at the age of nineteen, nor on the natural process of a girl turning into a teenager. The only time he consulted a therapist, on the instigation of his wife, then considering divorce, these two explanations were insinuated to him, and Jens Erik found them so hackneyed that he never went back to the therapist.

Instead, he blamed it on a photo, just one photo.

The photo had been taken years before Pernille was born. Jens Erik had not been aware of the photo's existence, as it had appeared in *Dagbladet Information,* a leftist newspaper that Jens Erik never read. It had cropped up later when, at the age of twelve or thirteen, Pernille prepared a class project on the Nørrebro riots of 1993.

When Pernille showed it to him, Jens Erik was surprised by the precision with which the photographer had captured his image, visor and baton raised, seemingly about to club a teenager—one of those *autonomes* infesting Nørrebro in those days—who was lying on his back, legs and arms flailing to fend off the blow.

The blow had never come. Jens Erik positively recalled that he had let the boy run away. But thirteen-year-old Pernille was not convinced.

Look, I still had hair then, he said to her, trying to laugh it off. It was a forced joke: his hair hardly showed under the riot helmet.

Your face is so full of hate, Far, Pernille replied in a hushed voice.

She had used the word that to her was the worst one could apply: *hadefuld*. Racists were "hateful", sexists were "hateful", the Danish People's Party was "hateful", Islamists were "hateful", Trump had been "hateful", half the heads of the nation-states were "hateful", billionaires like Musk and Bezos and Lai and Koplar were "hateful". Those days, Pernille had started to discover the world and she was convinced that it was a wonderful world, spoiled only by hateful people. And now, her father was hateful.

No, no, no, Jens Erik had wanted to say. That is not hatred on my face. That is fear.

But he could not say that.

How could he tell his thirteen-year-old daughter that her father, a trainee officer, then on deputation in the capital, having grown up in the small town of Grenaa and never experienced a riot before, had been frightened by what was happening on the streets of Copenhagen? The hooded young men, with tattoos and rings in their tongues and lips; the burning tires, the shouting and screaming. What was he, Jens Erik, doing here in these burning streets?

He had a provincial suspicion of Copenhagen and its inhabitants in any case. And to be thrown bang into the worst riot for years, when the police had to fire more than a hundred live rounds, no, Pernille, I was not full of hate, I was full of fear and my own inadequacy. I was acutely aware of my mortality, and your mother's, then a university student, vulnerable in some other corner of this alien metropolis.

But, of course, he could not say that.

He did not even formulate it to himself in those clear words. Those are the words of a novelist trying to put him into a book. Jens Erik was not a novelist. He was not a man given to elaborate explanations—to himself or others. He was happiest when he could settle an issue with a non-committal humpf.

Thirteen-year-old Pernille had gone on to write and submit her project, for which she received a 12. The highest grade.

He had forced himself to read it, disagreeing strongly with her interpretation of the police action—"police brutality" was the expression she used—and unable to stop himself from criticising her "somewhat childish impression of law and order". It was a heavy phrase coming from him. It fell heavily on Pernille.

A chill had fallen over their relationship, father and daughter avoiding each other's eyes for weeks, and Jens Erik felt that it had never really lifted. Even today, he suspected, Pernille saw him as the bullying policeman. A man who stood, baton-raised, to protect the status quo, and club the weak and the fallen.

The gradual dissolution of his marriage with her mother—who used to love Copenhagen just as much as Jens Erik hated it—had not helped either. When his wife, now ex, moved back to Copenhagen, one of her complaints against him had been his decision to ask for a transfer to Aarhus. When she married again within a year, he had felt no loss.

But when Pernille decided to join her mother, because she wanted to study in Copenhagen University, Jens Erik had been filled with a hollowness that still, despite years of habit, could suddenly empty his world. Anything could bring it on, but mostly it would be memories of places he had been with Pernille or things he had done with her: a girl on a swing in the local park, the brightly painted buildings of the kind of kindergarten she had gone to, a cat of the sort they used to have, a light-haired child picking berries by the roadside with her father.

It had happened so often that Jens Erik sold off the flat they had lived in—he had bought off his wife's share when they divorced, taking an extra mortgage—and moved to a village, Hjortshøj, just outside Aarhus, that held no associations for him. But even then, suddenly, out of the blue, the emptiness could hit him, and he would have to wait for a day or two before it passed.

He had decided to leave his Ford in the carport and take the tram. Despite years in police cars, he did not trust automobiles. Like all complex machines, they were not fully reliable. Not as reliable as his own limbs. But if one had to drive cars, and there was as little choice in the matter as there was in using computers, then Ford was the brand for him.

Jens Erik only bought and drove Fords.

He once explained his preference for Fords to Pernille: The Americans saved us during the World War.

Pernille had laughed: Far, the Soviets saved us more than the Americans did. Jens Erik had frowned, unable to let this go with a humpf. The Americans saved us from both the Nazis and the Soviets, he had said.

A few years back an exchange like this would have led to a heated argument between father and daughter, but ever since Pernille started doing her Ph.D. at Copenhagen University and going steady with her vegan rice-cake boyfriend, she had learned to pull a wry face and let matters drop. That had been the development of the recent past. My girl has grown up, he told himself.

How old was she now? Twenty-five? Yes, she would be twenty-six next year. His Pernille had grown up—learned to let me be who I am, well, some of the time. Something her mother never mastered, he would have added to a drinking chum, coming the closest to a complaint.

But he still missed the closeness he had with her before she discovered that photo at the age of thirteen. That little girl who would demand to be carried on his shoulders, who would watch him admiringly, sitting on her haunches, eyes big and unblinking, as he repaired something in the house.

Where had that girl gone?

~

When Gustave Brant died of comorbidities due to Covid-19 on 7th June 2020, or rather of related complications, he had been living in his hometown, Fegersheim (which you can reach from Strasbourg by the N83), for more than a decade, having retired there from Université de Strasbourg in 2007, and not many in his field (microbiology) remembered him, or, given the coronavirus mortalities in those days, had time to remember him. A local paper carried a short obituary, mentioning that he had retired as a lecturer, intending to continue his work on microbes. It did not add that he had subsequently not published anything. The research unit, Genetics, Genomics and Microbiology of Université de Strasbourg, held a commemorative webinar in his honor later that year, and with that Dr. Brant eased into the footnotes of academia, as do so many academics, to be remembered, once or twice at professional gatherings in the next few years, as a diligent researcher or a committed teacher, and not for any paper or book, which is a way not to be remembered at all.

Dr. Brant had never married and, as far as anyone knew, had not fathered a child, so his house and papers passed on to his two nephews and one niece. One of the nephews was a doctor in Berlin and could not attend the funeral—it was not an easy time to travel. The other nephew dealt in real estate in Fribourg and had planned to come to the funeral, but finally decided against it, given the restrictions on travel that were still partly in place. The niece, however, had more time; she was also a hairdresser in Illkirch, where she was settled with her husband and two children. She had cut Dr. Brant's hair too, had seen a bit of the quiet old man, who grew more stooped every year. She had been rather fond of her uncle. It was left to her to sort out Dr. Brant's papers. As was the custom, she employed a firm that settled estates, and they took care of inventorying the furniture, books, paintings etc., and disposing of the ones that could be sold, as well as putting the house on sale. The only thing the niece did not allow them to touch were the personal papers and photographs in Dr. Brant's small study, as well as his laptop. She managed to open the laptop and discovered nothing of interest in it. It appeared that Dr. Brant had not worked on any project for years, and he had the habit of printing out his files in any case. She took all the papers home, mostly for burning—if they were letters and old correspondence. She took out some family photos and put the other photos in a box, which was soon forgotten in her attic.

However, she collected the notes that Dr. Brant had made toward maybe an academic paper or a book and sent them to a couple of junior colleagues of Dr. Brant, not so junior as not to remember him though, as she hoped that they would be publishable. She could not make much of them, and it was obvious that the work was patchy and incomplete. But she hoped that perhaps his colleagues would see some merit in it and bring it out, maybe just as part of one of their own papers, with of course an acknowledgement to her deceased uncle.

As far as she could tell (for she read through the notes, some handwritten, most printed out), her uncle had, soon after his retirement, somehow obtained tissue from the body of a woman who was supposed to have died during the dancing plague of Strasbourg in the early sixteenth century. Her uncle had made rather copious notes about the plague, which, being historical, the niece could follow. According to the deceased man, dancing plagues had been common in Europe from at least the eleventh century to the fourteenth, but they had ceased afterwards—except in and around Strasbourg, where they were reported into the sixteenth century.

Her uncle had made a list of various dancing plagues—known as St Vitus's Dance—in Europe and some of them provided gory reading, making the niece shudder and causing her a nightmare or two. Towns she knew well, such as Cologne and Triers, had been badly hit by the dancing plague in the fifteenth century, causing dozens of deaths from sheer exhaustion. In Cologne, hundreds of afflicted men and women had rushed, dancing ceaselessly, from one sacred place to another, begging the onlookers to pummel them in order to cure them. In 1442, a monk had danced himself to death in the Swiss town of Schaffhausen. A woman in Basel had danced for an entire month until her feet were reduced to tendon and bone. But it was the 1518 outbreak in Strasbourg that concerned her uncle, because, as he wrote in his notes, by then the printing press was firmly established, and there are many written accounts of the people afflicted by St Vitus's dance, dancing on the streets, helplessly, perhaps soundlessly, until they collapsed of exhaustion, and then getting up again and dancing on for days.

But it was not the historical bit that interested her uncle. He was interested in the episode from a microbiological perspective, his field, and this is where the niece lost track of much of his argument and whatever evidence he claimed to have found. But from what she understood, it appeared that there are microbes that can influence the actions of their hosts. This slightly surprised the good woman, as she had been brought up to think of microbes—which she understood was another word for bacteria, or in any case, included bacteria and maybe viruses—as agents of disease. Parasites. They were best eradicated. Meister Proper! Sidol! But, according to her uncle, and it appeared that this was not a controversial claim, it was a claim that all people in his field accepted as true, that some microbes help plants and animals live in the way that they do. There were even some in our intestines, helping us digest! Mother's milk is so effective because of the microbes it helps feed and cultivate in the baby! That was cute, the niece thought.

Some other examples were less pleasant. Some parasites and microbes could make animals behave against their normal instincts. One of them could drive a mouse to a cat, because it appeared that the microbe or parasite or whatever it was—her uncle used technical names—could only reproduce in the guts of a cat. It lived in a rat but had to ensure the rat was eaten by a cat so that it could reproduce in the cat! Ugh, thought the niece. Then there was something her uncle called a trematode, which lived in ants but could reproduce only in sheep, so it got ants to climb onto blades of grass and hang there all night. All day this ant with trematodes in it behaves normally, but at night it does not return to the colony like other ants: it climbs on top of a blade of grass and hangs there, waiting for a sheep to come by and eat it. If no sheep comes by, the ant behaves normally the next day—it appears that the trematode does not want it to die of starvation, for then it would die too!—and then hangs on to a blade of grass the next night, and the night after that. Until a sheep eats that blade of grass. The niece shivered; this was like black magic! Invisible creatures doing black magic, though her uncle called the field neuroparasitology, which sounded worse.

It seemed to the niece that the uncle claimed he had retrieved evidence of a microbe related to this trematode from the tissue of the dancing plague victim that he had examined. In short, he was claiming that the dancing plague was caused by a microbe—for whatever reason, maybe it had to do, as is often the case, with reproduction, and there was some connection between that and bleeding from the soles of the feet?—and not, as had been argued in the sixteenth century, by possession, by God or Devil, or, as was argued later, by various psychological states of mind.

This was a frightening thought and caused the niece another nightmare or two, but she photocopied and bundled up the papers and sent them to the two professors at Strasbourg, whom she had called up first and who remembered her uncle, but both of them sent almost identical replies to her, with their due condolences, thanking her for the papers, expressing their inability to put them to any "good use", and returning the bundles to her. After that, she put the bundles in her attic too.

3

Macrobians

It is as if his mind and his body are two separate things, with conflicting ways of understanding a situation. He has noticed this in other people in the past: it sometimes caused them great harm. Women who let in a rapist despite a gut feeling of unease because their mind told them that there was no reason to fear a face familiar from the neighborhood; men who walked into a trap in a doomed bid to help a loved one, even though reason told them that it was a horrible mistake. Both could be wrong: emotion or reason. Neither could be trusted not to lie to the other.

The intruder alarm keeps shrieking.

Just some years ago, a situation like this would have sent Harris diving for cover even before waking up. But time and civilian life have added a layer of indolence, and fat, to Harris. Fuck, a voice in him whispers, fuck, not again, fuck, not now. He sits there, legs dangling out of bed, and peers into the murk of the room.

It is a large room, furnished in a retro-1960s style: untreated wood panels, furniture of metal, glass, and wood, though the preference is for black-and-white contrasts, not psychedelic colors. His curtains and carpets tend towards soft yellow and faint green. The most extravagant piece in this room is the four-poster bed with a Lucite frame and metal laminate accents. His house is a pastiche of the only part of his past Harris is willing to recollect consciously. This is what he remembers of his childhood home before his father left and his mother married again. And again. It was in another century, in another country.

Harris had retired early and well. His investments in IT and Big Pharma have continued to pay off, even more so after the pandemic. This faintly classical country house, white-washed and high-ceilinged, is his bit of heaven for the hells he has waded through, and sometimes dug deeper, in various corners of the world. Harris knows he is safe here. He had chosen one of the few nations to escape lightly, not just the consequences of the virus but of what continued to come after it, the accelerating roller-coaster ride of economies, turning entire nations into kingdoms run by oligarchs and corporate robber barons, under the thin veneer of elected Parliaments and free media. There was more. But here he could ignore it all. Just as he could ignore himself, reducing his past to this present, a present totally at odds with all he had been, a present in which he could be nothing, nobody significant, nobody who felt driven to make a difference. He has erased himself with determination, made himself utterly unremarkable, for he does not trust the original and the outstanding. This was the best country for it.

This was the suburbs of Viborg City in Denmark, a refuge fashioned for the rich and the elderly, who are always in need of safety, in the lush middle of a country that was itself a citadel, guarded equally by the vampire of free-floating capital and the archangel of welfare, a rare combination. Rows of solid houses with identical walls and hedges. Streets with only a person or two on them. He was safe in any case. They had deleted him from all files, except a master computer or two, which might as well not exist. Bits and pieces of his past survived in impersonal offices and individual memories, strewn across countries. Continents. These fragments sometimes returned to him in those nightmares, disjointed and without any sound, that he had finally learnt to sleep with. But in its entirety, his past did not exist anymore, except in the memories of two or three men and one woman, and of those only one or two might know, if they cared to find out from the pinnacle of their power in London or Washington, where he was and what he was called now.

Perhaps that is why Harris neither rolls to the floor nor grabs for the gun—an obsolete M9 Beretta, which he has retained from his training days. It now nestles in a holster taped to the underside of his bed. Even the prospect of touching it fills him with repugnance when, once a month, he takes it out and dismantles and oils it. It belongs to his past of being outstanding, remarkable—among many others, on all sides, who were outstanding and remarkable, which justified, to their minds, what they did to others.

Surely no one from that past can walk into this present.

Instead, he peers around the room, sensing rather than seeing its contours. He looks like any other middle-aged man woken up by a sound in a large "period" house, a dark-haired, broad-faced man with the beginning of jowls, partly hidden under a salt-and-pepper goatee. He is powerfully built, broad and wide-shouldered, dressed in only a pair of shorts, the strings of the shorts hidden under the belly. There are scars on his body; one of them is a bullet hole just under the ribcage, which has left an exit scar on his back too. Harris shakes his head a little, like a small dog drying itself. He is convinced that the intruder alarm has gone off on its own accord at four in the morning. It shouldn't have; it was the best one could get for money or love; or at least it had been thirteen years ago, in 2017, when Harris had refurbished and altered this house for retirement. A haze of light from the moon illuminates the thin curtains but cannot penetrate them. He can hear the elms swishing in the wind. The swans are quiet. Nothing seems amiss. Nothing except the alarm. Harris pulls on his silk sleeping robe, with a Chinese dragon on its back. He lumbers out to the panel under the staircase, stepping heavily down the stairs, noisily; they are of old wood and they creak. He switches off the alarm.

Harris is going up to his bedroom when he feels a draft. He never sleeps with any window open. That is one of his rules of survival, learnt ages ago, and now impossible to eradicate from his habits.

The draft is coming from the dining room. Picking up a golf club from under the stairs, because it is too late now to ascend the creaking stairs and retrieve his Beretta from under the bed, Harris tiptoes into the room. He is glad the wooden paneling of the ground floor was replaced when he moved in; the planks do not creak. It is darker in there with all the heavy curtains drawn, except at one window, which is a clear rectangle of moonlight. It is almost luminescent, but this is the moon in Denmark, and its light does not enter the room. It stops at the windowsill. The window is open, its curtain pulled aside. Harris can feel the prickle of hair at the back of his neck; he clenches the club, ready to swing. But he knows the voice even before he can understand the words. It is a voice no one could forget. No one who had heard it. And not many had. Or, not many who still lived, had. Low and rasping, as if the tongue was made of sandpaper. All emotion has long been drained out of that voice. It is the voice of a machine. But it issues from a human mouth. When had he heard it last? In Iraq, in Syria? It is a voice from the fragmented past, the gagged past, the past of voiceless nightmares. That collaterally damaged past.

For an instant, Harris wonders if he is not still asleep in bed, dreaming. But this dream does not carry the full horrendous load of an abstract nightmare (bodies floating, limbs unattached) that his dreams always bear. And it contains sound; the words are clear enough: "You sleep soundly, old man."

His nightmares are mute, and ghosts do not speak so clearly.

There is a click in the dining-drawing room, and a white light comes on. Someone has opened the refrigerator.

"Put that club away," rasps the voice from the past, "It is too dark to play golf."

Harris hears cans of beer being removed from the small refrigerator of his Turnidge cocktail bar. But it cannot be, he thinks; that voice was dead; that man died nine or ten years ago, in Afghanistan. It happened in the wake of the pandemic and was hardly reported, which probably suited everyone. Muslims had been replaced by a virus as the global villain by then, though with similar effects. Harris had read the short report online, two "American contractors" killed by a mine blast just outside Kabul; their full names and designations mentioned. Harris must have been one of the very few who could have paused over the names, one of them.

Harris inches towards the dining room.

It is as if the man in there, now closing the door of the fridge, has been reading Harris's mind.

"All of us die, my friend," the voice says, "There is no fountain of immortality. You died somewhere too. Or you wouldn't be here."

~

Herodotus writes that the Macrobians were the tallest and handsomest of people, and places them in Africa. They have been located in Somalia, Ethiopia, Libya ... and as far away as India, which, of course, is on another continent altogether. But one doesn't know for sure because, like all fabulous people, they have never been found.

They are a very prosperous and peaceful kingdom, writes Herodotus. Even their prisoners wear shackles of beaten gold.

Herodotus also narrates a story about the time when the Persian emperor Cambyses II conquered Egypt. He then sent an embassy to Macrobia, carrying costly gifts and urging the Macrobian king to accept the suzerainty of the Persians. The Macrobian king sent back an unstrung bow, with the message that if the Persians manage to string the bow, he would accept their suzerainty, but if they do not, then they should stay where they are and be thankful that Macrobians do not believe in intimidating and conquering other peoples.

The unstrung bow is, of course, a great staple of fabulous tales and ancient epics. The *Mahabharata* revolves around the stringing of a bow. Unstrung bows play decisive roles in the *Ramayana*. Homer's epics feature unstrung bows or the stringing of bows. Unsurprisingly, even later attempts at writing an epic, such as *Temora: A Epic Poem of Ossian*, feature unstrung bows.

The bow of the Macrobian king remained unstrung. No one conquered the kingdom, and now no one knows where it was. But another memory from Macrobia persists: the fountain of life. Herodotus writes that if you washed in that fountain, your flesh turned "glossy and sleek, as if bathed in oil, and the scent of a thousand violets came from the fountain". It was said that the Macrobians had found a way of doubling the human life span by bathing in this fountain so that all in that fabled kingdom lived to be at least a hundred and twenty years old. A look at mid-nineteenth century Brazilian newspapers reveals that obituaries of people reported to be stupendously old were listed under the heading *Macróbios*.

~

The light from the fridge is like a film of water on the wooden floor. It goes off with a slight whump. There is the sound of a chair scraping, a can opening with a fizz.

Harris turns around and puts the golf club back in place. When he enters the dining room the place is dark again, and he can barely make out a familiar silhouette at the end of the table. He had been a knobby man, towering, not thin but wiry, with more than a passing resemblance to Hans Christian Andersen, the Danish fairy tale writer. Maybe that is why his code name in the service had been Mermaid.

Harris used to think that they played such simplistic jokes when allotting them their code names. His, he thought, had to do with a superficial matter too. But now, years later, he is not sure. Perhaps all those interviews and tests they conducted before and after recruiting them did give them a kind of insight that the recruits themselves did not have. Perhaps Mermaid was a being who can live in two media; perhaps Carbon was a copy, something that refused to be original.

"Mermaid," Harris says in greeting, as he moves towards the light switch.

"Leave the lights alone, Carbon," the voice rasps. "It is best we do not see each other. We need not know what we look like now. Though I heard you grew a goatee. Hairy Harris."

Does the man have some special kind of night-vision gadget fitted into his eyes? If so, then they have devised something far more advanced than the outlandish wraparound goggles that Harris had used in his time.

Harris hesitates. Then he goes to the table and seats himself at the opposite end. Mermaid opens another can and, after a second, slides it towards him. It comes to rest exactly six inches from Harris.

"But Dr. Harris Malouf?" Mermaid laughs. "Why, Harris?"

"Why not?"

"It is a name I would not have thought up for you. You were never a Harris."

"Perhaps, that's why."

"Perhaps."

"And you, Mermaid? What do you call yourself now?"

The man takes a sip from his can before he answers.

"There is no reason for you to know. Yet."

"You are dead, Mermaid. I have retired…"

"Which means you are dead too, at least officially. The Big Death we used to call it. Remember?"

"Sure, sure. We are both fucking dead. So why the hell this visit?"

"You don't even read the local news any more, do you, Carb… Harris?"

"I had enough of the news when I was, as you put it, alive. I garden now. Sometimes. And I research and teach part-time."

"Cognitive anthropology. I have read two of your papers. That was less of a surprise. You were always our scholar, Harris. But here, of all places. Fucking here. The padded chamber of sanity!"

Harris drinks from his can, waiting for Mermaid, or his ghost (though Harris does not believe in souls), to go on.

"I need your help, Harris."

"Why me?"

"I wouldn't come to you if I had another option. And don't you think you owe me one?"

Harris keeps quiet: he owes Mermaid more than one. He owes Mermaid his life on at least three different occasions, on two different continents. If this is Mermaid.

Mermaid continues: "I am leaving a piece of paper here. Think it over. You have one week. You will find all the material in that box. But think it over, Carbon. Harris. Think it over. There is no compulsion. If you do not want to do this, you won't hear from me again. It is risky enough as it is. If you do not want to get into this, well, my old friend, just keep gardening. Forget this night. All of this just hasn't taken place. I was never here…"

"How did you find me, Mermaid?"

"Ah, Harris," Mermaid laughs, "Do you still believe in what we were taught? The secret handshakes and the forbidden fruit? So did I, my friend, despite what I heard and saw, I still believed in all that too. But then one day I read a book, a novel, by a French writer, someone called Doubinsky, and it changed my understanding of it all. You want to know how?"

Why is it that Harris feels groggy, slightly drunk? Is it that large slurp of beer this late in the night? He shakes his head to clear it.

Mermaid continues, without waiting for Harris to answer. He sounds uncharacteristically garrulous to Harris.

"You see, it is a novel set in the future. It features, if I remember correctly, a hero who has been fitted with an electronic shackle by the state. He cannot go anywhere without his minders knowing. He is a prisoner. But then one day, he just opens the shackle and throws it away. And you know what happens?"

Harris shakes his head again, more vigorously, not in answer to Mermaid but to clear the fog in it. It is Mermaid's voice, but this man does not talk like Mermaid, who was always taciturn. Have the years changed Mermaid too, or… ?

"Nothing. Nothing, my friend, nothing happens. The hero throws away his shackle and nothing happens. No one even finds out he has discarded it. The electronic shackle worked only because the poor bastard believed in it. That novel made me see things differently. The shackle was everything, or nothing. And what I am asking you to do is like that too: everything, or nothing."

Harris is having trouble concentrating on Mermaid's words. They seem to be receding.

"Let me repeat: you don't have to do this. But if you do, it will be the biggest thing any of us have been involved in…"

The voice grows fainter. Mermaid's outline seems to blur. Harris pushes away his can of beer in alarm. He grabs the edge of the table to steady himself.

4

Conquistadores

THERE were people who hated November. Jen Erik was not one of them.

This was the weather that reminded him of where he lived. This was real Dansk weather. It was as Danish as warmed-up *leverpostej,* as marinated herring on *rugbrød.*

You could complain about the darkness stretching into late morning and starting in the early afternoon, the slate-colored clouds weighing down on you all day, the rain that never fell and never stopped, the sun making a modest appearance maybe just on a day or two in the entire month. Or you could feel how small the world had become, as if the sky itself was huddling, and you had to just stretch your arms to touch all the sides. Jens Erik liked this sense of smallness.

Now, as he locked the door of his compact one-story detached house, *parcelhus,* as it was described in property brochures, something he did not bother to do when he was just visiting neighbors, he noticed, with the delight that he had always felt in the season, the leaves on the ground. There were so many colors on them. He liked the colors of autumn, though he never dressed in colors himself: white, gray, black, and brown were his choice, all subdued.

Pertentlig was the Danish word that described his wardrobe: it meant both "scrupulous" and "just so". He adjusted his sixpence cap on his head. He never went out without one. And no, he had worn them even before he lost most of his hair and started shaving his head.

I have to rake up the leaves, he told himself. They could not be allowed to blow into his neighbors' gardens. Many of the leaves had fallen from the towering maple in a corner of his garden, its broad purple blades congregating in corners and by the hedge, which was also shedding its small green leaves now.

Outside, there was no one on Mølleager, though Bente across the street was hoeing her flower beds before winter hardened the ground. She had wisteria plants that were Jens Erik's secret envy every summer: such a glorious shower of pure blue flowers that you understood why they were called "blue rain" in Danish!

Bente was at least fifteen years older than him and had lived alone in her house ever since her husband died of a stroke. This was before Jens Erik had moved to the street. She took care of her garden with a determination that even orderly Jens Erik lacked in his relationship to his flower beds.

Bente looked up, leaning heavily on her hoe; he waved at her. She shouted, See you on Saturday. He nodded, and straightened his cap. He had gotten used to walking her to activities in the local church. The tall, stark white walls of its tower were visible over the roofs from the corner. This coming Saturday it would host a presentation by a missionary who had returned from India and Bangladesh.

The talk was about migration, and the new hazards of life in these countries, which, as far as Jens Erik understood, had slipped steadily down the economic scale and up the criminal one since the pandemic. People were fleeing the encroachment of the rising sea in Bangladesh, and a human rights controversy raged over the possible use of drone patrols—equipped to shoot—by India, though some claimed more Indians were sneaking into Bangladesh to avail themselves of its better economy. Christians were being persecuted too, again, and this particular missionary had been ordered to leave Delhi within forty-eight hours for posting some videos of starving aborigines on Cinememe, the new craze that had supplanted TikTok.

All very violent and non-Danish to Jens Erik's ears. It was not the type of event Jens Erik would attend—he never went to church on his own anyway—but he had promised Bente.

He walked down the pedestrian-cyclist lane, noting the bushes with pleasure: he could recognize them from his childhood days. They were like cousins and siblings of old acquaintances. Their family resemblances reassured him.

That there was a row of blackberries, now dwindling to winter twigs with a few leaves still hanging on, but in the summer it would bear dark red berries, which children and adults alike would pick, carefully avoiding the thorns, and eat while walking by.

That plant out there, in the small kindergarten where the kids were playing indoors, was what Jens Erik knew as an *Ægte Syren* bush—an explosion of white flowers just a few weeks ago. He liked its English name, "Beauty of Moscow". His small collection of books was full of tomes on plants, birds, animals, gardens, and walks.

Further off were apple trees, closing down for winter too, and towering behind the houses on the other side of the road there stood the familiar elms, lean and steeping in the wind, rooks nesting in their topmost branches.

He passed a weeping willow, its trunk turning ghostly with approaching winter, its arms shedding and drooping.

It was a world Jens Erik knew well and could name with precision down to the small mushrooms on the ground: the edible ones, like Karl Johan, which might still be sprouting, as they lasted into October, even November these days, and the ones to avoid. His father had taught him to recognize them and he had tried to teach Pernille.

Just three cars passed him as he walked to the station, crossing a recently repaired wooden bridge for pedestrians.

Under the bridge, a small rivulet rippled over stones and into a pond across the road.

There were three ducks on the pond. Two were unremarkable. But Jens Erik could see that one of them was the Common Scoter. It was unusual to find the Common Scoter inland, but the sea was just two kilometers away. He paused to watch the ducks.

Jens Erik liked the emptiness and quietness of the place, something he had missed in his Copenhagen days and even more so on the two occasions when, succumbing to pressure from his wife and Pernille, he had taken the family to London. What clamor! What a crush! How could people live like that? Jens Erik shook his head and walked on.

LE1, the tram line to Aarhus central station, was no longer new, but the trams were well-maintained. As it was almost noon, the compartment was more than half-empty. Mostly old people—

some were around Jens Erik's age, but he saw them as old and himself as younger. They had aged before his eyes, while he still saw himself in his mind's eye, which is more resistant to time.

Up the compartment, there were some high school kids, playing truant obviously, who were the only source of noise. They were laughing and kidding each other. At least two of them were not Danish.

Oh well, Jens Erik thought, for Pernille would have corrected him, they were probably second-generation immigrants. But Pernille would have ticked him off about that too. She had done it in the past, despite the fact that almost everyone, including the newspapers, used the phrase, "second-generation immigrant".

Far, she had told him on more than one occasion, you are either an immigrant or you are not. You cannot be a second- and third- and twentieth-generation immigrant.

Well, what can we call them? Jens Erik had countered.

Pernille had an answer: First-generation Danes, maybe?

Jens Erik looked at the boys in his compartment. One of them was straddling the back of a seat, as if it was a fence, to talk to the boys sitting behind him. He was colored. Jens Erik felt that it was the two colored boys who were making most of the noise, moving about too much, speaking too loudly.

Couldn't they sit quietly and look out of the window at the fields and trees, the backyards of cottages with their broken garden furniture?

No, he shook his head and readjusted his cap, these boys were not first-generation Danes; they were second-generation immigrants.

~

Most people interested in the history of Conquistadores have heard of Juan Ponce de León, who voyaged to find the Fountain of Youth in 1513 and was probably the first European to set foot on the mainland of North America. Many places are named after him: Ponce in Puerto Rico, Ponce de Leon and the Ponce de Leon Bay in Florida, among others. The sixteenth century was a good time to look for things like the fountain of youth and the city of gold. Sailors often spotted mythical beings like mermaids and sea monsters. Most of these wonders were spotted in the new world, or en route to it. But in the seventeenth century, when mythical beings had become difficult though not impossible to report, a man from a dubious Creole background, who claimed he was from Puerto Rico, and a descendent of Juan Ponce de León, from a branch that had married into a Portuguese family, went looking for the Fountain of Long Life in Africa.

Don João Miguel, as he was generally known, had some money, and a smattering of languages, including Greek, and he based his plans on a careful study of Herodotus and his sources. This much is clear from his anotação, or those of his notes that have survived, though most historians consider them apocryphal, as they are not in the original but an early-18th-century copy made by a Jesuit priest. The priest attests to the authenticity of Don João Miguel's anotação, which he had seen in the library of the College of São Salvador in the Congo and derived his notes from. He claims that the ailing writer of those sheaves of anotação had met João de Paiva, the rector of the college, in 1639, and the legendary rector had even written about Don João Miguel's voyages in his (now lost) chronicle of the region. But the Jesuit priest made his notes in 1726, a year after the compilation of *Synopsis Annalium* by António Franco (1725), which, as everyone knows, was extensively based on João de Paiva's lost chronicle, and which makes no mention of João Miguel.

The Jesuit's notes from João Miguel's anotação reveal many things about the Congo region, but all of these also come to us from other sources, particularly António Salva's *Synopsis Annalium*. The only thing that is unique about Don João Miguel's anotação is his claim that in 1637-8, when he led a small expedition to the borders of the Kingdom of Matamba, then largely hostile to the Portuguese, now in modern-day Angola, he was given a map to the Macrobian Fountain of Long Life mentioned by Herodotus. This map was given to him by an old man who claimed to have drunk from the fountain sixty-nine years ago. He was then at least 127 years old, and he claimed that he would die soon, as he had no wish to return to the fountain, and only the water of that fountain, which bubbled up from deep inside the earth, contained the properties to prolong life. What are the properties, João Miguel had asked him? The old man had said that they were the souls of other beings, living deep inside the earth, which come to inhabit the human body and prolong its existence on earth. He knew, he had argued, because he has been carrying two souls ever since he drank from the fountain, one of his own and one of the other being, who was also him now, and he would like to relinquish both, for every life needs to end someday. We cannot choose how we enter the world, but we can choose how to leave it, the 127-year-old man had told João Miguel, through an interpreter of course, and drawn him a map of the fountain on a piece of leather. João Miguel also noted that, unlike other natives, who stank of perspiration or worse, this old man had a strong body fragrance that brought to mind the scent of violets.

Don João Miguel could not cross the Kingdom of Matamba then, given its resistance to Europeans, and had returned with the map to raise more money and men for another expedition. But he had died eight months later of a high fever, and the map had never been found, according to the Jesuit.

~

Hanif's red and white pølsevogn was not outside the station. This surprised Jens Erik, but then he had not been in town for a couple of months. He ought to find out if the guy had moved somewhere else.

Not that he would need Hanif as an informer again, for Jens Erik was on leave prior to early retirement. But he had known Hanif for decades, and it was something he felt obligated to do.

Much of Jens Erik's life, like the landscape he appreciated, came in small bundles of familiar acts and responses. He mistrusted the heroic and preferred the habitual. Even his conversation followed that pattern, for Jens Erik seldom spoke about things he did not know personally or well. And even then, mostly, in as few words as possible.

That is why, though Pernille never understood it, he did not discuss the resurgence of Islamism in Iraq or the intermittent racial conflicts in the US or the recent attempt on the life of the Saudi monarch or the latest billionaire fad of cryogenic capsules being sent to other planets, not even the various kinds of unrest that had followed the pandemic in many countries. That is why he did not talk about international migrancy, a condition he neither wished to imagine nor could imagine.

Matters concerned him only when they happened around him, and thankfully he'd mostly avoided bad things. Even the post-pandemic unrest had been mild in Denmark.

Jens Erik crossed the road outside the station with his straight, slightly stiff gait, watching with distaste as the young kids from the tram jumped the light before it turned green, then crossing into the pedestrian street, which was quite crowded. Jens Erik did not notice it much, as he was used to this street. He would have noticed a similar crowd in Copenhagen or London.

He checked his phone for the address that Pernille had sent him on SyncApp, a café by the riverside. Pernille had attended a birthday party and slept over at a friend's the previous night. She had arranged to meet her father for lunch before heading back to Copenhagen.

Should I insist on paying, Jens Erik wondered? Or would she find that too patronizing, now that she has a Ph.D. scholarship?

Jens Erik struggled to make up his mind on such matters. So much of what was just habit in the past, he felt, could be considered oppressive today. Jens Erik shook his head and continued walking in his military manner past the McDonald's and down to the riverside.

The river was more like a canal with cement banks, which were mostly lined with cafés, bars, and restaurants. It had been covered up and paved under a road in the 1970s. Then some bright chap in the government had realized how stupid that was. Soon it had been dug up and restored to being an actual riverside. Now it was the heart of the dining district of Aarhus.

Jens Erik crossed a bridge with the statue of a cyclist at one end and turned right.

Even though it was cold and the weather held the threat of a drizzle, there were people eating outside, wrapped up in the blankets handed out by the restaurants, under the awnings. Inside, the lighted cafés and restaurants were mostly full.

I hope Pernille has booked a table, thought Jens Erik. He did not relish the prospect of sitting outside under an awning. Sharing blankets was not him. He had never liked doing so even before the pandemic made the practice unthinkable. It was like being wrapped up in other people. People were good—at a certain distance.

The place was called Bistrot Hanne Hanne. Jens Erik wondered if Pernille and her friends would have considered it cool if the place was called Café Hanne. He smiled at the thought.

Pernille was inside, waiting at a table with a bottle of an elderberry drink and a tall glass. She had stopped drinking alcohol two years ago, much to Jens Erik's consternation. He took off his cap and entered the place.

The hostess at the kiosk inside the door—not older than twenty and looking like a poster girl—turned an inquiring gaze at Jens Erik, but he simply pointed at the table occupied by Pernille and proceeded to go there. Pernille stood up in the tiny space to give him a hug.

He had some trouble squeezing into his chair between the tiny table—could he even lean his elbows on it?—and the glass wall behind him. It was not his size and girth. No, it was one of those places. If you ate freely, you knocked a plate off the next table! And, oh no, the menu card—damn, Jens Erik muttered under his breath, what was this?—when a model-waiter came with the menu card. It was a tablet. Jans Erik let Pernille order for both of them.

He told himself: Just shut up and eat, *mand*!

The lunch proceeded without any friction. That is what went wrong. It proceeded too smoothly, and Jens Erik let down his guard at the end, after Pernille had asked for the bill.

It was unfortunate, he thought later, that the loud boys from his tram happened to pass by the restaurant just then. They paused under the awning, availed of an ashtray on one of the outside tables to stub out a cigarette, whooped at something one of them said, leered into the interior of the restaurant, and finally went on. They had probably been drinking a beer or two.

"Wish they would not do that," Jens Erik commented.

"Do what?"

"Those immigrant boys. They were in my tram. They draw attention to themselves. It gives people the wrong impression."

Pernille sat there, with the slightly baffled look that she often assumed when he said something wrong by her standards. He thought she would tick him off for calling the boys immigrants. But she had another point.

"Far," she said, "What is it that your immigrant boys are doing that similar Danish boys won't do? Why do you comment on them in particular?"

"It is simple, Pernille. When you have moved to a new place, you need to be more careful in the way you behave. People notice you more. You want to make a good impression. It is the same if you join a new class or office…"

Pernille made an exasperated sound.

"You hate people moving, don't you, Far? Even from here to Copenhagen…"

"I don't see any problem with staying rooted…"

She interrupted him.

"You have heard of Salman Rushdie, Far, haven't you?"

"Humpf ... Yes, the Iranian writer with an Indian fatwa in, when was it, the 1990s? Is he still alive?"

"The Indian writer with an Iranian fatwa. Ex-fatwa. Actually, he grew up in England."

"So, he moved," Jens Erik commented in a late and unsuccessful effort to lighten the discussion.

"Anyway, Far, he writes in one of his books that trees have roots, human beings have legs."

Jens Erik sipped from his coffee, hoping the waiter would come with the bill soon.

"You get the point, Far? Trees have roots, so they stay in one place; human beings have legs to move with, walk, run, travel, emigrate."

"Well, Pernille, human beings also have buttocks to sit on."

Humpf, said Pernille. Jens Erik did not notice that she sounded exactly like him. But he regretted the quip. He wished he had restrained himself to a simple humpf. It was his favorite word. What a perfect concise non-committal expression!

Pernille's eyes had glazed over.

In the past, she would argue or say, a favorite expression of her mother's in his last few years with her, "whatever," and walk away, but now she simply got this glazed look. Jens Erik knew that look. It reminded him of the time when, as a small boy, he would have nothing better to do than bounce a rubber ball against a wall. You did it mechanically. You started doing it without even looking at the ball, your eyes glazed.

You knew the wall was incapable of any surprise.

It was only when he was saying goodbye to her outside that Pernille asked him, "Are you sure, Far, that you have never discriminated between the crimes to solve, the complaints to follow up, based on color or ethnicity?"

Jens Erik reined himself in this time. He only said "humpf" and waved at her as she walked away, a tall, attractive girl with determined, angular steps. She walks like a man, he thought. He remembered that she had always walked like that.

It was his walk, his ex-wife had pointed out to him a long time back. She walks like you. He smiled.

5

Walt Disney

IF Walt Disney made a cartoon of Alvin, descending thousands of meters into the ocean at a point not too far from the famous islands that in 1835 provided Charles Darwin with the material for his theories, it would appear as a fat, podgy, white shark with a stubby fin. But Alvin was a submersible and this was 1977. It was carrying three geologists who would be the first to explore the hydrothermal vaults that they believed existed down there: vaults where water, heated up to 400 degrees Celsius, bubbled out of volcanic chimneys in the seabed. Alvin had powerful lights, for it was pitch dark down there. Not a ray of sunlight ever penetrated that far down.

It was darker than night. A night full of occasional shooting stars: bioluminescent creatures. Alvin sank farther down. The geologists eventually found the vents at a depth of about two and a half kilometers. But they found something else, something they had not expected. They found life! A profusion of species: clams, fish, crabs, pale shrimps. And rocks encrusted with hard tubes, ghostly white, with crimson tips: a surreally suggestive architecture that could have inspired Playboy photographers.

Life—in the lightless depths of the ocean, where the water could be up to 400 degrees Celsius? How could life exist here, and in such profusion, without even the possibility of photosynthesis? There was one explanation, of course: chemosynthesis. Way back in 1890, Sergei Winogradsky had proposed that some microbes could live solely on inorganic matter, liberating energy directly from them and not needing to use the sun's energy. In 1897, Wilhelm Pfeffer had coined the term 'chemosynthesis' for the creation of energy by the oxidation of inorganic substances. But surely that was all about microbes, those simple one-celled organisms?

It turned out that it was—and wasn't. Many larger organisms could use the microbes to create energy for themselves. Though Playboy worms were the biggest clue—or the biggest problem, for they had no mouths, guts, or anuses. Until, a few years later, a young zoologist, Colleen Cavanagh, unraveled their secret: they used bacteria, about a billion for every gram of tissue, to create energy from the sulphides that spewed out of the volcanic vaults. And worms were not alone in doing so. Over the years, other complex species, such as shrimps and crabs, have been discovered, mostly but not only around hydrothermal vaults, which use chemosynthesis to live and can do without sunlight.

~

When Harris wakes up, he is in his bed, with a strong sun beating on the curtains, filling the room with diffused light. The wind has stopped blowing outside. It promises to be a hot June day, as hot as it can get in Denmark.

Then he sits up. Why is he lying in bed? His last memory was of Mermaid, or the ghost of Mermaid, talking to him across the dining table. They had been sipping beer.

He is in his shorts. His silk sleeping robe hangs from a peg as it always does, the dragon on its back snarling at him. Had he not put it on when he had gone downstairs? Harris races down the steps. There is no one there. No can of beer on the dining table. Nothing in the wastebasket either.

A spot on his upper arm itches, and he scratches it absentmindedly. It hurts. He examines it. A red insect bite. Irritating, he thinks, and caresses the red spot tenderly.

He walks around the house. Spotting him, the swans think he has come out early to feed them; they come gadding after him. All seems to be in order. He goes to his study; everything is as he had left it the day before, but somehow he feels someone has been through his papers and files, opened and shut his computer. The order of his things is the same, except that it is all too well ordered, the edges too even, the mouse right in the middle of the pad.

Harris dismisses the suspicion: he is being paranoid. It must have been a dream. Not that he has ever had such a coherent dream. He has not heard a sound in his dreams for years now; mouths open and close soundlessly in them, men get blown up by minefields without a whisper, a drone comes screaming silently at him, there is a woman holding a child, dead in her arms, and wailing, soundlessly, while all around her, there is nothing but water, a woman Harris does not know, as he has never fought or killed out in the sea. Perhaps it was age; perhaps this is what happens when people approached sixty: their dreams start filling with ghosts and coming alive. Sound returns.

That is what Harris tells himself. Except: he does not believe in ghosts. He could not have survived in his profession if he had. But he also knows that paranoia is the worst enemy of people in his line, ex-line, damn you, he tells himself, and he has always struggled to resist paranoia. It is both the snake and the apple. It must have been a dream. At least his nightmares have turned coherent and stereophonic. He frowns.

He goes to the fridge. Harris has always been a methodical man. He counts things and keeps mental diagrams of how they are arranged without even being aware of it; that is just what he is, and what he had trained himself to become even better at. Unconsciously, he counts the beer cans in the bar-fridge. There are two missing.

Then he turns around and notices it: a crumpled piece of paper on the dining table.

Harris smooths out the chit. It bears a single line, printed in red in roman italics: *Can you ring to me when you have done the shopping and cleaning for week 14 and perhaps also had the time to go to the post office to put all those dutiful letters and bills in the box?*

Harris almost laughs aloud. A Samestic chit like this made sense if you wanted a message to remain unseen even when spotted. But a Sebald code? What the fuck? He would have expected something far more complicated from Mermaid. It makes him wonder: was the man Mermaid after all? A Sebald code is not something that a mathematical whiz like Mermaid would devise unless he was in a hell of a rush and utterly distracted. No, thinks Harris, no, not even then.

Harris puts the chit in his pocket. Then on impulse—impulse had saved him as many times as restraint in the past, and Harris has nothing against either—he takes it out, goes to the kitchen, rummages around for a matchbox, lights a match and watches the chit burn up into shriveled shreds in the basin. For good measure, he lets the tap run.

He does not need the code to remember the message.

He goes back to his room and takes a leisurely shower. In the mirror, he gazes at the white hair on his chest and the slight sag and love handles further down with an expression of wonder, as if he had just noticed them. Then, on an impulse, he shaves off his goatee. By the time he is dressed, he can hear the swans squabbling outside his main door. They are hungry. Harris has four swans, big bossy birds, their wings clipped, who can bite a watchdog-worthy chunk out of an intruder's thigh. Other people keep dogs; Harris keeps swans. No walks on a bloody leash, and you can leave them to fend for themselves for a few days. Also, they advertise his need for protection much less than dogs would, and they are just as effective.

Or, they should have been. Someone managed to get in last night. And leave, without any trace. Someone or something. Harris does not believe in anything without blood and bones, anything that does not bleed when shot. He has seen too many people who believed they were impervious to a bullet, either because they had a talisman or were doing their God's will, bleed to death in front of his eyes, scream as their fingers were chopped off or a pen was prodded into their spilling guts. He has done the occasional chopping and prodding himself.

He goes out and scatters some feed on the gravel of the driveway; the swans flap and feed, honking. He looks around. The lawn beyond the driveway is wet with dew, undisturbed. The gate is latched. The flowerbeds around the house do not betray any sign of having been trampled. Whoever left the chit must have levitated. But Harris knows that flesh-and-blood people can levitate too, or almost; all of them in Command Alpha were capable of entering such houses without leaving a trace. He doubts many people outside Command Alpha can do it. That is one reason why the man with Mermaid's voice could only have been Mermaid.

"PO Box 214". That is what the chit said. Harris is familiar with the old post-office building; he goes there once a month for the only letter he receives. It comes to his numbered box; he writes back to another numbered box, in a town in California. The letter does not bear a name, but Harris knows it is from the woman they had called Kath during his days in Command Alpha. Kathy. They arranged these numbered boxes just before they chose to "die". Kathy chose first; her need for analgesics was getting out of hand, she said. She called them analgesics. But of course, the drugs were a symptom too. She had never needed them before she joined Command Alpha. None of them had, despite having seen action with Navy SEALs, GIGN or Sayeret Matkal earlier on. Nothing had prepared her for the morass of Command Alpha.

Finally, like Harris, she had chosen what they used to call the Big Death: retirement into civilian life with the past erased and a new identity created for you. There was a large severance pay and a small "self-pension" from a private bank. They did not retire, because, technically speaking, they had already quit to join Command Alpha, quit in their early twenties from various branches of the armed forces.

There had been the Small Death too: those of them who were shot, stabbed, blasted, hacked, or killed in one of the thousand and one ways. And then there was what they called, ironically, the Un-Death: few people chose it. You were the Undead when you left Command Alpha for some other service, something smaller, less secret, less violent, with your years at Command Alpha replaced in your papers with a posting on deputation in British Honduras or some other untraceable, innocuous activity. Mermaid might have chosen it. He was the type. In which case the news item about his death on a mission in Afghanistan nine or ten years ago had been a plant.

6
Kathy

KATHY still has her first name, the name Harris knew her by, though her surname has changed, as have all her papers. But Harris would have trouble recognizing her: She'd had her nose changed, her hair was long and blonde ... She is not a close-cropped brunette any longer. Harris would, however, recognize her by her body, which is still compact and muscular, and bears a tiger tattoo, stretching from under the suprasternal notch, which the tiger appears to be trying to grasp in its open mouth, circling to the back, over firm buttocks and down one leg, around which the predator's tail curls and finally ends exactly at the talus.

Right now, that body is wrapped against the body of a man, fairly well-built, much broader and at least a foot taller. Kathy holds him as a woman might hold a lover: he is on top, and she has her arms around his neck, clasped tightly at the back, and her legs are wrapped around his waist. As the man is wearing only jogging shorts, and she has a red bikini on, they look very much like a couple in the throes of some rather hectic foreplay. The man pants and tries to squeeze his arms between Kathy's legs in an unsuccessful attempt to prise them apart. Kathy tightens her limbs around the man, her biceps and calve muscles bulge, causing him to gasp, emit a small scream of pain, and shout, "I give, I give."

This is what Kathy does for a living now. She wrestles men in private sessions. Sometimes she lifts them and carries them. Sometimes she lets them challenge her to boyish games of pull-and-tug or other ways of testing her strength. She charges $500 per hour. She does not want to do shitty jobs that pay $20 an hour anymore.

Her Big Death has not gone as well as Harris's: all that remains is a small private pension. The rest of the money went into bad investments and some expensive habits. Now she lives out of a camper van. Sometimes she goes on long drives, but rarely travels far from California for more than a few weeks. She needs the money. Not for food, gym, and the rest—her pension could be stretched to cover that—but for the drugs that keep her from going stark raving mad. Especially the new one that hit the black market two or three years ago: the wonder drug, Crobe, with no side effects, as far as Kathy can see, and a high that leaves you floating for hours in a psychedelic universe before returning you to balance and calm for days afterward. When it wears off, the calm rejoins the different broken bits of you—heart, mind, emotion, reason—and you need another dose.

Every time she retrieves and reads a letter from Harris, she cannot help wondering how Harris ever managed to make it through to the Big Death without drugs. Not even weed. Sometimes she wants to ask to him to meet. But they had agreed not to contact each another unless there was an emergency. And that is best: they have too many common memories. Of drones and murders, of killings and torture. But she feels the emptiness in her would be filled, or at least partly assuaged, if she could, just once, hold him in her arms, wrap her legs around him, as she does with these men, and not squeeze.

~

The year 2031 was a time of celebrations, as it marked the tenth anniversary of the first vaccines, not all equally effective, against SARS-CoV-2, popularly still known as the novel coronavirus, the microbe responsible for the Covid-19 disease, and millions of deaths in 2019–21. By 2031, memories of the dread that the virus had evoked in many circles had faded. Its after-effects had continued but were largely confined to those sections of society, the poor and the marginalized, and those parts of the world, the poor and the marginalized, whose plights had been habitually ignored for decades. The Covid-19 patients who claimed never to have recovered were often dismissed as freeloaders, trying to rip off the state, despite growing scientific evidence of the ways SARS-CoV-2 could affect the brain, leading to prolonged encephalopathy. There were even "virus revisionists", lately in fashion, who questioned almost everything known about pandemic: if they were from the Right, they saw it as a natural culling of the "unfit". If they were from the Left, they blamed it on the mismanagement of governments.

Many people were simply not interested in these dated, ten-year-old stories of suffering. Neither were they interested in connecting pandemics to climate change or human lifestyles.

There had been a boom in productivity from the year 2022, and the financial markets had thrived in recent years, with billionaires becoming even richer. In 2030, *Forbes* declared that there had never been as many millionaires and billionaires in the world. The article was titled "The Greatest Age of Prosperity Known to Mankind".

There was violence out there, no doubt (When was there no violence out there?). It was often reported in apocalyptic language online and in the few printed newspapers and magazines that still survived. Race riots simmered across America, no matter who was in power, mainstream Democrats or Trumper Republicans, and an entire generation had become used to it. There were bread riots in places like India and Brazil, but the governments blamed them on "mischievous" and "anti-national" elements, and business went on as usual in the polite circles. Boatloads of refugees continued to sink in the seas, and just in January that year an NGO ship, sailing the Mediterranean rescuing such refugees, had caught fire after a mysterious blast, killing fourteen people. The old Putin oligarchies in Russia were said to be unravelling and moving into "business" elsewhere. Israel was stuck in an electoral stalemate—after three elections—between two Zionist coalitions whose sole point of agreement was on the need to deport Palestinians. There were reports of increasing piracy off Africa, and a new reactionary movement in Saudi Arabia, though all this could be explained away. There were greater worries due to sinking coastlines and islands—especially as the Maldives had announced on 26th July 2030, during its Independence Day celebrations, that it would be procuring and arming ships to ferry its entire population to other nations unless the global community did something to help them within the next twelve months. Since January this year, a US carrier had been poised just outside its waters in response, though it was not clear if this was potential help or immediate warning. Of course, a new generation of climate-activist schoolkids had come up, but it was obvious that, like the previous generation, they would soon be tamed with student loans for university education and the pressure of careers.

In general, it was the best of times—for the people who count in the world were thriving. It was more than that. These people were euphoric. Despite continuing issues with GDPs, the financial markets were booming once again, and property prices rising in nine out of the twelve leading economies of the world. Above all, the silver bullet of vaccines had not only killed that werewolf, SARS-CoV-2, all the dire warnings of scientific Cassandras had been proved wrong. True, some millions had died, directly or indirectly due to the pandemic, but it was still much less than what had been prophesied. Best of all, the rise of various new vaccine technologies had assured the rich and the powerful that another pandemic was not just at least a century away, but would probably, like the last pandemic, cull mostly the poor, the aged, and the vulnerable.

Why, even the scare of 2028 had come to nothing. Virologists had warned of a new mosaic virus made up of H5N1, the "bird flu", and H1N1, the "swine flu". This had sent a ripple of panic in the scientific world and become a "Nostradamus moment" on social media, because, in his book from 2011, *The Viral Storm*, the virologist Nathan Wolfe had warned of exactly this combination.

Wolfe had noted that in 2004, H5N1 had a 60 percent fatality rate, but the rate at which it spread was low. On the other hand, H1N1 spread exponentially from 2009, though its fatality rate was only around 1 percent. However, Wolfe had noted, viruses are particularly good at swapping genetic material and creating new mosaic viruses. There was no guarantee that a mosaic virus made of H5N1 and H1N1, both endemic in the human population, would not combine the fatality rate of H5N1 and the ability to spread of H1N1. In short, it would be catastrophic.

Hence, with the discovery of a H5N1/H1N1 mosaic virus in 2028, this book—and its dire warnings—spread like wildfire on social media. As it turned out, the mosaic virus had combined genetic material in ways that made it both less deadly and less likely to spread, and the scare fizzled out. It was, the rich and the powerful argued, just another attempt by scientists and activists to put the brakes on economic progress, the only thing that could save mankind, perhaps by making undersea dwelling and farming possible or Mars inhabitable. All it needed was more investment, some vision and, of course, the occasional sacrifice by ordinary people. All the rest was just obstruction and fault-finding, mostly with dubious leftist roots. The innocuousness of the H5N1/H1N1 mosaic virus of 2028 contributed to the rejoicing that swept through the world three years later, at least in those circles with the wherewithal to rejoice. The world was thriving! Viruses were dead! Mars was awaiting colonization.

~

The post office is a mid-20th-century red brick building. Its exterior has been recently scraped of a century of paint layers and restored to a supposedly pristine state, one of those public works intended to rejuvenate the economy. It is in a corner of the town, not in the center, as one would expect, but then the town has grown and diminished with the ebb and flow of financial speculation in Copenhagen and other metropolises across the world. After every boom, it moved a bit westward, and each time a bubble burst, a bit of its eastern section turned into a ghost neighborhood. As a result, the building has ended up on the town's periphery.

You have no reason to cross it unless you take the eastern exit out of town, heading for Copenhagen, and in any case, not many people use the postal service anymore. Postboxes have gotten rarer over the years; Harris remembers a time when there was one on almost every major street. Now entire neighborhoods lack a postbox. He read online last week that three out of five small towns in America do not have a postbox at all—no postal service. He has seen children gaze without comprehension at them when encountering one at a station or an airport. Where they survive, as in Denmark, post offices have mostly become a cubicle in the supermarket. But here the local post office has survived because part of it was turned into a museum of postal history. Viborg City is that kind of place. Between the functioning postal section and the larger museum, there stretches a long and dark corridor where you can still, if you wish, book a PO box. Harris knows because he uses a box number for his correspondence.

PO Box 214. It is, not surprisingly, next to Harris's number: 215.

Too early to decide; the box can wait. Harris waits. Waiting is obligatory. People who do not wait get fucked up. He waits until it is his day to perform the one ritual that connects him to his past. He knows that the reason Mermaid, or whoever it was, has chosen the box in the post office is this ritual. Obviously, they know—when Harris had thought no one knew, except Kathy.

Harris has enough self-irony to laugh at this expectation, faint though it had been. Someone always knows. He has known that all his working life.

The copy Harris has made of an academic given his deep suspicion of "originals" has many advantages. It keeps him from thinking. It keeps him from remembering. It keeps him within the range of the deeply cultivated, the totally unremarkable, and hence that which is unlikely to add to the world's and his own nightmarish surfeit of bodies blasted, limbs torn apart. The only thing he does out of choice rather than routine is write anonymous letters, once a month. He exchanges them through his numbered PO box with Kathy. He often wonders about her: has she found something or someone to stay fit for? Kathy, with a tiger tattoo running down her back, had been the fittest woman he met in Command Alpha, more fit than most of the men in an organization whose fitness level was indexed against that of top Olympic athletes. But they never exchange photos. For all he knows, Kathy is an out-of-shape mother of two brats by now. She could have had babies: she had been around a decade younger than him.

This is the day he usually goes to the post office to collect his letter from Kathy, unsigned responses to the anonymous letters he sends to her numbered postbox in a town in California. Even this exchange of letters is bending the "advisory", which declares: "It is recommended not to contact your colleagues from Command Alpha after retirement, as that can compromise, you, them, or both." But they have no choice. They had seen too much to want to be reminded of it by being together, even if it had been possible. But they had also shared too much to let go of each other completely.

At the box, he stabs in the code. The box springs open and Harris retrieves the envelope. He knows it is from Kathy; no one else writes to this box. Then he closes the box again. He cannot help glancing at the box next to it. It is the second to last one in the row, the box listed in Mermaid's chit. Harris has almost made up his mind not to take up Mermaid's offer. The box is locked, of course, and Harris wonders, suddenly, if he can figure out the code to open it.

He tries some possible numbers: his real date of birth; his current date of birth. They do not work. He tries the code for Box 215, because, who knows, they might have it too? But no, it does not work. Then, as if it was a voice whispering in his head, he knows the code; it would be his registration number from Command Alpha. He tries it. Box 214 springs open.

Inside, there lies a folder. Harris takes it out: it is yellow and unmarked.

Harris puts the yellow folder on his dining table. He wonders why he has taken it out of the box and brought it home. He had told himself that he would just take a look at the content and then put it back. But he hasn't. He has brought it home with him.

Perhaps he would not have done so if the contents were more predictable. Or maybe he would have brought it home anyway.

The folder does not contain what Harris had expected, and he is intrigued. There is a seminar schedule, an international seminar on something called the "mind-body seminar series" held at Aarhus University, Denmark, in 2012. The seminar was called "Mind, Body and Soul: The Cognitive Sciences and Religion". Harris can imagine it was one of many such seminars spawned by

Islamic fundamentalism and the overlapping return to religion in the West in the first decade of the twenty-first century, with academics scrambling to both flow with the tide and not be sucked under by the waves.

A seminar program, and a few loose sheets containing abstracts of papers, plus a separate sheaf, stapled together. The names of all the speakers in the program have been highlighted in different colors. They are from various disciplines and universities spread all over the world. Nine are highlighted in red, four in yellow, and one in green. The folder also contains short synopses of their careers and "current status", and some photos. Harris can see that all but five of the synopses end with the remark: "Dead in natural but mysterious circumstances" or "Death by accident". Of the four that are still alive, three are marked as "untraceable" and the fourth, a Professor Dutton, as "confined to a psychiatric ward". These are the ones highlighted in yellow. The sole green-marked speaker is now a professor of linguistics at Harris's university, located in the Viborg City campus. Professor Horst Pichler. Harris has met him on some occasions: a large man committed to the hard sciences, swearing by Popper and with a tendency to make obvious puns. The location of Professor Pichler is probably the reason Mermaid approached Harris, but Harris also knows that it could not be the only reason: people like Mermaid had many contacts or could conjure them up.

Harris goes out to feed his swans. Then he pours himself a beer and takes the folder to the armchair where he usually does his reading. He changes into casual wear. The right clothes for the right activity: it is something he has learned to appreciate because he spent months in his working career wearing things he did not wish to wear. He skips the seminar program and the abstracts, and starts reading the thicker sheaf on the highlighted delegates.

7
Oil Rigs

I still cannot make up my mind about the water: is it gray-blue or green-gray? It changes with the light of the sky, the light that ranges from gray to golden. Why did I not notice this chameleon quality in the sea in St. Martin? Just as I did not notice anything about Kurt. Because, here, I soon began to make up my mind about Kurt. Ah, Kurt. My Kurt. Kurt of the golden syllables, the gossamer voice. Kurt of the clear blue eyes.

Kurt spent most of last evening in Vyachislav Mikhailov's room. His Michael, the tool pusher. But Mr. Watch is what I call him, for Vyachislav Mikhailov's job, I am certain, is to keep an eye on everything. Here and elsewhere; he is the only company man who flies in and out all the time. When he is here, Mr. Watch, I am convinced, also watches us, watches the rooms and corridors and spider decks, the closed sections, the helidecks up there, placed like two coins on the eyes of the dead. He watches the waves, the weather, the ships that occasionally cross the horizon, even when they are just specks shrouded in mist, unreal as paper boats. He watches, his gaunt pale face immobile, a dark woollen cap on his shaven head, his sinewy arms perennially folded across his chest, sitting or standing, always folded unless there is use for them. He watches. But he does not watch as your new boyfriend watched me when you were not around, Maman. He is not brazen.

That is not how Kurt sees it. He behaves as if he has found in Mr. Watch the big brother he says he never had. Mr. Watch is the man who has done things and been to places that Kurt has been unable to chisel into his incomplete novels. Anyway, that is what he made me believe earlier on. Mr. Watch has fought in the army; he has worked on rigs out here and in the Gulf; he has been a PMC in Iraq and Afghanistan. What is that? I ask Kurt. Private military contractor, he explains. Big business. A large chunk of the money that we plow into these dysfunctional countries goes into hiring PMCs. They are also employed on ships and rigs to fight piracy, especially after good old Trump, with international cooperation shredded beyond repair. Also big business. The guy knew his stuff. Chaos creates capital. If you have capital, O Divine Dulcissima. Many places it is the PMCs that keep everything running. Mostly ex-soldiers from our countries. You should hear the stories they have to tell!

Kurt launches into his novelistic spiel. When I met him first, I used to notice his clear blue eyes, which promised the horizon; now I notice his chiseled red lips, always slightly moist, which seem to have a life of their own, opening into a fathomless mouth full of words, words, words. You should be writing all this down, I tell him, silently.

For a writer, an aspiring one anyway, because he has never shown me his name in print, Kurt loves action: he treasures his Boker Scout pocketknife far more than any of his antique fountain pens or his Dell Precision 5 laptop. Not that he has worked much on his novel in our months together. I have never seen him writing. I am the one who uses the small library installed here, probably for the "guests", though the guests who come here, like the ones at the villa, are surely of the kind who display handsome bound editions without reading them. It is a strange library too, full of technical science books and cheap thrillers. There is a small film theater too. DVDs on a large screen. They need to have DVDs because, of course, you cannot stream anything here. No Wi-Fi out here, Kurt says. The only connection is wireless and the satellite room, and of course both are restricted. It surprised me when I arrived here: I thought the entire globe was wired. They must have a blocker installed: my phone and laptop catch nothing. DVDs are useful. Mostly the men watch them on their laptops in the rooms. I get to use the theater. Maybe the theater is a holdover from the time this rig was still producing. They must have had entertainment for the men. Otherwise, who keeps DVDs today? They died out years ago.

But what else can one do on this rig? It is a world without plants. Not even a potted cactus. Strange, isn't it? A state-of-the-art gym for the men, which I use only when Kurt goes with me, but no pots of flowers? Our sections are all heated. There could be flowers here. Outside, it is another story. It is often blowing so hard outside that one cannot go out for more than a few minutes. Wind from farther north, full of the ghosts of icebergs. The waves are like Kurt's spiels: monotonous. Sometimes the horizon lights up with colors, once even with lights moving across it, a glimpse of the northern lights, but it is rare. Even migratory birds do not usually stop here, as there are abandoned rigs in the region. Seals do clamber on to the lower decks sometimes, but you get tired of watching them after the first few times. They are not circus trained. Once, a week ago, there was a large owl. It sat up there, high above on the metal girders, and occasionally preyed on birds that resemble seagulls but are smaller, with black legs. They make a cry that sounds like "kittee-wa-aaake, kittee-wa-aaake". The owl was with us for four or five days. It left the bigger gulls and cormorants alone. Then one day it was gone, pursuing its migration to wherever it was headed. Not that anyone but I missed it. The "guests" never notice such things: they seldom go out on the platforms or walk on what Kurt calls the spider decks, a network of rusting ladders and gangways girding the rig almost down to the waves.

There are days when the "guests" are not here. Kurt calls them "guests". I think of them as "experts" or even, because it is so obvious, "doctors." The three who are regular visitors cannot be "guests" or "tourists". Why should anyone return to this rig? There is this very pink little man with white hair and the grayest eyes one can imagine; everyone calls him Professor. There is something ghostly about him, as if his face was slightly out of focus. He's the one who cannot drink a Riesling. Only chardonnays. Though he never takes more than a glass. And his two companions, a matronly woman with a permanent frown, around the same age as the Professor and I daresay secretly in love with him, and a much younger Indian man with the most astonishing potbelly in a skeletal frame that I have ever seen. It is as if the belly belongs to a different man. He is called Dubey. We had a Dubey in class. The Indian students called him Doo-bay. But here they all say Dub-eye.

Mostly, though I have little to do with the "guests" except during meals. I am kept busy cooking in my section of the galley—again Kurt's word for it. My job is to attend to the "guests". Your boyfriend would have been happy, Maman: this sullen gal's learnt to make 'erself useful doin' woman stuff. Unlike the men of the company, these are people who expect a better standard of cooking. Cook and clean; how can a poor young Caribbean woman, even one who studied and trained herself diligently to be a teacher or hotel manager, escape such duties in this world? But at least I do not have to cook for Kurt, Mr. Watch, and his men—the lot Kurt calls the "company". Does he mean company in the sense in which I was, once, company, good company, great company, or does he mean company in the sense of a corporation? I would have asked him such questions in the past. Now I just observe. Mr. Watch is not the only person who watches on this rig.

The dozen or so company men cook for themselves in their section of the galley, with Formica-topped tables and benches instead of chairs, their dining area separated from us by a glass partition. This partition, I can tell, is a recent addition, as are the upgraded rooms in the luxury corridors upstairs. My section of the galley has an almost state-of-the-art kitchen. Gantry, Kurt calls it. Again, an addition. It is a real pleasure working in it. You should see it, Maman. There is a room attached to the kitchen, decked up as a cozy restaurant. Even a small bar at the back. Kurt helps me when he has to, when there are too many "guests". But he spends most of his time with Mr. Watch and his men: the company. Or he disappears with his guests into a guarded and closed section, which you enter after crossing an open stretch full of leftover machinery and drums. This section is always kept locked, and I have been forbidden to enter it. The first day, that's where Kurt headed, the moment the chopper deposited us here, and Mr. Watch rushed out to the helideck and the two men embraced like long-lost brothers.

There is always at least one man guarding this closed section. Only Mr. Watch, Kurt, and the experts enter it freely, sometimes with a man or two to help them. It has a door like the ones you see in the vaults of banks in old films; you need to turn something like a steering-wheel to open it. "What's there?" I had asked Kurt on the first day. He had not answered me. "What's there?" I had asked him on the fifth or sixth day when Mr. Watch was with us for dinner. He sometimes eats with us, sometimes with the men. Kurt had not answered. There had been silence for a minute. Then Mr. Watch had remarked, in that unsmiling manner he has, his voice syrupy and dangerous at the same time: "Men's work. Not your concern."

~

Lenin Ghosh had never desired to climb mountains or go trekking in the wilderness. But he had done both for decades. It had all started in 1974, when Lenin was only nine years old. His mother was still alive, though she was ailing from the cancer in her uterus that would kill her less than three years later. They lived—both his parents were schoolteachers—in the small town of Phansa, which is the reason why the cancer was still undetected and would stay undiagnosed until the last months of his mother's illness. It was his mother who had set Lenin on his future treks and climbs. He had then been a roly-poly boy who spent his time reading science books (in three languages: Bangla, English, and Hindi) through thick black-rimmed glasses, and though he lost his fat in later years, Lenin never grew beyond five feet two inches or became visibly muscular. But villagers around the foothills of the Himalayas, especially in Nepal, which was not too far from Phansa, got used to the sight of this small Babu, tenacious if not strong, trekking along, digging up and taking samples around the roots of old trees, sometimes employing the locals to do the digging, but always under his watchful eye. What the villagers liked most about him was that, unlike other city-dwellers, he treated the trees and shrubs that he worked around almost as if they were sentient beings, capable of feeling and talking.

And that is how it had happened that summer afternoon when Lenin was just nine. The vacations had started, and monsoon was yet to descend. Lunch was just over. It was a furnace outside, but this room had a khus-cooler, the dripping weed-mat emitting its distinctive fragrance, and they always stayed in the room until the evening. Lenin was reading—he was always reading—a popular science digest, one of the few he had that also contained photos and illustrations. His mother and older sister were slicing mangoes, and passing them, in turns, to Lenin and his father, who was reading a newspaper. His mother looked up from her activity when Lenin laboriously turned a page—he could use only one hand as his other hand was sticky with mango juice—and remarked at a photo on the page, "That is Jogodis Chondra Bose, isn't it?"

Lenin read the caption. "Yes," he replied, "It says Jagadish Chandra Bose."

"Did you know that he was related to my grandfather?" she inquired, slicing another mango.

Lenin did not. His father looked up from his paper and added, "He died in Giridih, just around 200 kilometers from here."

That is what developed in Lenin a lifelong interest in the work of Jagadish Chandra Bose, especially his path-breaking discovery of the nervous system of plants, and took him, via a Ph.D. in botany from the neighboring Magadh University, a dissertation that he had written himself, to a job as a high school teacher—he did not have the clout to get a university position—which left him, a confirmed bachelor, with time to pursue his research. From the time he finished his Ph.D. to the winter vacation in 2004, when the minibus he was on plunged into a ravine in Uttarakhand, killing twelve passengers, including him, Lenin trekked, climbed, dug, sampled, and notated on every occasion that he could, and in the process almost missing his sister's wedding.

No one knew what he was doing. But in his mind, his work was a logical continuation of what Jagadish Chandra Bose had done. When he had started pursuing this line of research, which was cautiously mentioned and then safely circumnavigated in his Ph.D. dissertation, no one—at least in and around Phansa—had thought of the possibility. If Jagadish Chandra Bose had proved without any doubt that plants were sentient beings and could feel, then Lenin wanted to prove that they could talk too.

He did not like the word "talk", but that is what he had to use. The realization had come to Lenin quite early, when he was still just a college student, and had not read anything about the research already being done—though in a very early stage in the 1990s—elsewhere. Working on the nervous system of trees, Lenin had specialized in roots, which was the focus of his doctoral research, but that had led him on to fungi, especially mycorrhizae, or root fungi. It struck him as a coincidence that the word "mycorrhiza" was coined by Albert Bernhard Frank, who was essentially a contemporary of Jagadish Chandra, and the two had known each other. Quite early on, Lenin had begun to suspect that trees used their root fungi to communicate with other trees. Three years after finishing his Ph.D., on his second field trip in Uttarakhand, Lenin discovered a fascinating cluster of trees, some of them at least 200 years old: they were so intricately connected by root fungi that three trees in the cluster, which had been torn down by storms, one of them perhaps a century ago, were being kept alive by the other trees. Lenin returned to this cluster at least once every year, exploring and documenting it further every time.

When Lenin finally managed to obtain some recent papers on root fungi published abroad, he realized that the work he was doing was also being done—roughly around the same time—by others in Europe and America. This did not disappoint him. He had no desire to become famous. He did not think, even for a minute, that had he been living in London or New York, not in Phansa, he might have been listed among the pioneers of this developing field of research. He continued with his field trips and experiments. As far as he knew, this work was not being done around him, and that was enough to keep him going. Someone needed to do it here, he would have replied, if anyone had cared to ask him, just as his late father had always replied to friends who asked why he had taught all his life in God-forsaken Phansa: "Someone had to teach here."

8

The Visiting Card

It was none of his business.

Jens Erik was on leave—he had accumulated too many extra hours over the years—prior to retirement. About three years' worth of overtime. He could continue working until sixty and cash in those hours, but that was not Jens Erik.

He had always known that he would retire at fifty-seven, not the now-popular option of sixty for those who, like him, had managed to make the officer cut before turning fifty-seven. That gave them three added years of desk work, the work of secretaries, not of policemen, all for a higher pension. He did not agree with the new political fad of extending the retirement age to seventy, which was in the offing for most other professions, and then to, who knows, seventy-five, eighty? Humpf.

There was a time to work and there was a time to stop, and, as far as Jens Erik was concerned, the only people who worked until they dropped were people who had already stopped living. Jens Erik had not stopped living.

He had cousins he still saw. One of them, a widow now, lived alone in neighboring Lystrup, and he sometimes walked her dog for her. He would meet up with friends for a drink; two of them he had known from kindergarten. He had an uncle and aunt, both in their eighties, he still visited a couple of times every year.

He had his flat little house with its small lawn and beds of flowers; he had an allotment garden, a *kolonihave,* where he cultivated vegetables in the summer and maintained a greenhouse throughout the year.

He had been invited to five *julfrokoster*—Christmas lunches—this season. Three were still pending. He took trekking holidays up north or rented cottages in Skagen or on Bornholm, he belonged to a bird-watching club, he played badminton, a game you could enjoy with others but without intimate physical contact. His kind of sports.

It was a long if somewhat sedate list. It was the sort of list one does not notice from a distance. But it filled his life, and he saw no reason to work himself to death.

So he told himself, it is none of your business, *mand.* You are going to draw your hard-earned pension soon. Relax. Or as he put it, *slappe af nu.*

But he could not relax. He tried to push the image out of his mind, but his daughter's voice came up: Are you sure, Far, that you have never discriminated between the crimes to solve, the complaints to follow up?

I have not, he could have said with honesty. But then there were the Magic Gates, with their ornate, shining M. He could no longer avoid recalling that M. He had first seen it almost a decade ago—it was the last really cold winter he could recall: it had been on a visiting card clutched in the frozen hands of a corpse. He had been called to the beach. He was, so to say, the first responder.

That January there had been snow, and even the margins of the seashore had formed crusts of ice. Such winters were ordinary in his childhood and youth. But that was the last year he saw so much snow.

Jens Erik was not a climate change denier. No one who knew the land around himself could be, he always said. Climate change deniers are those who live in heated houses in cities and walk past bushes and birds without noticing them, without knowing them.

They are, he had once said to Pernille, and provoked a howl of protest from her, people who move too fast and too often—immigrants in their souls! They are so used to frequent changes that they cannot notice the climate, that slow old prehistoric reptile, changing. Because they have not known the land they live in, they do not notice how it has changed. One notices a change in the present only if one has a past to compare it to in the same place.

He had blushed, finding himself uncharacteristically eloquent on a topic.

You hate immigrants, don't you, Far, she had observed. He had humpfed, and stayed silent.

How could he answer that question? He was not good at putting his thoughts into abstract words. When he tried, he often tripped and fell into the wrong expression, especially with Pernille. But he felt that there was something to be said about staying in a place where you knew which berries to eat and which to avoid, where you could identify a bird hidden in a bush by its trill.

It had nothing to do with hating immigrants. Though he did not understand immigrants. Refugees he understood, but he could not understand why anyone would move by choice.

That January, he took a call from his boss telling him to drive to a pier in a stretch of the nearby Egå beach. A police car and ambulance were also being sent out, but he was closer. Someone had called to report what seemed to be a body in the sea.

Seagulls were hovering around in the low, slate-colored sky, cawing. Pushing past the brambles and rushes and over a strip of pebbled sand, where the thin ice crackled under his boots, he was the first one to reach the pier. He spotted the three women standing at one end of the pier, about twenty meters out in the water. There was a bench and railings out there, with steps leading down to the water.

The women were wrapped up now, but their hair was still wet, and he could guess that they had been indulging in a local pastime that was dying out: diving into the icy sea in the nude, usually early in the morning. It was said to be great for the circulation. Jens Erik had tried it a couple of times when he was a teenager—it had been a dare—but it was not something he would want to do as a hobby. Some people did though.

He heard sirens in the distance as he reached the women, one of whom, a tall lean blonde, pointed at the water under the pier. It was there, unmistakably, a body lying facedown amid the seaweeds, gently knocking against one of the legs of the pier.

The blonde shuddered. It was terrible, she said. Terrible. We were already in the water before we noticed, we noticed… it. She pointed, and shuddered.

I think there was no point calling for an ambulance, was there? One of her companions added anxiously. I hope we did the right thing? I mean, it is not as if one gets instructions about such matters anywhere.

She giggled nervously.

Then the blonde asked: Who is it?

Male, circa twenty-five years, Black, probably African. That was as far as the identification went following the post-mortem. There were no papers on the body. Nothing but a shred of a visiting card, which was mostly worn away by the seawater. That even the shred had survived was a miracle; the dead man must have clutched it like a lifeline. What was still legible were the words, Magic Ga…, with the M embossed in an elaborate, artistic style. The card had been clutched, with obvious desperation, in the fist of the dead man. Was it Magic Games? Was it Magic Gates? The eaten-away alphabet looked more like a "t" than an "m."

Somehow, he thought of it as Magic Gates.

It had not been Jens Erik's case. The homicide people had taken it from him and sent the body for a post-mortem. He might have followed the case out of natural curiosity because the circumstances were unusual. But whoever it was did not exist as a person in Denmark, or in Germany and Sweden, for the authorities had been consulted in these countries too, and the case had probably been filed away.

It was the only dead body he had ever recovered from the sea, yet he had forgotten about it. Until now.

Until the argument with Pernille, and close on its heels, there was something serendipitous about it, the missionary's lecture in Hjortshøj church, in which the Gates of Heaven were extolled as a connection to others in their essence, a formulation that had evoked a vigorous nod of affirmation from Bente next to him.

Jens Erik could still hear the missionary's sonorous, old-fashioned Danish phrases and Biblical quotations in his ears.

And God will open wide the gates of heaven for you to enter into the eternal kingdom of our Lord and Savior Jesus Christ.

The twelve gates were twelve pearls, each gate made from a single pearl.

And he was afraid and said, "How awesome is this place! This is none other than the house of God, and this is the gate of heaven."

The Magic Gates had come back to Jens Erik, leaving him with a choice: should he follow it up or forget it once again? Surely, there wasn't much to follow up? What could he tell his superiors? Surely it was best to forget it all once again?

Every second Friday of the month, Jens Erik met with his colleagues—ex-colleagues now—at Værthuset on Trøjborg. It was not a fashionable pub, and it was usually empty. There was a lingering smell of spilled beer and men's sweat in its wood-paneled interior that usually kept the young and women out of the place. You could find a table even on Friday evenings.

They had started meeting there about twenty-five years ago because two of them lived on that street, and in those days there could be a dozen of them in the bar every second Friday.

Now, there were only three or four. Some had retired, some had gotten divorced, some had married again, some had stopped drinking, some had started drinking so much that they needed to avoid pubs. Often, it was usually just him and Ulrik, who for years had been his best friend in the force.

Jens Erik took Bus 12, dropped off at the stop before Trøjborg Centre, and cut across the narrow residential streets to Værthuset. Ulrik was already there, at their usual corner table. He had a large

Carlsberg on the table. Værthuset only served Carlsberg, Tuborg, Albani, and one or two other Danish beers.

Jens Erik had never felt the need to cultivate a taste for German lagers, British ales, or Belgian monastery brews, as some of his friends had over the years. Neither had Ulrik.

There were three other people at the bar, regulars that Jens Erik knew by face but not name. They were not part of his group. They nodded to him. One of them said *God Dag*. Jens Erik wished him the same back, exchanged a word or two about the weather with the barman, who also knew him by face, and took his Tuborg back to Ulrik's table.

"You are late," Ulrik noted.

"Time matters less once you retire."

"Lucky bastard."

"You are one year older than me, Ulrik. You could retire too."

"Doesn't make any sense retiring before sixty. I mean both you and I did manage the cut in time. So why stop early? Fifty-seven is for plain policemen, not officers. Why not sit at a desk for three more years and get twenty-five percent more as your pension? Retire at sixty-eight I would say, if it was possible in our line, like it is for these bloody civilians. But before sixty, the fuckers effectively cut your pension."

"It is still more than enough for a single man, Ulrik."

Ulrik, like Jens Erik, had divorced some years ago and never remarried.

"Nope. I want to get as much as I can. I want to lie on my beach in Malaga with no worry on earth. I want to shut my eyes on my beach in Malaga and hear money tinkling into my pension account in Denmark."

Ulrik had bought a one-bedroom flat in Malaga. He spent his vacations there now. He kept urging Jens Erik to retire to Spain as well—the money carries a longer way, he noted—but Spain was far too hot for Jens Erik. He didn't say that: he just pointed to the pandemic summer of 2020, when poor Ulrik had been unable to vacation in his, then, freshly bought flat in Spain.

But Spain was not only too hot for Jens Erik. He also found the vegetation alien: Jens Erik had grown up being able to recognize the bushes and trees around him.

Some of his fondest memories were of his father and mother, both of whom had grown up on small farms in the days when small farms still existed, walking around with him, perhaps from the time he could toddle, and plucking off leaves and berries to tell him what they were and which ones could be eaten and which ones were poisonous. They would go mushroom picking, berry picking, and, with his mother, wildflower gathering every season.

He had done so with Pernille too: he had good memories of walks in the woods with her until she turned thirteen and grew sullen because of a bloody photograph in a leftist rag.

He had not been planning to ask Ulrik, but thinking of Pernille, brought it up.

"Do you recall that body we pulled out of the water at Egå sometime back?"

"The African with the visiting card?"

"Yup. What happened to it? You were on the case, weren't you?"

"Not really. It passed my desk. Not sure anyone was put on it. We just followed the routine process. Probably the case got filed away. They could not identify him. I remember that. He must have been illegal."

"Not many of those here."

"Thank God. They add to your work."

"Must have been washed up from Germany…"

"Nope. Not Germany. I recall they said it was from further up. A colder region. The North Sea, they suggested. I recall reading it in some file. Something to do with water in the stomach or the way he drowned, one of those egghead things. There was something weird about him though."

"The visiting card…"

"No, something else. It was something when they examined him before the postmortem … I remember talking about it. Yes, now it's come back. The guy had a scar, or maybe two, on his torso…"

"A scar?"

"A fresh scar, recently stitched up. As from an operation. But he had not died of that. He had drowned."

The bit about the scar surprised Jens Erik. He asked: "We did not follow it up even after that?"

"Maybe they did. But it came to nothing. I would have heard if it had. You know how it is: we have enough cases of our own, why worry about a stranger no one can even identify? Obviously not a Dane. There is only that much funding for all this shit."

~

There is a statistical correspondence between weeds and genes, wrote the eccentric Green philosopher, Professor Sue Evelyn Post, in one of her last pieces. By then, she had long stopped writing academic papers, having come to detest the tyranny of the footnote, as she put it, and had started writing, first, largely coherent essays, which were carried in some newspapers and magazines, and then abrupt notes, which either remained unpublished or appeared in offbeat online sites with a dystopian slant. This was one of those notes.

There is a statistical correspondence between genes and weeds, she wrote. Take Homo Sapiens. Over 98 percent of the DNA in a human cell is junk. DNA, we are told, codes us into existence. It is your DNA that shouts out to the world, "This is me". Except that it does not do so. What it shouts out is this:

xxxxxxxxxxxxTxxxxxxxxhxxxxxxxxxis
xxxxxxxxixxxxxxxxxxxxxxxxxxxxxsxx
xxxxxxxxxxxxxxxxxxxmxxxxxxxxxxxx
xexxxxxxxxxxxxxxxxxxxxxxxxxxxxxx

The x's are our junk DNAs. For a long time, they did not exist. After all, our DNAs were supposed to be the Digitally Programmed Book of Evolution, as divine as the Torah, Gita, Bible or Quran had once been!

When finally discovered and accepted, they were largely ignored: the description "junk" is an index of that. They were junk because they were not needed; they did not code for proteins. But only 2 percent of our DNAs coded for protein. So what were these "junk DNAs" doing, and how did they end up filling most of the human genome?

What was even more bewildering was the discovery that genes do not provide any explanation for the supposedly "greater complexity" of the Homo Sapiens compared to other "simpler" organisms. In other words, the number of genes that code for proteins remain around the same in a human being and a microscopic worm: about 20,000. The only genetic factor that increases as we move from simpler to more complex organisms is the number of "junk DNAs".

It is now also clear that many of these "junk DNAs" are genetic interlopers, absorbed from the genomes of viruses and microbes. Some "junk DNAs" simply keep these borrowed DNAs in control, but others perform more positive functions, such as coding for RNA or regulating gene expression, or keeping our DNA from getting damaged.

Now, what is curious is that the ration of weeds to "flowers" and other accredited plants is roughly similar: left to themselves, what we call "weeds" would comprise around 98 percent of our gardens. What purpose do these weeds serve? I would argue that it is as misleading to call them "weeds" as it is to dismiss 98 percent of our DNAs as "junk". And I would argue that the problem of ecology is deeply connected to the problem of biology. Without overcoming such glaring simplifications in both the areas—not just how we live but also what we are!—we are doomed as a species, because, unlike other species, we are a species that is capable of formulating concepts like "weeds" and "junk" and manufacturing the tools to eliminate both.

9

Mitochondria Man

Horst Pichler's office is square, orderly, and large, like the man himself. The glasses Pichler wears are heavy and square too. There are very few books on the shelves, but an elaborate filing system rests against one off-white wall and a couple of advanced recording devices, gleaming black, squat on a side table. On the desk stands what seems to be the latest version of a computer, thin like a mirror and with no wire connecting it to anything, not even to the flat, polished keyboard, totally dark now, in front of it. Apart from that, the desk bears only a few sheets in a corner and a couple of practical ballpoint pens.

Professor Pichler has pretended to recognize Harris more than he actually does. Harris could see from the tentative way in which he fishes for information that Pichler only knows Harris as one of the lesser faces scuttling around doing stuff that the greater dignitaries, like the Professor himself, cannot be bothered with. Untenured colleague-creatures.

"Coffee," asks Pichler, in his loud, buff voice, after the initial introductions.

Harris declines, as he is expected to.

"Well, what can I do for you?"

Professor Pichler is always direct. The large, square watch on his broad wrist indicates that time is of importance to him. It is seldom, Harris thinks, that one sees people sporting wristwatches anymore; apart from their inseparable iPhones, there are a whole lot of other devices—time-chip glasses, alarm pens, whatnot—that have replaced wristwatches. If you still wear one, you do so either because you are stuck in the past, which was the case with Harris, or because you need to make a point about your time.

Harris explains to the Professor that he is looking for the full proceedings of a seminar and has been unable to find them anywhere. He is interested in some of the papers presented there; he needs them for his ongoing research.

"I can see you were there, Professor. So I thought maybe I could borrow the proceedings from you ..."

"What year would that be? Which seminar?"

"Aarhus University in 2012. Mind, Body and Soul: The Cognitive Sciences and Religion," replies Harris.

Pichler looks puzzled. Then his face clears and he lets out a guffaw.

"Ah, the wacko seminar!" he exclaims, looking very amused. He leans forward and almost pats Harris patronizingly on the hand: "Don't worry, Doctor. You are missing nothing. Nothing ever came out of that one."

"No proceedings? No publications?"

"Nope. That was one weird team of wackos! They had no plans to publish. The seminar tag was just to enable them to meet, with university funding of course. These people were more like a kind of mutual-admiration club. You see them blossoming everywhere in academia."

"I looked at the seminar schedule, Professor Pichler. Almost all of them had major reputations in their fields."

"Oh sure, sure. They did. Not all, but most. I would not have accepted their invitation if they did not. I refer to papers by one or two of them even now. Some had been half-wacko from the beginning, if you ask me, like that Green activist-scholar, Sue Post. But a few of them had major work in their fields. Some even in cognitive studies, which was my pet project in those days, though all from different disciplinary fields. Wislawa Ostrowski's work on the cognitive beginnings of religious thought remains groundbreaking. Vijay Nair was once an authority in the field of parasitism, from where he entered cognitivism and, I am told, disappeared into Buddhism or something like that later on. One of them was a major neurologist, another had worked with Damasio. There was a biologist who had been a bright young hope once upon a time, which in academia means a decade ago. And that was the case, Doctor: this was all in the past by then. Every one of them published their major stuff in the 1980s and early nineties. By the time of the Aarhus seminar in 2012, these scholars had gone slightly off the loop. Not madmen-wacky, understand, but acad-eccentric. It happens. It can be innocuous, like Edwin Hubble pretending to be a British aristocrat all his life when he was an American farmboy. Or it can be crazier: you will recall that scientists like the Nobel Prize-winning Kary Mullis have believed in UFOs. Gustav Fechner believed in spirit-rapping.

Spirit-rapping! Oh, the list is endless. Once-brilliant minds can succumb to dumb, crazy obsessions."

If I may ask, Professor Pichler, interrupts Harris, in what sense were these seminar speakers crazy, and if you thought they were crazy, what were you doing there?

"I didn't know they were crazy. Not then. Not when I accepted. I discovered they were crazy by the end of that day's proceedings. They were crazy, you may say, along the lines of Mullis and Fechner."

They believed in UFOs and spirit-rapping?

"Not really. It was subtler than that. They were, many of them, working on reason and emotion. A lot on microbia and parasites too, actually, which I had forgotten, but I remember thinking that there had been a fair bit on fungi and parasites and whatnot, too. It struck me as a funny coincidence eight years later, during the pandemic. But reason and emotion are what I recall as the thread that interested me. Different fields, differing perspectives, but it often circled back to reason and emotion. All except one or two of them, who were basically non-entities; I think there was a historian who gave a paper on a dream by Descartes! And yes, that's why they had invited me; those days I had been working on the linguistic topology of reason and emotion. Dead end. I gave that up long ago."

"Reason and emotion do not sound crazy to me, Professor. Not unless Plato was crazy too, and half the scientists after him."

"Sure, sure. Not in that way. It is what they were doing with it. Do you have that seminar schedule on you?"

Harris took the sheet out of the yellow folder and handed it to Professor Pichler. Pichler adjusted his square specs and frowned at the sheet, with just a glance at his wristwatch.

"Hmm," he said, "Katsumi Takewaki, let's see, no, no recollection, could hardly understand his English in any case ... The guy was a nuclear physicist, I think. He spoke of dark matter and whatnot. George Sutton, ah, yes, bonkers, absolutely bonkers. Had done good work in psychology too once, with Damasio I think, but bonkers by then. He gave this paper on UFOs or something like that as psychosomatic entities. Popper would have turned in his grave. Totally unfalsifiable! Let's see ... no, do not recall what Lars Larsen said, Danish guy, do not know his work in any case ... He was the host. Something on Descartes and his dreams. The soft humanities. Not a real scientist. Unremarkable, totally, like most Danes after Bohr. But Ostrowski, Wislawa Ostrowski, I remember her paper. I must say I had gone to the seminar largely to meet her. I was not here in those days; I was an associate professor in Munich. I made time for the seminar mostly because of Professor Ostrowski. She had not attended conferences for years, and then suddenly there she was, a scholar of her reputation, legendary for some, at this small invitation-based event in the backwoods of academia. I had to go when they invited me. Wislawa must have been in her sixties then, but she was a sprightly and sharp woman. Straight like a ramrod. Hair still dyed blond; traces of her famed beauty showing through the wrinkles and engrained in her posture. You know, when I was a Ph.D. student, it was said that audiences never knew what question to put to her because her beauty and bearing distracted all men, and the few women in the audience, from focusing on her presentation! Sexist I suppose, but true. I had people vouch for that. I recall her paper quite vividly. It was so disappointing. She appeared to have gone into Oriental mysticism and such rot. Essentially it was all about the transmigration of souls, but cast in scientific terminology. I know the Polish have a natural affinity for such stuff, Madame Blavatsky etcetera, but still… Wislawa Ostrowski! What a fall was there, my countrywomen! Let's see, who else, Vijay Nair … yes, Vijay I knew from before, our paths had crossed; we were both promiscuously interdisciplinary, and he was an authority on parasites. But—this will give you an idea of how crazy brilliant scientists can get—he spoke about parasites or microbes from outer space, and how they have influenced the evolution of human beings. Symbiogenesis was bigger then, Margulis et al., well … let's say Vijay was drunk on symbiosis. He saw it everywhere! Like some crazed fanatic hearing Jesus all the time. Everything, from the human body to the universe, was an ecosystem to him. Not metaphorically, which would be fine, but actually. Bonkers, totally bonkers!"

Pichler hands the sheet back to Harris with a laugh and a gesture of lighthearted despair.

"But Professor Pichler, there is a convincing argument that microbes have a symbiotic relationship with complex organisms. No one really denies it."

"This was about humans, Doctor. It was not about worms, rats, and shellfish. And it was all conjecture. You can put conjecture in a novel or film, fine, but keep it out of my laboratory, thank you, at least until you can formulate some falsifiable statements. Anyway, the one good thing to come out of that virus crisis in 2020 is that all such goody-goody, airy-fairy stuff about how we have to live in balance with our microbiome and virome has been starved of funding since then. The silver bullets of vaccines and drugs work better, as granddaddy Pasteur knew two centuries ago."

Harris wants to interrupt and say that, actually, Pasteur believed that most microbes were not harmful, and some could even be useful. But he does not want to antagonize this opinionated man. It is a retirement policy with Harris to avoid conflicts; he has waded through enough conflicts, real conflicts, not wordy ones, in the past. Instead, he asks: "You do not have notes from the seminar, by any chance?"

"Threw them away, threw them away ages ago. Why keep rubbish? Rub out the rubbish is what I say."

Then he paused. "Hey," he said, "That brought up something. I was asked about the papers many years ago too. Weird. I just remembered it!"

"Do you remember who asked you, Professor?"

Pichler shrugged. "It was at a conference, two or three conferences, actually. Different people. Now it comes back. Yes, I remember wondering then why, suddenly, there were two or three people asking me about it in conferences one after another. Young researchers. Not people I knew. Ph.D. students probably, maybe seven-eight-nine years ago. I had forgotten all about it."

Harris gets up to go. That is all he had expected from the professor: some surviving notes and papers. He is not surprised that Mermaid's men had sounded him out too, years ago. It makes sense.

Professor Pichler stands up with an effort. As they shake hands across the broad and almost square table, Pichler offers some consolation. "You are wasting your time, Doctor," he says, "Nothing useful came out of that seminar."

"Are you in touch with any of them now?" asks Harris.

"I wasn't even in touch with them then!"

"You wouldn't know what happened to them?"

"I guess they retired or are teaching in some hole. I do not recall seeing anything new in print by any of them for years now. Why?"

"Just so. I looked them up. Most of them are dead. They died over the past few years. In different places and at different times. Sometimes in odd circumstances."

Pichler looked surprised. "All of them?" he asked.

"Six or seven out of the lot, the majority," Harris replied.

"Vijay too? I used to know him."

"He disappeared in India."

"He was not from India. He grew up in England; he worked mostly in Germany and the USA."

Harris essentially paraphrased the information in the yellow folder for the professor: "Vijay Nair went to India a bit before the pandemic and settled in Calcutta. He got involved in leftist activism, was branded an urban Naxal, who were then being hunted down by the Indian government. Two years after the pandemic, he went into the countryside in Chotta Nagpur. It is a wooded, hilly region still inhabited by aborigines; lots of intermittent conflicts between the aborigines and mining corporations and what they call the land mafia. Before he disappeared, Vijay Nair had built up a kind of reputation as a sort of spiritual-cum-political leader among some of the agitating tribes. The police blamed his disappearance on the aborigines and arrested five of them, accusing them of being Naxalites. That is what they call any far-left revolutionary group in those parts, but there is a better chance he was abducted and killed by some land or mining mafia. But he has some sort of following. It is reported that he kept—keeps—appearing to his followers even now."

Pichler shook his head. "Sad. It is a sad world," he said.

Harris is certain Pichler does not know more than he has revealed. But he feels he owes him at least one correction, despite his retirement policy.

"No, Professor, it is a crazy world," says Harris, as he leaves the square and orderly office.

~

Kathy had done odd jobs. The best option for someone like her would have been to find work as a PMC. Kathy knew that many people who retired from the services ended up doing such jobs. Some were paid excellent salaries as private military contractors, if they worked with the syndicates protecting things like oil refineries in the Gulf or gold mines in South Africa, which were increasingly under attack by rebels or pirates or other syndicates. But there was no way Kathy would go back to a life that would remind her of her Command Alpha years. She knew she would go crazy if she ever had to go back to that kind of life: no drug would save her.

The other option was to work as a security guard in America. There was a growing craze for highly trained security guards among the very rich. New billionaires, in particular, paid a good salary, perhaps because it signified status. But the idea of protecting a billionaire or a family of billionaires did not appeal to Kathy. She had seen the ones protecting the Trump family on TV: they were dressed up in liveried uniforms with logos!

She did work as a security guard for a supermarket chain for a couple of years and grew sick of apprehending poor people, who stole to survive, or bored middle-class shoplifting kids, whom she could not really blame because they were from circles where stealing had been legalized for generations. What was Wall Street speculation but a kind of stealing? One day, Kathy had enough: while locking up that evening, she filled a trolley with food, rolled it to the corner outside the supermarket where a dozen homeless people slept, and left it with them. Then she got into her car and drove away for good. They could try to arrest her on one of the false identities she had handed over to them when applying for the job. "Good luck, fuckers," she shouted at the rambling ugly supermarket building, and gave it the finger.

She had come across the idea online, when she came across a site that offered domination, playful wrestling, professional wrestling, lifting, carrying, and muscle worship with women. They were looking for women like her. She had applied. She had quickly accumulated what Bo, the transsexual ex-wrestler who ran the site, called a "clientele".

~

The swans came waddling to meet him as he got out of his car. They flapped after him to the main door, long necks craned towards him, demanding food. There was always enough for them to feed on in the garden for days, but they had become accustomed to being fed by Harris.

Inside, he took the yellow file out of his suitcase and walked with it to the study table. He knew most of it by heart now. It had been a week since he had taken it out of PO Box 214. He had gone to Professor Horst Pichler on impulse earlier that day. Or, was it because he was impatient at not hearing from Mermaid?

His mobile rang. The calling number was blocked. Even before Harris picked up the phone, he knew who it would be. The grating voice left no doubt.

"Snooping around already?" said Mermaid.

Harris waited for him to go on.

"It is good you have taken up the case, Carbon."

"Have I?"

"You went to see Pichler."

"I might have discussed university matters with him."

"You did not."

"So?"

So, you should meet someone.

One of your men? Not you?

Not me. Not one of my men. I don't have any organization behind me this time, Carbon, so there is no fallback. Nothing. Some backers, but no one who can save your ass. Don't say I did not warn you. But you have to meet someone close to me. Someone to help you with the legwork.

Why not you?

There are reasons, Carbon.

There are always reasons, Mermaid. Why me then?

What do you mean?

Why did you contact me? Why not one of the 100 other henchmen you no doubt have in your hatch.

I needed someone close to Pichler.

Ha. You don't expect me to believe that. You know as well as I do that Pichler has no idea what all this is about.

He is alive, isn't he? The others are dead, mostly. Dead in natural but mysterious circumstances. You have the file, Carbon. Pichler is alive; something or someone is keeping him alive.

His ignorance, probably.

Ignorance can be an answer too. We wanted someone who could keep an eye on him easily, naturally.

You don't expect me to buy that, Mermaid. You could have planted someone in his bloody office. Child's play for you. So why me?

There are reasons.

Give me one.

Give me time, Carbon. Just nose around, online and elsewhere. Carefully. Nose around and give me time.

Give me a reason, Mermaid. Or I won't see your man.

There was a pause. Then Mermaid said, softly: "Would you believe it if I said that you are the only person I could trust?"

"No," replied Harris.

"There," said Mermaid. "What did I say?"

Then he added: "There is a letter. You know where. Be there at noon tomorrow. Ask for Mr. Atkins. Say Nicholson sent you."

The line was disconnected.

The address in his box had been of a secondhand bookshop off Istedsgade in Copenhagen. For decades until the first years of the millennium, Istedsgade had been the hangout of prostitutes and drug addicts. And the poorer colored immigrants, of course. Then in the first decade of the twenty-first century, students and such safer kinds of bohemians started moving in; the drug addicts and whores were pushed to a few street corners, the dingy shops started being replaced by franchises, and the ethnic restaurants got swankier.

Taking the back gate out of Copenhagen main station and walking up Istedsgade, Harris noticed that the process of gentrification had stalled, maybe even backslid in recent years. The road and the narrow streets shooting off it still had a mix of posh places and cheap outlets; students intermingled with immigrants and the obviously unemployed and blatantly unemployable. This was good, Harris thought, as he caught, passingly, the sweet smell of weed. But he knew that the causes were not good: it was not the acceptance of difference but the pandemic-related gradual impoverishment of many. Just outside the station, a gaunt Nordic-looking man in blond dreadlocks turned to address him but then changed his mind; Harris looked a little too much like someone who could be a retired cop or army officer.

The shop was a short walk away from the station, down a side alley. It was a corner shop, probably the only one left behind from an older time, sign faded, glass windows grimy, a newspaper rack just inside the door, shelves stacked haphazardly with books. After Harris's eyes got used to the dark—almost grainy inside—he went to the counter where an old woman well past seventy sat knitting. She was Indian; she did not look up. Mr. Atkins, said Harris, stifling a smile. Mermaid loved these boy's games.

The woman did not look up even then. Her hummingbird fingers paused for a second in her knitting. Then she nodded towards a curtain; there was a door at the back of the shop.

Harris went through the door and entered a completely different kind of room, where everything was clean, orderly, and modern. The filing systems, the racks of files, the metal-and-glass-topped desk, and the computer. Mr. Atkins was a small man with an incredibly round head, balding in the middle. He sat behind the desk—which even had boxes marked "In" and "Out" on it—in a black leather swivel chair. There was a whiteboard, with bills and papers stuck on it with magnetic holders. Sam had his back to Harris. The papers and photos stuck on one wall were the only bit of disorder in the room.

Harris drew back one of the smaller chairs on his side of the gleaming desk, loudly on purpose, and sat down. The man swiveled around, slowly. Everything about him was round: his head, his eyes, his body, the bald patch on top of his head.

"Nicholson," said the man.

"Nicholson," agreed Harris. But when he extended his hand across the desk, the man folded his hands in response. "Namaste, I stopped shaking hands during the pandemic," he said. In another man, this would have sounded cold, but Atkins made it sound inoffensive, maybe even affectionate, as if it was full of concern for you. "Sam to friends," Atkins added.

He spoke with a genteel English accent, as if there were marbles in his mouth. Despite occasional years in England, Harris still had to strain to understand this accent. No one in Command Alpha spoke English like that, but Harris had come across the accent in strange places, most remarkably in the voice of a large and scarred Pathan warlord in Pakistan.

"I have been instructed to tell you all I know about the university case," said Sam. "Coffee?"

"Yes, thanks."

Sam pulled out a drawer and removed a tray with a thermos flask and two small Chinese cups in it.

"But before you tell me about the university case, I need to know how you came into it," Harris added.

"I used to work with Nicholson... the man you call Mermaid. Some other name, but I am supposed to say Nicholson to you. He was my boss."

Harris's surprise must have shown; Sam did not look like he could ever have been part of any wing of Command Alpha.

Sam noticed the surprise. He smiled, pouring strong, thick coffee into the cups.

"Not where you worked with him, whatever on earth that was. Later."

He pushed a cup over to Harris.

"Guess you don't know," Sam continued. "About eight or nine years ago, Nicholson became the head of a unit that was created in 2015. I was already there. Nicholson took over in 2021, I think. I continued to work under Nicholson until I retired two years ago. Heart trouble. I was one of their data men."

He held up a hand to stop Harris from speaking.

"Let me tell you about the unit. It will help you understand the university case. Our unit was, is, called SAW. The Section for Anticipatory Warning. Set up essentially as a consultancy, one of those semi-governmental ones, but it is not really just that. It was essentially a post-9/11 idea, a section containing people retired or semi-retired from different wings of intelligence and police, solidly backed by data experts, with the brief to keep an eye on any developing threat. It has offices in three cities on three continents. All the registered good guys are into it, Americans, EU, Israel, even Brexit Britain. Because it is a consultancy, we manage to rope in the Chinese and Russians too, when required. What it does is piece together unconnected information and try to establish a pattern. If a pattern starts forming, it looks into it to see if there is a threat, a mechanism, behind it, or if it is sheer coincidence. I don't know if Nicholson still heads it. He might. Or he might be elsewhere. I left. Now I basically do a bit of private data investigations from my office here. Usual stuff, corporates checking one another out, estranged couples wanting to find out what the other person is really worth, stuff I can mostly do from this office. That was my mother you met outside."

Harris was surprised. He could not associate this very English-looking, marble-mouthed man with the Indian woman knitting away at the counter.

"It's a quiet life. I have always liked the quiet life," Sam continued.

"So do I," Harris replied.

Sam inclined his round head, as if bemused. Then he continued: So you see, SAW does exactly the kind of thing that this university case seems to be. Different news reports, here and there. We, the data people, would crunch it through our computers, trying to establish patterns. Suddenly there is a pattern. Professor George Sutton, a once-renowned American behaviorist, falls from the tenth floor of a New York hotel in March 2019. Suspected suicide but no suicide note, no real cause to commit suicide except the mild one of a career going gently downhill for years. Ronny Krishnan, South African neuroscientist, drowns during a vacation in the Caribbean the next year. No body recovered. Lars Larsen, a retired professor in history and religion studies at Copenhagen, trips over something in his summer cottage, and is found dead by his wife when she arrives the next morning, neck broken. Early 2022. Dr Julia Yong takes early retirement after the pandemic and disappears. Wislawa Ostrowski, legendary scholar in her field in her days I am told, dead of an overdose it is rumored, but again no suicide note.

Harris interrupted: "There was a police report in that case. It did not specify any drug."

"No," replied Sam, smiling a secretive smile, the smile of a man enjoying the story he is telling.

"Actually," he added, "it did not specify anything. It simply conjectured. Nothing really suspicious in all these cases, but then one of us unearths—we are good at this kind of stuff—something that makes all of us sit up: all these people attended the same seminar in Denmark. For many of them, it was the last seminar they attended: a kind of swansong for careers on the decline. We pass it on to Nicholson. He sets other people to work on it. Half the time all this comes to nothing; the other half, it can be useful … mostly it reopens closed files in police offices, and in that case, we just pass it back on to other departments. Consultancy, you know. Sometimes though, it can help prevent terrorist strikes and such stuff. Hence our acronym, SAW."

"You left one out: Katsumi Takewaki, the Japanese braino."

"He was still alive when the initial report was compiled and passed on to Nicholson. He died later. One or two others I cannot recall. Derek Dutton had already been confined to the loony bin, true, but Vijay Nair was also still in the jungles of India. He disappeared soon afterwards. All this happened after I left SAW."

"So, that is what Nicholson and your SAW do. But how come you are doing this for Nicholson? I doubt SAW is the kind of organization that subcontracts."

Sam laughed.

"It isn't. Nicholson came to me unofficially. He has gone to you unofficially. See, there was more of it. You know all about intelligence chatter, don't you? It was big even when you were active. No one talked about it, no one does even today, but you had agencies eavesdropping on social media, chat rooms, phone calls, emails, and whatnot; their automated systems filtering for suspicious words. Well, in the 1990s, or was it a bit later, anyway, there was a version of it developed to predict and prevent pandemics: it was called viral chatter. Old Trump and his lot did away with the funding for it much before 2019, or perhaps that shit-storm could have been ducked, but we at SAW revived an intelligence version of viral chatter later on. A smaller, honed version: our purpose was to look out for biological weapons being developed by terrorists or hostile states. Well, there was an uptick on the scale of viral chatter around the same time, and then that too went quiet. We needed further sampling but were never allowed to follow it up. The strings of organizations like SAW are pulled from so many different army headquarters and corporate offices that you cannot tell who is really calling the shots. Part of the reason you got out, I think. Part of the reason I got out, to be honest. Nicholson did not get out. He is not the type. But Nicholson does not trust his own people at SAW, or wherever he is now. Strange, isn't it?"

Then he raised an eyebrow at Harris, and added, musingly: "You wouldn't call Nicholson paranoid, would you?"

"No," replied Harris, "No, that I wouldn't."

Harris was thoughtful when he walked back to the station from Sam's shop-office. The envelope that Sam had handed him on his way out contained the usual stuff: an untraceable Bitcoin credit card issued by an obscure Swiss bank, some passes and identity cards, all made out for Harris, and all seemingly genuine. Some had expired; obviously Mermaid had a kind of added identity created for Harris elsewhere. What they used to call the buffer bio. Harris wondered why. Was it just to keep him safe?

What Sam had told him made sense. It explained the schoolboy-ish cloak-and-dagger methods employed by Mermaid-Nicholson to approach him. But it also made Harris worry; if Nicholson did not trust his own people, then Harris was in deeper waters than he wished to enter. He had not chosen the Big Death on a whim. There was another worry too: Nicholson could not be doing this all alone. If he had, he would not have managed to get the Bitcoin credit card and identity stuff made for Harris. It was not the kind of thing that Nicholson, despite all his connections, could organize on his own. At least one or two powerful people, or organizations, were behind him—in the shadows.

Sam had told Harris more. Like Harris, Sam was convinced that whatever, if anything, was behind the deaths, Professor Horst Pichler was not part of it. Sam's opinion was based on the data he had processed, as he had never met Pichler. "But differing patterns," Sam had told Harris, "Two major differences: number one, the others stayed in touch with one another, maybe not as a group but in twos and threes; number two, the others appear to have fallen out of the academic scene, no publications for years, retirement or move to a less prestigious institution, while Pichler stayed where he was, publishing, networking, getting a full professorship, politicking in universities."

But were these differences enough to exclude Pichler as a suspect? A suspect? A suspect for what? How could a man who had been in other places have managed these murders, which were not even classified as murders? Takewaki, for instance. He had been hit by a speeding car in Tokyo, and Harris knew from the yellow folder that Pichler had never been to Japan, not even for a conference.

The man with the blond dreadlocks was still at the station, his back to Harris, but as Harris passed him the man stepped backward suddenly and bumped into Harris. "Watch your steps, man," the guy with dreadlocks said in English, "You steps on the people, the people steps on you." At that moment, Harris saw a woman, maybe in her thirties, watching them from across the road. Her dress was old-fashioned but very elegant. She was of such remarkable and unapproachable beauty that even Harris was distracted. She looked vaguely familiar. He stepped back to mumble an apology to the man with dreadlocks, which the man laughed off, as he shuffled away, eyes fixed in the direction of the woman.

When Harris looked across the road again, the woman was nowhere to be seen.

~

It is one of the last years of peace, though the news from Germany is not good. Some Americans want to stop Hitler; most want to stay out of the war. But we are a long way from the war that is brewing in Europe. It is a log cabin, built twenty miles away from Boulder, Colorado, then only a city of 20,000 or less. Not far from the cabin, the white waters of St. Vrain Creek, called a river locally, burble over rocks, flanked by tall thin trees and bushes. There are fish in the creek. Just outside the log cabin, on blocks of woods around a bonfire, sit five young men and two women. The fire is fed with recently chopped wood in which the resin fizzles, sparks splutter. They have blankets. It is chilly, but not dark yet. The cabin belongs to the man, decades senior to them, they all call the Doc.

They are students at the Medical School of the University of Colorado at Boulder. A couple of them have brought along their fiancées. They are waiting for Doc to come out from the kitchen in the log house, where, with three helpers, also students, he is roasting two ducks, which he shot that morning, and boiling potatoes. He is also preparing plates of pickled herring and dried codfish. These are Swedish delicacies. Doc's parents were from Sweden, as all the students know. They are holding mugs of mulled wine. Most of them are already a bit drunk.

Doc comes out carrying a plate. His helpers follow him. The roasted ducks and potatoes, with a brownish sauce, will come later. They are greeted with a cheer. Someone tosses more wood into the fire. Doc is a tall man, with dark blond hair that is cropped closely on the sides, so that his head appears longer than it is. He has a wide forehead, high cheekbones, a wide mouth. He wears a laboratory coat. He always cooks in a laboratory coat.

"Have to use it for something," he answers when students ask him about this idiosyncrasy of his. Doc is known as an eccentric: this log cabin that he has built up here, helped by his students, the drunken parties that he throws, the glögg that he serves, his poker games, his Christmas parties, his lectures which can sometimes be totally soundless, as he simply dissects a cadaver, surrounded by students, and then fires off staccato questions at students, whacking the ones that give bad answers on the chest: that, after all, is Professor Ivan Emmanuel Wallin.

He is a legend among his students. He is a scandal for the scientific world outside. Some of his colleagues whisper about him in Boulder too. He is called the Mitochondria Man. Most of the students here are too young to remember that he had published a series of papers in the early 1920s—that is almost two decades ago. The papers had stirred up a hornet's nest in academia. And provoked much derision. Doc never talks about them anymore. Only a few of his students know what the papers were about and why they had created a controversy. The ones who do have looked it up on their own. He had conducted his research in his usual eccentric way, not in some proper laboratory, but in a shed behind the school's classrooms. He had been ostracized by the scientific community.

His claims had been grandiloquent. He had claimed that the human cell—that all cells of multicellular beings—contained bacteria. That mitochondria—the "powerhouse of the cell", as all school books stated—had descended from a bacterium consumed by another bacterium, millions of years ago, and that this ill-digested cannibalism had marked a gigantic leap in evolution. He had argued that bacteria were not the agents of disease, made to be annihilated, as everyone knew—the only good bacterium is a dead bacterium! This upstart scientist from the backwoods of academia had even claimed that bacteria were us, that, in a way, we, we human beings, homo sapiens, the pinnacle of God's creation or of Darwinian Evolution, or, why not both, we were essentially the creation of bacteria. And he claimed that he could culture mitochondria outside the cell ... in his ramshackle shed behind the classrooms!

Surely his samples were contaminated? It was impossible to culture mitochondria outside the cell because, as everyone knew, the instructions for 95 percent of the proteins needed for it reside in the nucleus of the cell. They were right about that. Even those of his students who were aware of his work knew that his critics were right about this. No wonder Doc never discussed his research anymore. He taught, and he involved himself in administration. He dissected cadavers without a word of explanation, in a concentrated frenzy. He whacked students on the chest for wrong answers. He threw drunken Christmas parties. He built a log cabin with his students and went hunting for ducks with a double-barreled shotgun. He fished out here in the wild.

And sometimes, when slightly tipsy, he played Swedish folk songs for his guests on his piano.

10

Seeing is not Believing

We flew to the oil rig via London, where I spent a long weekend, my first outside the islands, shopping lavishly on Kurt's card. One of his cards. He let me keep the card to use on the way back. But he had already started changing. He was mostly away from our five-star hotel—on business, he said. He had less time for me, or not unless he wanted sex. From London, we flew to Moscow, and from there to Yuzhno in Sakhalin, an island peninsula on Russia's northeastern seaboard. This was the dump with bars. A tough town, dependent almost entirely on the oil economy and crime, from what I have seen of the bars on the two occasions when, perhaps to restore my sanity (or his), Kurt has choppered me down there for a night or two in a hotel. It is from a private helipad in what seems to be a farm out of town—though what farming can take place in those parts?—that we are always transported to the rig.

I had not expected something so huge, so solitary, as the rig. The thing rose in the middle of an endless expanse of water, buffeted by wind and waves. Its sheer size took me by surprise. It did not look like something that men could have built. How could you build something like that out here, in the middle of nowhere? It was as if a weirdly assembled spacecraft had landed in the ocean and stood now on surprisingly thin metal legs. The platform was a jumble of metal, some dismantled, some transformed, both futuristic and brutally primitive at the same time. There was so much metal all around—the floor, the walls, the slippery grill walkways—that the men wore leather, steel-capped boots much of the time. Kurt had a pair for me. I hated them and resolved to keep my sneakers on indoors. I was nervous about the place. I still am. It looked solid and vulnerable at the same time, under those vast skies, with waves crashing on its spindly legs.

"Is it safe?" I had asked Kurt.

"Oh, you needn't bother your pretty head about it, my Mālum Persicum. You do your cooking and keep our guests happy and let the men do their work. It is just three months anyway, maybe four, and you'll make what you would in two or three years on St. Martin."

When I appeared about to respond to that, he added, "Let me assure you, it won't explode." And at that, Kurt and Mr. Watch uttered that complicit chuckle they engage in, mostly at my expense. It is not often that Mr. Watch laughs, so I suppose the joke must have been a good one.

Kurt and Mr. Watch have known each other for years, I am convinced of it now, Maman. Mr. Watch is the one who flies in and out all the time. The rest are mostly here. They are all men, tough-looking young men of all or any ethnicity, organized by their Japanese "foreman". That is what Kurt and Mr. Watch call him: foreman. Mister Hiroyuki. That's all he is called, always with the Mister. Maybe because he speaks with such a careful British accent that you almost imagine a bowler hat on his large, round head. Chinese I thought the first time I saw him, but Kurt corrected me: "Not Chinese, Japanese, and not just Japanese, Gokudo. Didn't you notice the tattoos?" And Kurt proceeded to tell me, with obvious relish, what the Gokudo were. Evidently, they were enjoying a major revival as "protectors" in the post-pandemic age.

That is the company, headed by Foreman Mister Hiroyuki. Then we get the guests. These are very different, usually much older than the company men. Some are obviously scientists, but not all. Some seem to be just affluent men and, very rarely, women. Kurt claims they are rich tourists, out for an experience on a rig, but they seem too preoccupied to be on vacation. They have the aura of men at work. They even do the gym as if it is a job to be done precisely. They do not lounge around like your boyfriends, Maman. They are mostly white, though the color does not matter. You can tell that they all belong to just one race: the race of the powerful and the privileged. It is one race; it just happens that there are far more whites in it than blacks. They come in groups of three or four. Only one group returns regularly. We can have two or three groups staying here at the same time, or they can come after one another. Most seem to stay here for just a night or two, and some seem distinctly nervous while here. They spend much of their time in the closed section during the day. Then they go away. One or two return. But only one group—two men and a woman—comes here regularly and seems delighted about it. My job is basically to keep all of them happy in the luxury rooms. Their job—and I am sure it is a job now—is in that closed section next to the galley that is always guarded and I cannot enter.

That the job is an important one is evident from the rooms they stay in. These are different from our rooms. Even Mr. Watch's room is like the one that Kurt and I have. They are exactly like economy hotel rooms. Think of Cabinn, for instance. Tidy little rooms with pull-down bunkers, fitted study tables, compact toilets and bathrooms. I guess that is how the workers lived on this rig in the days when it was producing oil. But the rooms for the guests have been ripped out and redone. They are not economy hotel rooms; they are closer to five-star hotel rooms, with all the amenities, including well-stocked room bars. They are all on one floor, just above the galley and the men's quarters. Only Kurt and I have a room—an ordinary one—on that floor, perhaps because I am in charge of keeping the luxury rooms clean, the room bars stocked, and the guests happy. Kurt helps occasionally, and I can always ask Mr. Watch to send one of the company men to help, though I avoid doing so. I do not like being alone in a room with any of Mr. Watch's men. They carry guns, visibly when on guard duty, but always as a bulge in their jackets. There is even a surveillance drone that they send out at times.

It was only in my first week that I asked the most obvious questions: what does the company do? What is it that the guests do? Why do the guests hardly ever go out on to the spider decks for a view? Kurt told me again, with growing impatience, that this was all an unusual vacation, arranged for the rich who wanted to experience living on an offshore rig in a desolate part of the North Sea. But he could not sustain that explanation after a few days here, and the only time I pressed him, he replied in his elaborate manner, all M'ladies and Sugars and Latin, that it was best for me to count my silver and rest my brain, for I was getting four or five times what I would in St. Martin. Knowledge, he noted, is troubling, and dangerous. That was when I realized that Kurt had deceived me: he had not taken this up just because some people at a party in his old villa—the one he used to take care of—had given him a better job. He was much more involved than that. He was part of the "company". I feared then that I was not here for just three months. I had heard of various kinds of slavery—it had been rising for years, the papers wrote: Was I, in effect, a slave? Would I ever leave this abandoned oil rig alive?

And then I saw something.

~

It had been a close call. She could have killed the man. This is only the second time that it has happened to her in this new profession. Most of the men who book her for sessions like being overpowered and defeated by her. They seldom call her Kathy or Kath; they call her "Goddess", "Amazon", "Athena", "Superwoman", "Miss America", and they would be disappointed if she turned out to be less strong or skilled. But once in the past, it had been different, and then again it happened yesterday.

The man had been small—perhaps an inch taller than her—and sinewy. She could see he exercised, but she had wrestled with stronger, bigger men. He had started off by teasing her, taunting her for being too small. "I will go careful on you, baby," he had said. This sort of taunting was unusual. Most men were more likely to gasp in admiration at her musculature after she took off her clothes, and mostly their admiration was genuine, as Kathy did not look big or muscular with clothes on. But once in a while, there would be a man who would challenge or tease her about not looking big enough: are you sure you can handle me, little woman? And usually that was play too.

This man was different. He grappled Kathy with an intensity that should have warned her. When she made him tap out twice in less than five minutes, once with a chokehold, and once by squeezing his head between her legs, he got more vicious and desperate to win. Sometimes, there were men like him, men who disliked the ease with which they were overpowered, and usually Kathy relented, and let the men go on for longer before making them tap out. She did so with this man too, letting him slip out of various wrestling holds for the next ten minutes, but that did not assuage the man's ego: he started swearing. Kathy disengaged from him and told him that she did not put up with real violence, physical or verbal; that was not what the sessions were about.

The man did not stop. He came swinging at her, calling her a bitch, a dumb dyke, telling her she was cheating. Kathy did not box. It was too dangerous, and the nose job had cost her a fortune. She backed away. Take your money and go, she told the man.

"Fucking lousy lebby," the man shouted in response, "What you need is a real man's dick in your ass." And he started fumbling with the buttons on his shorts, swearing. That's when it went black. The next thing Kathy remembered, she was holding the man in a chokehold, and the man was twisting, turning, unable to escape, and then just flapping about like a fish out of water before suddenly going limp. Kathy let go of him immediately. She slapped his face twice. The man coughed and retched. Kathy picked up her clothes, got into her sandals, and hurried out of the hotel room. She pulled on her dress as she made her way down the corridor, even as a couple of guests looked her way.

Dammit, she said to herself, I could have killed the fucking bastard. I need Crobe.

Driving away, she remembered similar blackouts in the past. They had been the secret behind her Big Death. She was more shaken by the recurrence than by what the man had tried to do. Those manic blackouts in moments of crisis. That was the reason she had left, to seek some semblance of sanity in drugs and the Big Death. She had not left because she could not take it anymore, as Harris had. Or not only because of that. Unlike him, she had not been the intellectual type. She left because she could not control herself all the time. Those moments her mind did not recall but her body reacted, when her body became nothing but the deadly machine it had been trained to be. She had to drug herself for days. But then Crobe had come along. Mysterious Crobe, sold to her by her dealer some years ago. Try this, sweetheart, he had said, it costs a fortune but has no aftereffects. What is it, she had asked. No one knows, he had replied. It just hit the market.

Now, only the translucent tablets of Crobe could calm her down, for days, sometimes weeks, before its effects wore out, always without warning.

Dammit, I should not have stopped taking that fucking shit just because of the fucking money, she thought. She rolled down the window. "Fucking shit!" she shouted into the rushing wind. "Fucking shit! Fucking shit! Fucking money!"

~

Jens Erik walks into his old police station, and his colleagues, those two not busy at the counter, come to him and say: "So you missed us after all, didn't you?"

"Yes," Jens Erik jokes, "I missed you so much that I think I will return to work for another year." Then he asks if the "boss" is in.

"He is, but busy with some visitors."

Jens Erik says he will wait.

Jens Erik has never liked the "boss". He is a Turkish man—"Far, he was born here! He grew up here! *For fandens!*" (Jens Erik can hear Pernille exclaim in his head.)—a Turkish man, he repeats to himself, Aslan Barzani, four years junior to Jens Erik, or is it five years?

Jens Erik is convinced that promotion was bestowed on Aslan for his ethnicity; some politicians evidently thought that a chief with a Turkish name looked better in newspaper handouts! Aslan became the station chief a few months before Jens Erik applied to go on pre-retirement leave.

But there had always been subdued antagonism between the two from the earliest days when Aslan had been occasionally partnered with Jens Erik. Aslan tended to address him as "Jens", prompting him to point out that the "Jens" and the "Erik" came together in this case, shouldn't you know that despite your Turkish background? At which Aslan would politely note that actually he was Kurdish-Turkish, and Jens Erik would humpf. But this was years ago, when Aslan had been junior to Jens Erik.

Now the man was the station chief.

Jens Erik is invited into their cubicles by a couple of old colleagues, but he is a stickler for rules and insists on sitting in the visitor's section. It is almost empty. There is only one woman, with a blackened eye, in there.

When Jens Erik is called into Aslan's office, after a wait of fifteen minutes, the "boss" gets up and comes around to shake hands, addressing him carefully as Jens Erik, and asking after his daughter, whose framed photo had always adorned Jens Erik's desk. Every person who worked with Jens Erik knew that the man doted on his daughter.

"What brings you here, Jens Erik?" asks Aslan when the men have settled into their chairs.

Aslan's office, Jens Erik thinks critically, as he always had in the past, is not a police officer's room. It lacks all the usual trophies, souvenirs, sporting and old boys' photographs.

The desk is bare apart from a computer and two plastic containers for paper. A pen holder, containing three ballpoint pens and two pencils. A pink post-it note pad next to it. There is a small filing system in one corner. The walls are totally bare, except for an old, framed, police-issued public health poster from the pandemic of 2020. No sign of any weapon, not even a painting, anywhere in the room.

It could be the office of any mundane secretary, except that Aslan does not even have a family photo anywhere on his desk.

But there is an office dog next to Aslan; a robot designed to look like a dog and used to send messages to other people in the building. It had been introduced around the time Jens Erik applied for early retirement, and if they had not granted his request, he suspects he might have, for the first time in his career, shot something down. He looks at the office dog with hostility, but the stupid robot has been programmed to respond to human stares by shaking its wire tail.

Aslan obviously does not mind the dog. Jens Erik shakes his head. People are different, he tells himself, feeling magnanimous at the thought.

Aslan is waiting for him to reply.

"There was a case," Jens Erik says, hesitatingly. Then he cannot bear it. He points a finger at the dog and asks, "Does that have to stay here?"

Aslan smiles. "You never really liked the idea," he notes, and then he adds, "Can't blame you. They wiped out a lot of secretaries." Then he tells the robot to go to desk 21 and await a note from the officer there. He knows that there is no one at desk 21 today.

Jens Erik relaxes a bit after the office dog tap-taps out of the room. He explains to Aslan, "This is about a case, much before I retired, a man, a negro (he notices Aslan hide a wince: the word, Jens Erik believes, does not have any bad connotations in Danish) who was found dead in the sea. I had been the first respondent."

"I remember," Aslan replies. "From the beaches in Egå."

"I can use some information about the case."

Aslan frowns. Jens Erik sees him frame the question—Why?—and then refrain.

Jens Erik is surprised by this restraint from a man who, when junior to him, had provocatively called him "Jens" for years. He was prepared for the why. He was expecting to be stonewalled, and perhaps even wanted it to happen, relieving him of the responsibility that he had assumed, this sleuthing that had arisen as a vague compulsion within him, an urge he did not understand.

He had reasoned it out, and his mind agreed: the dead "nigger" was not Jens Erik's problem. He had also seen enough murdered Danes to suffer from a bleeding heart over someone who was not even from Denmark! That is what he told himself. And yet, some unknown part of him replied: humpf. It was a deadly word. No one, not even Jens Erik, could argue with it.

Aslan clicks on to the computer. It has an eye-scanner for entry. He types in a couple of code words and looks desultorily at whatever appears on the screen.

Jens Erik cannot see it; he is sitting on the other side of the desk. But he can see Aslan grow interested after a minute of moving the cursor down with his antique black mouse on a blue mat. Aslan pulls his chair closer to the screen and spends five minutes reading the screen.

He frowns and looks quickly at Jens Erik. Then he taps in more codes or requests for information. He frowns again and gets up.

There is a window on one side of the office. It has plastic shutters on it. Aslan pulls up the shutters and looks out for a few seconds. Jens Erik waits quietly. This is more interesting than anything he had expected. He had expected to be fobbed off with a why. But this? This was interesting.

"Jesus," Aslan mutters. Jens Erik is always taken aback by this expression—always in English—by Aslan. He wonders if this man, obviously not a Christian, exclaims "Jesus" just to irritate Danes.

Finally, Aslan returns to his chair and sits down.

"It's strange," he says.

Jens Erik waits.

"You remember that the case was passed on to the homicide section, and then it was passed on to Copenhagen, because it involved an untraceable foreigner."

"Yes."

"Well, that's it."

"That's what?"

"The case seems to have disappeared. We have the initial reports here, we have the record of it being moved on to Copenhagen, and then the file has been shut."

"I guess they couldn't find anything. That's what we heard."

"Yes. But there is no concluding report. Nothing. It has just been shut down. No one got back to us, which would be procedural. Things don't happen like that here. We follow due process, you know."

~

"Why are you so interested in this negro's death, Jens Erik, *mand*?" Jens Erik asks himself, as he waits for the bus to Hjortshøj.

The tram lines stretch behind him, and then there is a paved public space with sporting sections, where some young men in trendy sportswear, mostly second-generation immigrants, as Jens Erik obstinately calls them, are playing basketball. Behind them there is the water, blue in the bay, with factory buildings and dock cranes beyond the library building on one side, and expensive flats and corporate towers, all glass and metal, on the other. There are gulls, white in the sky. Further off a yacht, gleaming white too. It is an unusually still day.

Am I bored with retirement already? Jens Erik wonders.

But he has a full life, friends, neighbors, hobbies, *kolonihave, parcelhus* with a garden. Why should he be bored? Was he just curious? Or, he thought so, didn't this prove that he was not a bigot? Why was he so concerned about an unidentified dead "negro"?

What Jens Erik did not think about, for he was not a man given to intricate self-analysis, was Pernille, his daughter, whose voice he kept hearing inside his head.

He did not imagine that this voice, which he heard only as Pernille's, had also become, over the years, one of his voices. Just as he could not imagine that he might be doing this in one final bid to justify himself in the eyes of a girl, now a woman, who had turned away from him in disappointment and, yes, maybe even momentary revulsion at the age of thirteen, when she had discovered a photograph, a single photograph, in the pages of that leftist rag, *Dagbladet Information*.

But while Jens Erik did not think of these explanations, his hand searched in his pockets for his phone, ostensibly to check if the bus was late—it was two minutes late—and then, unthinkingly, called his daughter.

Pernille picked up immediately. She was at work. She was surprised, maybe even a bit worried. Jens Erik was not the kind of person who just called. But Jens Erik assured her. All was fine. It was just that he had some work in Copenhagen and he would be taking the train there sometime tomorrow.

Could he sleep over at their place tomorrow night?

Jens Erik had not thought of saying this to Pernille. He had not thought of going to Copenhagen.

But the statements came out fully formulated, as if a part of his brain, some secret part, had been mulling over them. And as he switched off, he told himself, yes, why not? Why not go to Copenhagen and ask some ex-colleagues and old friends about the dead body, that nameless black man?

Then, he corrected himself. The nameless negro, he told himself, as the bus pulled up, driven by, who else, an immigrant!

~

Seeing is not believing. Decades later, after she retired as a banker in Harare, having also done stints in Johannesburg and Dubai, that is what Maita told others was the essential lesson she learned in school, and it was a lesson that stood her in good stead throughout her career in the commercial world, from 1985 to 2026, for she always understood that the capital she handled did not exist, that it had never existed and would never exist, not even as money, and that its non-existence was exactly what made it real. For, if it had existed, if it could have been touched and seen, then there would have been less reason to believe in it. If it had existed, it could have been destroyed.

Seeing is not believing.

This lesson Maita credited to her science teacher in secondary school.

It was lucky Maita came to attend Mt. St. Mary's Mission School. She was one of the scholarship students that the priests took from outlying villages, and it was only her second week at the school. The science teacher had a degree from Harare, in those days the biggest city Maita could imagine. She was in awe of the school, her classmates, who seemed to know so much more than she did and express it with so little effort, and above all the science teacher from Harare.

The class subject was botany. The science teacher was telling them about plants and fungi. Mostly, fungi are to plants what parasites are to human beings, Maita can still recall him saying. There were illustrations on the walls: he had unrolled a chart. It was about fungal parasites of plants. It illustrated the kinds of fungi that destroyed the crops and trees of the local ecosystem. It had been printed by a department—Maita thinks it was the agricultural department, but she is not sure—some years back: in 1961. Maita remembers the year because that was the year of her birth.

Maita had been a wide-eyed, quiet student from the day she had joined the class. She had not uttered a word of her own. She had enough to do: scribbling down notes in her copybooks, for everything happened faster in this school than at her previous one. During recess, she sat by herself, mostly gazing at Mt. Rusunzwe, which rose behind the school buildings. Somewhere beyond it, she knew, was the village where she had grown up until she had been taken to an orphanage. Later one of the Fathers brought her to this school because of her extraordinary ability to memorize Bible passages.

But that day, as the science teacher spoke of fungi and plants, for the first time since she had joined the school, the subject took her back to her childhood in the village. And so she spoke unprompted, almost unaware that she was speaking.

"The village elders where I grew up," she told the teacher and the class, "said that fungi are the beard of trees: the denser the beards, the more vigorous the tree."

The teacher looked annoyed, and then bemused. "Luckily, we cannot see parasites," he joked, "Or your wise village elders would be putting them into their beards to grow more, what did you say, more vigorous."

The class burst out laughing.

Maita never said another word in class for the rest of the term. She had learned a lesson: Seeing is not believing. There was no truth in things from that point on. She never pursued science as an advanced subject, so she never discovered that her villagers were right in a way. Not all fungi are villains. Trees use fungi to grow networks for nutrition and communication. With the help of mycelium of the appropriate species, trees increase their root surfaces so they can reach more water. A fungus in Oregon extends for more than two thousand acres and connects dozens of trees. It is around 2,500 years old. There are fungi that transmit warnings to other trees or that dissolve nutrients that trees can use. All this with fungal threads growing into tree roots, a vast unseen beard under the ground.

If Maita had pursued Science further, she might have had trouble believing in Capital as numbers, like digits, as something that was real because it did not exist. She might have seen its underground roots. She might have seen other things. But it would not have made her a good banker.

11

Cowboys and Red Indians

THE Harper Behavioral Anomalies Rest House (HBARH) is a private facility, tucked away in the countryside outside Camberley. Harris drives into town from London, guided by the GPS in his rented Peugeot. He crosses the town, as HBARH is on the other side. He drives past rows of deteriorating dark red houses with peeled white windows and sills, and through about ten minutes of fields and tall trees, before taking a right turn, per the instructions of his GPS, and reaching the grounds of the Rest House.

The house is situated among pine woods and has long views. It stands well back from the road. There is a small parking lot in front of the three-story building, and on the side a garage for two large vans, both backed out right now, bearing the HBARH insignia and acronym. Surveillance cameras are everywhere. A surveillance drone follows Harris's car for a minute and then whirrs away.

On the other side, a terrace walk leads to two clay tennis courts; Harris can see there are woodland walks through pine trees and banks of rhododendrons on that side, extending to the back of the house. There are no walls or wires around the grounds, which is surprising to Harris, but then he reasons that this is not that sort of mental asylum. It is for people with money, people who would not climb over walls—because their families can afford to pay for a pair of attendants to watch them twenty-four hours a day. There would be guards here, but this was not Brazil or the US, not yet, so they would be invisible until required.

The large, heavy wooden main door is not meant to be opened. There is a smaller side door on the left, more recently installed. Harris goes through it to find himself in a reception that reminds him of five-star hotel receptions. All polished glass and burnished wood, with two smart-looking women, dressed like efficient secretaries and not like nurses, behind the counter. One of them has a startling head of reddish-golden hair, the kind of hair only successful models can afford. She is the one who looks up as the door tinkles and Harris walks in. Harris offers his card. She asks him to be seated and gestures at the plush sofas, around a low table that holds some newspapers and glossy magazines.

"Dr. Stewart is expecting you. He will be here in a minute," the redhead says. "Would you like some coffee or tea?"

There is a coffee-tea-hot chocolate dispenser against the wall near the sofas: Harris notices that it gives you a dozen options.

Harris declines. He waits for ten minutes before Dr. Stewart shows up. The doctor is a young man in his late twenties with a furtive manner, as if he is always considering whether to duck into an alley or doorway. He hardly even meets Harris's eyes while speaking, preferring to look at the folder in his hand, the floor, or the walls. He gives Harris a debriefing on what to expect and what to do. "Ignore him if he says anything about microbes and Indians," he says. "Indians? Red Indians," Dr. Stewart explains, and then coughs apologetically; "American Indians," he adds. "Professor Dutton suffers from an obsession with American Indians ... and microbes. There is no logic in the connection," he explains, smiling furtively, looking away.

Then he leads Harris through what seem to be thickly carpeted five-star hotel corridors, with spacious common spaces scattered here and there, corners equipped with vending machines and armchairs and window views, deceptively barred. They go up a broad flight of stairs and down a similar corridor until they reach a suite bearing the name "Professor Derek Dutton". Dr. Stewart presses the buzzer.

A man, built like a wrestler, opens the door. He has been expecting them and leads the way, wordlessly, into a large suite, its walls almost totally covered with framed posters or paintings, all featuring American Indians or related themes. There is a portrait of Chief Geronimo holding a single barrel gun, two large paintings of heavily armed cavalry mowing down spear- and bow-wielding natives on horseback, and framed posters of old films like *Soldier Blue* and *Dances with Wolves*. Harris looks around for a John Wayne poster, but there is no John Wayne, not a single John Wayne, which is surprising. He knows from experience that white people who have a thing for the Wild West are always rabid John Wayne fans. Harris recalls reading about a John Wayne revival in recent years.

There is a study on one side of the suite, with mostly books on yoga, nothing scientific at all, except a very state-of-art computer, with a printer and various other gadgets attached to it, and a state-of-art kitchen on the other side. Farther on, there is a very clean bedroom section, and beyond it a small white terrace. The terrace looks out over the lawn at the back. Harris can see one of the tennis courts. The only thing remarkable about the terrace is that it is totally caged in, with glass—unbreakable, Harris is certain. In the terrace, on a cushy meditation mat, sits a man with a white beard. He is dressed in one of those saffron gowns that Indian sadhus wear. Two or three years back, Harris remembers reading, it had been turned into the compulsory color for school uniforms in all public schools of India. An act had been passed in the Indian parliament. There had been an op-ed in *The Guardian* fuming about it. But Professor Dutton is obviously unaware of the politics of that color. He is sitting in the lotus position, his eyes shut.

The wrestler says, "Dr. Dutton has just finished his yoga. He needs a few minutes to wrap up his meditation."

He waves Dr. Stewart and Harris into some chairs against the wall of the terrace. Derek Dutton continues to meditate for another five minutes or so. He opens his eyes slowly and smiles at Harris and Dr. Stewart. Harris has never seen a lunatic look saner. Dr. Dutton is much thinner than he had looked in his photo in the yellow file, further dwarfed by the wrestler who helps him rise to his feet. Stewart introduces Harris, who is pretending to meet Dr. Dutton as part of a research project. Dutton holds up a hand for silence. The man is every bit the eccentric British aristocrat, descended on both sides from half the royal families in Europe, it is said, that Harris has come to expect.

The wrestler seats Dutton, supporting him by an arm, as if he is something breakable, in a chair which he has dragged to face Stewart and Harris. Then he fetches a wicker table from inside and puts it between them. Finally, he returns with a silver tea set and pours them three cups of herbal tea. All the while, Dutton sits in his chair, fingertips touching one another, eyes closed. He opens his eyes, picks up his cup, takes a dainty sip from it, and looks at Harris. Yes, he says. His eyes are a washed-out blue.

Dr. Stewart uses the pause to excuse himself. He promises to meet Harris at the reception, in an hour, and leaves. The way he says it is intended more for the wrestler, who now knows that Harris is allowed only an hour with the patient. The wrestler stands behind Dutton, hands folded across his broad chest, face impassive.

Harris then goes through the motions of introducing himself and his fictitious research, complimenting Dutton on his scholarship, which is proving so invaluable to Harris. Dutton waves away the compliment. His hands are dainty, mostly skin and bones. Harris feels they might be translucent against a light.

"Nothing to do with me," says Dutton. "I left it behind ages ago. Ages."

"But Dr. Dutton, your paper on the mind and the body, the one that came out in the *Journal of Cognitive Sciences* ..."

"In 1989," Dutton interrupts, dismissively.

"... your work in general on how the body thinks, the alternative cognitive structures of our membranes as you put it somewhere. And then from there to symbiogenesis ..."

"Papers in 1992, 1993, a book in 1994. I left it all behind. I was playing with the toys of a child." Dutton closes his eyes, touches the tips of his fingers together, and looks faintly amused, as if remembering a private joke. There is the trace of a lisp in his speech.

Then he leans forward, pushing his face so close to Harris that Harris recoils slightly. The pallid blue of Dutton's eyes seems to deepen. When he speaks, his breath brushes Harris's face.

"Ask me why I left all of it behind. Ask me what you really want to ask me," Dutton hisses.

Without waiting for Harris to put the question to him, Dutton continues, his face still disturbingly close: "I left it all behind because it had been done. It had been done ages ago. The answers were all there, known for centuries, centuries, it is just that we were not looking at the right evidence. And I left it because, because the murderers, the cowboys, came back with the first pandemic… There was no point… no point… They would make dynamite of everything I could give them…. They murdered the answers… They shot down the Indians… They bombed Hiroshima…"

Dutton's excitement has mounted. He is speaking in sentences that seem to have no punctuation. The wrestler behind him unclasps his arms, shifts his weight from one leg to another. As if on cue, Dutton leans back again, his eyes drain of color, and he picks up his cup of herbal tea. The cup shakes just a bit, a slight tremor.

The next few minutes, Dutton lets Harris speak, only occasionally intervening, feigning disinterest. His interventions are measured, scientific, technical. Then, suddenly, he turns to the wrestler and says, "Why don't we have any shortbread here? Would you mind getting us some shortbread?"

The wrestler goes into the rooms and comes back.

"I cannot find them," he says on returning.

"Well, get some then. I want to serve my guest some shortbread," Dutton insists, sounding like a petulant child.

"I am certain we had a packet. I will ring for it."

"Ring for it?" Dutton sounds even more like a spoiled child whining for his toy. "They will take an hour to send it up. Go and get it for us, will you?"

The wrestler hesitates. Dutton's thin, delicate features look like they would crumble into a screaming fit. The wrestler shrugs, and says to Harris, "Stay with him. I am back in five minutes."

The moment the wrestler leaves the suite, Dutton leans forward again, his eyes deepening, his breath on Harris's face.

"Bloody idiots," he hisses. "They do not let me talk about it. They think I get too excited, that I am crazy..."

"But," he adds, "You will understand. You will understand why I left, I left all behind. I discovered... I discovered... The Truth. And I refused, yes, I refused, to be part of another massacre of Indians."

Later, Harris is not sure how long Dutton spoke. His words were so packed with meaning—though none of it made sense—that Harris could not be sure if the wrestler-nurse was back in two minutes or five, six, maybe seven. But time passed, time flew, and then there was the sound of the front door opening.

As if on cue, Dutton relaxes; his eyes fade and he sinks back in his chair. The transformation takes half a minute or so, as the wrestler opens cupboards in the small kitchen. Harris hears the sound of a box being violently ripped open. The wrestler enters, bearing shortbread on a silver plate. Harris realizes that Dutton has some kind of fetish about silver. He probably refuses to eat off anything else.

Harris prompts Dutton to return to his talk about his experiments. But Dutton shakes his head. He is reclining in that limp way that seems to come naturally to the British upper class. "Maya," he says, "All is maya." Then his eyes assume a sly gleam and he looks at Harris, man to man. "All the laboratory I need is here," he lisps, jerking his bird-like head in the direction of the glass and the lawn below. It takes Harris a second to realize that

Dutton does not mean the lawn; he means his yoga mat on the ground. After that, Dutton refuses to talk. Harris asks him about the 2012 seminar in Aarhus, but Dutton does not respond. Harris keeps fishing for a few minutes, met by monosyllabic responses or silence and an enigmatic smile from Dutton, tapering thin fingers touching at the tips, eyes half shut. The wrestler shifts on his feet.

They still have around a half hour of his time left, but Harris knows that Dutton will not talk any more. He takes his leave—Dutton absentmindedly offering him a limp handshake—and wanders out in the plush corridors. He meets an old lady in a thick nightgown. She is wearing a wig. Accompanied by a matron, the old lady is obviously a resident; she asks him, suspiciously, what he *might be* doing there. "Visiting Dr. Dutton," says Harris, not able to think of anything else. "Ah," the old woman looks enlightened. "Shame on you, young man, shame on you," she scolds. "You should come more often."

She wags a finger at Harris's back as he descends the stairs.

Dr. Stewart gives him the medical lowdown on Dutton once again, which is of no use to Harris. Then he walks Harris, avoiding eye contact all the time, to the door of the reception, almost offers him a handshake, changes his mind, gives him a grimace-smile instead, and withdraws. Outside, a semblance of sunshine is falling on the parking lot. One of the vans in the garage has been driven out, and is being loaded, methodically, with patients and their minders out for a trip. Dutton is not one of them.

As Harris backs his Peugeot, he catches sight of a woman in an old-fashioned dress standing at the edge of the grounds. She is too far away to be seen clearly, but her dress is the same as that worn by the exceedingly beautiful woman he had seen on his way back from Atkin's in Copenhagen. Harris is startled. He parks his car again and gets out. But the woman is nowhere to been seen.

Harris spends half an hour walking around in the grounds and scouting beyond it. He does not spot anyone in that dress.

The sight of the woman and time wasted trying to locate her has prevented Harris from doing what he had intended: find a parking spot on the country road and make a verbatim record of what he remembered of Dutton's monologue while the wrestler-nurse was away. The vans have driven away. He gets back into his car, drives out to the nearest picnic spot, and starts dictating into his mobile phone. But much of the monologue seems to have slipped away even further. What he manages to recall is less than a page when finally transcribed and added to the stuff in the yellow folder. And it makes even less sense than it had when tumbling out of Dr. Dutton's mouth.

"The answer has been there, staring at us for years, decades, centuries… Religions got it, and lost it in rituals. Philosophers got it, and lost it in sophistry. Poets got it, and lost it in prose. Scientists got it, and lost it in method … And then they came, the cowboys, always the cowboys, their guns blazing. Their only drug is a bullet … There is always a duality. There is only singularity … You cannot laugh when you think. You cannot think when you laugh … In the depths of the oceans, there is a worm that is blind. No sunlight reaches it. It is not alone. There are crabs down there. They are blind too. No sunlight reaches them. Their food is made by microbes … Then the idiots talk of symbiosis, and you say that is a simplification. Then the idiots talk of dysbiosis, and that is a simplification too … It is the job of idiots to talk. Wisdom lies in silence … Because otherwise, the cowboys come, guns blazing, guns blazing … Do you know that

200,000 Indians were massacred after the fall of Tenochtitlan, and 250 as late as 1890 at Wounded Knee? That is their only answer. Shoot it down. Silver bullets. The only good microbe is a dead microbe ... Why tell them then? Why tell the cowboys? Wislawa told me that; lovely, ethereal Lava. That's what her friends called her. Lava. But by then she had stopped erupting. Oh no, she was not the spitfire she had been when young. That is what she told me when we met last. She said, the truth is best hidden. She said, they sensed it, the ancient sages ... But we are not prepared. The truth should not be told, or they will shoot it down. They will smelt it into gold. The cowboys will come on their bridled horses, guns blazing, guns blazing..."

~

She looks out of the window with its cracked blue panes and can see glimpses of the agricultural fields through the thin screen of trees that remains around her cottage. It had been built by her great-great-grandfather right in the centre of a coppice, but the coppice has since been shaved away, generation by generation, as the village fields spread further. Her father tried and failed to get the coppice, what was left of it thirty years ago, included in Poland's many new afforestation programs. Now just a scatter of trees are left around the wooden cottage. They have not been cut because they are on her land. They are an eclectic combination of ash, elm, and willow. There is a towering oak, which is being consumed by the oak wilt—she can tell from the discoloration of its leaves—and she has asked the nearest forest department for help. This is the only oak left in or around the village. They should do something. The oak is also where her father had built her a small treehouse, which has since collapsed, though a few planks and ropes remain hanging from the gnarled branches.

This was the cottage her parents had retired to. She had hardly visited them in those years. She was already abroad: it had been a brilliant trajectory for her, from Warsaw to Cambridge on a scholarship, and then to Harvard, where she had received her first tenure. She had come down and stayed with them during Christmas or Easter some years. They had seemed happy to her, satisfied with the cottage, which, apart from electricity and piped water, had been maintained as it was. Her father loved old things and gardening. Her mother loved books. Then her mother had died of a heart attack, and two years later her father had committed suicide with an overdose of sleeping pills. Their village friends said, he did not like living on after your mother. The doctor said, he was suffering from clinical depression.

She did not know much about not wanting to live on without your partner. She remembered all her partners, even the Hollywood star who had, for a short while in the 1980s, brought her out of the realm of journal attention into the limelight of tabloids and society pages. Strangely, it had reinforced her scientific reputation in academic circles. But not one of her many partners, some charming, some beautiful, some brilliant, had ever left her lonely for long. Life, she had told herself years ago, when she was considering moving to Cambridge, is purposive. That is what distinguishes life from non-life. The smallest microbe has a purpose; the biggest lump of gold lacks a purpose. Life becomes meaningless only if you lose sight of the purpose of the moment. I, she had told herself, a brilliant young student in Warsaw, with half her professors in love with her, I know my purpose. Life will never be meaningless for me.

Clinical depression, she understood better. Anhedonia. Her father had clearly suffered from it the past two years, though he had hidden it from her on her two visits. Or had he hidden it? Could it be that her visits had given him the interest that he lacked in life after her mother's death? In those days, she did not allow herself to think of it. Her work had been intensely clinical. She had been working on dopaminergic pathways; she had been a staunch advocate of cingulotomy as the final treatment for acute depression. Perhaps it was her father's depression and suicide that had sent her on the trajectory that she pursued after that, a trajectory that made her leave Harvard, and then move to successively smaller universities, until she was here, back in the spare cottage of her ancestors.

Purpose, she had learnt, was not enough. All life has purpose, and purpose gives meaning. But purpose on its own is not enough. Because various purposes can clash or combine. That is also why clinical explanations are not enough. She is still a trained scientist, a clinician at heart, but long ago she started focusing on what clinicians always ignore: how subjects with exactly the same biological causes end up having very different trajectories in life. There is no gene for crime, no center of depression. Some of what happens to human beings is like gangrene; you can cut off the infected appendage. Much of what happens to human beings is not like gangrene. It is unimaginably complex: a tightrope walk on a network of purposes, balancing one's own pole of purpose. She remembers talking to Vij and Sumi about it for hours. Days. They were the ones who had followed their common discoveries to their logical limits. Maybe Derek too, but Derek was always eccentric. A rich aristocrat who dabbled in science when it took his fancy. She last heard that he was in some kind of asylum. As for the others: they all had bits and pieces of the jigsaw. They did not dare follow the evidence to its logical conclusion, because then they would be left with so little: no certainty, no conclusion, no, not even a self as they understood it. They pressed forward and balked. Not one of them was as daring as Vij and Sumi. She misses the two for a second, and then the feeling passes, because she can sense them again. They are with her, one part of her. This is something she learnt only in this cottage.

She knows they must have taken precautions like hers. She walks out to the porch and looks down the graveled track leading away from the cottage. There is no one there. She has to tread carefully on the planks of the cottage here. The porch, with its old filigreed and carved wooden panels and posts, is unstable. She had it reinforced when she moved in a decade ago, when she still had savings. Now, she can only watch it rot and fall. It won't be long. No, it won't be long. They will come for her soon.

She walks out into the trees, letting their greenness fall like a blanket on her. In her long, flowing dress, she drifts like a ghost among the trees. They have their purposes. The insects and birds in them have their purposes. So do the microbes and fungi. And she has her purpose. It is not what she thought it was when she packed her bags for Cambridge as a confident twenty-year-old. But she is prepared. She has burned all her papers and notes. She has erased all her files and thrown both her laptops away in a dump. She does not need them. She did all this almost a year ago. Since then, she has been waiting for them to come.

12

Person/Paradigm

Two days later, back in his villa on the outskirts of Viborg City, Harris gets an email. It has been sent from a burner email account. Harris does not even try to trace it further. Whoever sent it was not an amateur, and it would be a waste of time. Instead, he spends more than a day trying to decipher the single sentence contained in the email. But it is not a code. It is just a sentence. An instruction that does not make sense: "Scoop up some water and weeds from your pond, put it in a glass jar, and then perform that most Herculean of tasks: patient observation."

Harris tries everything on it, ranging from something as simple as the Caesar Shift to computerized and even chemical codes, such as the logic governing the Pioneer Plaques. Everything he remembers from his training days with Command Alpha. Nothing gives him anything other than the obvious words of that sentence. So, as the sun climbs to its zenith, though largely hidden behind a thin gauze of clouds, he decides to walk out and do as literally instructed: fill a glass jar with water and weeds from his pond.

His swans come waddling up to him as he approaches the small pond. It makes him realize that he hardly ever goes out for a walk in the garden these days. The grass is showing signs of neglect. Bushes need trimming. The apple trees in the corner need pruning. Harris can call the gardening firm he occasionally employs, but he decides against it. If this is paranoia, he would rather be paranoid—he does not want unknown people on his property right now. Instead, he ignores the swans and fills the jar with water and weeds. He takes it back to the house, puts it at the head of the dining table, right where Mermaid had sat on that night, and looks at it.

The water is fairly clear: this is a region rich in ochre, but limestone had been added to the pond to neutralize it. Harris can see green and brown weeds, which he tries to identify with the help of online pictures and information. This is difficult enough. Then, as he looks at the water through a magnifying glass, he spots other things, including what appear to be larvae. This is not a jar of water; it is an entire ecosystem. Harris knows that much. It is like being asked to look at a tropical forest for a single clue: the proverbial needle in a haystack. What is it that he is missing out?

And then the obvious word strikes Harris: Herculean! What, he asked himself, would be Herculean in a small jar of pond water? Which of the tasks of Hercules? Harris recalls some of them: the slaying of the Nemean lion, the capture of the mad bull of Crete, fetching Cerberus from the underworld… But Harris is a methodical man: he googles up the twelve labors, and the answer is the second one. Why hadn't he thought of it? Nothing else fits this small jar of water and weeds, not one of the other eleven labors of Hercules. But the second one does, in a way: the slaying of the nine-headed Hydra of Lerna! Harris picks up the jar and looks closely at the undersides of the weeds, and there they are, small green-brown blobs: hydras. He sits down and observes, as instructed. The water in the jar settles down, the leaves and weeds grow still, and slowly one of the hydra unfolds into a thin stalk with tentacles, a ghostly arm reaching out. It waves weakly in the water. Harris peers at it through his magnifying glass.

What now? He wonders. What message does this hydra hold? What message can one of the most common water creatures in the world hold, a simple creature that has survived unchanged for 500 million years? That it is primitive, or that, having survived so successfully, it is highly modern? That it can regenerate, like the mythical Hydra? That it is related to jellyfish, and can kill small aquatic creatures with its chemicals, like the famous poisonous breath of the Greek Hydra? No, these were generalities. The clue needs to be something more specific. Harris has no idea what it is. The variables, Harris thinks, are too many, as he finally goes to bed. He smiles at the word, "variables". The variables were always too fucking many.

It is well past midnight when a thought wakes Harris up out of a seemingly deep slumber. This happens sometimes. He does not recall dreaming, but here he is, wide awake with that single thought that his mind should not have had if it was really sleeping deeply. A thought that centers around the last word he had in his mind when falling asleep: variables.

He goes to the list of dead, missing, retired and damaged scientists in Mermaid's folder. One of them had been a biologist. That is the thought that had woken him up. One of them had been a biologist.

There she is: Dr. Julia Yong. She is not one of the dead; she had disappeared. She had taken early retirement in late 2020, when the coronavirus crisis was still raging and Donald Trump was refusing to vacate the White House. Soon afterward, she had moved to Honolulu, where she had grown up as a child, and essentially dropped off the face of academia. A few years later, it had been reported that she had gone out on a walk and never returned. Could he find her, if she was alive? Harris is not sure in what state he would find her. Was it worth a delay of weeks, and surely Mermaid would have looked, with all the forces at his beckoning? No, thinks Harris: that would be a waste of time.

There is something else he could do. His full access to library and scientific publications might be the best place to search first. He needs to search for any research that Dr. Yong had done on hydras.

It is not difficult to find: hydras were central to Julia Yong's last known field of research, an area she had explored for around a decade, but published only one paper, in the second year of research, on it. It started with a quotation:

"The history of any organism is often depicted on a family tree. Family trees usually are grown from the ground up: a single trunk branches off into many separate lineages, each branch diverging from common ancestors. But symbiosis shows us that such trees are idealized representations of the past. In reality, the tree of life often grows in on itself. Species come together, fuse, and make new beings, who start again. Biologists call the coming together of branches—whether blood vessels, roots, or fungal threads—anastomosis. Anastomosis, branches forming nets, is a wonderfully onomatopoetic word. One can hear the fusing. The tree of life is a twisted, tangled, pulsing entity with roots and branches meeting underground and in midair to form eccentric new fruits and hybrids." (Lynn Margulis, *Symbiotic Planet*, p. 52)

It was not an unfashionable quotation from the period. Margulis, Harris is aware, had come back into the warmth of academia, despite scientific scepticism of the Gaia thesis, in the initial decades of the millennium. Harris believes that Margulis and her branch of research would have been bigger today if the pandemic had not diverted attention—and funding—to better ways of killing microbes, viruses and any other being, visible or invisible, threatening the safety of humankind. The big corporations had grown even bigger on this promise: make mankind safe forever! Some peripheral leftist sociologists even called it the shift from capitalism to "safetyism."

But there had been only one paper on hydras by Dr. Yong. This—it was a pattern Harris had noticed in other scientists from the seminar, all except Professor Pichler—had marked her fall from grace in academia, and finally, probably, her retirement. A decade of research, with only one paper, and that too published in the second year? This was the equivalent of jumping off the Eiffel Tower in academia.

The research had started well. And hydras had started it off. Dr. Yong had initially joined a team led by Professor Thomas Bosch, who, in the beginning of the millennium, had made a significant discovery by studying the hydra, these primitive animals that had been around for 500 million years. This was more than a hundred and fifty million years before the earliest dinosaurs appeared. And hydras were still there, hugely successful, fully adapted, sixty-six million years after the last dinosaurs disappeared, or survived only in the metamorphosed forms of birds! Was it correct to call hydra "primitive"? Bosch did not think so. He was more interested in learning how an organism like the hydra, containing just two layers of cells, every one of them exposed to the outside, had survived and thrived? Being so vulnerable, why hadn't it died of infections, of disease? After all, as Bosch was quoted telling an interviewer, the hydra is "just a slimy epithelium sitting in a hostile environment".

It was the answer that Bosch and his student Sebastian Fraune came up with that had initially drawn Dr. Yong to their research. Soon, though, she had moved away, in the third year, after her first and only publication in the field, and set up on her own, moving progressively downwards to smaller institutions, as funding for her experiments and patience for her research dried up. It was again a pattern Harris had noticed with the others in the list.

The answer Bosch had come up with was part of a larger change in research in those days, essentially a rewriting of the history of life. The hydra, Dr. Bosch and his team had discovered, did not survive and thrive because of what it was on its own. It did so because of its ability to harbour distinctive sets of microbes in its own body, microbes that sustained and protected its exposed cells. This was not surprising. By the time Dr. Bosch and his team made this discovery, it had been established that microbes—and even the viruses with them—were not the singular villains that many considered them to be, at least since Louis Pasteur, though Pasteur himself had not taken such a one-sided view. Scientists knew that the human body contained 30 trillion human cells and 39 trillion microbial cells, many of them performing useful functions for human beings. A series of scientists had traced various forms of symbiosis between animals, plants, insects, and microbes. The human had not just come to occupy a zone of indiscernibility populated by what had been considered non-human; the human was itself also that zone. The idea of the microbiome had come to be accepted. It was generally acknowledged that the animal body—including the human body—was not the master of all it surveyed, a crusader slashing through evolutionary dangers; it was more like an ecosystem, with the immune system working as a thermostat rather than a silver bullet. All that Bosch and his team knew, and what they discovered about the hydra simply added to the area of knowledge.

What took the matter a bit further was their observation that related species of hydra, brought up in the same environment, fed the same nutrient, kept in identical plastic containers for decades, nevertheless cultivated distinct sets of microbes. This was shocking, to say the least. These "simple" organisms were selecting the microbes they wanted in and around their bodies? In human terms, they were constructing their own identities? How did an animal that did not even have a brain manage to do so? Not once, not twice, but across generations? How did two Hydra species, for decades submerged in the same environment, still select a different set of microbial companions, finely honed to fulfil their different needs?

By the time Dr. Yong joined the team, research had progressed further. It had become obvious that the ability to select your microbial companions existed in other organisms too. Microbes did not just infest us; we selected some of them over others. Or, we did so under healthy conditions. Many of our diseases, it was being argued in those days—before the virus crisis muffled the arguments, given the political need and economic impetus to manufacture silver bullets once again—had to do with a mutual failure, a dysbiosis rather than symbiosis between organism and microbes. It was this that had drawn Dr. Yong to the research.

Except that she had taken it further. Much further. Even as scientists were struggling to come up with hard evidence—and finding them painstakingly—in simple organisms, Dr. Yong had started speculating about human beings. That is the impression Harris got from the few peer reviews of her funding applications from her last years in academia that he could access. "Conjecture" was a word often used to dismiss her proposals. "Speculation" was another word. They were not "falsifiable", as one, kinder, rejection put it.

What had Dr. Yong been speculating about? It was not clear, not even in her own proposals. But it was obvious that she essentially wanted to study the impact of microbes on the evolution of human intelligence.

~

Jens Erik got off the train at the main station in Copenhagen in a foul mood, but then he had boarded the train in a foul mood.

He had almost forgotten to book a seat. The policy of not being allowed to board a train without a seat reservation had started during the pandemic, but it had been continued on long-distance trains afterward, with the seat reservation price increasing slightly every couple of years. This had kept the ticket price from rising substantially, which was a good election gambit.

But it was not the price that upset Jens Erik. He was used buying a ticket, finding a seat if and when you could, and shifting between vacated seats and the corridor if the train was crowded. He had refrained from arguing with the ticket collector, for Jens Erik was at heart a policeman, and knew that rules had to be implemented as part of your duty, whether you liked them or not. He had simply got off that train and caught the next one an hour later, having booked a seat. But he was annoyed by the whole experience.

And then the Hovedbanegården at Copenhagen?

He had never liked the place. It always contained too many people in too much of a hurry. It was always dirtier than all other stations in Denmark, and Jens Erik knew why, though Pernille would not agree: because you only care for places that are strewn with your past. You pick up those pieces of your past and tidy them away. But the people here? Why, their pasts were mostly strewn in other cities, even other countries!

Now it had started looking seedier, more cluttered with people who seemed to have even less to do than in the past.

Jens Erik knew from his deputation in the city, and the cop friends he had, who for some weird reason chose to stay on or move back to Copenhagen, that the main station had always been a hangout for loafers and drug-addicts. They said it had been worse in the past, when the area behind the station was frequented by prostitutes. Jens Erik humpfed.

It was around four in the evening, and Jens Erik had told Pernille he would reach her flat on Falkoners Alle in Frederiksberg, an autonomous municipality bang in the middle of Copenhagen, sometime around nine. He had no intention of having dinner with her boyfriend, the rice-cake vegan! Instead, he had arranged to meet with some cop-friends for a beer. He had come to consult them anyway.

Jens Erik left the station by the back exit, as the main police station where he had friends was about half a kilometer behind the station. He stepped out into a colorful mix of people, some wearing Asian or African dresses. But the person who caught Jens Erik's eye was a tall, gaunt man, very Scandinavian-looking, but with long cane-rowed and beaded hair. Jens Erik shook his head. Why couldn't people be what they were? He adjusted his cap for reassurance.

The café was just a few minutes' walk from the police station, across the broad boulevard. It was part of the theme café chain that started soon after the pandemic, as the Universal Restaurant and Café Corporation (URCC) slowly bought up privately owned restaurants that went bankrupt in 2020 and 2021. The one here was called "Farmyard", in English, but Jens Erik recalled it as a place full of old sofas and mismatched chairs that had, before the pandemic, been a popular haunt for students and bohemians.

Now it was all polished wooden panels, stylized faux-stone fireplaces—electric fires that looked like real logs burning—and farmyard décor that had obviously never been used by a farmer.

The bartenders wore cowboy hats.

The waitresses wore checked red or blue dairymaid dresses, which drew attention to their bare arms and legs, and (aproned) breasts. They were the reason why this was a favorite haunt of Jens Erik's pals, most of whom were men in their fifties.

Word has gone around that Jens Erik, good old grouch from Aarhus, was in town, and his friends—some posted elsewhere in the city—have dropped in, sometimes for a quick beer, sometimes to have a bite with him. There was the kind of artificial bonhomie that only a reunion of old friends evokes.

Jens Erik sounded all of them out about the "nigger"—he did not have to rephrase it differently in this company—but they either did not pay attention or dismissed it with a "shit happens" shrug. In general, the reactions were of bewilderment, amusement, uninterest. One of his old friends put it all in words as he left after a quick beer. He patted Jens Erik on the shoulders and quipped,

"You need to get yourself a hobby or a woman, old man! It will take these dead old cases off your mind."

The only person who seemed to consider it an issue was Anne Mette Sørensen, with whom Jens Erik had often been partnered in a patrol car, and who, like Jens Erik, has not scaled the heights of the profession but managed to reach high enough to get those last few years of desk jobs. Though, unlike Jens Erik, she has stayed happily married, with three grown-up sons, all of whom are policemen, two in traffic, and one in homicide.

"I will ask Jonas," she told him later in the evening, when only four of them were left at the table, "That's the boy, my son, the one in homicide; now, he is definitely going places. He has been promoted and commended more in a decade than I was in my entire life."

"Now, don't mention me," Jens Erik said.

"Oh, I never mention you," Anne Mette laughed, and they clinked their glasses.

~

I saw something, Maman. But even before that, I had heard something. Both had come about in the same way, through the ventilation panels.

Ventilation is a major issue on oil rigs. So is fire, Kurt had told me, and seepages of noxious gases from the lower decks. All the floors, of which the bottom ones were sealed, had elaborate ventilation. The air ducts ran under the ceiling on each floor, powered by purge and pressurization systems and a three-stage air filtration system. The corridors being used, the rooms and galley were studded with ventilators and axial fans. It was all a bit dated, according to Kurt, but it was convenient for me because I realized that the air ducts for the galleys and the company rooms below ran right under my feet at times. I discovered this because, when I was cleaning one of the rooms, I heard a murmur of voices. I put my ear to the floor and realized that the voices were coming from below. There must have been a ventilator panel just below me, opening into a room on a lower floor.

After that, it was relatively simple to examine all the rooms as they were emptied or occupied and find one with a panel in the floor that could be leveraged. The first time, I just removed the panel, and was too frightened to do anything more. I could see the air duct was large enough for a small person like me to crawl into. I did not dare do it immediately. I put back the panel and covered it with the carpet. But I kept that room locked, not giving it out to any guests in the future. I had the keys to the rooms in the luxury corridor anyway, for it was my job to tidy them up, and Kurt was hardly around during the day. He was always with Mr. Watch or one of the men, or in that closed section barred to me. It was the closed section that bothered me. I wanted to know. It could be necessary for my survival.

Two days later, I returned to the room. I had my cleaning clothes on, and this time I locked the door behind me. Then I put the broom against the door handle, in such a way that it would fall if someone tried to open the door. That might give me the signal to crawl back. I pulled back the carpet, removed the panel, and crawled into the air duct. It was cold in there. Next time, I thought, I would have to wear a thick sweater. I also knew I had to be careful. If I could hear them when they spoke, they would also be able to hear me if I made a noise.

I silenced my pager and pocketed a small flashlight and a kitchen knife in case I encountered rats or insects. But there were no rats on the rig, and there didn't seem to be spiders either: the ducts were almost sterile. Once inside them—there was enough space to crawl on all fours in some sections, and on your belly in other parts—I realized that I could not use the light freely: a light showing from the ventilators would be a dead giveaway. And, mostly, enough light filtered in from the ventilators for me to get by.

Each day that I went into the air ducts and crawled a bit farther, I got a better idea of what was below me. Soon I knew which ventilators let out into the rooms, which into the galleys, and which into that secret chamber. I was afraid of going into the area above the secret chamber because, mostly, the experts were there. Mr. Watch was there when he was with us. Kurt was there. But that is where I heard it from. It was unmistakable: the sound of an animal in pain. The sound of an animal being tortured.

Now I knew why even the door to that section was so heavy—and always guarded.

It was unbearable after that. One of your men, not this one, Maman, used to call me Miss Pokey Nose when I was eleven or twelve. I guess he was not wrong. I just had to know what the secret chamber contained. I could not look through the ventilators in that section during the daytime. There could be men in there: the experts spent a lot of time in there when they were not eating or sleeping. Also, it was at the other end of the corridor, about as far away from our room and the luxury rooms above as possible. Crawling there took at least fifteen minutes, and I could not afford to be down in the air ducts for more than half an hour or so during the day. Kurt or someone might need me. They did not necessarily use the pager every time. There was only one option. I had to go down there during the night when everyone was asleep, the secret chamber locked, and the two or three men on guard were posted as lookouts outside, mostly to keep watch on the ocean. But to go down there at night, I had to leave the room I shared with Kurt—and hope that Kurt would not wake up while I was away for at least an hour, perhaps more. It was too risky.

Maybe I would not have done this even two weeks ago. But by then I did not trust Kurt. I also, to be honest, resented him for bringing me here on what, I was certain by now, were false premises—and promises. In a moment of bitterness, I told myself that I had not turned out to be so different from you, Maman: Kurt, after all, was like the men you had always collected; men who promised one thing and did something else! I kept this resentment to myself, which was easy because Kurt was hardly ever with me—except for meals and in bed, when he would still, like most men, make love to me without stopping to ascertain my mood. No, I would not have done this two weeks ago, but now I knew what I had to.

Kurt kept his sleeping pills in a plastic bottle in the shelves to one side of the small sink in our bathroom. He took a pill almost every night, but I knew that it was not sufficient to keep him from waking up: it just enabled him to drowse off again. What, I asked myself, if I doubled the dose? I considered trebling it, but then shrank back from unintended consequences: I did not want to harm Kurt. But doubling the dose? That should give me at least two or three hours when Kurt would be certain of a deep sleep.

It was simple to crush the pill and add it to his food. No, Maman, don't raise your eyebrow at me. I had to wait for the right evening. Often we ate downstairs in the galley. It was always after the experts had eaten in the dining room for them, attached to my section of the galley, when I and sometimes one of the men, depending on the number of guests, had to serve. Sometimes Mr. Watch and Kurt would eat with the experts too. But there were also nights when I just carried a tray upstairs because Kurt had stayed in our room, working on his laptop. There was no Wi-Fi on the rig, but I am certain they could dock their laptops somewhere in the control room—a facility kept secret from me. So I waited for the evening Kurt would be upstairs. It came three nights after I had heard the animal moaning.

Everything went according to plan. I let him sleep for half an hour and then shook him. "Kurt," I said, "Kurt. Sweet Kurt." He murmured, turned over and kept sleeping. I waited for another five minutes. I also left a note I had already prepared by the bedside, informing Kurt that I could not sleep and had gone for a walk in the upper deck (the lower decks were locked and forbidden), something I did often enough during the daytime. That, I hoped, would give me an excuse if things went wrong. Then I tiptoed out of our room and down the luxury corridor—some of the rooms were occupied—and into the room, I had begun to think of as my access room. I had to move noiselessly, but rigs do not have wooden floors, and it was quite easy.

I locked the door behind me, put on the kitchen overall I kept in that room—there could be traces of dust and soot in some parts of the air ducts, especially above the galleys, which I would have to cross. Then I lowered myself into the air ducts. I had to move more cautiously this time. The slightest noise could be heard, if I was above a room occupied by one of the men. Noise carries at night. Mr. Watch was luckily not with us that night; he had flown away on one of his regular trips to wherever. I did not even take the torch or a knife with me, as I was afraid of them clinking against something as I crawled. I proceeded very slowly. It took me about five minutes longer to reach the part where the secret section began. I saw it from a distance: bright ribbons of light were pouring through the ventilation slits in that part.

They left many parts of the rig lit during the light, all of it powered by the powerful generators whose hum matched the sound of the waves on still nights. I knew they left the secret chamber lit too, but I had no idea it was so strongly illuminated. It was as if all the lights were switched on in the section. This solved one of my problems: I had not been certain how much I would be able to see.

It took me some peering through the slits before I got an idea of the room below. But it was clear right from the start that this room—hall would be a better word—was different from anything else on the rig. How can I describe it, Maman? What it reminded me of most was a hospital operating theatre, perhaps because there were two shiny metal tables—exactly like operating tables—in one part of it. There were lots of monitors in the room, things with lights and electronic screens, with strange gadgets and tube-arms attached to some of them. There was a kind of glass cabinet, about man-size, made totally of glass or some other transparent medium, with tubes attached to it, all of them hanging free, and wires that led to some of the computers.

I had never seen a room so chockfull of scientific equipment. But that was it. There was no one in the hall. No human being—and definitely no animal. Where had that sound of an animal in pain come from?

Then I saw it. I had taken it for shadows thrown on the wall, distorted by the slits through which I was peering into the garishly lit room. I could see it only from one of the ventilation panels because it was on one side of the room. What I had confused with the ventilation slits or shadows were metal bars. Actual bars.

There were three doors with bars on that side of the hall. Each door was about four feet in height, and it must have been especially installed because there were no other such small doors—like that of a cage—anywhere else on the rig. What was contained in those barred rooms—or cages—was mostly in shadow. The light from the hall did not carry beyond the first three feet or so, from where I was perched, where it drew a pattern of bars on the floors of the cages. There was something disturbing about them. I felt a grievous sense of wrong, even anger. It reminded me of how you could never bear to see a bird in a cage, Maman.

I concentrated on the three cages. Slowly, I felt convinced that at least one of them contained movement. It was the middle one. I kept looking. There was something in that cage. An animal. A large animal, something like a chimpanzee. I was convinced of it. I lay down flat on my belly, rested my chin on my hands, and kept watch. I must have spent at least one hour, I told myself. That meant that I still had about an hour. Maybe two. I watched.

Nothing happened. The lighted hall exhaled emptiness. The seconds ticked away; the minutes started to stretch. I struggled against drowsiness. Just when I was about to crawl back, there was a sudden movement in another of the cages, one of the two I had considered empty. Two thin arms reached out to grip the bars, and a face appeared behind them. I almost cried out in fear. It was a devastated face, a face torn by disease and pain. But it was not the face of any animal, not just any animal.

It was, or it had been until recently, a human face.

~

Absolute temperatures are still stated in units of kelvin in his honour. There are about a dozen physical phenomenon and concepts named after William Thomson, Baron Kelvin. Born in 1824, with a heart problem that nearly killed him in his childhood, Lord Kelvin's career is a good example of brilliance in the sciences: his mistakes match his successes. Most famously, he dismissed Röntgen's discovery of the X-rays as a hoax, but later accepted the scientific evidence. However, he remained convinced that a heavier-than-air aircraft was not possible. He died in 1907; it was four years after the first flight by the Wright brothers.

As famously, Lord Kelvin doubted Darwin's theory of evolution, based on his (correct) calculation of the relatively short period when the earth has been habitable. It was this that made him offer a conjecture about life on earth that, in later years, was roundly scoffed.

Life, he claimed, arose elsewhere.

The earliest record of this conjecture is provided to us by Dr. Alan E. Wallace, who reports visiting the great man in his laboratory, overlooking the River Kelvin, in Glasgow. Thomson, in those days not elevated to the peerage—he was the first British scientist to be thus honoured—was looking out of a window, according to Dr. Wallace.

He waved Dr. Wallace into a chair and kept looking out for a long time. Then he turned to him, and without preamble, said, "It cannot be possible. The earth has not been inhabitable long enough for life to evolve as Dr. Darwin proposes. I have always had trouble reconciling his theory with the facts. But I got the answer right now. The current of the river gave me the answer. Look how it carries leaves, twigs, and detritus from a long way off to us and beyond. Why can't life have come to us like that, from another planet?"

In later years scientists poked holes in this theory. The most obvious one being that of its circularity: it did not really explain the origin of life. It just postponed the explanation. But for Lord Kelvin that was not an objection, for he did not feel any need to explain the origin of life. He only wanted to explain how it came about on earth. As for its origin, he had no doubt: life was created by God.

Strangely, in the first years of the millennium, about a century after his death, the tide of scientific opinion turned again, at least in some circles. The notion of panspermia was evoked. It started way back in the 1970s, when Fred Hoyle and Chandra Wickramasinghe proposed that dust in interstellar space was essentially organic. This was later proved to be correct. The possibility of the seeds of life being interspersed throughout space was back. But these seeds of life, it was obvious, could only be microscopic, something like viruses. Hoyle and Wickramasinghe even contended that these interstellar life forms continue to enter the Earth's atmosphere and are responsible for both epidemics and genetic novelty.

This was more controversial. But by the first decade of the new millennium, it had been reasonably ascertained that the units of life—"seeds", according to some; "carbon molecules", according to others—do exist on meteors and elsewhere, and all genetic material, including human DNA, contains segments from other life forms, including microorganisms.

Lord Kelvin would have grunted approval. Of course, it depended on your paradigm: it meant something, or it meant nothing. Or, just possibly, it meant something else?

13

Woman in the Long Dress

SAM Atkins is at his usual place, behind the desk in his neat office at the back of the cluttered shop, manned, as it was last time, by his knitting mother. He does not look surprised to see Harris. He pretends not to notice the terseness in Harris, who has a quarrel to pick with Mermaid. He cannot reach Mermaid, so it has to be Atkins. Harris is almost angry, angrier than he has been for years. He has been thinking about it for days, ever since he returned from England. That woman in the long dress. The irritation shows in his voice. But Atkins does not look surprised to hear the irritation in Harris's voice. His round marble eyes gleam beneficently; his mouth retains the marbles of genteel intonation.

"Tell Mer…tell Nicholson, tell him from me, that he has to stop having me trailed. I won't put up with it," blurts out Harris, refusing to sit down.

Sam Atkins waves at Harris to be seated. Wordlessly, he withdraws his thermos of coffee and pours them a cup each. He pushes a cup over to Harris as he had last time.

"I can assure you that Nicholson is not having you followed," he says. "He trusts you and, in any case, he knows you would spot it."

"Someone has been following me," Harris insists, "A young woman, probably in her late twenties..."

Sam Atkins blinks.

"Are you sure?" he asks.

"I have seen her twice. Very pretty. Extremely pretty. In an old-fashioned dress..."

"A long dress. Floral pattern..." Sam interrupts.

"Yes," says Harris, his irritation creeping back, "So you know her."

"No, I don't." Sam looked thoughtful, "And neither does Nicholson."

Then he rummages through one of his drawers.

"Recall Wislawa Ostrowski, the Polish prof?" Without waiting for Harris's reply, Sam Atkins continues, still rummaging in his drawer, "You have seen her photos, haven't you?"

"There was one in the yellow folder," Harris confirms.

"I know the one. A lecture photo from when she was in her fifties. For a woman famed for her lectures and beauty, there is almost no photograph of her from before. She was never the social media type. We have photos of her only from around the time she became a professor, in her forties, and before she finally quit academia and went back to her parents' cottage in Poland. She had maintained it after their deaths, spending longer and longer periods there with the years. She died soon afterwards, as you know. Of an overdose, they think, in her parents' bed." Sam took something out of the drawer. It was a black-and-white photo.

"This took time to recover. She was in her twenties then," he tosses the photo to Harris.

Despite the lack of color in the photo, Harris gasps at the resemblance between Professor Wislawa Ostrowski and the woman he has seen twice. Even the dresses are similar.

He sits down without noticing it.

"You mean, her daughter has been trailing me?" asks Harris in bewilderment.

"If she is as young as you say, she will need to be her granddaughter," replies Sam.

"But Ostrowski never married, I remember reading it in the file."

"You remember correctly, my friend. Lots of broken loves, lovers galore, but no marriage, no child. She was a spinster dedicated to science."

"An illegitimate child..." wonders Harris aloud, but then a thought crossed his mind, "How did you know that the woman I had seen resembled Ostrowski?"

"It's happened before."

"It's happened before? To you?"

"To the man from SAW who had the case before you."

"I think it is time you told me more," says Harris. All the anxiety he has been feeling for weeks now had formed into a knot in his stomach. He can feel his fists clenching.

"I think it is time I ask Nicholson," Sam agrees.

"What happened to the man?"

"He went crazy soon afterwards. He shot down some innocent passersby and then turned the gun on himself. It made the news. Or it didn't. Some say what made news was not news. Who knows? I suspect it has something to do with Nicholson coming to you, to me. Remember, the Houston curbside shooting, as it was called? That was it. Only, of course, his connection to SAW was never revealed."

Five days later, a thin yellow file is put in Harris's letterbox sometime during the night. He discovers it when he checks the box, after feeding his swans, later that day.

The File:

[Pages redacted] of reports prepared following the incident in Houston when [name blacked out], code name Agent A-43act, in a moment of insanity, turned his service revolver on pedestrians, killing four and wounding seven, mostly women, before shooting himself, by placing the barrel of his revolver in his mouth. Death was instantaneous on the discharge of the bullet in the revolver.

Background Information

Agent A-43act was born in [lines blacked out].

Pater: An army officer, discharged with honor after a non-combat injury suffered in Kuwait.

Mater: Secondary school teacher, not retired.

Family reported to be religious, very active in their local church. Also, involved in a group from their church that meets every evening and prays for the immediate return of the saviour, believing that this would only take place if sufficient numbers of Christians prayed for it on a daily basis.

Relationship with family: A-43act fell out with his parents, before joining the army. Objected vociferously to his parents' religious beliefs during high school. Conflicts over his clothing choices and music. Reports of daily arguments, some of them relating to A-43act's promiscuity, until A-43act graduated and left home for good. He was subsequently enlisted [lines blacked out; pages redacted]

Career at SAW

Agent A-43act had an exemplary career at SAW. Involved in several major projects, especially [lines blacked out]. Considered a reliable colleague and a competent investigator, specializing in fieldwork. Adjectives most commonly applied to him by his colleagues: "pragmatic", "trustworthy", and "systematic". [Pages redacted.]

The Final Case

[Lines blacked out.] Referred henceforth only as Case X, this involved the investigation of [words blacked out] seminar proceedings in Aarhus in 2012.

Reason for investigation: Most of the seminar participants have since died or disappeared. Further reference to the case in files [line blacked out].

Description of activity: Agent A-43act entrusted with field investigations in February 2023, worked on the case right until his suicide in November 2028. His state of mind (Ref: File [line blacked out]) at the commencement of his investigation was certified as stable plus. Despite [lines blacked out] period of absence, there were no psychological or other issues. However, as the investigation proceeded, Agent A-43act showed clear evidence of psychological ill-health, even, in retrospect, paranoia and a kind of inverted religious mania, following the said period of absence. At the time when he killed the passers-by and himself in Houston, on 2 November 2028, he had been asked to go on leave (with pay) by his SAW mentors. Various factors, including his religious childhood, estimated to have played a role in this unexpected deterioration in Agent A-43act's behavioral patterns and mental regime.

Probability: Death of one of the individuals (Professor Katsumi Takewaki) under investigation triggered a degree of paranoia and religious mania in Agent A-43act, though colleagues contested this by noting that A-43act was not unused to such tragedies as part of his work for SAW and other agencies before it. At 45, which was A-43act's age in 2028, his colleagues argue in his defence that he had vast experience of the mortality of fellow humans and he appeared to be in full control of his facilities.

Comment: Despite above, indications that the death of Professor Katsumi Takewaki in Tokyo seems to have affected A-43act deeply, confirming in him a growing suspicion that he was being followed by a young woman in an old-fashioned dress and, in particular, giving this suspicion a strange religious turn. He also complained, less frequently, of another trailer, a vaguely described man of indeterminate age, whom he once referred to as his evil twin.

Description of the Tokyo event: [Lines blacked out] After he had exhausted all clues in Europe and USA, and after he had shown some initial evidence of paranoia—he had observed to his superior that a woman in a long dress was following him, though this had been dismissed and proved wrong by arranging for A-43act to be double-trailed—A-43act flew into Tokyo to meet Professor Katsumi Takewaki, who had recently retired and returned to Tokyo after a distinguished career as an astronomer. Agent A-43act's reports on his meetings with Takewaki were irregular and caused the first serious round of worries among his superiors at SAW.

Comment: Takewaki suffered from mild paranoia and this triggered off something latent in Agent A-43act. His reports filled with suggestions of people who could read his mind, and the mystery woman recurred again and again in them. At least twice, he suggested the existence of a spirit world. In his last report, he stated that "the borders between our world and the spirit world have been weakened, and now they can come and go amongst us more freely than hitherto." His reports had already started filling with Biblical intonations.

Departmental response: Ordered back to base by supervizing officer. Obeyed order, but claimed to have witnessed the death of Professor Takewaki. This could only have been a hallucination because A-43act left Tokyo on 12th October 2028 and Professor Takewaki was run down on 14th October.

Unresolved matter: Agent A-43act's report on the death of Professor Takewaki reached the desk of his superior at least an hour before the official intimation of the professor's accident arrived from Tokyo. Agent A-43act could only have known of it from other sources, but if he had other sources, he refused to divulge them to his superiors.

Comment: Agent A-43act's report on Takewaki's death tallied with the police report from Tokyo, except on one significant fact. The police report classified it as a hit-and-run: Takewaki had gone for a walk and had stepped off the pavement, when a car turned the corner rashly and hit him. However, A-43act's report specified that Takewaki walked to the middle of the uncrowded road and waited for the car to come and hit him, because he had decided to "move on". All this was refuted by the Tokyo Police, though the driver could not be identified or arrested.

Departmental process: Agent A-43act investigated by colleagues on his return, as recorded in file [line blacked out], and cleared of any suspicion, but advised to go on leave. This he did on October 21. Also submitted to regular therapy and returned to his residence in Houston, which he shared with his wife and daughter, then in college.

Therapy report: Therapy sessions seemed to be proceeding well, though A-43act did on occasion continue to show evidence of paranoia—once he said that he was "still being watched"—and traces of religious mania (particularly a deep interest in what he called "the spirit world"). In his daily life, though, it appears that A-43act kept a tight hold on himself. His wife did not feel that A-43act had changed drastically or was paranoid, but she did consider him "tired, pre-occupied and over-wrought". According to his therapist, A-43act was improving.

Fatal event: However, on the afternoon of 24 November, A-43act pulled out his service revolver (which he should not have been carrying) and started shooting at passers-by in a mall in Houston. He appears to have aimed at women in long dresses. He continued the shooting on the street outside the mall. However, by the time the police arrived, he was sitting on the curb, looking dejected and lost. He held the police at bay by poking the revolver into his own mouth and threatening to shoot himself. The officers, tipped of his identity, tried to talk him out of it. He gradually grew calmer and agreed to put down his revolver. He took the barrel out of his mouth and lowered the revolver, slowly. He said, clearly and distinctly, "There are angels and demons." Then he laughed, put the barrel back into his mouth and pulled the trigger.

Conclusion:

Agent A-43act suffered from religious delusion caused by a difficult childhood and triggered by work-related trauma. Case was investigated by his immediate superior [words blacked out], and no further anomalies were discovered. Case is closed by order of [words blacked out].

~

Anne Mette Sørensen called up Jens Erik about a week after he returned to Hjortshøj.

He had spent the week trying to get the dead "negro" out of his head.

He had tidied up his garden, worked on the *kolonihave* that he maintained, which had been neglected recently, and where two trees, both pear, were not thriving: Jens Erik suspected it was a fungus, but he had not been able to locate it, and, like most people he knew, he did not believe in blasting the roots of the tree or its trunk with just any fungicide.

Smide barnet ud med badevandet, his father had grumbled whenever he observed people use pesticides too readily. In his father's generation, it was more common: there was a blind faith in using chemicals for gardening that had waned in recent decades.

Jens Erik had dug up some of the roots of one of the afflicted pear trees, carefully, often with an old spoon to avoid destroying their ends. It had taken him an entire afternoon, but he had been unable to find anything unusual.

One day, he had invited Bente and another single neighbor over for a grill and beer evening.

He had gone bird spotting for a whole day—it had been lightly overcast and had drizzled intermittently, which was the kind of day Jens Erik liked—with some club members in Egå Engsø.

Then, one evening, as he sat in his own garden, with a Tuborg Classic in hand and a defrosted, oven-warmed kebab-pizza—he had not felt like cooking—in front of him, his phone buzzed.

It was Anne Mette, his ex-colleague from Copenhagen.

She asked him about Pernille, and told him about her three sons, and their five (in all) children, and joked about the extent of her much older husband's retirement boredom—that man had worked till he was sixty-eight, Jens Erik told himself and refrained from humpfing. That was the kind of person Anne Mette was: if you did not know she was a career policewoman, you would consider her a traditional housewife, and now, of course, a loving grandmother. Then she got to the point.

"I asked Jonas," she said.

Jens Erik had discussed the "case" of the dead "negro" even with old Bente, who was frightened by it all and told him to stay out of it: "Who knows what happens in those lands?" Jens Erik did not have the heart to point out that it might have happened in this land. But at the moment Anne Mette called, the case had slipped Jens Erik's mind.

"Jonas?" he echoed, "Asked what?"

Anne Mette thought he did not remember who Jonas was, and explained that Jonas was her oldest son, the one in homicide, and, well, that unknown African man—Jens Erik smiled and reminded himself that Anne Mette was always, as he put it, politically correct: "You know that case you had asked me about, well, I asked Jonas if he could find out a bit more about what had happened."

"Ah," said Jens Erik.

"He did. And he asked me not to get into it. The case was a strange one, he said. It had been closed from the top."

"From the top of the police department?"

"No, from the top of the state."

"Parliament? Ministers?"

"Yes. And even further up."

"What is further up than the Parliament, Anne Mette?"

Anne Mette laughed. "You do live in your own world, don't you, Jens Erik? Any idea what's been happening the last few years?" she said.

Then she added, "But Jonas is a good boy, so he looked in sly at the files. It is all codes and this and that, but Jonas, I told you, is up there with the kings and queens of codes. So he took a look. It wasn't actually illegal, he told me; we use those databases for our work anyway. He was surprised that very little work had been done on that case, almost nothing, before it was shut down. But the autopsy report was there. And guess what?"

"I am too old to guess, Anne Mette."

"The man had organs missing."

"Yes, I was told of a scar too, but why…"

"Oh Jens Erik, don't you see it: there is a huge market in organs. We keep hearing of clandestine traffic in organs. Millions, they say. Syndicates running it. Billionaires involved: they want to live forever, you know. Or at least for another ten years, one year, two weeks… Especially now, what with the virus and the resulting unrest, frightening rich people away from going to places like India and Nigeria for the transplants. We hear that transplants are done in Europe now…"

"That's all conspiracy stuff, Anne Mette. Internet rubbish. They cannot do it in any European country. It is not possible. We still have law…"

Anne Mette laughed again. She laughed for a long time. "Jens Erik," she gasped. "Jens Erik! You will be the death of me!"

Then she added, "Jonas said something else. Skip the organ. It was too freshly removed for the chap to be out swimming though, if you know what I mean. But the forensic report, according to my boy, showed evidence of autoclaving and microbial cleansing. You know what that is?"

"Humpf."

"No need to humpf about it, dear Jens Erik; I did not either. It was cutting edge stuff, still is. It appears that all species, and even individuals in a species, have their own selection of microbes and viruses. Jonas said microbiome and viromes, I think. These are new concepts. What they mean is that our bodies host millions of microbes, including viruses, and their combination, if we could trace all of them, are as distinctive as fingerprints. Or that was the impression I got from Jonas. Now, this is where we get back to the real world: the organ transplant business has a problem with this. Because, you know, viruses and microbes could be transplanted along with the organ. Jonas is a bit of a nerd, you know; he is a six-foot-two nerd! He went on a mansplaining spiel about this! Something about two corneal transplantation patients who died of rabies passed on inadvertently from the donor. So, the organs people have a system, it is still illegal in most countries because it appears they end up killing good and bad microbes in one fell swoop, and that is harmful to the donor. Anyway, they have this technique of subjecting organs to microbial cleansing. This man's body had been subjected to vigorous microbial cleansing. It had been scrubbed like mad, mor, in the words of Jonas, who thought I would understand it better in housekeeping terms. Evidently, your victim's microbe count was so low that it was like a genocide of microbes had been committed in his body."

"So?" Jens Erik found himself resisting these facts. They did not belong to his world, his Denmark.

"So, there are two things, dear Jens Erik. First, the victim had been prepared for organ transplantation. All of him. That is the only explanation. Second, many of the techniques of microbial cleansing are not permitted in Scandinavia, and it requires equipment and expertise that cannot be carried around on a yacht. It is cutting edge biology. It cannot be done out there in the North Sea, mor, Jonas said."

"Humpf."

"Humpf forsooth! Oh yes, and Jonas also said that such bodies have been recovered in the past too, bodies with organs missing. In Scotland, in Sweden, in Holland. Always off the North Sea. But the last time such a body was recovered was in 2022. Nothing after that. He suggested the business was over. They shut it down for some reason in 2022 or 2023. So you can forget it and sleep in peace again. At least that North Sea business."

"What business, Anne Mette?" Jens Erik could not help saying, though he knew what the answer would be.

Anne Mette started laughing again.

"Humpf," said Jens Erik.

~

Kathy bought her red Chevrolet Silverado a decade ago, brand-new. It was a very popular model at the time. She had also bought a studio apartment overlooking a beach, partly paid with her severance money. And she had invested the rest of it. It would have been enough to keep paying the mortgage and lounge on the sands until the end of her days. Everything had been planned out. But then the crisis years of the 2020s intervened, and by 2024, her investment had disappeared. She never understood how, as some millionaire speculators were also making billions from the general misery. But the consequences she understood: She could not afford to pay the mortgage. She sold the apartment—for a lot less than what she had bought it, and used the money, after paying off a hundred bills, to buy a camper. And that is where she had lived since then.

But even owning a camper was expensive these days. The police were often "supervized"—that was the term politicians used after the austerity riots of 2025—by corporations, and they had an incentive to collect camping and parking fees… and, ah, fines. The camping lot Kathy used was an old private one, run by an American Indian couple on reservation land, who charged low and fixed monthly rates, but only allowed people they liked to use the lot. For some reason, they had liked Kathy. That is one reason why she seldom took the camper out, preferring to drive around in her now rather battered, slightly dented Chevrolet.

She is driving from the Rancheria in South Sacramento County to the capital city, and can see the large resort and casino, which was to be inaugurated in the year of the pandemic, and has, given the consequences, been struggling to survive since then. The tribe is now under pressure to sell it to a corporation. Corporations have bought most of the land, and much of other countries too, entire nations, it is rumored, with the few exceptions being the old social democratic nations of Europe, and even there, from what Harris writes and what Kathy reads between the lines, the government is more of a polite pretence. Kathy has driven this route hundreds of times, and she has seen the land change like the skin of a diseased animal: patches of fur and splotches of naked, exposed, festering skin.

It is something she remembers from her years in other countries, in Afghanistan, Syria, Iraq, Libya, Yemen. But there the land had been scarred with war: there were burned hulks of cars and buildings, there were craters from bombs between stretches of sand, sometimes trees, sometimes even gardens, or a miraculously intact neighborhood. But here there had been no real war. Instead, the land was now dotted with resplendent villas and entire gated neighborhoods where not a blade of grass was out of place, and then there were the broken neighborhoods, the dilapidated houses, the shanties and campers, the men and women burning with anger. Anger at what? Anger at everyone else, also at her, or her battered Chevrolet, anger at themselves, their perceived enemies, their friends, their wives, even their children ... and Kathy checked to see that the gun in her dashboard was loaded.

She is driving to Sacramento to buy more Crobe—she has run out again—and check her postbox.

~

Only once in his life had Professor Katsumi Takewaki experienced the reality of the universe, of the galaxies and the stars, and it had been a kilometer deep inside the earth. This is what he would say to his students, sometimes eliciting a suppressed smile from these brilliant young men and women who believed either that reality was not a scientific term or that they were on the verge of grasping it.

It had been in the days when Professor Takewaki was still considered one of the five top astronomers of the world. About a decade before his scientific reputation had declined among his peers, though, unlike many of the Aarhus group, he had been savvy enough to ride his institutional standing to retirement. He had done so not because he cared for reputation any longer, but because he knew it afforded him a degree of safety. It was a shield. It would give him the time he would need when they came for him, as, he was certain, they would one day—and it did not matter who 'they' were, Japanese or American, government or corporation, policemen or gangsters, or all of them rolled into one indistinguishable bolus.

Even though Takewaki's research background had been nuclear physics, he had made his name as an astronomer. It was in that capacity that he was involved in the project to find dark matter and dark energy. This was like finding a haystack in a needle. About 68 percent of the universe's mass is dark energy; about 27 percent is dark matter. The remaining five percent is us, stones, flesh, plants, fungi, microbes, planets, stars, everything we can touch, feel, see, hear: the needle. The haystack is totally invisible.

As the Swiss astronomer, Fritz Zwicky, had shown back in the 1930s, this invisible haystack made us possible. Our galaxies and clusters of galaxies were rotating too fast. The known mass in the universe was insufficient to hold them together. Something else was keeping us from flying apart, disintegrating into smithereens and gases. And then Albert Einstein had shown that light was curving much more than it should, given the visible mass of the galaxies. Something else was there, and that something else was the haystack: it was 95 percent of what was there. We were the needle lost in it.

How do you register what is all around you but cannot be seen? Well, one way is to trace its impact on what can be seen. And that had taken Professor Takewaki deep into the earth, where the impact of invisible mass on "visible" subatomic particles could be traced with the least interference and greatest accuracy. A blip on a screen, like a shooting star in the sky. That was reality, he would say to his discreetly smiling students. Professor Takewaki had been one of the pioneers who developed muon tomography and other ways of recording the presence of dark matter through its impact on "visible" matter, or, as scientists termed it, baryonic matter.

But it had all started ending for Professor Takewaki when he met Wislawa Ostrowski at a post-conference party. Or maybe it had started ending earlier on, when Takewaki began wondering about how the invisible influences the visible, a line of thought that took him first to religion and then, finding religion either muddled or rigid, to various kinds of philosophy—and, finally, to psychologists who diagnosed him with "mild paranoia". Those trips into the womb of the earth were supposed to have triggered his mild paranoia.

He never told them about his discussions with Wislawa and the others she slowly collected around them. He never even mentioned the Aarhus seminar. If he had, they might have wanted him committed to a mental asylum. It would have reassured them. Because he was no longer thinking of dark matter, or not just, or not only.

14

Jyoti Lankeshwar

I return to my room, where Kurt is snoring loudly. I am totally shaken by that riven and torn but obviously human face. Was it a man? Was it a woman? I could not tell. My hands are trembling, and I almost turn to Kurt, to hold him, to have him hold me, when a voice in me points out that Kurt must know. Kurt must know about that man, and whatever was happening in that chamber, that hall full of computerized equipment and with three cages on one side of it. I shrink away from him. But that act sobers me up: my hands stop shaking, and I tell myself, Michelle, you are alone here. It makes me think of my mother. Yes, of you, Maman, how, though I had never realized it earlier, you were the one person, I, all of us, all my siblings, could trust. Your men came and went, but you were always there, inattentive at times, irritable too, but there. There is no one on this rig I can trust. It is as if that thought was a pail of cold water thrown on me: I wake up, focused entirely on my own survival. I knew then, as I know now, that I have to ensure that I did not betray what I had discovered by the slightest change in my behavior towards Kurt.

The next day is mostly sunny. This is unusual in these parts. The sky is a washed blue, with dark bundles of cloud scudding across it in one direction, as if the world under the horizon was on fire. Two of the experts leave by chopper after breakfast. This leaves me with more free time. But Mr. Watch is not back either, so there is a chance that Kurt might laze around me, instead of hanging around Mr. Watch, and when Kurt lazes around, sooner or later, he wants sex. I have never denied him sex before; I had no real reason to do so, and Kurt, like all the men I have known, is easy to please. Even on slow days, it takes just a bit of absentminded effort on my part. But I am not in the mood for even absent-minded effort anymore. I want to evade his attention at least until I am more in control of my emotions.

I go out for a walk on the upper deck. It is made up of metal sheets and metal railings. This is the only one I can access. Tip of the oil berg. Yes, one of Kurt's expressions. There are three decks below it, all forbidden to me. The bottom one, which Kurt calls the spider deck, is only a few feet above the water. I can see from here that it is always wet. Seagulls wheel and float both above and below me. There is a cormorant sitting on one of the metal girders further down. I miss my owl: the only land bird I have seen here. Four of the men are there on the spider deck. Despite the cold, three of them are in bathing shorts. The three jump into the water, splash around for a couple of minutes and clamber out, shivering. They do it for a dare once in a while. They scuttle away into some heated room, laughing and talking. At least they have someone they can talk to. I talk to myself these days.

The day is a clear one, but there is nothing to see, apart from these seabirds. The water stretches endlessly all around us. Its usual gray-blue, more gray than blue, has a greenish sheen today. The sea is unusually still this morning, stretching to the horizon, where it merges into a light shade of blue. That is the sky. There is nothing to be seen, except, a kilometer or maybe ten kilometers away—distance is difficult to evaluate without a backdrop—three brown pencils sticking out of the water. If the day had not been so clear, I might not have seen them. I know what they are: the legs, leftover by Shell, I think, of an oil rig similar to this one. An abandoned oil rig. It, unlike this one, belongs to no one now.

Until I had come here, I had not realized that the oceans were full of such abandoned oil rigs, some partly dismantled, but with tonnes of metal left standing in the water, polluting it—there are no coral reefs here, but I remember reading at school that the easiest way to kill a coral reef is to drop a nail of iron on it. As for this one—I look down at the second spider deck, where one of Mr. Watch's men is standing guard—it was supposed to contain some leftover crude oil and chemicals. Enough to poison a small town, Kurt had laughed when he had told me. It was all down there, somewhere. But, Cura Pastoralis, we are almost our own empire. The company has sole rights here.

There is some commotion down at the deck below me. The guard is speaking on his walkie talkie. I cannot hear him. The sea is quiet, but it is still loud enough out here to prevent conversation from carrying. The wind is blowing too; it is always blowing. I huddle down in my thick leather overalls—you need them to go outside—pulling the parka-type hood over my head, and watch.

Four other men come out on the spider deck. Two even have bulletproof vests on; all are carrying automatic guns. They usually do not take out the heavy guns, only a guard or two carries them. The way they run out, and then crouch down, aiming their guns out into the water, anybody can see that these are men trained by some military or the other. It is when I follow the trajectory of their guns that I see it: A small ship, a speck, near the horizon. It seems to be heading towards us. But this is unusual. Fishing trawlers stay away as this region, Kurt once told me, had much of its sea life driven away by the seismic soundings used to detect oil. It seems to be the case in those parts of the ocean where oil rigs are established. But that does not mean nothing comes near us. Occasionally private fishing boats and yachts have come to within a kilometer of the rig without any such reaction by the men. There must be something about this ship that I, using only my naked eyes, cannot see. It is not a fishing boat or a luxury yacht. That much I can see.

The ship comes closer, and now I can see it resembles a gunboat. Is that a turret of a gun poking out of it? I cannot tell. But if it is a gunboat, it should be flying some national color, and there is no flag on this ship. No flag at all.

The five men stay in position, as I suppose it would be called, for almost an hour, guns trained in the direction of the ship or gunboat. Then after crossing the three rusted pencils sticking out of the sea, the ship changes tacks and starts moving away from us. It is only then that the men below me relax.

Pirates are always a possibility, Kurt would have told me if I had asked him. I had believed him in the past. Stories of offshore piracies had increased in the newspapers in the past few years. I knew that. But now I would not believe the explanation, not entirely. Especially not in these parts, off the gated continent of Europe. I find myself repeating what Maman's current boyfriend always said while watching reality shows on TV: Truth is a fuckin' rich bitch.

~

When Harris returns from the university, having finally taken leave for the rest of the year, pleading a health complication—not that anyone cares about contract teachers—the swans trail squabbling after him from the garage to the front door. He realizes he has again forgotten to feed them this morning. He is fetching their feed from the pantry, when the phone rings. It is the landline, not his smartphone. Mermaid is prompt, thinks Harris, picking up the receiver. But it is not Mermaid Nicholson. It is Professor Pichler.

"Sorry to disturb you at home," says Pichler. "I did try your university number first. They gave me this one."

"I have been away."

"Something came up. I thought you should know. It is about that 2012 seminar you came to ask me about."

"Yes?"

"I had forgotten. But there was another man at the seminar."

"Another man? In the audience?"

"Not the audience. It was a closed seminar. This man gave a paper, oh well, a talk in any case. About himself, I think."

"Why isn't he listed in the schedule then?"

"He wasn't an academic. Actually, I think the others raised money for him to come and give his talk privately; the university would not pay for him. I think one of them, it might have been Derek Dutton, he had inherited a fortune, was related to royalty, you know, paid for him."

"Who was it?"

"You won't believe it, but then it was a weird crowd."

"Who?"

"Fred Butcher."

"Who? Harris knew he had heard the name but could not place it immediately."

"You know. The author."

"Fred Butcher, the sci-fi man?"

"Bingo."

"What was he doing there?"

"No idea, Doctor. He rambled on about his latest book, which was about parasites from outer space or something like that. They listened to him with rapt attention, believe me. Well, I thought you might want to contact him: these writer fellows are supposed to be very scientific and keep notes and all, you know. The, ah, research for their novels, I am told!"

Pichler rang off with a laugh.

It does not take Harris long to google the book. In 2011, Fred Butcher had published a novella titled *Microbia*. It was about a meteor carrying some deadly microbes from outer space into some town in Kansas, where a group of high-school students... Harris does not read more. Fred Butcher is easy to locate. Though his novels are often set in the US or Nigeria—he was born in the latter and did some of his schooling in the former—but he now lives in Maida Vale, London. Harris searches for Fred Butcher in Maida Vale. There are two Fred Butchers in Maida Vale, their numbers listed. But one of them is Fred C. Butcher. Harris hopes Fred Butcher is not so big as to need to hide from his fans. It would save him a lot of time, for, of course, he will get the number of the correct Butcher in due course: no personal information is sacrosanct, if you are willing to pay and take the right routes, all of them semi-legal, all of them leading to the heart of some very legal multinational corporation.

Harris calls the number. A male voice answers. Harris asks for Fred Butcher, the author.

"Speaking," replies the voice.

Harris introduces himself, switching his discipline to comparative literature, and requests Butcher for an interview. He explains that he is working on a paper on contemporary sci-fi scare narratives.

"Scare narratives, uh?" says the voice, "You mean you need to read books to be scared? Boy, just go out on them streets. Read Parliament proceedings."

But Fred Butcher gives him an appointment for later that week. Harris doubts that any author can resist the flattery of a paper, no matter what they claim in public. Another damn flight, Harris thinks. Why didn't the bloody pandemic create more leg room in planes? If anything, they appear to have become even more crowded after 2021.

Fred Butcher lives on the fourth floor of a very respectable-looking building, down a quiet avenue lined with trees. This is where quiet affluence resides. Harris can see it in the small cafés and restaurants that dot the area, the kind of dogs being walked by the residents, the lack of loiterers at the corners.

The author buzzes him in and is waiting in the lobby when Harris steps out of the lift. Harris realizes he should have googled a bit more about Fred Butcher. The sci-fi tag is misleading: Fred Butcher is a large, heavyset black man. He looks like an ex-boxer.

"No trouble finding the place?" asks the author.

"Not at all," Harris assures him.

"Easy to find," says Butcher, leading him to the flat, whose door bears a silvery metal plaque, proclaiming "F. Butcher, Author."

"Call me Fred," Butcher adds.

The corridor leading to the sitting room is lined with books, not arranged on shelves but piled one on top of another, in some places up to shoulder height. The sitting room looks like a colonial room from Kenya or Zimbabwe, hung with masks, and with spears and daggers arranged in patterns. There is even a set of antlers above the door, and what looks like a leopard skin on the sofa. The sofa and chairs are heavy and Victorian; the tables ornamental and antique or pseudo-antique.

Fred notices Harris observing the room. He waves his arms around in an expansive gesture. "My heritage," he proclaims, "Bought secondhand in London. The revenge of a man who had to change his name to publish. Whoever heard of a bloody Nigerian getting popular in these parts as a Science Fiction author? It is not magic realism, mind you! Not even Africanjujuism."

He waves Harris into a sofa, fetches a bottle of white wine from the fridge, pours them two glasses without asking, and says, "Okay, now, shoot man."

After the initial pretence of asking him for personal information and comments on his writing, none of which he needs, Harris mentions *Microbia*.

"Ah," says Fred, "Scare fiction. The Naturalism of our Age. Now you talkin' some, man."

Harris has noticed that Fred Butcher switches from a clipped Oxbridge English—he had studied at Oxford on a scholarship—to exaggerated "Black English" at times.

"My second novel; my first semi-bestseller. I have had a few other semi-bestsellers since then, you know, the kinda book that keeps 'em agents and publishers happy but does not get the writer enough to ignore the bitches."

"It came out in 2011, didn't it?"

"Thereabouts. I was young, twenty-eight or twenty-seven methinks."

"It remains my favorite, Fred," Harris hazards, "The notion of microbes from outer space..."

"A common enough notion in sci-fi, man."

"But you made something special of it," Harris insists, "It looked like it was based on real research."

"Naw, man. All bunkum. I mixed up bits from the *New Scientist* with New Age spiritualism, that's all it was."

"It does not show. I felt it was all based on research, something that might have happened and was kept from us, you know, the general public."

Fred laughs and drains his glass. "You were not the only one," he adds, "There were these eggheads, I think the very year after it had come out... Wait a sec."

Fred leaves the room and comes back in a few minutes, waving a crumpled, yellowing sheet. "I always keep the stuff," he says.

"Writers are supposed to take notes of new ideas and stuff, aren't they?" Harris replies, inadvertently echoing Pichler.

"Naw, man. Would go blinkin' crazy. You heard that one about old Einstein meeting a brilliant young scientist in a party? The young scientist would scribble something in a diary every few minutes. What's that you doing, asks Einstein. I keep notes of all my new ideas, replies the young scientist. Surely you do so too, Professor? he asks Einstein. Naw. Don't need to, says Einstein, you see I have had only one or two new ideas in my entire life."

Fred places the sheet on the table in front of them. Harris can see it is identical to the seminar schedule that he has. But he does not say anything.

"Them there eggheads, when was it, yes, 2012," continues Fred, "They got me over to this dingy little town in Denmark where shops stayed closed on Sundays, paid for me, put me up in a Radisson hotel, first time I was pampered like that by academics. They had me talk about my novel. They thought I had done research too."

"Literature people?" Harris feigns ignorance.

"No, man. The hard stuff: psychology, chemistry, anthropology, cognitive sciences, whatnot. Top names too in their fields, I gathered. Asked me a dozen questions about my non-existent research. Hung on every word I uttered. Well, most of them in any case. There was one, a big man, German I think, where is he here, yes, here (Fred stabbed at a name on the schedule), Pichler, he was obviously bored; I think he fell asleep ten minutes into my talk. I distinctly heard him snore."

"Did you stay in touch with them?"

"Naw, don't think I did. Maybe an email or two of thanks, but that was it. Separate worlds, separate ways. All that just came back because of what you said. Did not even remember it until you asked me about *Microbia* and the research that went into it. Zilch, man, zilch research, all a figment of my writerly imagination."

"What is it that they wanted from you?"

"No idea, man. But I went for the usual obligatory dinner with them, and they kept talking about mitochondria."

"Mitochondria?" Harris recalls Dutton rambling about mitochondria too.

"You know that little bit in our cells. The powerhouse of the cell, as we were told in secondary school ..."

"Mitochondria? I thought you said most of them were not even from Biology."

"Oh, they were a pretty eclectic lot. Most of them anyway. I sorta liked 'em, y'know: reminded me of writers, the creative sort, when they are not bitching about one another."

"What was it that fascinated them about mitochondria?"

"Oh, I suppose I got some of that. You see, the mitochondria is basically a cell that was gobbled up by another cell millions of years ago. A microbe ate another microbe, and after eons of the earth being populated only by microbes and viruses, we came into being: multicellular organisms. A kind of alien in us, who is us. They were interested in aliens in us. That is what fascinated them about *Microbia,* I gathered. They also spoke a bit about how our DNAs contain bits and pieces from outer space. That woman, she must have been a looker when young, was still very impressive then, the Polish one…"

Butcher looked at the seminar program again and found the name.

"… Professor Ostrowski. She even gave me a paper she had written about interspecies DNA-transfer, star dust and such stuff. It was unpublished, she said. I gathered no one wanted to publish it."

"Do you have it?"

But Butcher had not kept it. "You could only carry that much back on Ryan Air flights, you know. I always leave all that stuff, stuff I know I will never read, behind in my hotel room. I keep the schedules, in case a prospective biographer pops up one day, but I toss the rest away," he replies, and pours himself another glass.

~

Jyoti Lankeshwar was not a scientist. She was a journalist from Assam, and her surname was derived from a famous temple in that state. In September 2027, she was gunned down by unknown assailants in the office of the radical feminist and Marxist weekly that she had founded in 2017. The assailants were never traced. Her weekly folded up after her murder. There were some protests. There are still some online protests on her death anniversaries. In the year 2028, to mark her first death anniversary, some of her friends collated and edited a selection of her essays, for the first time translated from Assamese and Bangla, the two languages she employed for writing, into English. These were essays in which she had interviewed various radical thinkers and leaders, ranging from professors to grass-root activists. One of the essays was the last extant report on Vijay Nair, once a major scientist, now a folk-leader in Chotta Nagpur. Lankeshwar had met him in the year 2025 in a hamlet about two hours away from Ranchi. The essay was titled, at least in the English translation, "The Scientist Sage".

The Scientist Sage

The old Mahindra jeep we were in could go no farther. The last five or six kilometers, my Maoist companions informed me, could only be negotiated on foot. And I had to keep my mobile switched off all the time, until I returned to the jeep. "Are you sure you want to go on?" they enquired, because I was a city person, and dressed in a rather elaborate sari. I nodded, slinging on my sleeping bag.

We had been hearing of Professor Vijay Nair—they knew him as Firangi Baba in these parts—since 2021, when he had been associated with post-pandemic labor unrest in the state. In 2023, the government had put a small bounty on his head. Since then, he had gone underground. He was said to have a faithful following in the tribal villages of these parts, though it was uncertain if that was because of his political radicalism or because of mystical mumbo-jumbo. Lately, there had even been rumors that he was considered an incarnation of Birsa Munda, who had led the greatest tribal uprising against upper-caste landlords and the British in the late nineteenth century. At a very young age, he had been betrayed to the British and had died in mysterious conditions on 9th June 1900 in Ranchi Jail. The British had attributed his death to cholera—the coronavirus of the time—but there had been no symptoms to suggest it was cholera. Birsa Munda has long been revered as a God in these parts.

As I trekked through the brownish wilderness—it was mostly shrubs, stricken trees and rocks—I asked my tribal companions about their Firangi Baba. They told me lots of stories. How he had led them peacefully in the early years, sometimes aweing the police officers and mining contractors with his fluent English—hence, the name Firangi Baba; how he had the ability to foresee every attack by the authorities or mafia henchmen; how he could leave his body and return to it. It was the usual stuff of admiration and superstition, and, as an atheist, I bore it only because I sympathized with the cause and wanted to meet the leader who had galvanized these tribes. Also because, as I knew, Vijay Nair had once been a world-renowned scientist. But when I asked my companions about this, they seemed to have no idea. "Doesn't he tell you anything about science and technology?" I asked them. They shook their heads. "So, he only talks about

God and religion?" I added, trying to keep the scoffing out of my tone. No, they replied, he never talks about God or religion either. What does he talk about then? I asked. They thought for a while as we walked on, and then one of them replied, hesitatingly: us. He talks about us.

The village was in a stretch where the shrubbery grew denser. Vijay Nair was sitting outside his hut when I reached him. He was sitting on a small mat, out on the ground. It was still only afternoon, and the huts of the village were small and bare—but surprisingly clean. I have often observed that tribal villages in the interiors are usually very clean; they get dirtier the closer they are to urbanity. Nair had a white turban wrapped around his head and was wearing the kind of loincloth that the men traditionally wore in these regions. He was bare-bodied, wearing rubber chappals, and had two or three days of white stubble on his cheeks. A dark man, with no fat on him anymore—his earlier photos from academia had shown a podgier person—it was true that he resembled the photos and paintings of Birsa Munda that I had seen. I suppose if Birsa Munda had lived that long, because Nair was more than double the age that Birsa Munda had reached.

"I have read you." That was the first thing he said. He said it to me in English. Actually much of our conversation was carried out in English, though we occasionally used words of Hindi and Bangla.

I have read you, he said, looking at me with penetrating eyes, the eyes of a professional godman. Did he say it just to flatter me? Nothing is more flattering to a writer than to be told that someone has read her. I felt immediately hostile to him.

"I do not write in English," I replied curtly. In English.

"I do read Bangla," he said, smiling. Then he added: "I know you do not like me."

"How do you know that?" I asked him.

"You are an atheist. You think that despite my politics, I am a religious fraud."

The way he said it, directly, his dark eyes twinkling, somehow removed the bile of hostility from within me. I laughed.

"Well," I said, matching his directness. "Aren't you?"

He closed his eyes and thought for a while. Just when I thought he was upset and ignoring me, he opened his eyes and said to me, "I recall reading that you are a science graduate. Physics, actually."

I was surprised that he knew so much about me. I nodded.

"Then you know something about quantum physics," he observed.

I waited for him to continue.

"You know that every quantum entity can be described as both a wave and a particle. In common-speak, we say that a quantum entity is both a wave and a particle, which also means that it is neither just a wave nor a particle."

"Yes, I mumbled, not really getting what he was leading to."

"So," and his black eyes twinkled as he explained. "So, when we say that quantum entities are both wave and particle, we are using the words we have at hand, words we know, the world we can see or imagine, to describe something else. Something that evades us. Something we do not have words for."

He waited for me to think about it.

"You see," he said after a while. "What else can one use but the words that one has, the things one knows? Metaphors, all."

"Yes," I conceded. I could see what he was saying.

He looked at his watch. He was wearing one of those old-fashioned watches, on a metal chain around his left wrist, the kind of watch that needs to be wound up.

"You have to start back in two hours," he told me.

"No, I don't," I replied. "I have my sleeping bag with me."

"Tonight is dangerous," he said, looking serious. "They will come for us by dawn. We have to leave this village. The tribals have to disappear into the forest too, or they will get punished."

"Ahh, the seer," I said, unable to suppress my skepticism.

"I have my sources," he replied, smiling.

"In the police?"

"Somewhere," he said. But ask me your questions.

"Well," I replied, "I guess I have only one question: how did a world-famous scientist end up becoming not just a wanted radical but also a sage, the reincarnation of a God?"

He closed his eyes again. This time for longer, as if he was communing within himself. Then he looked at me and said: "It started with my research."

What he told me next is still fuzzy in my head, and I am not sure I have managed to get everything down. I was taking notes, but he used too many words I did not understand. There was no question of switching on my mobile, not even on flight mode, and recording him, for they were reasonably afraid of being traced. It was common knowledge that Vijay Nair's band of fugitives did not use any electronic device. So the reader would have to forgive me for what seems unclear, and I suspect most of it does. But this is what Professor Vijay Nair, now Firangi Baba, radical leader, wanted as a Maoist agitator by the government and revered as an incarnation of Birsa Munda in many tribal villages, told me that afternoon, as the crows cackled, the mynahs chirped, the sparrows hopped, and, I could see now, the villagers went about calmly collecting their few goods in preparation to melting away into the forest.

"It started with my research in embodied cognition. I was one of the pioneers in the area, but of course it was all in the last century. You know what it is? Well, at its simplest, it is the theory that we do not just think with our brains, we also think with our bodies. The kind of body we have determines, to a degree, how we think. Our body encodes information about the environment and determines the possibilities and constraints of how we deal with it. Not everything goes through the brain, or only through the brain. The brain is not a CEO, as they want us to think. Now, this is obvious enough in beings like octopuses, whose neurons are spread throughout their bodies. Unlike animals, octopuses have brains, so to say, in each of their tentacles and in their body. But animals, especial us, brainy-us, have brains, though of course that is not the only colocation of neurons that we have. Moreover, the robotics of our bodies also determine how we react to the environment: we do not just walk because our brain orders us to do so; we walk because we have the right kind of joints and limbs. So, that was what I was working on, ages ago. It led me to other things. One of them was this: why is it that human beings reason, as it was often put in the past, and other animals do not? Despite Swift's Houyhnhnyms, post-modernists and what not, this is still true. Animals think. Some think in complex ways. But if you define reason as abstract thinking—thinking involving abstract concepts, thinking such as multiplying and dividing, thinking that goes beyond language to artificial grammar—then human beings are the only species that qualify. Isn't that strange? I am not talking of thought, or even complex thinking. All sentient beings feel and think. Even beings like octopuses, who split from our evolutionary tree before our worm-like common ancestors had evolved brains, have brains—very different from ours, spread throughout their bodies, but they can only be called brains, just as the blue-green blood of octopuses is blood, and their three hearts are still hearts. All living beings are purposive, most living beings communicate in some form, or feel, or think. Baboons who place boxes on top of each other to reach a fruit, or birds that do not just remember where they have stored food, but also which hideout contains food that will rot first—all of them think in complex ways. In an early paper, I had even argued that some modes of complex thinking in other animals are not accessible to us. But only we, Super-Sapiens, have abstract reasoning. Isn't that remarkable? Evolution has developed eyes, limbs, wings, brains many times: not one of them has a single evolutionary source. They have evolved many times and in different ways. There is only one evolutionary gambit that is singular, something that happened only once: the eukaryotic cell, when one cell engulfed another cell, leading to a chimeric cell containing mitochondria. That was a once in a planet thing, and then this: abstract reason. Why? How? That is what moved me away from embodied cognition: it marked the beginning of the end of my career because I asked myself: What if? What is it that makes abstract reason possible only in us; not intelligence, not thinking, not feeling, which animals and cephalopods have, but abstract intelligence. But the hypothesis I had was too far-fetched. I was out in the cold. For a while, I felt lonelier than ever, because science is not individualistic, no matter what they say; it is communal. Then I discovered others who..."

At that moment, one of the men in the village came up and whispered something into Vijay Nair's ears. Nair closed his eyes and listened. He kept his eyes closed after the man went away. It looked as if he was trying to listen. Then he opened his eyes and said to me, "We have even less time than I thought."

"I will come with you," I said.

He shook his head.

"There is not much to be added, not much that can be said. Quantum physics, you know. Even if I could put it in words, I wouldn't. Can you think of all the harm that would have been avoided if brilliant, well-meaning idiots like Bohr and Einstein had kept their words and equations to themselves?"

"So much good too…," I objected, scandalized.

Vijay Nair shook his head. "No," he said, very decisively. "The harm will always outweigh the good unless…"

He got up, folded his blanket neatly, and waved his arms in the direction of the villagers assembling in a knot. "…Unless every one of them has an equal share in the good," he said, and walked briskly away from me to join the group. I made to follow him, but one of my companions restrained me. "We are leaving," he said. "Now."

We drove back to Ranchi that evening. Just outside the city, I passed a CRPF regiment containing armoured vehicles. It was heading out. Just as Vijay Nair had prophesied, a major combing operation, involving CRPF units and aerial support by the army, was launched in that region at midnight. Five Maoist terrorists, it was announced later, were killed, and eleven arrested, including three women. Vijay Nair was not one of them.

15

The Mired Brain

Jens Erik knew he had to see Hanif, the Bangladeshi *pølsemand*. If there was any news in the immigrant world, and the craziest rumor or conspiracy theory, Hanif would have heard of it, in person or online, where he seemed to spend all the hours he did not work. Though it was another matter whether he would pass it on.

Jens Erik had worked often enough with this short podgy man, with a broad smile and bad teeth, with soft, servile manners, and he knew that this was a man who knew more than he told, who was far tougher than he appeared to be. Jens Erik shrugged: he would need to be, wouldn't he?

He wished that Pernille would understand: In his own mind, Jens Erik did not patronize immigrants; he did not underestimate them; he just wished they had stayed in their homelands. The world would be a far better place if people stayed back and took care of their own homes and gardens, as Jens Erik did. And their small *kolonihaver*, if they could afford one.

Hanif's sausage wagon had not been at the station when Jens Erik went to Copenhagen or returned, so there was a good chance the man had changed to some other spot or retired. He must be almost Jens Erik's age, probably older, though did these immigrants ever retire?

They were every modern politician's dream, Jens Erik told himself, and humpfed.

The Turkish café in Bazar Vest was not crowded at that time of the afternoon, though it seemed to be to Jens Erik. Three was a crowd to Jens Erik. Though he sat there at an inside table, holding a glass of Turkish coffee, only in the company of one. The other man was Hanif.

It had not been difficult to find Hanif. Jens Erik had called up and asked a couple of other immigrant contacts from his policing days, and the second one told him: Hanif, the pølsemand, had sold his sausage wagon and bought himself an electronic kiosk in Bazar Vest.

"Now he was Hanif, Bill Gates II," the man had said, and guffawed into his phone.

It made sense. Hanif had always loved electronics. Jens Erik vaguely recalled being told that the man had come to Denmark, decades ago, with an engineering degree from Dhaka.

Hanif had also loved his own cuisine: his only complaint about the pølsewagon had not been the sausages, sacrilegious pork mostly, that he served in toasted bread husks or with soft bread, but—as he had often complained to Jens Erik in the past—the fact that they could be "improved" with just "a dash of imagination and spices", but the only time he had evidently tried to do so, he had lost half his regular customers. The move to Bazar Vest, full of Eastern eateries stinking to the high heavens of spices and shops selling everything under heaven (at suspiciously low prices), would obviously satisfy both these cravings of Hanif; it would be, Jens Erik chuckled to himself, the closest that man would allow himself to come to retirement.

The kiosk was a small one in a corner, next to a large shop selling sundry goods, but mostly food-related, including a large collection of bottled spices, canned juices of exotic stuff, like guavas and mangoes, and bags of grain. Hanif, who had grown a little podgier and balder, was ensconced behind its counters, surrounded by electronic gadgets on shelves, tinkering with an open smartphone, magnifying goggles wrapped around his eyes.

He took off the goggles to see Jens Erik, emitted a whoop of genuine pleasure, and came around the counter to embrace the much bigger man.

Jens Erik acquiesced to the embrace, a mode of greeting he had never favored and had scrupulously avoided during and after the pandemic.

But this was Bazar Vest: it had its own native customs.

Bazar Vest had once been an abandoned factory building.

An outbuilding at the front, not used for anything, still had a towering industrial chimney, visible from a long distance. It had been at one end of the city, but, by the 1990s, the neighborhood had become the "immigrant suburbs" of Aarhus. Houses and apartment flats had come to surround the abandoned factory, and the stretch of land around it.

Then in 1996, a housing company, Olav de Linde, describing itself as a "private integration and employment project without any official funding", turned the factory into a collection of shops and cafés, all of them, inevitably, owned and run by the immigrants in the neighborhood—and their children. Second-generation immigrants, as Jens Erik calls them. First-generation Danes, as Pernille insists.

The initiative had grown, more shops had been added; it now stretched over eleven thousand square meters, mostly full of people who, at first glance at least, did not seem Danish. Turkish and Indian restaurants, vegetable sellers, greengrocers, bakeries, meat shops, grills, carpet and rug merchants, shops offering anything you can think of, though mostly on the cheaper side, café and kiosks galore; it was the rest of the world, conveniently packaged away under a rooftop in one corner of Aarhus.

Outside, you had cars playing loud music; inside, there were old men hanging around and talking almost in whispers to one another, women in all kinds of attire. If you listened, you heard other languages, though mostly Danish is what dominated, for there were quite a few Danes around, feeling like tourists in Bazar Vest, and in any case the only language in common between most of these people from different nations, and their children who had grown up in Denmark, was Danish.

Jens Erik had never been able to make up his mind about this place.

But that is where he sits, in a Turkish café, drinking Turkish coffee, a few feet away from a glass cabinet displaying the sort of sweets Jens Erik would never eat. But the coffee is not bad. He concedes that much to the Pernille voice in his head. Of course, he has been here before, but only in uniform, and hence he had never tried their coffee. Jens Erik is strict about such matters.

Hanif doesn't have a coffee in front of him.

He has a very impressive phone, the flashiest and flattest Jens Erik has seen for years. He has a large glass of cola. He also has a succulent shawarma sandwich in a plate and has taken such a big bite of it that it is a minute before he can speak. Then he answers Jens Erik's question.

"It has never been a secret," he finally says. Jens Erik looks away.

Hanif drinks from his glass and continues: "It has never been a goddamn secret, except for you guys. Half the people here must have heard of it." He waves his arms around, indicating the two young men, with tonsured heads, in keeping with the fashion, behind the counter, the Somali or Yemeni family at a table farther back, the stream of men and women, one in a chador, two in shorts, walking past in the corridors outside.

"What has not been a secret?" Jens Erik asks.

Hanif dramatically lowers his voice. Why lower your voice, Jens Erik wonders, if it is not a secret, but he does not say anything. These people just love drama—and conspiracies. No wonder their countries are full of both!

"You read the goddamn papers, Jens Erik," Hanif whispers, "You know, they talk of refugee smuggling routes, what not..."

"Yes."

"Well, this is one of them, my friend."

"In the North Sea? In the North Sea? What do they do, put refugees in deep freeze and ferry them across?" Jens Erik is entirely skeptical.

Hanif lets out a guffaw.

"Yes," he says, "Yes, that is what they actually do! Or, did. Only, not all of the goddamn refugees, choice pieces of them." He points to another counter with kebab on skewers, slices of meat, samosas, falafel. "Choice pieces, you know: like kidney, skin, eyes, heart..."

"You are talking organ trade?"

"You have no idea, Jens Erik!" Hanif sounds excited, despite himself. "You have no idea! This thing was big before 2020. It had been going on for years, but we started hearing about it around then. I remember being told of it a few months before the virus hit us. That is why I remember when I heard of it. Then I started paying attention. We heard of men and women—young ones, always healthy ones—disappearing."

Jens Erik starts to interrupt, but is waved into silence by Hanif, who continues: "These youngsters were always promised another life, another identity. They disappeared, and there was nothing one could prove. All had contracted with just one tourist agency: that is what they called themselves. They were getting across illegally in any case. And often their relatives assumed they had just gone underground. It happens. People are smuggled in somewhere, you do not hear from them for a year, two years, ten years, and then they contact you once they have the papers. But in these cases there were weirder rumors. There was a travel agency in Dhaka, with a branch in Nairobi, maybe elsewhere too; it was called Magic Gates, and it insisted on men and women going thorough medical tests. They even paid for it. The agency, not the, ha, tourist. Paid for it, mind you. And all the men and women who claimed that they had been given perfect health certificates simply disappeared. Whatever route, whether they were smuggled by sea or land, whether it was via Russia, or Greece, or directly to the US, whatever the modus operandi, not one of these illegal immigrants was ever seen or heard from again ..."

"What happened to the agency, what was it called?"

"Magic Gates. Everyone knows. They closed in 2021 or so, soon after the pandemic. Some people had tipped off the police in Germany or Sweden or Nigeria, and it was said the police had tipped off the agency people. But then, a bit later, there were rumors that the people behind this agency are still around and involved in something bigger."

"Something bigger?"

Hanif toys with his phone. He seems to think. Then he looks Jens Erik in the eyes and says, "Something official. Bigger."

"Why bigger?"

Hanif stares at Jens Erik. Then he answers, seriously: "Because it is quieter."

Then he returns to his jovial manner and waves his short arms around once more. "You won't call this place quiet, will you, my friend?" he asks.

Jens Erik, who has been struggling to hear Hanif over the terrible cacophony of people talking, shouting, listening to music—so unDanish!—shakes his head.

"Well," Hanif continues chuckling, "If you go to these new malls in town, they will be quiet, much quieter. Last time I was in one of them, I fell asleep on a bench. It was that quiet. Why, my friend? Why are they so quiet? Because that is where the real money is, not here!"

~

Kathy pulled up in the mostly empty parking lot behind Walmart just as the sun was about to set. It was one of those evenings when the wind seems to hold its breath. Even the clouds, scattered like a flock of sheep, did not move.

This was one of those monster Walmarts spawned by the post-pandemic phase of government-funded economic revival. They were everywhere, these gargantuan enterprises, all owned by the same handful of oligarchies. This one had the façade of a palace from the Arabian Nights, with colored lights for jewels embedded in its pasty walls. It was the only palace most people shopping here—or living around it—would ever enter. It was the kind of thing that would upset Harris. That, she suspected, was why he chose not to retire in America. Denmark enabled him to pretend. Make-believe, Kathy thought. Make-believe. He had his own drugs. They were just not the kind one injected or ingested.

Kathy rolled down her window and sent a text message to Blondie. Then she activated her localization app. Now Blondie could find her in this sprawling parking lot. Blondie was her dealer.

The motorcycle cop pulled up after twenty minutes. Kathy expected him. He was young, muscular, and beautiful like a film star. Maybe he had come here hoping to become a film star? She held out her papers; he looked at them, tipped his visor at her, and kicked off again. This was Blondie's security check. All cops around here, Kathy knew, were in the cut. There had been bad cops in the past, but the last few years of privatization of the force had taken care of that: now, there were no bad cops; they were all part of the game.

Five minutes later, Blondie's hot-rod BMW two-seater pulled up and parked next to Kathy's Chevrolet. Blondie was appropriately named: he was the most blond man Kathy had ever met. He was silver-blond. Even his eye lashes were silver. His eyeballs were yellowish too, and Kathy could not tell if they were natural or the creation of special lenses.

"What is it this time, sweetheart?" he asked Kathy, "The usual?"

"I had a blackout," Kathy said.

"You probably tried to wean yourself off it, Beauty," he replied. "I have heard that from others too. It grabs you."

"You said it does not have any chemicals. Nothing addictive."

"Nothing addictive that we can find, lady. Let me assure you: the boys have been trying to decipher this shit for months now, and we cannot find anything. They say the Mexicans had three labs looking into it. No clue. It is all an innocuous blend of natural stuff, the sort bodies have in any case. If we could find the secret, we would produce it ourselves. It costs us a fortune to buy it too."

"Who are the people behind it, Blondie?"

"No one knows. They say it is all Big Pharma. Russian, Chinese, Israelis, our own people. Global shit. Big Pharma on speed. Some say, they are developing something bigger, and this is just pilferage. People making a bit on the side. Some say, it is an experiment. In that case, Sweetheart, you are a guinea pig. I take it too, so I am a guinea pig as well. It is all quite spooky: not every dealer has access to it, you know, and things have happened to dealers who got too nosy."

"It is far too costly."

"Your choice, baby. Free world, you know. I have all the other stuff too. You name it."

"No," replied Kathy, "I'll stick to Crobe for the time being."

She handed him an envelope. He looked at the notes it contained but did not count them. "You should get into the Bitcoin scene, lady. It would be easier and safer," he said.

"Safer?" Kathy laughed, "Is anything unsafe for you, Blondie?"

"Safer for you, Baby. No one carries much cash anymore."

"I am sure I am safe as long as I am dealing with you, Blondie."

"You got a point, lady. You got a point."

Then he started his engine, waved at Kathy, reversed in a rash curve, and revved away. Five minutes later, the motorcycle cop was back again. He asked for Kathy's papers, dropped an envelope of pills into her car in the process of looking at them, returned the papers, tipped his visor again, and rode off into the sunset. Everything, Kathy muttered to herself, is well with the world.

~

I am obsessed with the closed section now, the chamber of instruments in which I had seen that caged being. Whenever I am down in the galley—it lies across an open stretch at that level, cluttered with leftover bases from machines that have been dismantled and removed and huge metal containers from the past—I have to force myself to look away from its vault-like door, always guarded by one of the men. I do not want to betray my curiosity. I crawled there one more night, having overdosed Kurt in a drink, and spent an hour looking through the slits of the ventilator. The cages are there. Or the small rooms with cage-like doors. The blinking instruments, the clean, antiseptic hall, the shiny operating tables, the glass cubicle. But that is it. This time I do not detect any movement in the cages, no noise, no sound.

I am trying to resist the temptation. I know it can mean my death. "Kuriosity killed de kitten, baby," Maman's boyfriend would sing-song when my studying on the kitchen table irritated him. I am trying to resist the temptation of crawling in there during the daytime, when one or more of the experts, with or without Kurt or Mr. Watch, is working in there. Then I would know what they do! The other men seldom go there, though they guard the door night and day. If they go in, it is for an errand,

and they are out soon. They almost pretend as if it does not exist. Even Mister Hiroyuki hardly ever goes in there, or at least not for long. It is only the experts who spend hours in there during the daytime. Sometimes Kurt; often Mr. Watch, when he is here. What do they do?

I know I won't be able to resist the temptation. I fear it will be my death. And I tell myself, if you have to take the risk, wait, wait at least until Mr. Watch is away again. It is Mr. Watch I fear most of all.

There is a storm the next day. It is my fourth storm in the weeks I have been here, but it is much worse than the first three. I know it is going to be bad, because of the way Mister Hiroyuki is marshalling his men. The generators are put on double watch, as is the control room upstairs. I have never seen men with so much armor in real life: policemen in St. Martin do not have such weapons. Are they going to shoot the storm, I wonder. They remind me of TV reports on invading armies in the Middle East, or on the recurrent race riots across America. They have done this in the past too. But this time I know something worse is expected, because Kurt starts talking a lot about storms. I know this about Kurt by now: he talks a lot when he gets nervous.

Now he starts spilling over bits and pieces of information. All through the day it goes on in the kitchen, in the rooms, even in the corridors. Every time he is with me, a sculpted fact comes out of his sculpted lips. I wonder if he talks like that to Mr. Watch or Mister Hiroyuki, and I conclude that he wouldn't; he has another persona with them. But with me, he is a voice: I hear the phrase in my inner ear, "He is very little more than a voice," and I am sure it is from some book I have read, it has been said about someone else; I cannot recall the book, but it sure does apply to Kurt. All day, deep into the night and next morning again, until finally the storm blows up, with forty feet waves buffeting the rig, which, as Kurt has informed me, is around eighty feet above sea level, which is unusual for a rig built in the 1990s, why, in the 1950s, they built rigs that were just thirty-forty feet above sea-level, it is only after 2005, remember Hurricane Katrina in the Gulf of Mexico? No, you won't, were you even born then? No, you couldn't have been born then, I was twelve or thirteen, I recall, my father was into oil, so was my grandfather, did I tell you? I remember Katrina, she knocked out at least sixty platforms, including two of ours. Katrina was the first nail in the family fortune, then came Rita, then came others, not hurricanes, but worse, much worse in 2008, my father made mistakes, but it was after Mademoiselles Katrina and Rita that they made it compulsory for platforms to be at least ninety-one feet above sea-level, not that storms were unknown before that, not anywhere, and definitely not in the North Sea, it is calmer now than it used to be in the nineteenth century and further back, did you know that? In 1720, a storm in the North Sea demolished a coastal hill of sand and blocked, for good, an entire fishing harbor near Rattray Head in Scotland, further back, in the sixteenth century, the entire town of Skagen in Denmark had to be abandoned, and well into the nineteenth century, its buildings were still awash with sand, there is a painting of the church in the nineteenth century, still smothered with sand, that was a bad century, another North Sea storm flooded all the major towns of Holland in that century, Amsterdam, Rotterdam, others, anywhere up to half a million drowned, we are living in a lull… though now it is acting up again I think, not climate change, that is all leftist bullshit, these things come in cycles, that is what they do, they come in cycles, gyres said the poet Yeats, turning and turning in a widening gyre, have you read Yeats?

And so on and so on, one immense jabber, a mouth, a dapper mouth, that is what Kurt was, and he went on and on in my company, until the storm hit us the next day. There was the initial fizz of rain on water. Then the waves started rising, compact and almost foamless.

Mr. Watch took the only expert with us at the time to the small bar, leaving the rest of the rig to Kurt and Mister Hiroyuki to manage. He was probably trying to distract the scientist from the waves, which were frightening to look at. Even if you are eighty feet above sea-level, it is frightening to look down on armies of forty-foot waves marching on you and smashing past the spindly legs of the rig. The color of the waves changes too—they are now a dark gray, almost the color of the clouds above, but with edges that flash like steel. The lowest spider deck was submerged, but there was nothing there. The sky was an admixture of purple and black. And at the height of the storm, you could not hear people more than a few feet away from you, not even in the insulated sections, well above the waves, that were the living quarters. Some men were wearing water-vests, and the laboratory section—for that is what I now called, to myself, the hall in which I had seen that animal-human face in a cage—had been locked. I wondered what that being in the hall was doing. Was it shrieking, panicking at the sounds… if they reached the section? And was there only one?

The storm waned much faster than it had hit. It had taken a full night to build up, but suddenly, within an hour, it was gone. The sea grew calm, a few rifts of lighter blue opened up in the clouds above. Towards the sun, the sky turned into the palette of an impressionist. The seagulls came out again. How do these birds survive such storms, I wondered? The lowest spider deck became visible once again, foaming and draped in weeds. It seemed intact to me.

It was only then that Mister Hiroyuki and two of his men unlocked the laboratory hall and entered it, closing it carefully behind them, as they always did. As I was in the galley having a coffee with Kurt, who was talking less now that the storm was over, or because Mr. Watch had joined us, I could watch the three men go in. Two minutes later, one of the men came running back. He was agitated and probably overlooked my presence at the table.

"One has broken away," he blurted out, "Cut himself out, or maybe something collapsed at the floor level in one cell."

Mr. Watch got up and pulled the man away from our table, but as they left, Kurt tagging along, I heard him ask, "Which one?"

And I thought I heard the man answer, "Number 3."

If I had any doubt about this place—and Kurt—it disappears over the next few hours.

First, they order me not to leave my corridor or the galley. Oh, well, they do not really order me: they advise me, things are broken and dangerous after the storm, do not go out, we are looking into it... and of course they find things for me to do. That is the easiest and oldest way to order a woman, isn't it? Set her tasks. Cooking, cleaning, tidying up. I obey them. But I have lived on the rig long enough to find spots from which I can watch without being seen. And I sometimes see what they are up to.

I see two of the men put on night-vision goggles, take up their automatics, and descend into the lower level. Maybe more go down from other sides. There are eleven men in all, not counting Mr. Watch, Kurt and Mr. Hiroyuki. I overhear Mr. Watch monitoring them on his walkie talkie. This goes on for about an hour.

I scrub and clean and keep an eye out. I peel and cook, and keep my ears cocked. Then I hear shots from below. Two, three quick shots, then a pause. It sounds muffled, but you can hear it clearly enough. Then one more shot. A clear, decisive, singular shot.

I do not have to hear more. Later I think: they did not even bother to use silencers. I am sure they have silencers. They are well-equipped. If they have night vision and bullet-proof vests, they must have silencers. But they did not use them. Obviously, they are not afraid of me hearing them shooting. Is it because they think I am so dumb—being pretty has its advantages—that I would not understand?

Or is it because they know that, no matter what, I won't be speaking to anyone else? Maman, I whisper when alone in the room, Maman, are you thinking of me?

~

Back in his house, the swans mobbing him, Harris paces up and down the garden. There is something wrong about all of this. It is not the seminar or the material he has collected about whatever those eccentric eggheads were doing. All that has started making sense. It is not clear yet, but it has started making sense.

What does not make sense is his involvement. What does not make sense is why Mermaid came to him, and why it has all been conducted in this elaborate manner? Also, what happened that night, the chit, the beer? It seems to be a kind of game. But why should Mermaid be playing a game with him?

Mermaid is a killer, Harris knows that. So was he himself. So was Kathy. So were all of them in Command Alpha. Each one of them, a cold-blooded killer: that is what they were trained to be. Fuck the ideals, the reasons, the excuses. And yet there were people in the squad he would trust to death, and others he would not. Kathy, he would trust. Mermaid, he would trust.

"Why should Mermaid be playing a game with me?" Harris mutters, and kicks at the gravel.

He has trouble sleeping that night. And when he falls asleep, he is woken up by his soundless nightmares. Especially the one he cannot place, because it features a woman he is sure he does not know, holding a child, dead in her arms, and wailing, howling soundlessly, while all around her there is nothing but water. Endless, the water stretches. Dark green and endless. And the woman, a large, older woman, holds the inert body of the child, and howls in grief.

Harris has seen many people hugging dead bodies—sons, fathers, mothers, friends—and shrieking into the day or the night. Some had been shot by him or his companions in Command Alpha. But this is not one of those memories—because Harris has never been active out at sea.

He knows he is there in that nightmare. He is watching the woman wailing; she is wailing without a voice. And then, suddenly, soundlessly, the skull of the woman bursts open like a melon. That is always when Harris wakes up.

~

The "mired brain" was a concept that Professor Wislawa Ostrowski floated in what was her last published paper, way back in 2020 during the pandemic, though it had appeared in such an obscure journal brought out by a small Chinese university, and the concept died at birth. It was based on the notion of the "wired brain" that was, and continues to be, extremely popular in scientific, theoretical and, above all, financial circles. The wired brain, as we know, refers to a direct link between our mind and its processes and a digital machine, a link which can enable us to use a thought to trigger events in material reality. You would just need to think to switch on the coffeemaker when you got up in the morning. Optimally, this could be done with nothing attached to your head, though right now that is not considered an option. The "wired car", for instance, currently said to be under development by four different and competing manufacturers, could be run just by your thoughts, though attempts to simply open and shut car doors recently failed spectacularly at a demonstration event, because, experts later explained, the presence of observers "disoriented" the heavily wired driver.

In her paper, Professor Ostrowski had argued that the brains of many organisms were already "wired". They were wired by microbes: hence, the switched "m" of "mired brains." She noted that this has been an evolutionary necessity for microbes, which monopolized the earth for billions of years before the first multicellular organisms evolved, and which still, in terms of biomass, far exceed multicellular life and continue to be hosted by and in every form of life. Since microbes generally cannot move on their own accord, they have had to strategically alter the mental processes of their hosts in order to spread and survive.

Professor Ostrowski had listed the usual examples known to science in 2020. Microbes induce human beings and other animals to cough, sneeze or vomit in order to spread. Some, like the rabies virus, alter behavioral patterns, such as preventing the host from drinking or swallowing, so that the host is driven to attack and bite and thus transmit the virus to others. But more crucially for the Professor's hypothesis, some microbes alter the "normal" behavior of their hosts. Usually examples of this tend to be of the sensational kind, such as that of the feline parasite, *Toxoplasma gondii*, which infects a wide range of animals but cannot complete its life cycle unless it lands in a cat's guts. This parasite has found ways of doing so if it ends up in the wrong animal. For instance, it spreads through the nervous systems of rodents infected by it and hijacks their brains. Mice infected by it develop a fascination for cats. Instead of running away from cats, as they have all their lives, such mice run towards cats, with disastrous consequences for themselves, but of course a fertile future for the parasite.

Professor Ostrowski had listed other such examples, in smaller organisms, such as ants and worms and some kinds of trees, but she had argued that such examples are partly misleading. They are, as she put it, "newsworthy", and they have blindsided researchers to many examples, the vast majority, when microbes alter the behavior of their hosts with no bad consequences to the host. Or even with good consequences in some cases. The "mired brain" already exists; what we lack, she insisted in that paper, are means and the will to access it, and that in turn had to do with our failure to consider microbes as partners in the evolution of life. Accepting that while some devices enabling a semblance of the "wired brain" have been developed—such as MIT Media Lab's "Alter Ego", developed by Arnav Kapur, which is a "wearable silent speech input-output device, attached around the head, neck and jawline, that translates your brain centre impulse input, on conscious motivation by you, into words on a computer, without vocalization"—Professor Ostrowski noted that the idea of the "wired brain" remained more exciting as heavily-funded vision than poorly executed reality. She expressed the belief that more—and better—results could be achieved by focusing on the concept of the "mired brain".

Examining the editorial records of the small journal in which this paper was published, it is clear that the editors had asked the once-renowned professor to revise her paper twice, before finally accepting it for publication. Both the revisions had to do with her speculations—"speculation" was the word used by the editors in their emails—about the "mired brain" in Homo sapiens. The published paper had no reference to the effect of microbes on human beings, let alone the human brain, apart from that one illustration of microbes making us cough, sneeze or vomit, and the passing allusion to the rabies virus.

~

Jens Erik had insisted on the office dog being sent out.

Aslan had obliged, as readily as last time, which indicated to Jens Erik that the man, despite all his bureaucratic ticking of boxes and political correctness, did find at least this addition of "robotic dogs" to police stations—they had been sanctioned by an act of Parliament as part of rampant post-pandemic digitalization—partly a joke.

This was, of course, very different from Jens Erik's reaction, when he was still working and had read of the act being passed: "I will kick the butt of the first blasted metal dog that comes to my desk." Luckily, their production had been delayed, and Jens Erik had gone on early retirement before they were introduced.

But, watching the dog clunk away on metallic feet, wagging its wire tail, Jens Erik was mystified by the very fact that he was here at all, in this bare office room with just a poster framed on the walls! Why had he come to Aslan Barzani?

He knew the reason he had given himself last evening, as he sat down to a solitary dinner of rice and meatballs in curry sauce, bought readymade from the SuperBrugsen and heated up in the microwave. It had to do with the way his friend, Ulrik, had reacted when Jens Erik narrated Hanif's organ trade theory to him. Or not reacted.

They had met in the usual pub two days back. Værthuset. They had been alone; no other colleague had turned up. Late in the evening, when both had consumed three or four beers each, and Ulrik had been rebuffed by the only woman in the pub, a morose-looking female in her forties, who was steadily drinking gin and tonic at the bar, Jens Erik had finally blurted out Hanif's story to him. Ulrik had listened without interrupting. Then he had drained his glass, stood up and said, "Shouldn't we go somewhere where there are at least some skirts to watch?"

Jens Erik had gardened all that day.

He had dug out old plants, raked up leaves, cleared under his hedge, weeded the lawn, though it could have waited.

Gardening had always been Jens Erik's escape from the problems of the world. When things looked unmanageable, as during the last years of his marriage, or when he felt dejected by his lack of progress in his career, he had taken to the spade and the shovel.

It had helped him stay calm, this effort to create a small world: not an orderly world, Jens Erik knew that there was nothing strictly orderly about gardening. It was something else.

He remembered his father, a man who had grown up in a farm and never fully stopped being a farmer, working stolidly in his garden in his spare hours. He was a man of even fewer words than Jens Erik, and perhaps the only complex thought, or probably long sentence, he ever spoke—or, in any case, the only one that Jens Erik remembered—was this one: "Son, you do not go into a garden to boss plants about; you go to have a conversation."

Jens Erik had always managed to get a whiff of this conversation when working in his garden. Not the full conversation—he was not his father—but a feeling of it, like a sense of words being wafted by the breeze from across the hedge.

But now, despite throwing himself into the gardening, that remembered body by the shore was pissing him off. .

People should die in their own fucking countries, Jens Erik thought, as he picked up a plastic bag of soil. In the hole he had dug to unearth a shrub, he could see a worm cut in two. He covered the two wriggling halves with dark, loose soil.

He needed to talk to someone who would listen. Someone in authority. *Hva' fandens, mand!* he said, out aloud, put aside his gardening implements neatly in the shed, and went inside to start thawing the food.

That is why, eating his meatballs and rice in curry sauce later that evening, Jens Erik had thought about who would listen to Hanif's story. If Ulrik did not listen, who else? Strange as it was, Jens Erik was determined it should be followed up. But who would take it seriously enough to follow it up? And the answer had come to him: perhaps only an officer who was, as Jens Erik put it, a second-generation immigrant! Ergo: Aslan Barzani.

Now, fifteen minutes after the robotic office dog had been sent out on another impossible mission to a vacant desk, Jens Erik finished narrating the story.

He told Aslan everything he had found out, only not naming his colleagues in Copenhagen. Having put it into words, Jens Erik was surprised by how thin it all was—why it did not take him more than fifteen minutes to narrate all of it. He felt embarrassed. Surely Aslan, who was listening with his eyes closed, elbows on the desk, face cupped in his hands—Jens Erik found it offensive!—would burst out laughing.

Why the hell did I have to come to this immigrant to embarrass myself? Am I turning senile?

And Aslan did laugh. One short ha.

Then he opened his eyes. "Jesus," he said, leaning back in his chair, "That is one helluva story, Jens Erik. They would put me in a lunatic asylum if I took it to anyone further up!"

Jens Erik got up abruptly to leave.

But Aslan understood the reaction. He got up too, and said, "You misunderstand me, Jens Erik. I think this should be investigated. Let's talk a bit more about it."

Then when Jens Erik had returned to his seat, Aslan added, "But you know that I cannot act on it officially. No one would act on it. There is so little to go on, and, if as your Copenhagen friend says, there are people who shut down the investigation last time, then there is even less of a chance. I mean, they will shut me down too. We will have to find other ways of checking it out. Or at least satisfying our doubts. I do have an idea."

Then he paused and added: "I gather you do not believe all that "bigger thing" stuff: you think they are still out there, transplanting organs, just doing it quietly now, maybe taking care of the bodies in other ways?"

Jens Erik nodded and waited for Aslan to outline his idea.

~

The nightmares are back, his soundless mental-scapes full of blasted limbs, exploding bodies, and, increasingly, that plain-looking matron cradling a small child and howling soundlessly, surrounded by water. He was once prescribed sleeping pills, but Harris mistrusts drugs. He never took them. Now he heads for the only sedatives he uses: they are in the small bar installed in the drawing room downstairs.

It is still dark. He has left his phone upstairs, so he cannot check the time. There are no clocks on the ground floor, and the timer on the oven has not been set for years. He walks about in the dark. The years in Command Alpha have given him a degree of night sense; he even suspects that he, like others in the force, has learnt to see better in the dark. If you stop depending on your eyes, you discover that the body sees too, he remembers his night-vision trainer tell them. Some organisms can see through their skins.

Harris likes walking around in the dark. He reaches the bar, traces its rich wooden surfaces with one finger. This was once a tree. There is a strong wind outside; he can hear the trees. Harris pours himself a cola in a tall glass and adds a generous splash of rum to it. He puts in two ice cubes, looks for a lime in the fridge, does not find it, and takes the glass to his study.

He sits down at his desk in the semi-dark. The folder is lying there, on top of his laptop. Small differently colored lights twinkle here and there in the room: from his desktop computer and other devices, such as the Wi-Fi comport, in the dark. It is easier for him to see in this room. He does not switch on the lights. He does not need to look at the file. He needs to think.

Much of it is clear to him now. This is how he sees it: A group of scientists, with hare-brained theories, chanced upon something. What was that something? It happened during or around the pandemic. That much is clear. It has to do with microbes and other such matters. Was it a virus? Was it a vaccine? There is money in both. And only money—a lot of money—could have landed them in trouble. Because sometime around and after the pandemic—the one death before that seems a coincidence to Harris—things started happening to them. Individually. Nothing too glaring. Nothing that would be noticeable. So whoever had them in sight was not ordinary. This was some powerful government or organization. Intricate planning. What is it that these manipulators want? Harris thinks it is some kind of bioweapon, a virus they can use as a bioweapon. Only massive destruction carries so much money. Only millions of deaths interest governments and corporations. That is what he thinks.

What he does not understand is Mermaid, and why Mermaid brought him in. It is obvious to Harris that all he has unearthed over the past few months could have been discovered by Mermaid and his men. Harris is under no illusions about his sleuthing abilities. Even if Mermaid did not trust people in his organization, he could have done what Harris had been doing on his own. So what was the need to involve Harris in this cloak and dagger game that feels slightly false, slightly exaggerated?

Harris sits there at his desk, sipping slowly in the dark, until his glass is empty. Then he goes upstairs again, lies down in bed, and falls asleep almost immediately.

One of his soundless nightmares wakes him up at the first light of dawn. He cannot sleep again. He grabs his phone and sees that he has been called, from an anonymous number, five or six times. Who could call him this late in the night—or so early in the morning? There is no one who knows him that well. Could it be Mermaid?

Even as he is thinking about it, the phone buzzes again.

It is a man's voice. It sounds educated. It says, abruptly: "You want answers, Dr. Malouf? Kamchatka, Yuzhno, Five in the evening next Wednesday." It repeats: "Kamchatka, Yuzhno, Five in the evening next Wednesday. Alone."

Silence.

~

It always took a full day or more for Kathy to come out of the hallucinogenic effects of Crobe, which, at least in her case, transposed her to places she had never visited, and showed her people she mostly could not recognize. Most people, Blondie had informed her, needed longer, three, even four days. Some did not hallucinate; there had been cases of paralysis and coma, though the authorities remained unaware of their source, for nothing chemically incriminating had been discovered in Crobe. Just a translucent capsule, resembling those cod-liver oil pills sold in supermarkets. It was not a psychedelic, dissociative or deliriant. It was actually nothing but a suspension of organic material. There were no refined chemicals in it, only chemicals found in a natural state in the world. Why was it so effective, and so diverse in its effects? She had asked Blondie once. How does it work? And Blondie had laughed. How do we work? He had said. Blondie, like all the dealers she had known, had a bit of the philosopher in him. How do we live? There is nothing in us that is not there in stones and earth and water. But they are dead and we are alive. It's magic, lady!

This time, perhaps because she had abstained for too long, it hit Kathy for longer. It transposed her to some kind of an underwater kingdom, full of miraculous flowers, and beautiful, long-haired women in flowing robes. It was like a 1960s costume drama set in some ashram, except for the saffron; the robes were translucent and multi-hued. She woke up to the ordinary world only on her second morning. For almost two days and nights, Crobe took over Kathy's mind: filling it with images, sounds, numbers, figures, colors, beings that she had never known. That was what she felt. Everything was fresh and new. Everything was alien. But, strangely, it was not hostile. It was not frightening. What was most addictive about Crobe was the way the images and sounds culled by it in the mind found a reverberation deep in her, in her heart. It was an exciting kind of peace, and she never felt like eating or leaving her camper as long as Crobe kept unfolding, like a blossom, inside her, petal after petal.

And then, within minutes, it disappeared. It was like water seeping into desert sand: there one moment and gone the next! But it was not really gone. Kathy still felt it in the calm that descended on her. It left her united. The feeling lasted for a week, sometimes nine or ten days, and then slowly she started coming apart again. The sand grew dry. Soon it was blowing in her face. It started with her sleep getting shot, as it had been in her last years with Command Alpha, before she started taking pills and then stronger chemicals, until finally she had come to Crobe. A drug that was not a drug. But it did not last forever. Her nights grew sleepless again. There were bouts of anxiety. Then there were moments of anger, violent anger at anything: the color of a curtain, a buzzing fly, a window that did not open easily, a rash driver. Perhaps everyone felt this anger in today's world, Kathy thought, but she could not allow herself to do so: she knew she was trained to be a killing machine. She would never be able to save up for her old age, which would come sooner or later, if she had to keep buying Crobe, but was there any other option? It was that, or homicide. And if she killed now, it would not be dismissed as duty—or collateral damage.

Yes, she needed more money, but she would still not have agreed to follow the man who knocked on her camper door late in the night. She had been sitting there—in the after-calm of the Crobe—writing to Harris. There had been no letter from him for three months or so. And then the man had knocked. This was a safe camping lot, but it was night, and she had not opened the door. Who is it, she had asked, staying away from the door, in case this was someone with a shotgun. One never knew.

She had finally opened the door because it was a voice from the past. That he knew where she lived did not surprise her. Such things had stopped surprising her a long time ago. But she would still have said no to him—despite the money offered, which would tide her over for a year or two—if the man had not mentioned a name. She had no desire to handle a gun again, except in self-defence. Not even for this man, no matter how important he thought the mission was. She did not feel gratitude for anything in the past, to anyone from the past: they had all done what they were paid and trained to do. She had saved some; she had been saved on occasions. It was all part of the job. They, he, she would have killed just as readily, if required. No, past obligations were not enough. But something was. No past leaves you totally free. There are always strings. Some thing. Some person. Only one, for her. And the name he uttered was not to be denied.

PART II:

LIMBO

THE place reminds Harris of his first "expedition" with Command Alpha. Harris and Kathy had been added to the group, replacing two previous members consumed by the Small Death. It had been an elaborate process, involving retraining with the entire unit for five weeks in discreet locations in Saudi Arabia and Israel. That was the process: members were not just plugged into each of the five units that comprised Command Alpha. The entire unit was retrained. The logic was that the unit had to be able to act as one, and newcomers, no matter how carefully selected, had to be "absorbed" before the unit could be sent out again. Then, with Mermaid as the unit head ("Colonel" was the official designation), they had all been flown to Baghdad. The year was 2004. Their commission was to silently weed out three top Ba'athist officials who had gone underground, separately, in the surrounding towns. It was less than a year after the fall of Saddam, and Baghdad was still raw. Most of the men there were like Harris. You looked at them up front and you saw army men; you looked at them from the back and you saw hardened adventurers. Years later, when Harris returned to Iraq for other missions, it had all changed, and the camps were full of contractors and officials—some Iraqi—who had obviously gone to the best universities in the US and UK. People like Harris were there to protect them and, when necessary, give them a competitive edge. But in 2004, these sophisticated people were yet to descend in sufficient numbers on Iraq, and, later, on Syria and Libya and other places; Yuzhno reminds Harris of Iraq in 2004. The bar—Kamchatka —confirms his impression.

Something like an elk's head hangs over the barman, who might have been called fat if he had not been so thoroughly scarred and tattooed. He is fat like a Sumo wrestler. It is a condition one does not feel inclined to joke about. Almost all the tables are occupied, despite it being only late afternoon, mostly by men who look like they have stepped out of a Western. One is even wearing a Stetson. But Harris knows they are on leave from the oil rigs studding the region. All except two of them—who could be Cossacks, or Mongols, or Chinese—are white. The three women in the room are obviously prostitutes. One has purple hair. One is black. She is the only black person in the room. She is hanging on the arms of one of the men at the pool table further back. There is more smoke in the room than Harris has encountered in any bar since his Big Death. If they have a rule against smoking in public in these parts, it is obviously not implemented. There is even a jukebox in a corner. As the crowd is almost entirely at least ten years younger than Harris, the number playing is unrecognizable to him.

Harris asks for a whiskey. "Bottle?" mumbles the sumo wrestler.

"Double peg," replies Harris. "On the rocks."

He suspects there is no point asking for a specific brand. The sumo wrestler plunks a glass and two bottles on the counter. Harris does not know either of the brands. He points at the bottle that is emptier.

There is an empty table not far from the entrance. He takes his drink to it and sits down facing the door. One of the women sidles up and asks, in a hoarse voice, "Drinking alone, mister?" She speaks English. Harris ignores her. She stands there for a moment, then shrugs and moves away.

Harris knows it is the man the moment he enters the bar. It is the way he looks—like a film star, that aura of privilege and power. Blue-eyed. Chiseled lips curled into something that stops a millimeter before turning into a sardonic smile. A Burberry trench coat, and under it, even before the man unbuttons the coat, Harris knows there would be even more expensive and immaculate clothes. The man takes off his black frame wool hat and looks around. He spots Harris on the second survey, nods slightly, and goes to the bar.

"You should try the local brew," the man remarks, after he has joined Harris with a Carlsberg and introduced himself as Kurt. He speaks with a slight New York accent, but it is overlaid with years of elite education, perhaps decades of East Coast breeding too. Not an adventurer, not a mercenary, Harris tells himself. A contractor. Someone out here to make the big bucks after we have dug the mines, laid the trails and shot the red Indians.

Kurt tries to start some small conversation about the region, but Harris cuts him.

"Just call in the people who are waiting outside," he says.

"What do you mean?"

Harris points at the coat hanging from the back of Kurt's chair now.

"Warm, but not warm enough for the cold out there, and there was no parking space on this street."

Kurt smiles. He pulls out a thin, sleek phone and calls.

"You will need to talk to him yourself, I am afraid," he says into the phone. Then he puts the phone away and smiles again at Harris. It is a smile Harris cannot decipher. It is not the smile of the confident and privileged man who had walked into the bar. There is something out of character about the smile.

The tall and wiry man who strides in is from a different class altogether. Even the other people in the room sense it. Or perhaps they know him. There is a slight lull in the hubbub, as if a famous person—or a dangerous animal—has entered the room. Even the men at the pool table stop for a second. The new man stops on entering, folds his arms around his chest, and slowly surveys the room. He notices them. Then the conversations resume, and the man takes two or three long strides to their table. He does not offer a hand.

"I apologize," he says. "I stopped shaking in 2019. But it is a pleasure, Mr. Malouf. I am a great fan of your career. Or should I call you Carbon?"

Then, giving Harris a moment to absorb the revelation, the man adds, "I am Vyachislav Mikhailov, Michael to friends, though Kurt's cute girlfriend here calls me Mr. Watch. She thinks I do not know, but, Mr. Malouf, let me assure you, it is my job to know everything."

~

I know something is up. Yesterday, the doctor with the gray eyes—they never call him anything other than "Professor"—and his assistants, Elizabeth and Dubey, flew back in. I sometimes feel like taking Elizabeth aside and talking to her, as she exudes a sense of loss, a heavy woman limping on arthritic joints after the limber Professor and Dubey, but she studiously ignores me, even frowns at me if I smile at her while serving, as if I was some kind of low-life. These are the three who are regular; all other experts come and go, seldom to return. Mister Hiroyuki, talking like an English butler and looking like a Gokudo gangster, took them immediately from the helicopter pad to the experimental area, and they remained closeted in there until late in the night.

And then this morning Mr. Watch and Kurt left in the chopper. Kurt said they would be back by midnight, so they were probably going to a place nearby, perhaps Yuzhno. That was fine by me. I could now crawl into the air vents and watch what the Professor and his assistants actually did. I had never had such an opportunity before: Kurt and, often, Mr. Watch were always around at least during the daytime when the experts were on the rig, and the few occasions I had peeked in, the sealed section was bereft of any ongoing work.

I wait until I have served them lunch. Then I tell Mister Hiroyuki that I have a splitting headache and will lie down in my room this afternoon, so could they just buzz me if I am wanted? "Take a nap, dear," replies Mister Hiroyuki, in that posh accent, with a polite bow. His genteel mannerisms are frightening in a man of that girth and with those tattoos. "Take a nap. Our guests will be occupied until late." That is exactly what I want to hear.

What I see in the sealed section that afternoon I will not be able to forget as long as I live. Which, I fear, will not be that long, Maman.

There is a woman on one of the operating tables, or whatever it is. They had already been working on her by the time I managed to crawl through the air vents and reach my vantage point above the room. There are tubes and wires attached to her head, to her wrist, to her upper arm, to her neck. The woman herself is firmly strapped to the table.

She is a wasted human being. The gate of one of the cages is open. They must have pulled her out of it. It is the cage in which I had seen that half-human face on the first night I was here.

But she is human. Her hair is awry and knotted, her clothes torn and crumpled, her face devastated: the face of someone in chronic pain. But she is human. She can even talk. Or she is talking when I first catch the action in there. It is strange. Dubey, the skeletal Indian assistant with the immense potbelly, is showing her some charts. He asks her a question. I can hear it clearly. "What is the answer?" he says. The woman does not respond. Dr. Dubey raises his voice; he has the voice of a child, shrill and high-pitched: "What is the answer?" he repeats. "What is 10 plus 23?"

When the woman does not respond again, the other assistant, Elizabeth, scowling deeply, hands Dubey a metallic rod. It reminds me of the new shock sticks that have been added to the batons of all police forces in the world. I have seen them work on demonstrators on TV news: they give an electric jolt, which can be calibrated, by turning a dial, from just an unpleasant shock to a knockout blow. Elizabeth hobbles quickly away, back to the screens she had been watching. All those wires and tubes attached to the woman on the table connect to monitors and computer screens that the Professor is intent on. Dubey pokes the woman with the rod. This time it is an unpleasant shock. The woman winces, her face contorts, she gasps. Dubey waits for a few seconds and repeats his question. The woman shouts out the answer as Dubey raises the shock stick again: "Thirty-three!" Dubey tucks the rod under an arm and puts a tick on the chart he is holding. Then he continues, and the woman answers, correctly every time as far as I can guess from the responses below me, because sometimes the woman's voice is too low to carry clearly to me.

"Fifty minus ten?"

"Forty."

"Four multiplied by three?"

"Twelve."

"Ten divided by two?"

"Five."

"Five hundred plus three?"

"Five hundred three."

Simple arithmetical questions of the sort posed to primary school children, though I can see that the woman is not delinquent. This is not an intelligence test. They are testing something else. Then Professor Gray-Eyes makes a gesture and Dubey puts down his chart. He goes to a device on an adjoining table. It looks like an old-fashioned film projector, the type they used for home movies in the last century. A box with a tube sticking out on one side. Dubey switches it on and clicks a few buttons. An image forms just above the woman. It starts with a few spots of light and then takes the shape of a rabbit. It is a holographic projector. "Rabbit," says the woman, without even being asked. She obviously knows the routine. Dubey presses a switch. The image dissolves, and another forms.

"Goat," says the woman.

Another image.

"Wolf," says the woman.

Professor Gray-Eyes leaves his revolving chair by the monitors and comes to the table. He strokes the woman on her forehead. The woman tries to turn her face away, but even her head is trapped, strapped down by the forehead and neck. She can do nothing.

Professor Gray-Eyes says something that I cannot hear. He always whispers, even at the dining tables. A whisper is his normal voice. The woman jerks, as much as her straps allow her, which is not much. She is obviously frightened of what is coming. Dubey and Elizabeth are tinkering with the monitors now. Elizabeth prepares an injection, but stays away from the woman, not looking in her direction. She hands the syringe to Dubey who injects the woman in the forearm. The woman shudders. I can sense the shudder despite the straps.

Professor Gray-Eyes pours out a cup of coffee from a thermos flask that they always fill from the machine in the galley. He holds out the cup for Elizabeth, who declines with a shake of her head. Now she is observing the woman on the table, focused on the tubes attached to her head. Dubey accepts the cup. "Five minutes," he says. "Three should be enough, but let us give her five." Professor Gray-Eyes nods and pours himself a cup.

Five minutes later they go through the mathematical routine again. But this time they only get grunts and snarls from the woman. They jolt her with the shock stick twice, but the response does not change. Then they try the hologram machine. A bird forms above the woman. She makes animal sounds. The image changes. There is a tiger head, snarling, above the woman now. Peering down into this cavernous hall, where the artificial white lighting dims the lines of hologram, I am strangely reminded of Stone Age paintings on a cave wall. But it has a different effect on the woman: she goes berserk. She screams and contorts. It almost looks as if her frail, wasted body will burst the straps, such is her terror.

I am taken aback by this primal fear, her shrieks of terror, and I recoil physically. Do I make a sound? Suddenly the Professor looks up exactly at me. He cannot see into the air vents, but his strange gray eyes seem to penetrate everything. He stares in my direction for close to half a minute. Then he looks away and says something to Dr. Elizabeth. The hologram is switched off. They return to work on the strapped woman and the monitors. But I am so shaken by the stare that seemed to see me through plastic and metal that I crawl back, as fast as I can, to the guest room, tidy myself up, and sneak into my room. I have a splitting headache. I take a pill and go to bed, covering myself with more sheets than I need. I am too numb to even think of Maman.

~

Aslan Barzani's friend looks like his twin to Jens Erik, but then they do all look alike, don't they? I mean, Jens Erik tells himself, if they are the same size, it is difficult to tell them apart. He can hear Pernille laughing at that. He smiles to himself. This identical friend is the idea Aslan had mentioned in his office some days ago.

"You are Kurdish too?" Jens Erik asks the man, who has introduced himself as Mehmet Something.

Aslan answers: "He is Turkish." Then he adds with a sardonic smile: "But a good Turk."

"Fuck you," Mehmet tells Aslan.

The man walks him down the pier to a yacht. It is called La Göke, written in dark blue on its white flanks. It seems to Jens Erik to be around twenty meters in length.

"The woman in my life," says Mehmet, indicating the yacht with an expansive gesture. "I divorced twice for her."

Then he looks closely at Jens Erik.

"Have you ever been out in the sea?"

"A vacation or two."

"How many days?"

"A whole day once."

Mehmet laughs. "This will be tough on you, man," he says. "Eight days, we are going to be out for more than a week. Believe me, you will wobble on the ground for a month afterwards. Bit of advice from an old seadog: keep a vomit bag in your pocket all the time, and vomit in it, or in the water, or into the jaws of a shark, but whatever you do, do not throw up on my girl here."

He stroked the side of the yacht with affection, the way Jens Erik had seen people stroke a dog or a cat.

~

Harris looks at the man, Vyachislav Mikhailov, Michael to friends. He does not seem to be the kind of man who would have many friends. Kurt, sitting next to him, seems to think that he is a friend. Kurt, Harris is certain, is mistaken. Someone like Kurt would never be a friend to Vyachislav Mikhailov. But there is another element in Kurt's blue star eyes when he looks or says anything to Mikhailov: respect. That element is appropriate. Mikailov is a dangerous man. But he is more than that, or he would not know Harris's code name from Command Alpha: Carbon.

"Mr. Mikhailov…," Harris begins. He is interrupted. "Michael," said Mikhailov, "Michael to you."

"Thank you, Michael," says Harris. He is playing it safe. He does not feel he is in any immediate danger. They would not have invited him all this way out, possibly close to their lair, if they just wanted to bump him off. But he has to ensure he does not make a mistake. "I fail to understand how you can be a fan of someone who does not even have tenure, and has spent most of his life teaching on contract here and there..."

Mikhailov smiles. It is more of a grimace.

Harris continues: "But I am happy you came to see me, for the matter about which you called, you or the gentleman here, that matter interests me ..."

Mikhailov smiles again. Only his lips. There is nothing in his eyes. Kurt starts to say something, but is silenced by a glance from Mikhailov. Then Mikhailov places his hands, which he had kept folded, on the table. They are big hands, heavily veined, with visible scars.

"Let me tell you a story, Carbon," he says, stressing Harris's codename. "The Greeks used to call it limbo. But we have other words for it. Whatever the word, you know you have reached it when you do not really know where you are. That is your state now. Or so it seems. I will call you Harris from now on. Why bring up past names, past games? I will tell you a bit about myself. I started off in the Seals. Then I moved to Alpha. Yes, I was in another of its units; I rose to be its commander. Colonel. As you will recall, the units were not supposed to know each other; they were never deployed together. Back then I still knew where I stood—though, looking back, I can see that it was my first step into limbo. Because Command Alpha both existed and did not exist. I suppose that is why people like you left: you wanted to exist again, and I must say I am impressed by the career—or, shall we say, careers that you fashioned afterwards. I meant it when I said I am a fan. But the step into limbo is immutable: once taken, you can only disappear with every other step. That, I know now, is in the very nature of things.

You must have felt reality slipping through your grasp. Nothing, no false identity, no degree, no change of name, no new career can arrest that. Perhaps you knew this would happen. Perhaps that is why you crafted two careers: a visible one and a hidden one. That impresses me, that kind of foresight."

Mikhailov raises his glass and pauses, perhaps hoping for a response from Harris, but Harris raises his glass too, politely, in a gesture that means nothing. Both take a sip and return the glasses to the sticky table. Mikhailov offers his grimace smile again and continues: "Unlike you, I did not know this when I left Alpha—another step into limbo—for something similar. They proliferated, these organizations. You know how it was. Governments and corporations had been in bed for decades: now they were producing hybrid offspring. Mutants. You thought you chose the Big Death? But no, you did not choose it. You were encouraged to choose it, I am certain. You had as little choice as those of us who fell to the Small Death. But I, the Undead, thought I had choice. Volition. So I moved to something else when they asked me to do so, something even deeper in limbo, something where you could not tell what was government and what was corporation. The mutants had proliferated. They had become invisible. This must have been after you left, during and after the pandemic. What a virus it was; it changed everything, and no one has noticed it even today. I did not know this then. I won't even name the organization I moved to, for that deep in limbo nothing exists. Only one of the cases I had in that organization deep in limbo concerns us. There were dead bodies."

Harris has been in such situations before. Not all his interlocutors had been so eloquent, or had spoken English. But it is not a new situation. His body, his senses, have already remembered. He sits there, seemingly relaxed, appearing to listen only to what Mikahilov is saying, but he is registering other things too. First, the way Mikhailov sits, arms folded, like a Buddha statue, conveying a sense of calm, as his voice drones on: "Bodies washed up in Germany, Scotland, Russia, Denmark. All around the North Sea. Not many, but often enough to attract Interpol, and then to be passed on to us. We thought we were Super Interpol, cloaked in greater powers and the cape of invisibility. License to kill and all that. James Bond, but with greater impunity, more gadgets. I was asked to look into it. These were not drowned sailors or vacationers. They were not white, most of the time. Not many, you understand, just one here, another there. But enough. And curious. It was obvious they were coming from the North Sea. Why were mostly black and brown young men and women turning up, dead, on the coasts of the North Sea? It is not on any immigrants smuggling route. The routes on that side are overland."

Second, the fact that not one of the prostitutes has approached the two new men. "And," continues Mikhailov, "There was another curious factor: the bodies were invariably of young people, and had organs missing. They had been thoroughly prepared for transplantation. Actually, so thoroughly had they been cleansed of microbes, the bad and the good, that, if they had been allowed to live on, they would have died of diseases, indigestion, and a hundred ordinary things. And just as invariably, these were people who did not exist in the region. You look surprised. Yes, organs missing. Not just missing, neatly, scientifically removed. It was obvious what was going on: organ trafficking. With the kind of powers the organization had, it did not take me long to assemble that jigsaw. Young immigrants and refugees were being smuggled in, and their organs removed for transplantation. It was, as you know, big business, and grew bigger during and after the pandemic, when the rich started avoiding trips to private hospitals in poorer countries, and "clean" organs became even more expensive. So, someone was providing the service at closer range. Instead of moving the patient to, say, a private hospital in Delhi or Nairobi, someone was moving the donor to a site in the North Sea. It did not take us long to locate the business. It was global, run under the banner of a tourism agency called "Magic Gates". It had offices in India, Nigeria, and other places. It offered a door to other worlds."

Third, the decibel level around them seems to have gone down. Harris knows that this could not be because people have left the bar; he sits facing the door. He notices that there are two vacant tables near them now. Some clients have edged away from their corner, as if they do not want to overhear whatever these two men might be telling him. This tells him a lot about Mikhailov, who is still talking to Harris as if narrating barroom gossip: "A magic gate. But it hardly worked with tourists. We discovered that it was a front for the smuggling of immigrants and refugees. Not just any immigrant or refugee: only healthy young people. It ran expensive health tests on the selected candidates, telling them that they had to be healthy to survive the smuggling route. It seemed convincing. A new world beckoned. They entered the magic gates. And they arrived in another world. The question was: where was this world? Where were these young men and women transported to? Given the operation, and the scatter of the bodies recovered, it had to be in or around the North Sea. I reasoned that it would not be on land. Because, in that case, the bodies would be disposed in other ways, and in any case they will not reach so many different coasts, always at different times of the year, depending on the currents. Also, land means authorities, eyes, scandal. The operating theatre had to be in the North Sea. There were not that many options in the North Sea. Whoever was running Magic Gates had been stupid or lazy. They should have disposed of the bodies in other ways. They had assumed that the sea would hide all the bodies, and it probably hid most of them. But the sea did not hide all of them. Nature is careless. It threw up a few on the coasts around it. They had made a mistake. Because there is not that much in the North Sea. Tourism all along the coast, fishery over the waters; the few islands all known and inhabited, or protected as wildlife reserves. Where could they be? Not on ships, because ships have to go to port somewhere, and in any case they would be too unstable for an advanced operating theatre. There was just one other option: oil rigs. I knew that this could not be on any working oil rig; these are places teeming with people. But there were abandoned rigs. I had my men do a survey of the possibilities. Most had been partly dismantled. But there were a few that were entire, at least on paper. One of them was too old. They used to build rigs very low in the past, and such rigs could get denuded in storms. It would not be an option. No one would put a state-of-the-art operating theatre on a rusty rig which might be submerged by a wave. But there were others. I made my report. I submitted it to my bosses. And then *they* came to see me and I realized why I had been in limbo. I had been in limbo because the real world—the world in which people took decisions and did things—was elsewhere."

Mikhailov pauses and drinks deeply, and the film star next to him looks up, his eyes wide in awe, the eyes of the faithful being told of a miracle. Focus on the Buddha, Harris tells himself, because this film star is froth. This time, having put the glass back on the table, Mikhailov does not fold his arms again. He puts them on the table, as if about to get up, but then he proceeds: "And these five people, who came to see me, were from that world. I cannot give you their names. But if I did, you would recognize them. Each one of them. Oh yes, I am certain of that. These are legends, giants: one from the corporate world, amongst the richest men on earth, another a highly decorated general, a senator, even a prime minister. It was in New York, there was a global conference going on, and not all of them were from America. But our meeting was invisible. Actually, you will never find a photo of these five men—sorry, one was a woman—together. And there were more of them. Why did they come to see me? Because they could use me. They could have ignored me, but they, as they told me, needed people like me. And that, Harris, is the reason we came to see you. There are various ways we could have dealt with your interest in the Aarhus seminar, but all of them would have been messy—and you are a man we can use. Kurt, can you fetch me a beer?"

As Kurt jumps up to oblige with scout-like enthusiasm, Harris remarks, "Michael, you still have not told me what I came out here to learn."

"It is coming," replies Mikhailov, folding his arms again. "You see, Kurt there was in charge of the oil rig. The famous five who met me in New York, wanted me to work for them, locate the rig, and make Kurt—shall we repeat a cliché?—an offer he could not refuse. Because they wanted to use the rig for something else, something that, despite their powers, they could not do in their own countries and bases. Why, you would be wondering, why the rig? Why that rig? Well, it already had what they needed, a state-of-the-art operating theatre, microbial cleansing facilities, which they could turn into something else, the right location, far out and not too far, a ready system to obtain, shall we say, volunteers for the experiments. But there was another decisive factor. Because you know, one of the conditions of limbo is that reality always takes place elsewhere, and all of them had to keep the rules of whatever limbo that they sustained. They were masters of being in limbo, but they could be so only if the condition of being in limbo stayed in place, undetected even by people like you and me who worked for years at its edges. But they held out a hand to me: they offered to pull me to their side, so that I could both be in limbo and step into reality. What was that reality? I cannot describe it to you, but I suppose you can guess. It was the reality in which large stretches of the Amazon are sold off for profit, oil spills into the ocean, protesting workers are shot, journalists disappear, people lose their jobs, and yet the stock markets thrive, even prosper, and governments get elected and re-elected: it was that reality. It was unavoidable because it was reality. Only a fool would shut his eyes to it. I am not a fool. These were the people—and there were maybe a dozen more behind them—who made that reality possible, and that is why the rest of us lived, no matter what we did, in limbo. People like you and me, Harris, we are not meant to live in limbo."

Kurt returns with two beers and another whiskey for Harris. Harris does not say anything. He waits for Mikhailov to resume.

"My friend Kurt here was surprised when I turned up on his rig. I think he and his partner, who unfortunately is no longer with us as he took a view that did not mesh with my view or Kurt's, had been running a cosy little gig. Especially our friend Kurt here, who has an eye for fit young black women. You see, it was a side diversion for him. You should see his latest, the girl Michelle: she is enough to make a seventy-year-old man feel seventeen. Well, he could have them, and then give them, shall we say, a new life—usually in the bodies of rich white women twice their age. It was good business. But it was also fraying. Too many bodies had washed up on shores, and though Kurt and his partner had contacts, we could easily have allowed honest police officers in, say, Germany or Denmark—there are still a few idiots who think that limbo is reality—to create trouble for them. So Kurt took our offer. He had an operating theatre already in place, and the rig was beautifully located: far enough, but also accessible by chopper. And we paid him a good sum. His partner agreed too, but then he changed his mind when he saw what we were doing. It was far less gruesome than what they used to do, if you ask me, but for some reason, the man had an attack of conscience. He thought his four or five hired guards would be able to protect him and his rig. That is what happens when you live in limbo, even if it is at the edge. You underestimate the force of reality."

Mikhailov breaks off to drink from his beer. The way he drinks beer reminds Harris of Mermaid: there is no trace of pleasure on his face. He is drinking, as Mermaid used to, because it is part of the job: he would drink water, beer, wine, or a cocktail of poison with the same lack of interest in the beverage, as long as he felt that he had to do it.

"You have told me what your friend was doing. But you still haven't told me what you are doing now," Harris notes, neutrally.

"That is something we can only show you. No, Michael?" Kurt replies this time. He sounds anxious.

"But why should you want to show me something that is, obviously, so far outside the confines of the limbo I live in?"

This time it is Mikhailov who replies: "Because we can use someone like you. You belong to reality. And because we do not want needless trouble."

"Trouble?" Harris scoffs. "What trouble can I give an organization like yours? I know you are not making up everything, because you have the connections to find out about my Command Alpha background. The edge of limbo, as you put it. But even with that Command Alpha background, I am just a part-time lecturer now, and if my investigation is causing you trouble, what is there to prevent you from arranging a small accident? We all know how these things happen."

"It would be too troublesome to arrange a small accident for you, my friend, for if it was not foolproof, and often the best laid plans of mice and men... you know, someone might come looking, and then we would have to arrange another accident, and another accident," replies Mikhailov.

"But it can be done," Harris insists.

"Yes, my friend, it can be done. I daresay, it might have been done if you had only that cover as a university lecturer."

"What do you mean?"

"We have looked a bit deeper than that, Harris. Give us some credit." Mikhailov says, staring hard at him. "We know of your other career, the career for which you must have left Command Alpha. I said I am a fan of you. Who wouldn't become a fan of perhaps the greatest and most unknown hired assassin in the history of the profession?"

~

I must have dozed off, though I wake up with the feeling that there is a woman in the room, and that she is looking down on me with pity. Sleep-fogged, I think it is Maman, perhaps because she has brought with her a feeling of safety than most of us associate with our childhood, and then realize it is someone I had never seen before.

That is when I wake up. There is no one there. But, for a moment, it is as if the presence of the woman fills that small room with comfort, and then I panic because I think I have slept for too long. The artificial lighting inside the rig does not allow you to distinguish between night and day. I grab my phone and look at the time. It is late, but not too late: only around five in the afternoon. I have to get dinner ready by seven-thirty. There is more than enough time for it. But Kurt had also asked me to prepare an extra room, and I haven't done that yet.

I am serving dinner to the experts—Mister Hiroyuki has joined them, which he does only when Kurt or Mr. Watch are not on the rig—when I hear the whirring of the chopper. I put out three more plates on the next table. There is space for only four on each of the three tables—everything is screwed to the floor—in this section of the galley. The part of the galley where the other men eat has benches and long tables, but this section is designed to resemble a restaurant. The food is always served on hotplates, and the guests help themselves. My job is to keep the bowls warm and replenished and pour the drinks.

Jerk chicken with rice and peas—your favorite, Maman—though the rice is in two versions, plain and coconut basmati. That is what I have cooked. Professor Gray-Eyes only eats coconut rice. There is a side dish of my thick lentil and dumpling soup for Dubey. Dubey puts the rice in his bowl of soup and eats it with a spoon. He is a vegetarian. This evening all three of them—Mister Hiroyuki seldom speaks and never shows any emotion—are talking a lot. It is mostly in snippets of Scientish. That is what I call it, Scientish. It contains words and phrases like orthogenesis, junk DNA, progressive differentiation, microbiome, Hodgkinia in the cicadas, endosymbiosis, holobiont, mitochondrial networks, peptidoglycan, microbial graffiti, autoclave … These, of course, are the ones that, because of their similarity to normal words or due to a memorable sequence of sounds, somehow stay in my memory; there are many more that I do not even register!

Kurt and Mr. Watch walk in with a man who has never been here before. He looks distinguished, and could be an expert, but you can tell he is not just a scientist or a doctor. The way he walks, his massive build—even his middle-aged girth cannot hide the power of those limbs and muscles—and, above all, the way Mr. Watch watches him all the time while appearing not to watch him, and the look in Kurt's eyes. Have I told you about the gleam of hero-worship that shines from Kurt's eyes when Mr. Watch, in one of his expansive moods, tells him a story from his past, stories that take place in distant lands and usually under a hail of bullets? Kurt has a bit of that gleam when he looks at the new man. As for Mr. Watch, he is wary, respectful and wary. That is not how he looks at any of us, not even at the experts. Sometimes, maybe, at Mister Hiroyuki. But not the rest of us. Whoever this man is, he is not just another Professor Gray-Eyes. Could he be my escape route from here? Or will he be my executioner? He has that look.

The man is not introduced to anyone, though everyone greets him: the scientists from where they are, Mister Hiroyuki getting up and offering a respectful bow. They must know who he is. Kurt, Mr. Watch, and the new man settle down with their plates. It is only then that he looks at me. It is a quick look, for a second perhaps, and it seems to me to be exactly the same look that the strange woman in my dream had given me. They start talking. Mr. Watch calls the man Harris.

They leave soon after dinner. They go back to the closed section: the laboratory. For that, after all, is what it is. It is clear now. Even Mr. Hiroyuki goes this time. This is unusual. He usually stays out, supervizing the men or, yes, meditating on a mat. Mr. Hiroyuki is a great yoga enthusiast. But this time he goes with them, though with no enthusiasm. Kurt lingers for a moment to give me an absent-minded kiss and say, "Go to bed, Sugar. I will be late."

I tidy up. Then I go upstairs to our room. I am tempted to crawl through the air vents and peer into the laboratory. But I do not dare do so with both Mr. Watch and Mister Hiroyuki down there. Especially, Mr. Watch. I have a dread of him. And the new man, Harris, who knows what he is? Do you dare put your trust in another strange man, gal, I ask myself. I think of you, Maman, and I know the answer.

I force myself to read a bit in bed. Not on my Kindle: I am out of stuff on my Kindle. And nothing that would upset your boyfriend, Maman. No Dickens or Morrison. It is a potboiler. That is the only kind of book I can read now. There are a few in the library. Old paperbacks. I can read them and think at the same time: I always think of how I can get away. Some of these novels are full of great escapes: people clinging to helicopters, swimming through the seas, digging tunnels, tumbling down mountains and surviving. People snatching a gun and shooting themselves to safety. People being rescued by secret agents. It is all weirdly reassuring. And thoroughly unbelievable.

I fall asleep reading the novel. I have various dreams. I am running down one of the beaches in St. Martin. My mother is making callaloo soup. I am attending a class in my old school. I am sleeping on the silk sheets of the villa that Kurt took care of.

Broken dreams. All of them broken by a woman in a long dress, the woman I dreamt of sometime back, the strange woman, I can see she is white now. She interrupts every dream. She comes into them unexpectedly, silently, and looks at me: it is a calm, reassuring look. Not a pitying look as I had thought earlier, no, it is a calm, reassuring look. It seems as if she wants to say something to me, but then that dream breaks, and I am in another dream. When she enters that dream, the same thing happens. It breaks just as she appears to have found the words.

I wake up when this happens for the fifth or sixth time. I wake up feeling that someone is in the room. Kurt must be back, I think. I feel groggily in the bed next to me, but there is no one there. I wake up completely, and switch on all the lights. It is past midnight.

There is no one in the room.

~

Jens Erik leaves with Mehmet and Aslan only the next day, as some provisions must be bought. To Jens Erik, it appears to be mostly crates of beer.

As they glide out of the harbour, Mehmet turns to Jens Erik and says, "You know, this is the first time that I am in this baby without a baby. But Aslan says you have to hunt for oil rigs."

"Abandoned ones," Jens Erik explains.

"There are dozens out here. Do you know which one?"

"Aslan tried to get a list..."

"There isn't any list. Not of the abandoned ones anyway. They do not exist. I could have told you so."

Aslan interrupts them. "Well, there are navigational charts with dangers marked on them. There are some records. We have marked out a few for you."

Mehmet looks doubtful. "It is huge out there," he says, "You know the North Sea is bigger than Germany, almost as big as France!"

"We have an idea what parts to look at," Aslan replies. "If what we looked up about currents and season is reliable."

~

Kathy watches his back, as he gets up to fetch the tray of food from the McDonald's counter. He still walks the way he used to, a bit stiffly, which is deceptive, she knows, because he can be extremely supple in action.

This is the first time she has been in a McDonald's for around a decade. It is almost unrecognizable. She knows that they changed their signature uniforms soon after the pandemic, when there was a period of nostalgia for a cleaner past.

He returns with the tray. The packaging has become not just more traditional but also demonstrably ecological. The tray too. "Wonder about the beef," she says.

"What?" he asks, unwrapping his burger.

"I wonder if the beef has become ecological too," she elaborates.

"I am very sure, I am very sure," he replies, sardonically or absentmindedly.

Kathy looks around. There are only three backpackers, college kids probably, at a table further off, and a large, tattooed Maori-looking truck driver at the counter. Outside the sun is strong, and she can see the highway gleaming across the parking lot. An old, dented Ford Endeavour stands in the lot along with two other cars and a truck. They have been driving in the metal gray Ford since early morning. She is sure that he has chosen the kind of car least likely to attract attention: he probably has some algorithm to figure that out too.

"Why didn't we catch a flight?" she asks him. "This is a long drive. And in that tin-can!"

"I will get your new papers only in Chicago," he replies. "Then we are catching a flight to Europe."

"No one is watching out for me," she remarks. "I am not you. I am one of the late Mr. Trump's losers."

"You never know what they don't know; you never know what they know." He replies, after a pause, during which he looks like he wants to say something else too.

They munch morosely, like any long-married couple with nothing left to say to each other. The Maori driver takes his tray to a table in another corner. She counts seven cars pass on the highway. Two of them are the latest redesigned Humvees preferred by the rich, both with blinking surveillance jammer gadgets stuck to their roofs. She smiles at the thought. The rich: their paranoia and their faith, both slightly at a tangent from reality, both expensive.

He is speaking again, without looking up: "I would have saved time if I could. We have only until Thursday, maybe Friday. We need to get there, find an access. Believe me, I hate the time we are wasting on this drive. But we cannot take any chance. There is no net under us if we fall. Not this time. And that would mean the end of him too. A horrible end, Kath. I am sure of that."

There is a long pause again. She sips her cola and counts some more cars. The Maori driver is joined by another man, a white man this time. They seem to know each other. They share the French fries.

"Do you think he will ever forgive you?" she asks.

"You cannot forgive people if you are dead."

"No. If this works? If he survives?"

"Well, I expect some backing there too, Kath," he responds with a wry grimace. After all, you are the muscle on this one.

~

Harris has watched it for hours now. It is fascinating in a horrible manner: their ability to turn off the rational faculties of the woman and accentuate her emotional responses by just injecting her with a fluid. Harris knows all about the prefrontal cortex, but the Professor assures him—and Dubey regularly draws his attention to the screens attesting to the fact—that the woman's prefrontal cortex has not been tampered with. "Entirely intact," Dubey assures him, "See, see, look at this..." The Professor smiles. It is a divine smile. Elizabeth ignores all the men, except the Professor, concentrating on her work. The strapped woman counts, multiplies, screams, weeps. They wait for the effects to wear off. The Professor times it. It takes about an hour. "We need to reduce it," says the Professor. Harris has not been introduced to the Professor. Dubey says Sir. Once or twice, Sirji. Maybe they assumed he knows who the professor is, for Harris finds the face familiar, and he is certain that a bit of googling would throw up the answer. He has to hide his true feelings. He has done bad things to living beings in the past. He has killed and tortured. But he finds this spectacle deeply disturbing. The strapped woman screams, weeps, trembles, counts, multiplies, divides. Is it because she is a woman, and not identified, rightly or wrongly, as a terrorist or an extremist or something like that, as Harris's victims had always been? No, that is not it. It is more than that, more than just the pity of the spectacle. It is the explanations—purely scientific—that the Professor offers, and the explanations—purely practical—that Vyachislav Mikhailov, Michael, offers. Kurt and the Japanese gangster do not say much. Harris patterns his face on Michael's; his years of experience with Command Alpha stand him in good stead. He lets them demonstrate the great achievements. But, after the first round of demonstration, his mind is on other things.

Two things. Two unrelated things. Or are they related?

First, Michael's revelation of Harris's career as a hired assassin. He knows that this is a decisive factor. Without it, they might have tried to bump him off; even his Command Alpha background might not have made them hesitate. But with it, he is a mercenary, and a useful one. That is why he is here, and not in a gutter with fifteen holes in his body. What does it mean? Because of course, it means more than even Michael realizes.

And the second is this question: Is this all? Is this woman the end result of all those papers and brave hopes of the group of eccentric, perhaps brilliant, researchers who had met in Aarhus years ago? For by now Harris can piece together their hopes. He can see how, from different sides, different fields, they had converged on the same matter: how human beings think and feel? Or, as some of them would have said, what human beings are? Or maybe even the bigger question: what is life? Despite the paucity of written texts by them in their last years, they had been a courageous lot, willing to make mistakes. They had hoped for so much: to understand the link between thinking rationally and feeling, to figure out aspects of the evolution of life, to prepare the human being in such a way as to use the good microbes to control the bad ones. Each had his own vision of a brave, new world.

Their diverse, sometimes rambling, sometimes cryptic, observations and discoveries have cohered in this woman—this woman is proof of their conjectures and hypotheses—but what is being made of her is something entirely different. What would they have said to this experiment—and its purpose, as tabulated by the people behind Michael? Is that what Niels Bohr, Albert Einstein, and J. Robert Oppenheimer must have felt when they were told that atom bombs had been dropped on two Japanese cities? Harris can recall the crazy words of that mad scientist he had spoken to, what was his name, Dutton: "They would make dynamite of everything I could give them ... They murdered the answers... They shot down the Indians... They bombed Hiroshima."

When they finally stopped displaying their successes on the strapped woman, it is past midnight. Harris is shown to his room by Kurt. It is next to the rooms occupied by the scientists. His small suitcase has already been placed there. Harris is sure they have checked it for weapons. But he is not carrying any. They probably know it. It is sheer craziness to fly with a weapon—even a pen-knife—these days.

It takes time for Harris to fall asleep. He keeps thinking of the woman. He keeps thinking of her "purpose". "Purpose" was Michael's word. Dr. Dubey had used "significance".

How excited many of the Aarhus group would have been if they were here! They would have argued voraciously, but they would also have felt redeemed. Harris knows that.

They would still have argued. Oh yes, they would have, because they had various hypotheses, each one usually to do with the field they came from. Was it a meteor from outer space that had brought it to earth? If it was like a virus, surely that would be a possibility!

Was it the decisive factor: the moment when the Homo sapiens species achieved its name, its "wisdom"? Or had it happened earlier, with homo erectus, or the intermediate Homo antecessor, and Homo sapiens triumphed, also over Neanderthals and others, simply because they were the best host? Was part of the meteor still embedded in Africa, capable of effects that were considered wondrous? Was it the source of the legends about the fountain of life? Was it where the notion of "souls" and "rebirth" came from? Was this just another kind of microbe, like the millions that enable us to digest our food or enable trees to communicate with each other, like the mitochondria in our cells, a microbe that somehow passed itself on, could reproduce only in the human brain, or some human brains, and in the process effected it, bestowing the kind of abstract reasoning on human beings that no other animals have? For, as some of them had argued, is it not strange that of all the millions of animals who share everything with human animals, only the human species has abstract reasoning? Isn't it strange, as Harris had himself realized so often in the past, that our emotions and reasoning are often in conflict, and both can be wrong? Oh, those crazy scientists and thinkers from the Aarhus seminar would have argued like mad!

But they would have been excited to see that the "microbe"—or whatever it was, for its chemical properties were elusive, only its effects observed or effected, and either of the options changed it, something that had made Dubey wax eloquent about quantum laws—they would have been overjoyed to see that this "microbe" in the human brain had been confirmed by human intervention. But what, Harris wondered, as he finally fell asleep, would they have thought of the reason Michael—and the people behind him—were investing billions into this secret project? What would they have thought of Michael's precious "purpose": By controlling the "microbe", we can control every single human response in the world! It wasn't even the bioweapon Harris had imagined. It was something more sweeping than that. Think of it, Harris, Michael had whispered, approaching the closest to excitement a man like him could achieve, "Think of it, you would not have to pull the trigger, you could get your target to hallucinate and shoot himself. Harris, my friend, you will be out of a job pretty soon!"

~

At breakfast, the new man, Harris, looks at me. I am used to men looking at me. They usually start from my breasts and then slowly move their glance upwards or downwards, depending on their particular fixations. They try to catch my eye somewhere in that elaborate process of undressing my body. But that is not how this man looks. He looks when he thinks I am not aware. He does not look at the obvious targets: boobs, legs, buttocks, arms, and shoulder, face, or, though I do not wear anything too revealing here, stomach. He looks at a point just above my head. It seems as if he is thinking, wondering what to make of me. Or, is he wondering what to do with me?

The men leave for the laboratory soon after breakfast. All except Mister Hiroyuki, who goes off to supervize his men: they are expecting a shipment of something. It is nothing unusual. Unusual shipments come at night, by helicopter.

I know Hiroyuki and his men will be busy. They never come up to my floor in any case. Do I dare creep into the air shafts and spy on what is happening in the laboratory? With all six down there, surely even Mr. Watch would be too preoccupied to pay attention to imaginary sounds? Not that I make any sound anymore; I know the contours of those shafts as well as the back of my own hands. I am torn between my desire to know—it is not lazy curiosity, for I know that my future might depend on whatever is happening down there—and the shackles of fear. I examine the matter rationally. There is no reason to be afraid, I tell myself. It would take much longer for any of the men to leave the laboratory and come to this floor than it would for me to crawl out, at least to the room from which I enter the shafts, and I can always pretend to be dusting it. If I see one of the men leave, I will just climb back out, I tell myself. But my sense of dread, of premonition even, is greater this morning. So is my urge to know. It is my life, I tell myself. And coolly, carefully, cerebrally, ignoring my thumping heart, I will myself to go down the air shafts.

It is not a woman who is strapped to the board this time, tubes and wires running out of her. It is a man. I am not surprised: I always thought that they had more than one captive in the cages. I had heard different sounds during the nights I had spied on the place.

But this man could just as well have been the woman: his face is just as devastated. It is clear they have done the same things to him that they did to the woman. However, when I peer down, they are not doing anything to him. All the men are clustered around the screens, where Professor Gray-Eyes is explaining something to them. He always speaks in a whisper, and his sentences carry only in words to me. All I can tell is that he is directing their attention to two sets of screens and graphs, one of which depict the man's "biological functions" and the other depict his "macrobic output". I do not hear this well enough. Did he say "macrobic"? I have heard of microbes; I have never heard of macrobes. He must have said microbic.

I am thinking about the matter when something totally unexpected happens. Elizabeth walks away into a corner of the hall, hobbling as quickly on her arthritic joints as she can manage. This should have warned me. Mr. Watch takes out a small, snub-nosed pistol—I always thought he went about armed everywhere—and shoots the strapped man in the head, twice. The pistol is not silenced; it makes a low coughing sound, but I am sure it does not carry outside this padded laboratory. All the inhabitable sections—both the floors—are soundproof. They always are on rigs, I have been given to understand. But the laboratory is more than just soundproof. It has been designed to prevent any sound from exiting. Not that anyone would care. I admire myself for not jumping or letting out a shriek. I am tougher than I thought I was. Or maybe I have a greater drive to survive. I look on.

The professor is pointing to the screens again. Elizabeth has returned, but is watching the screens, her broad back turned to the body on the table. Even I can see from here that the screens and graphs with what the professor had called the man's "biological functions" are tapering off. Soon they are flat or have stopped. I understand that this means the man is dead. "Biologically dead, you see," Dubey states the obvious in his high woman's voice.

"But see here," he adds, directing Harris's attention in particular to the other set of screens and graphs. The lines and dots there are still fluctuating, moving. Whatever they depict is not dead. But whatever they depict is also in the dead man, for all the wires and tubes lead to that dead body, with two neat holes on one side of the temple and just a bit of blood dripping from the table to the floor.

"It takes time to die. We cannot find it yet, but we can manipulate its effects on the host; we can even tabulate its death. Once we registered activity for 103 hours after the host was biologically dead. It varies widely. We don't know why. We have figured out how to kill it too, which proves its materiality, and, believe me, that is something you cannot even imagine!"

It is Dubey explaining. He sounds gleeful. The Professor and Elizabeth are doing things with what appears to me to be a huge helmet, of the sort that astronauts are supposed to wear. Like everything else in this room, it has tubes and wires, some attached to screens, some to the almost man-size glass cubicle that I have always wondered about. The helmet is heavy and probably fragile. Both the Professor and Elizabeth handle it with care. They carry it to the dead man, but then Elizabeth shudders and asks Dubey to help her. As soon as she is relieved, she walks back to the screens again. With Mr. Watch's and Dubey's help, Professor Gray-Eyes inserts the dead man's head into the helmet. Then they tighten straps, so tightly that if the man had been alive, he would have surely suffocated.

Now it is the professor explaining again, and his words mostly do not carry to me. His assistants are doing something at the panels to which some of the wires and tubes from the helmet go out. It takes a minute or two. "Watch now," the Professor says, loudly enough for the words to carry to me. He directs Harris's attention to the screens again, the ones with the moving lines and dots. Even as I look, the lines start getting more accentuated, the dots moving all over the screens. If it was a heart graph, I suppose it would resemble an attack. This continues for a few moments. The graphs and lines get more and more frantic and then, suddenly, they start flattening, calming down. That is when the Professor points at the glass cubicle. All the men turn towards it. At first I see nothing, then there is something like a glow in it. Rather dots of light, shades of light in phases. Something starts forming. At first, I think they have switched on the holograph machine, but no, this is lighter, more discreet. An outline forms: that of a man. Its features become clearer. It strikes me that the thing in that glass cabinet has the dimensions of the dead man on the table, but no, it is just my imagination: it has a vague humanoid appearance. Then suddenly it disappears. All the men turn to look at the screens. The lines are dead now.

"There is no reason for it to assume that shape," Dubey speaks excitedly, "But it always does before it dies. A kind of projection, because we are yet to find any unusual biological or chemical residue. Often it is just a glow, a small haze, something like bioluminescence. But sometimes it very visibly takes the shape of its host. In a couple of cases, even the face was recognizable. Strangely, it is not just the shape of a human body, as it was this time; in some cases, it appeared to mimic even the clothes worn by the host. This time it went quickly; once it had lingered for seven hours, four minutes, and twenty seconds."

It is then that I notice it: a dull red spot not two feet from me, slightly behind me in the air vent. At first, I think it is my eyes playing tricks, transferring a dot from the screens below into the space behind me. I blink. The spot stays where it is. Is it an optical illusion?

I reach towards the dull red dot. No, it is not an illusion. It is attached to a small gadget that, I am certain, had never been there before. I touch the gadget, as it is too dark in here to see it clearly.

I feel around it. It takes me two minutes, but I am certain what it is. It is a camera.

I am being filmed.

~

The night was difficult for Jens Erik. He had never slept on the waters. But he finally fell asleep around two in the morning, and when he woke up at five, he felt curiously refreshed. The queasy feeling in his stomach had disappeared too. What he had found most difficult was going about without his cap, for the wind and the motion of the boat were sometimes enough to blow it off his head, and finally he had put it away for good.

A bit later, as he helped himself to a second chunk of bread, put two slices of cheese on it, and smeared it with marmalade, Mehmet looked at him, from over his cup of strong Turkish coffee, and said, "How come you have not thrown up yet, Jens Erik?"

Jens Erik held up the bread, poised to bite off a sizeable chunk, and answered: "I am a Dane."

Mehmet laughed. "Yes," he said, "We Turks and Danes are born with sea legs. But you should have seen this landlocked Kurd the first time he came with me…"

"It was stormy," Aslan protested.

"Shut up! It was just you, Kurdish landlubber!"

Jens Erik wonders what Pernille would have said to these two men.

~

The thing forming in the glass panel shakes Harris. It was more of a shock than Michael taking out a .38—Harris made a note that it was pulled out from an area around his left shoe—and shooting that poor bastard on the table. Harris expects something like that from people like Michael, just as he expects syringes and screens from people like the Professor. But that hologram-like being—undoubtedly a replica of the dead man—that formed for a few seconds in the glass cubicle and then dissipated, that was unexpected. What was worse was that, in the moments when the apparition was at its clearest, there was a glow around it, a freshness and beauty that reminded Harris of the woman in the mysterious long dress that he has seen on some occasions.

Michael is explaining now.

"You see how it works, Harris," he says, as Kurt walks in with two men, who start putting the dead body in a plastic sheet with a zipper. "We can do almost everything: we can influence it when the body is living, kill it when the host is dead. The Professor is still unhappy, because he has not managed to really locate it in the brain. He says he still has to figure out things, like why it assumes the shape of the dead host for at least a few seconds before it too dies, but who cares about such matters. Not me, not my syndicate. What we care about is almost here: the professor assures me that in two years, maybe three, he will have devices that will enable us to influence it, and hence the host, from a distance. No more tubes and syringes. We will be able to do it from a distance, or with a pill. Do you know what it means? We can make individuals behave rationally or emotionally, we can determine their reactions, get them to kill someone or buy something. In short, we can control them. That is what my syndicate is interested in. And that is another reason why we want you with us."

"I still do not see why you want me with you, Michael," Harris replies, "I mean you say it is all mostly ready, so why bring me into it? What can I do that you cannot manage on your own? You and your powerful syndicate."

Michael looks at Harris for a second and then gives his slight smile. "Let us take a walk on the deck, my friend," he says, "I will explain, and we need some fresh air."

When they put on their heavy outdoor jackets and climb the stairs to the top deck, where the wind is blowing hard enough to knock a child into the water, it is well past noon. Above them, there rises one of the helicopter decks. The other one is at the other end and has the helicopter that brought Harris to the rig still parked on it. Below, the sea is roiling. "Lunch," Michael says, "will be served at one-thirty. Routines help on a rig," he adds. "Even on active rigs, the men never stay for more than four or five months at a stretch," he explains. "Here we stay for six months. Mr. Hiroyuki and Kurt you have met. This is their semester, as I guess you will say in your university. Then there is another team. I remain common, of course, and the scientists, who come and go ..."

"What about the woman?" Harris asks.

"What woman?"

"That pretty one who cooks for you. Kurt's girlfriend."

"Do you want her? It can be arranged."

Harris shakes his head.

Michael looks down into the sea. It is a clear day. Harris can see up to the horizon, where the gray-blue of the water fades into the blue of the sky. He notices what looks like the remains of another rig almost at the horizon but appearing much closer in the thin cold air. There are seagulls; they seem to have colonized the unused sections of this rig. They are mostly flying below the top deck, where Harris and Michael stand, attracted by the boat docked at the foot of this rig; Hiroyuki's men are unloading crates from it. They have a small crane too, in that section, but it is not being used right now. The seagulls are creating a ruckus. It is strange to see seagulls from above.

Michael shrugs.

"Forget Michelle. Forget women. Not worth the trouble. Let's talk about you," he says. "Let me tell you what you can do for us. You and your syndicate."

"My syndicate?"

"Someone like you never works alone, my friend."

"It is not often that I get to know of someone like you, Harris," Michael proceeds. "You see, Command Alpha and all that, well, it is not ordinary, but there are some of us out there, some still working for governments, some as mercenaries, some as security guards, some as whatever: you, I thought, were actually an academic. You had covered your tracks about your other work very well."

"To be honest, Michael, it does not exist."

Michael laughs. "Yes, it doesn't, except in one record. And not many people can access it. But, as we said in the force, they..."

"... always know," Harris says, completing the phrase.

Michael laughs again. It is more like a rasp. "Yes, they always know, but they seldom care. Why is that so? I used to think about it. Was it because they know so much that they cannot choose? Maybe that was the reason ten, fifteen years ago, when you were active. But now, my friend, the reason has changed."

Michael waits for Harris to say something. But Harris just stares down from the deck, at the water and boat below. Mr. Hiroyuki's men have finished their work. They are clambering out of the boat; two of them still talking to one of the people in the boat, a large man. Harris, unconsciously, counts the men in the boat. It is just his old training. There are four. One is at the motor. One stands just behind the man talking. He is tall and thin, and wears a khaki safari hat, probably strapped under his chin. Then there is a smaller man further back, wearing a hoodie, obviously keeping an eye on everything. The lookout. They are all too far down for Harris to make out their faces, even their bodies are stick figures, further foreshortened from the top.

Michael continues: "Now the reason is that they cannot do anything without someone like us winding them up. They are wind-up toys, all these governmental bodies, secret agencies, Alphas and Betas, all those fancy acronyms. We do the winding up..."

"We?"

"My syndicate. Your syndicate."

"You keep mentioning my syndicate, Michael. What do you know about it?"

"Harris, let us be honest with each other: you would not be who you are, there would not be a file like that on you, and nothing but a file like that on you, you would not have spent months tracking the Aarhus seminar matter, you would not even have come to Yuzhno if you did not have a syndicate behind you. And that is why we decided to bring you in."

The two men below return to the deck. One of them tosses the mooring rope back at the men in the boat. The motor starts. The lookout at the back of the boat is the only person who does not move. He retains his posture, deceptively relaxed, watchful. Harris finds the posture of the lookout strangely familiar.

"You see, Harris, we are on the verge of a breakthrough that will change the world. They talk of the wired brain and what not. But this is bigger than that: we are tinkering with the wires already in place. We can cut the human mind in two. We can make the subject totally rational or entirely emotional. We can manipulate them to hallucinate, and kill others or commit suicide. We have tried it. We even tried it on an agent one of those toy agencies put on our tail. We had to abduct him because, as you see, we can still not do all this from a distance or with a pill. It will come, the Professor says, three years, maximum. There are ways. But we are not there yet. We had to abduct the guy, and we sent him back: he did exactly what we wanted him to do."

Harris stands upright and shifts his attention back to Michael. "What did he do?"

Michael gives his rasp of a laugh. He is obviously enjoying this. It is probably not that often he gets to talk about all this, Harris thinks, and not to a person whom he obviously considers a peer.

"Oh, nothing much," Michael explains, "He sort of saw things, shot a pedestrian or two, and killed himself. Religious mania, his toy organization finally decided. They had to reassure themselves. I will show you his file someday."

"But why me, Michael?" Harris asks, as he bends again to lean on the railings of the deck. The boat is pulling away now. Mr. Hiroyuki's men are no longer on the deck below.

"Because of the future, Harris," Michael replies. "Because we are the fittest, you, me, our people, and it is time the fittest ran this world. We have out-competed the rest in our fields, but we are hobbled by rules, regulations, constitutions, laws: all the weaponized mediocrity of the masses. This thing, this new knowledge will allow us to manipulate the masses, so that we can be what we are. No pretense. No bullshit. We know the possibilities. We know who will buy this evolving technology from us. Politicians who want to get votes; governments that want to control dissent; corporations that want to sell their products, armies that want soldiers to fight like demons … or run away like children! The great generals of finance, the great generals of armies: the fittest, the best of competitors. The possibilities are endless for us now. Finally! And we know that we will need to work with other syndicates to make the most of them. We definitely do not want you lot, whoever you are, for we know you are not one of those toy organizations in the governments, we do not want you lot creating a needless stink. We do not want to fight our like: the fittest. There will be enough to go around—the entire world, my friend—and we are willing to share. We are willing to share the world."

The boat has pulled away some distance now. Two seagulls have followed it away from the rig, and are circling over it, screaming, hoping for scraps. The figures on the boat are smaller. The tall man walks the large man into the cabin. The lookout is still where he was in the boat. He seems to be holding a pair of binoculars. It is too far to be certain, but Harris is convinced that he is looking up at the rig.

Harris smiles. It has started making sense now.

"Let's go down and celebrate with a whiskey," he tells Michael.

~

I return to my room, and then go down into the galley to prepare food, worried. If it was a camera, I have been recorded and, sooner or later, someone will check the recording and come knocking.

Perhaps that time when Professor Gray-Eyes looked up … maybe he had heard me or noticed something? They must have installed the camera after that. I had never expected a nerd like him to be so sharp! The runt! I wouldn't mind dosing his meal with some arsenic!

But if it is not a camera, what could it be—and why was it installed right there? And what do I do? Do I coast along, in the hope that the recording will be missed, or that it was not a camera but, somehow, something else? Or do I try to escape?

Escape where? I laugh at myself. Escape where, gal?

If I could have managed to escape, I would have done so days ago. I know the rig quite well, for I have spent my free time trying to work a way out, and I suppose I could hide away for a day or two in the closed sections. But what use is a day or two? I have seen them go down and shoot that escaped prisoner. It had taken them less than a few hours.

There are not that many people on the men's side of the galley. Only one of them, slicing and cooking. The others are helping unload the boat, apart from the usual two or three lookouts. Can I sneak into the boat? I consider and abandon the option. Even if I could evade Mr. Hiroyuki's men, I would be discovered on the boat, and why should people supplying this place ferry me to safety? I would be turned over, or probably just thrown overboard. That is the kind of people they are. No, there is nothing I can do. I have to wait. If I try to do something, I will just cut the time I have. And time is all you have, gal.

I throw myself into the cooking. Cooking reminds me of home now. It reminds me of you, Maman. It helps keep me sane.

The day passes. The boat unloads and goes away. No one says anything unusual to me, not even when I serve dinner that evening.

If they know, they are keeping it quiet. Or maybe they have been too busy to check the video recordings: the men unloading that boat, Mr. Watch showing the new man around or whatever it was he was doing, Kurt helping out the scientists in the laboratory. I have also seen Mr. Watch and the new man sitting in the small bar we have further down and clinking glasses, a sight that sent a chill through me.

I put extra effort into the dinner. The plan had been to make something bland and European, but earlier on the men had unloaded a crate of things I had ordered, and it included bottles of cassereep sauce. So I think, why not, if it is going to be my last meal on earth, or one of my last, why not make something you love, gal? So I make Guyanese pepperpot, with fresh bread and Basmati rice. It is not the way we make it on St. Martin, but I came to love the Guyanese version in catering school. There is a cauliflower and potato curry for Dubey, who does not eat meat. Strange, that this big-bellied man, who can do such horrible things to other human beings, does not eat meat! The process keeps me engaged and I almost stop thinking of my plight.

There is nothing else to do but wait and act normal. I spend a sleepless night—Kurt stays out until late once again—but I put on a brave front at breakfast and throw myself into cooking for lunch the next day. It is more difficult now. I cannot distract myself with cooking any more. The suspense is killing me, and I consider confessing to Kurt. But, no, that would not work. I make a rather flaccid lasagne—there is a vegetarian version too—and salad for lunch. But when the time comes for food to be served, and the men enter the dining room next to the galley, a storm is forecast. Nothing dangerous, I hear. But it sends Mr. Watch, Kurt and Mr. Hiroyuki rushing off to separate sections of the rig to check on things. This is routine: they check the guard posts, the generators, the helicopter stowage, the control-radio room, and other areas every time there is a storm warning.

The new man, Harris, and the three scientists stay in my part of the galley, the decked restaurant-like section, replete with a small bar with armchairs and a magazine rack at its back. On the other side, across the glass panels separating us, I can see the men drifting into their much larger dining hall. Outside, in the corridor connecting the two sections and leading upstairs and out, there are coffee, soft drink, and chocolate machines. It is also my job to keep them replenished.

Harris is talking to Professor Gray-Eyes. They have opened some chardonnay as they wait for me to serve. The professor rarely drinks, and never at lunch, so they are obviously celebrating something crucial.

Professor raises his glass. "To a new collaboration," he says.

Harris and the Professor clink glasses.

"When did you get into this, Professor?" Harris asks.

"2020-21," replies the Professor, sipping from the glass. He pulls a face—though I know this is an expensive French bottle—and needlessly swirls the wine in his glass. "I was working on the aftereffects of Covid-19. Then Dr. Danielopoulos came to me. He was one of that Aarhus lot. He came to me with all of what he had on their research. Chap was out in the cold. He wanted me to get him a job. I did. In my laboratory, because I found what he told me interesting. You see, it was close to what I was working on: how a virus affects the human mind. With Covid-19, it had started interesting a lot of us. Dr. Danielopoulos said they were not dealing with a virus, nothing so simple, and he was right: I did not believe him then, but I think he was right."

"And then you went to Michael and his people."

"Oh no, Michael's people, as you so quaintly put it, were already there. Michael came a bit later. But his people were there: I was working in one of their institutions. I was leading it."

"I suppose, then they started contacting the others from the Aarhus seminar—leading to the, ah, the accidents."

"Not really. Two of them were already dead. Suicide. Jumped off a building. The other had drowned, I think. Though maybe they tried to get him. I am not sure. I do not bother with these manual matters. But they did botch up Larsen. They tried to get the others too. It did not work. Vijay Nair had disappeared into the thickets of India; he got a reputation of having become some sort of a communist sage. They sent a team to retrieve him, but he was running from the Indian forces, and he evaded them too. He had some aborigines helping him. Then, of course, there were reliable reports that he was killed, by the Indian forces or some mafia, and that was it. Except that lately there are again reports that he has been seen in those parts: his followers believe he is a saint and can manifest himself. It is all bullshit, but given what we know, I think Michael should send a team to investigate again…"

"Wislawa Ostrowski?" Harris asks. I notice that he is hardly sipping from his glass. He might just be touching the wine to his lips and putting the glass back on the table. Strange, I think. Who are these people, I wonder, as I prepare the food. They think I cannot overhear them in the kitchen. Or maybe they do not care. I do not like this conversation. I do not understand what they were talking about, but if Harris and the Professor know the same people, it is clear to me that I cannot count on any help from this new man. He is one of them.

"Oh, they almost got her. If only they had!"

"What happened, professor?"

"They located her in her parents' cottage. Of course, they went with the local police: they always work with local authorities. She did not seem surprised. She asked them to give her five minutes to pack a few things, and they allowed her to go into her bedroom. They found her five minutes later, lying peacefully in bed, stone dead."

"Suicide?"

"That is what they wrote in the report, I think. Drug overdose, or something. But no, there was no trace of anything: she appeared to have just laid down and willed herself to die. I wish I could have examined the body immediately, but it was too late; the local authorities did not want a scandal and they started playing by the rule book. It was weird. So was Takewaki. The Japanese collected him for us. We did it very carefully. We did not want him to do a Wislawa on us, so we stayed out of it. He was being flown, by the highest Jap authorities for consultations, but somehow he knew. He came along. And then—the Jap agents escorting him are not sure, because it appears not one of them saw it happen—he stepped off the curb and into the path of a speeding car. They just saw him being flung away, and they could not even tell which car had hit him. They said it was as if their brains were befogged for a few seconds."

"So you did not get any of them? You had to recreate all of this from scratch, on the basis of what Danielopoulos told you?"

"We got one of them. Julia Yong. They picked her up and brought her here. We had it set up by then. We were experimenting on other subjects. Dr. Yong was a windfall. She was, shall we say, not too cooperative, but there were ways out. There are always ways out." He pauses, as I walk in with the lasagne and salad. The professor is smiling his ghost of a smile, which is more a loosening of facial muscles than any real indentation of the lips. Dubey gives out a high-pitched giggle. They stop talking. Then as I walk away to the kitchen section, I hear Harris say, "What happened to Dr. Yong?"

"She is around. You have already met her. We do not need her anymore, but we have kept her. Nostalgia, you might say. I am too soft-hearted, as Dubey always tells me. By the way, Dubey we need more subjects. Kurt has to get us some more before our next trip."

"I will tell him."

"Dr. Danielopoulos?" This is the new man, Harris. Asking again about common acquaintances. They have too many acquaintances in common. My heart sinks.

"Ah, no. He left us. He caught a deadly infection: the worst a scientist can. What do you call it? Ah, qualms of conscience. It was fatal."

Dubey giggles again. I walk in to replenish their glasses and check the bread basket. Elizabeth is gazing at the Professor with abject admiration. I hate the look; I have seen it on my mother's face too often. Yes, your face, Maman, for months after a new man entered our lives. I am convinced our Elizabeth is in love with this sexless man. She would do anything for him. Who is more dangerous, I wonder: giggling Dubey or this plain, dumpy, gray woman in love with the brilliant professor? As for Harris, he appears unaware of my existence.

The scientists and the new man, Harris, have almost finished lunch when Kurt comes back. I can tell something is wrong. He purses his thin lips when he is upset or angry. He looks exactly like a small boy about to throw a tantrum over a broken toy.

"You have to help me with something," he says to me.

I do not like this. I try to get out of it.

"I am busy serving the guests, Kurt," I reply, lightly, in the girly way men prefer.

"No time," he says, grasping me roughly by the arm. "It cannot wait."

"Kurt!" I exclaim, and shrug myself free of his hold. I turn my back on him. The girly gambit did not work. "Is there anything you want, gentlemen?" I ask the diners. Professor Gray-Eyes makes no response. I am not sure he knows I exist. Elizabeth and Dubey shake their heads. But I had asked the question for the new man. I had hoped against hope that he would side with me, help me stay in this room, find a chore to detain me. But he seems preoccupied, as if he is thinking about something else. I am not sure he even hears me.

So when Kurt says, "Come now," and pulls me by the arm, I go with him. I do not like his tone. But what else can I do?

As I leave the galley, I see Mr. Hiroyuki running into the other section. He is asking the men there if they have seen so-and-so. But Kurt ignores him, he marches me past the galley, through the corridors. He is aiming for the deck portion outside, and I point out that we are not wearing our outdoor jackets. "I should put on my lead-tip shoes, Kurt," I say, turning girly again, "Or, you know, I can slip on the deck. I will just run up and get them from our room." He replies that we are not staying out. He marches me across the open section, full of screwed-down debris from the past, and to the sealed section on the other side, the laboratory. I am Kurt's property here; no one pays us any attention. The guard opens the bank-vault door for us.

I am terrified. Yes, I am terrified, Maman. Now that I am being taken there, I do not want to enter this place. It is like the mouth of hell yawning for me.

"Kurt," I exclaim, as sweetly as I can manage it. "You know I am not allowed to enter this section, love."

"Now you are, Honung Dear," he replies, and laughs.

Then he almost shoves me inside, and the impassive guard closes the heavy vault-door behind us.

~

Aslan and Jens Erik had spent a week looking up the currents in the North Sea during certain times of the year. The dead man would have been carried by the currents, and there were only that many currents and they only flowed along certain routes during a season. It had been Jens Erik's idea. He had done most of the research too, not trusting a second-generation immigrant to know much about nature in or around Denmark.

They had managed to narrow it down to two possible regions. About a tenth of the North Sea. But even that was the size of Denmark. And by their third day, when they had located the steel legs of only one abandoned rig, Jens Erik suspected that it was too much to cover.

It did not help that Mehmet spent the better part of the morning trailing a school of salmon. He let Aslan take care of the yacht while he fished. Mehmet was a dedicated angler.

"Don't you need a license for this?" Jens Erik asked Aslan, as Mehmet cast, and reeled out and reeled in, and cast again, and swore expressively in three languages.

"Not my jurisdiction," Aslan replied with a shrug.

Jens Erik would have said more, but just then Mehmet let out a whoop. He had hooked one. "What a beauty, what a fucking beauty," he was shouting. "Shit, shit, take it slowly boy, take it slowly!"

~

Harris has been listening for it. The prophesied storm is convenient. Perhaps, after all, it will work out. He has pilfered a kitchen knife and dropped it into his left boot. He has to be careful when he moves, a kitchen knife, unlike in films, is not something you drop into your boot, but he might need a weapon. If he is right, it explains everything—including his brilliant career as a hired assassin. Though how…? It makes sense, all of it, all of this wild goose chase. He is so intent on catching the signal—what would it be?—that he does not pay attention to the small altercation between that boy—he thinks of him as a boy, though the man is probably in his forties—and the beautiful Caribbean girl who cooks for them.

She is the only one who does not fit. He feels sorry for her. But he has felt sorry for many in the past. Fathers, mothers, friends, nieces, nephews, sisters, bystanders. Collateral damage. People in the wrong place at the wrong time. The world is full of collateral damage. It was one of the things that made him seek the Big Death—not the damage, for he had become used to it, but the suspicion that it was collateral to… to nothing, to emptiness. Collateral to collateral. There was nothing but collateral. Collateral after collateral, nothing direct, nothing primary. No lineal.

The boy walks away with the girl. Harris ignores them. The boy does not matter. He is watching out for something else; he has to stay alert for Michael and Mr. Hiroyuki. They matter, not that boy. Not these scientists. No, not even that beautiful girl who has just left them.

And then he sees Mr. Hiroyuki rush into the men's section of the galley. It is clear that the man is perturbed.

"Excuse me," Harris says to the scientists. "It has been a long day. I need to lie down for a bit."

He slips off his jacket, hanging from a peg. He moves towards the door, slowly, so that the knife in his boot does not cut him, so that he can hear Mr. Hiroyuki as he passes. Mr. Hiroyuki is asking about a man, maybe two of his men. There are two men missing from the guard posts.

Harris suppresses a smile, drops his jacket, bends down to retrieve it and slips the knife into a pocket. Then slowly, like a man exhausted and sleepy, he walks down the corridor and ascends the stairs to his floor.

In his room, he closes the door. He cannot lock it. His door does not have a lock. But he would not have locked it in any case. Then he puts on his jacket. He arranges the knife in a pocket, and keeps his hand there, around the hilt of the knife. He puts on his outdoor shoes: they are heavy boots. He sits down in a corner. He does not need to put on the jacket and boots. The heating is on. That is not the reason why he puts them on.

The reason, he knows, will reach him soon. If he is right. He listens.

~

Kurt is livid. Strangely, he reminds me of Maman's boyfriend when he gets mad at us—or her. I know the danger I am in, but I cannot help laughing. There is something about Kurt in anger that reminds me of a spoiled child, incensed at the world not obeying him for a change. There is something hilarious about my white prince looking like Maman's boyfriend!

"Why," he shouts at me, his face suffused with blood, pink, "Why did you have to pry and crawl…?" And then, because he cannot help himself, he adds in a caustic note, or what is caustic in his mind, though it sounds like a whining child to me: "Miss Prometheus!"

I try to make light of it: "O come on, Kurt," I reply, laughing, "Anyone would be curious! You made such a bloody mystery of this section."

"You fool, you do not know what you have gotten into!" he screams at me. His eyes turn round like coins, as they do when Mr. Watch or Mr. Hiroyuki narrate some story, always a bit beyond my hearing, to him. The small boy being let into the secrets, real or concocted, of adults! That is what sets me off. I cannot contain my growing merriment—perhaps it is also a kind of nervous reaction, the release of tension, the tension of weeks, for now I know I have come to a crossing—and I burst out laughing. I laugh, almost hysterically.

At first, Kurt looks surprised. Then, suddenly, he grabs me by the throat, both hands around my throat, and starts choking me. Kurt is a big man, but I am not exactly a shrinking violet, and I could knee him between the legs and escape. Moreover, though Kurt does not know, choking someone with your fingers is not particularly effective. But I let him do it, shake me up a bit, get rid of his childish anger, and then suddenly I let myself go limp. He is surprised, and cannot hold me up with his hands. He lets go of me and I collapse at his feet. I lie there, pretending to be out cold. I think that is safest. He might relent. Gather me up. After all, he has brought me here after watching the camera recording; he has not turned me over to the others. He has also fucked me religiously for months now. Surely he will be moved by my plight in his manly hands?

But that is not what happens. He stands there for a few seconds, and then pushes me with a foot. A foot! I could have killed him for that! But I lie inert, knocked out cold by the virile pressure of his powerful fingers, obviously. How can he doubt that? That's what happens to us weak little women when big powerful men attack us, no?

Surely he will gather me up, breathe or kiss some life into me?

No way. The dickhead! He grabs me by the arms and starts dragging me towards the cages. Two of them are open. I know what he is up to now. Is that what he did to all the other women he brought here? Is the woman in the only cage that is still locked someone he had fucked like he fucked me, called Saccharum Officinarum or Celestial Coelestis? My anger builds up, but I am not a fool. I moan and let him drag me across the room. I know he will have to pause at the doors of one of the open cages, as they are two low for him to enter without first stepping in and then pulling me through. I think, if he goes in first, I will slam the door on him and lock it. That would give me a few minutes, maybe hours, for the laboratory is sound proof. He could shout all he wanted; they will never hear him unless someone entered the hall!

But Kurt does not drag me in. He lets go of my inert body at the entrance of the cage, then he goes around me, and starts pushing me in with a foot. Well, I say to myself, too bad, Boy. I will have to kick you in the balls now.

And that is what I do.

I know I have to be fast and decisive, for I do not want him to come after me with that precious Boker Scout pocketknife that he always carries around. I let one of my legs bend under the impetus of his push and then lash out between his legs. It catches him unprepared and squarely in the middle. He gives a cry and goes down clutching his manhood, and I roll away. He is on the ground on his knees, one arm supporting himself and one hand soothing his appendage. I know I cannot let him get up. I grab a tabletop or instrument stand on one side, lift myself up, and swing at him with both feet. The kick lands squarely on his back. I have strong legs, but that is not what knocks him out cold. My double-legged kick throws him forward against the metal walls, face first. He gives a grunt and collapses. There is a bruise on his forehead, blood is trickling down his nose.

Is he dead?

I suppose I should have checked like a good girl, Maman. But then, I could have died like most good girls. I am more interested in not dying myself.

So I get down on my buttocks and, using both legs, shove and push his body into that cage he was going to put me into. He groans as I shove him through. So he isn't dead. I close and latch the door, fetch the key from the peg where they hang in a bunch, and lock the cage. Goodbye, Saccharum Officinarum, I mutter.

But what do I do now? I could not just walk out of the laboratory. The guard would check. And if I stayed here, I would be just postponing the inevitable. I look around the hall. There is no other exit. Could I climb up and break into the air vents? They are reinforced and look solid to me in this hall. I doubt I could break or unscrew them.

Then Kurt groans again, and I look back at the cages. One of them is still open. That is the one from which that man had escaped, the one they had shot and killed in the lower levels. Have they sealed the hole he had made, or whatever it was he had wriggled through? I crawl in and look. It is dark, but the refracted light from the garishly lit laboratory enables vision. The hole is in the floor of the cage. It has been closed with a heavy sheet of metal, just pushed on top of it. I push it away. The hole drops into the dark below. I do not know what it holds. But it leads to the water, and there should be lifeboats at the lowest levels. In any case, the water, though too cold to swim in for more than a few minutes, is still an escape route. There is no other escape route for me. I bend down and look into the hole and see only a faint light on one side. More like a suffused glow than a light. It is probably the daylight. I know that whatever the hole contains, men have gone down it to the lower levels, and returned. True, they had protective clothing on. That reminds me.

I clamber out of the cage. There are laboratory suits hanging in one section of the hall. Masks, gloves. They offer some protection. They are also warmer than my light woolen jacket. I pull off my light jacket and I put on the smallest lab coat hanging there. It is only a bit loose. Then I cram myself into the biggest one I can find. I ignore the masks but stuff a pair of gloves into a pocket. I am as isolated as I can be.

Kurt is moaning in the cage now. He will soon be shouting.

I think of the other cage, the one with the woman. I unlock it. I call to the woman to come out. There is no response. It is unlikely she would come out of her own; I am sure she has always been dragged out. And I am wearing laboratory clothes. She would be frightened of me. I also do not have time to waste. I toss my light woolen jacket into her cage, as a goodwill gesture perhaps. Escape, I say to her, escape through the hole in the other cage. Then I clamber into the other cage.

Kurt is cursing now.

As I drop through the hole, he starts shouting.

~

The fourth day, Jens Erik, despite himself, pointed out the school of salmon crossing the stern of the yacht. Mehmet would not have seen them otherwise; he had been taking an afternoon nap in the hold. But Jens Erik could not help himself. The salmon they had caught and cooked on Mehmet's state of the art grill had been arguably the best Jens Erik had eaten, and he had grown up on salmon and pork!

But that was another three hours lost. Though this time Jens Erik did not notice it pass, and he was there beside Mehmet, helping him reel in another. The yacht had a monstrous freezer. They prepared the salmon and froze it down. The offal they threw into the water, like yesterday. Jens Erik was hoping to see sharks devour them, but the intestines and scales just floated for a while and then sank into the clear water.

They cooked what has left of yesterday's salmon that evening, as the sun settled into the sea, turning it a flaming orange, and Jens Erik wondered why he had never done anything like this before and how he had thought, just some days ago, that Aslan and Mehmet looked alike, for they were actually so different from each other.

~

The door to his room opens slowly. Harris stays where he is, hand gripping the kitchen knife in his pocket.

Then the door stops opening.

Harris knows the voice.

"Time to go," it says.

"How the fuck did you find me?" Harris says.

"It is something new, Carbon," Mermaid says, stepping through the door and closing it. "It is called a nanotracer. You plant it in the body of the target with a syringe." Mermaid is dressed in a diving suit. But the suit is dry. He has been out of the water for some time.

"On the night you drugged me. I was the fucking bait." Harris remarks, not getting up yet.

"Yes. No time to explain. You have work to do, people to meet." Mermaid says, handing Harris a M9 Beretta with a silencer and two extra clips, from a bag on his shoulder. He is holding a more recent and deadly looking automatic in his other hand. "Your favourite, if I remember correctly."

Harris gets up and takes the handgun.

"When this is over, Sir," he says in a voice from Command Alpha, "You will have to permit me to slug you one."

Mermaid grunts.

"Orders?" Harris asks.

"You have done enough," Mermaid says, "Kathy is setting the explosives down below. This fucking research has to be stopped, and the bloody authorities cannot do it. We have about thirty minutes. In a few minutes, the boat will become visible again. Sam is holding a gun on the skipper. He is keeping the boat just below the horizon right now. I need to neutralize the key figures before that. The plan is for Kathy to set off some explosives when Sam reaches us, enabling us, perhaps, to reach the boat and get away. But you can stay out of the gory bits. Just point out the key figures to me."

"In for a penny, in for a pound. Anyway, you will need a hand. They have discovered that two of their men are missing."

"Damn!"

Then Mermaid adds, "You will be out on a limb. I am not working for any governmental organization, Carbon. We are just a group of individuals. There is nothing behind us."

"Why?"

"Because the syndicates are everywhere. In every organization, every governmental body. CIA, Mossad, EU, Pentagon, Parliament, whatever. You involve anything organized, and they get wind of it. I will tell you more about what they did to that agent whose redacted file I had sent you..."

"I think I heard a bit about that."

"So, they even boast about it! That is what they have become. They run the show, and they can only be fought in secret. Person to person. All official organizations are tainted. That is why we had to set you up in this elaborate manner..."

"...a mercenary? Dammit, a paid assassin? The greatest in history?"

"That was the icing on the cake. They would not have grabbed you without that. And we could not have traced you to this place. But, no time, Carbon, just point out the kingpins..."

"These people are deadlier than that, Mermaid. You will need a backup. And there are a couple of ladies I want to help out."

"No heroics, Carbon."

"Never. I like living too much."

~

It is darker down here than I had imagined. There are things lying about. There are cables and wires dangling. I am certain the wires do not carry any electricity from the generators up there, but I still avoid them. Some metal sheets in the walls have warped, and they can slash me. I explore this section, trying to find a way to descend further. I am looking for the staircase signs. I find one, but the door has been welded shut. I move on, as I do not have the strength or the tools to open it.

There are rooms that might have been offices: some still have posters and papers, faded and torn, tagged to walls and bulletin boards. I accidentally kick something on the floor and it rolls away. I pick it up. It is a broken radio. One room still has chairs and tables, all screwed into the floor, like almost all the equipment on this rig. There are mattresses and sheets in one corridor. There is something ghostly about such detritus; the space feels haunted. I shiver from something more than the growing cold and hurry away.

There is a door with illegible signs on it. I turn the handle and, to my surprise, it opens. I half-enter a large room that must have an opening somewhere further on, because there are seagulls nesting in it. The floor is layered with birdlime and balls of feather. There is an overpowering smell of fish, but it is warmer in here than in the corridors. I look for the opening. It is a small window-like panel, at the far end, that has broken away. But it is too small for me to squeeze through, and in any case I cannot drop out from here: I would smash on to the rods and decks further down. The seagulls have turned their heads as one and are watching me. A seagull makes an aggressive move towards me. It is their territory. I back away, hurriedly closing the door behind me.

A dead end. I cannot go farther on this side, so I turn around and explore a different corridor. Then I find it: another staircase sign and this time a door that has been chained shut. I was looking for something like it, because I knew that they would keep a door or two accessible. There is only a metal chain, with an ancient, rusted lock, holding the door shut. I look for something to break the lock with. I find a piece of wood, the remains of some furniture, but it splinters after two blows. I need something heavy and metallic. It takes me some time, but I finally find an iron rod. I lever it into the lock and strain. It bursts open with surprising ease.

I descend to the next section, further down, stepping gingerly on the steel stairs leading to it. There is more light here, refracted from holes in the floor and the sides. It is colder too. I can hear the sea more clearly. I put on my gloves. It smells strongly of chemicals and oil. This level is littered with debris I cannot even identify. It is not furniture and posters or a broken radio, as in the section above. These are metallic leftovers from instruments dismantled and removed, or broken equipment left behind when they abandoned the rig.

I pick my way carefully through all this debris, taking care not to make any noise. I dart and crouch and dart. Some of the floor is slimy with mould and seaweed, which indicates that water gets in here during storms. I am afraid of slipping and knocking myself out. These sneakers are not what I should be wearing. I am afraid of touching some deadly chemical left over from the past. I try to avoid touching the sides.

Am I in what the men called the module deck? I have no idea.

And then the shooting starts upstairs.

~

Were they even looking for abandoned rigs anymore? On the morning of the fifth day, they had found another one. This one was almost intact, better preserved, or less dismantled, than the other one from some days ago.

Mehmet did not want to take his precious baby too close to the rusting metal hulk. Aslan and Jens Erik had taken the lifeboat out to the monster, a giant with its legs in the sea. It was covered with bird shit, its metal legs rusted and carbuncled. There were jellyfish in the water around it, all kinds. Birds rose from its collapsing upper levels. Jens Erik knew them: seagulls, cormorants. There were at least two smaller skuas, their distinctive white marking showing as they fly up. There was an entire colony of fulmars on one side.

This was a world Jens Erik knew: the world of birds. Danish birds. Or birds from the Danish coastline and outlying islands. He had gone birdwatching almost all his life. He almost forgot the purpose of the trip, and started pointing them out to Aslan. Despite himself, he started telling Aslan things about the birds. Some he had been told by his father; some he had told Pernille.

"Look, Aslan, look there, do you know those birds?"

"Seagulls," says Aslan, uninterested. "No, those are not seagulls; those are fulmars. They look alike, but you can tell them apart from the way they fly, and their tube noses. It is weird they are here, because they breed on cliffs. Maybe we are not too far from land?"

"And there, the dark, long-necked one, that is a cormorant. The cormorant has an interesting history, Aslan. Their ancestors can be traced back to the dinosaurs. The Japanese have been using cormorants to fish for one thousand and four hundred years or so. The ancient Egyptians used them for fishing too."

Aslan looked bemused by this sudden garrulity on Jens Erik's part, but he did not look interested. He was more occupied with noting the structure of the rig. They were happily talking at cross-purposes: "Look, Jens Erik, up there, that is where they must have had a helipad. And there, do you think that was a dock for boats?"

Jens Erik has overcome his initial dislike of Aslan—actually, though he would never use such an emotionally vibrant word, he has quite started "liking" Aslan and Mehmet. They allowed you to be who you are, unlike the women in his life and their rice cake-eating partners. Humpf. Despite all that, Jens Erik remained convinced that people should stay where they were born. But Aslan was born in Denmark, he heard Pernille object in his head. "Yes, yes," he said, and uttered it aloud, startling Aslan. He completed his answer to Pernille silently in his head: Yes, but his father, unlike my father, was born elsewhere, and the birds he loved are not to be found here. It is simple as that, Pernille! Love is a growth; it cannot be transplanted.

He liked that sentence: Love is a growth; it cannot be transplanted. He wished he could talk like that in real life and not just in his head. He was happy Pernille was not around to pick holes in his argument.

They rowed the lifeboat around the rig, keeping some distance from it. It was clear no one had been there for decades.

Aslan halloed. It was foolhardy: he had only his service revolver to protect them. But the place looked uninhabited. Aslan halloed again. There was no reply.

"We are coming up," he shouted, in English this time. Some more birds rose into the air.

"I would not trust any of the stuff there," he said to Jens Erik. "Would you?"

"Not unless I was a bird," Jens Erik answered. They turned the lifeboat back towards the yacht, where Mehmet lolled, listening to Turkish songs.

~

Mermaid and Harris slide down the steel stairs. There is no one in the corridor below. The galley section is empty.

"The lab!" says Harris and moves towards the exit. But Mermaid restrains him with a gesture. He points to the floor above. "Deck," he says. They run back up. As they run through the corridor, past the door of his room, a door further up moves slightly. The door opens and two men step out. Harris is leading, and they hesitate on seeing him. That gives Mermaid the second he needs. He shoots both of them with a shot each. He was never one to waste ammunition.

They run to the deck at that level, keeping undercover. Below them, Mr. Hiroyuki is herding the scientists across the open space that had once been occupied by the derrick, and is still cluttered with remains of dismantled metal, their bases welded or screwed into the floor, and even a couple of immense container-like objects. He is moving them towards the safety of the laboratory, whose bank-vault door is being opened by the guard. Harris points to the short figure of the Professor. "Get the man at the door," says Mermaid as they unscrew their silencers—which would make for less accuracy at this distance. Mermaid aims at the Professor. They fire at the same time. Mermaid hits the Professor. Hiroyuki, for a man so heavy, ducks immediately, fires in their direction, and dives behind some drums. Harris misses the man at the door, who wrenches open the door and dives in. He is out of practice, and a handgun is not accurate at such distances.

There is a moment of silence. Dubey is crouching, cowering on the floor, either petrified or unsure if running for cover would be safe. Elizabeth is holding the Professor in her arms. Then she starts screaming. Elizabeth is a large woman, and the professor looks like a child in her arms. Behind them, after a stretch of metal, there is water, gray-green and endless. It is a scene that seems familiar to Harris, but he recalls why only days later. "Assistants?" Mermaid asks Harris. Harris nods, not really understanding the question. Mermaid shoots both Elizabeth and Dubey down. "We have to stop this for good," Mermaid says as explanation. Harris looks away into the gray. He wishes he had Mermaid's certainty. Is that a boat at the horizon?

Then they hear a click behind them. Mermaid tenses, about to swivel around and fire.

"I would not take the chance," a voice says behind them. "There are three of us."

Harris recognizes the voice. It is Michael's. Mermaid looks at Harris without moving. He is waiting for a signal. But to take a chance with Michael behind them would be sheer suicide. To surrender would at least buy them some time, for Michael will not shoot them down without finding out what it was all about. He is a man who knows only syndicates and believes in shadows.

Slowly, Harris puts his handgun on the floor.

~

The shooting up there frightens me. It is muffled down here, but it is clearly gunshots. What is happening up there? Should I go up and check? Are these policemen?

But if these were policemen, there would be sirens, loudspeakers. I have not heard any. I continue groping, as silently as I can, towards the North side, where I think there are lifeboats. I turn a corridor and there is light. I move towards it. But not noisily. I know I have no friend but myself… and stealth. Once in a while, I talk to myself in the voice of my mother. "Shape up, gal," I say. "Shape up. You owe it to yerself."

And the corridors down here are worse. There are things, broken machinery, canisters, drums, shells, weeds, lying about. I am close to the sea. It is damp and chilly here. Despite my two layers of lab overalls, I can feel the cold cutting into me. Then I come out of an entrance and find myself on a trellised floor. It is like the decks above. You can see through the metal networking of the floor. The water is less than twenty feet under me.

But I can also see out, on to the sea on that side. The sea is calm despite the storm warning. There is a mist building up. That is good. But I do not like what I see out there. I see a boat. Still a long way off, but a boat, and heading for the rig. I am certain it is the boat that had docked—this is the side of the docking port—and unloaded the supplies earlier today. It is still way out, but it is coming back. It will reach the rig in fifteen, twenty minutes. Maybe a bit longer.

I cannot escape from this side. I would be spotted by the men on the boat. I plunge back into the dark corridors, running for the other side of the rig, trying not to slip.

~

The next day was no better, and Jens Erik could see that Mehmet was tired of hunting up abandoned rigs. Mehmet thought the two policemen were on a wild goose chase. He was teasing them about it occasionally now, referring to them as the "Discovery Duo" and the "Tracking Two". Clearly, he would have preferred diving or tracking and photographing dolphins with his new Nikon Coolpix P2000a. They even passed two dolphins, but he had to leave them behind.

Instead, the two policemen made him head for another spot, traced on his navigational chart. The abandoned rig they finally located was only pillars of steel. By then it was afternoon. But the sun was gone. There was mist building up on the horizon to the north. Mehmet cut the engine. "Let's have lunch," he said. Then he added, "There has been a storm warning. Maybe we should head back closer to shore, in case they up the grade."

But Jens Erik was not listening to him.

"What's that?" Jens Erik said, cupping a palm to one ear.

The answer came in a few seconds. It was a helicopter. It flew out of the mist on the horizon. It came diagonally towards them and then headed towards what Mehmet knew was Russian waters. "That's a Mil MI-16," Aslan noted, observing it though the binoculars. "Transport," he added.

"What was it doing here?" Jens Erik asked again.

Aslan was looking in the direction from which the helicopter had appeared. It was hazy at that distance.

"I think there is something there," he said. "Can we get a bit closer?"

~

Michael and his two men walk Mermaid and Harris down one of the steel stairways and on to the floor where the dead bodies of the scientists lie in a jumble. Blood has seeped out and started to pool. There is no one else in sight. Then Mr. Hiroyuki steps up from behind the steel canister. Two other men step out from cover on the other side. The vault-like door of that laboratory opens, and another man steps out. He is supporting Kurt, who looks like he has run into a locomotive. His face is all bloody. One eye is swollen shut. He is limping and swearing.

"Where is the girl?" That is the first thing he screams on stepping out. "Where is the fucking bitch?"

But Michael silences him with a gesture. He orders Harris and Mermaid to turn around and face him.

He laughs when he sees Mermaid's face.

"You?" Michael says, "I thought you were incorruptible, Mermaid."

Mermaid does not seem to be able to place Michael. But Harris answers for Mermaid. He wants to buy time, and he can do so only if he has something to sell.

"Not for the price my organization offered him, Michael."

"So what is this about?"

"I suppose," Harris says, "That my people want to buy you out."

"Buy us out? But we were willing to collaborate with you! I told you: there is more than enough for everyone."

"I guess my bosses do not believe in sharing, Michael. We are very competitive."

Michael pauses. Then he shakes his head. He asks Hiroyuki: "Do you believe him?"

Hiroyuki shrugs. He has stayed near the metal canisters.

"I don't believe you, Harris," Michael says, "I don't believe you. Ask me why?"

Then he points at the three scientists and the pool of blood.

"That is why," he says. "If they wanted to take us over, you wouldn't have shot them. You have set the project back by decades."

Then he steps closer to Harris and suddenly back-whips him with the hilt of his automatic. As Harris falls, one of the men steps up and kicks him. Harris curls into a ball. But the man does not kick again.

Michael addresses Mermaid. "Your turn to speak, Commander. Who are the people behind all this?"

"CIA ..."

Michael starts laughing. He shoots Mermaid in the leg, still laughing. Harris makes an attempt to move, but the man standing over Harris pushes the muzzle of his automatic against his temple.

Michael ignores Harris. The shot has brought Mermaid down to one leg. It would have thrown most men to the ground. But Mermaid is still on one knee, the other leg stretched. It is bleeding from the thigh. Michael moves up to Mermaid and pokes his automatic's muzzle into the wound.

"No more games, Commander. It cannot be CIA, Pentagon, M5, KGB, Mossad, anything in any government worth a fuck, or we would have known. So tell me before I shoot again, who is behind you jokers and why?"

Mermaid has his eye on Harris. He is waiting for a signal. Harris knows that soon it might be too late. His gamble to buy time has not paid off. It would be suicide to try and rush Michael and his men, but do they have any choice? He doubts Kathy would come up to check; she has been told to plant the explosives and wait near the docking area for the boat, and, like all of them, she would follow her orders.

Then it happens. Harris sees it from a corner of his eye. The girl creeps out of the open door of the laboratory and runs for the railings. She seems to be hurt, crouching. She runs, stumbles, gets up and runs again, her woollen jacket flying. At this distance, she resembles a bird with a broken wing. Harris can recognize the jacket. She had been wearing it when the boy had dragged her away from their dining table.

Kurt recognizes it too, and with a curse he sets off after the fleeing girl.

The man with the gun against Harris's temple swings up to shoot at the girl, and Harris kicks him in the knee, grabbing his gun. He can see Mermaid grapple with Michael too, who had also been distracted for just that millisecond. But even as Harris fights, he has no hope. He can see Hiroyuki and the two other men approaching them, carefully because there are guns being grappled over, but purposefully. They cannot shoot from where they are, but once they get close, they can easily shoot Mermaid and Harris without any fear of missing. It is only a matter of seconds.

But then there are shots from somewhere else. Harris sees one of the men fall. The man tussling with Harris kicks him but loses grip of the automatic in the process. The man dives for cover in one of the entrances on that side. There is another shot even as Harris swings up the automatic. The man dives and scrambles to safety. Harris rolls with the automatic, for now he is prime target for Hiroyuki and the other man. But the covering fire—surely it must be Kathy?—saves him. He manages to drop in behind some leftover machinery, the base of a crane or something like that.

Only Michael and Mermaid are left struggling on the open deck. Both sides cannot shoot at them, as they are in a tangle. Then there is a shot. One of the two has pulled the trigger of the gun they were fighting for. The two figures cease struggling. Both do not move. Has the bullet passed through both, killed both? It could easily happen with these automatics. They lie in a heap, sharing the essential anonymity of death. But of course, even if one of them was alive, he would not get up—let alone reveal that he was alive. To do so would mean getting shot down by the other side. He would be a sitting duck.

Harris scans the deck for Kurt and the girl. They are nowhere to be seen. He last saw them running towards the other end of the rig. The girl was running as far away from them as she could get.

After all the shouting and shooting, the silence is immense. Even the breaking waves seem to have been silenced. Only the seagulls are wheeling everywhere and cawing, expressing their indignation at all the noise.

~

I reach the other side. I am almost there. I can see the light at the end of this corridor. The shooting upstairs has intensified. But I am not paying it any attention. I am heading for the light.

Then there is a moment of silence, or maybe it just happens in my head, because the next moment the firing resumes. I am tired and despairing. There is no end to this. I collapse in a corner, squat on my knees, rock myself. I chant a song from my childhood. A nursery rhyme that we had learnt in school because it mentioned St. Martin. It was not our St. Martin, but we felt it was. I rocked and sang to myself:

Oranges and lemons
Say the bells of St. Clement's.
You owe me three farthings
Say the bells of St. Martin's.

When will you pay me?
Say the bells at Old Bailey.
When I grow rich,
Say the bells at Shoreditch.

When will that be?
Say the bells of Stepney.
I do not know,
Says the great bell at Bow.

Here comes a candle to light you to bed,
And here comes a chopper to chop off your head!

Chip chop chip chop, the last man is dead.
Chip chop chip chop, the last man is dead.
Chip chop chip chop, the last man is dead.

I do not know how long I stay like that, rocking and shivering and muttering my song over and over again. I am jolted back by a series of bangs. Even I can tell these are not shots. They are explosions. They seem to come from one of the levels here, not up there, but down here. Maybe just above me, maybe even this level.

I turn to look behind me in the darkness, and I spot the glow. It is moving towards me. It is a ball of fire.

I run. I run desperately for the light at the end of the corridor, even as I hear, and then feel, the ball of fire gaining on me.

~

Mehmet cursed. He restarted the engine. He mumbled, "you and your fucking rigs," and turned the yacht around to head in the direction from which the helicopter had come.

"I don't think there was anything marked out there in the maps we looked at, was there?" Jens Erik asked Aslan.

"There is definitely something out there," Aslan replied. "It's probably a rig."

"What else would it be?" Mehmet shouted to them. "A fucking UFO? A floating brothel?"

~

Harris feels the blasts. The explosives have gone off. Mermaid had planned this as the distraction that would enable them to escape, but of course it has all gone wrong. It went wrong with the storm warning, and the discovery of the missing guards. The explosions do not shake the rig. It is far too massive for a few explosives to do much more than start a fire. There is a jet of flame that shoots out from one of the hatch-holes farther up. Then nothing.

He hears Kathy yodel. It reminds him of the times they had fought together. That was always her cry when a job was done and they were on their way out.

Except that this time they are not on their way out.

Then an automatic clatters to the floor from behind the canisters shielding Mr. Hiroyuki.

"That's my gun," Harris hears Hiroyuki shout. "I am coming out. Do not shoot me, and perhaps all of us will get out of this alive. Shoot me, and you will have to shoot down every remaining man of mine. Understood. Understood?"

"Deal. No shooting anyone," Harris shouts back.

The bulk of Hiroyuki emerges and moves towards the two entangled combatants on the deck. One of the two men stirs. He gets up, with some effort. It is Mermaid. Both Hiroyuki and Mermaid stand facing each other. Neither is holding a weapon.

"I am a professional," says Hiroyuki. "My men and I only die for money." Then he points at the body of Michael. "Our paymaster is dead."

Hiroyuki continues, loudly. He is making a speech for Mermaid and Harris, and also his men. "You can fight us, for whoever has paid you. But we are still at least four, maybe five. We will get you, or one or two of you. Is it worth it? Is the money you are getting worth it?"

He waits. There is no answer.

"You let my men go. They will leave their weapons here. You let them go to the helicopter up there. I will go last. Then you can do what you want here. I am done with this place. Deal?"

Mermaid nods.

At a signal from Hiroyuki, his men toss down their automatics and leave for the stairs, one by one. They keep to the winding deck staircases, so that they are visible until they reach the helicopter deck.

"Never liked this bloody place," Hiroyuki says, when he finally walks away.

~

I dive into the water just ahead of the ball of fire. I smell my hair burning. My outer overall is on fire too, but it fizzles out in the cold green water. I dive under and hold my breath for as long as I can. I expect the rig to blow up. But nothing happens. The ball of fire shrinks and disappears.

Was it just some gas igniting?

I swim back to the rig. I know I cannot last in this cold water for more than half an hour, if that. I have to get back on the rig. I climb back.

I am shivering. Then I sense the heat from further in. I crawl back. Some of the railings feel warm. I crawl into the corridor. It is strangely warm there. I look up and see the fire through cracks in the metal floor above. But I stay there. Letting the fire warm me. I stay there for five minutes, maybe ten, maybe fifteen. Or is it longer? It is almost as if I fall into a pleasant stupor.

Then I shake myself out of it. "You are not gonna die out of sheer laziness, gal," I tell myself in your voice, Maman, "Not now. Not after all this shit." I crawl out again and start looking for a lifeboat. I cannot find any. I had expected lifeboats on the other side, where they have the docking port. But surely there would be some elsewhere too, I hope against hope.

~

In fifteen minutes, it was clear even to Mehmet that there was a rig out there. It would probably take them an hour to reach. He could have gone faster, but he was in no hurry, just another fucking rig, it could wait.

Then Jens Erik said, "Is that a boat heading away from it?"

"Looks like it," Aslan replied, as he had the binoculars. Then he exclaimed, "There is smoke coming out of the rig."

Jens Erik looked disappointed. "Oh well," he said, "It is probably an active rig then."

Mehmet perked up at that. "So, should we forget them?" he asked. "Let's stop and grill some salmon."

"A bit closer, if you don't mind. We need a better view." Aslan replied. "It looks weird, the way wisps of smoke are coming out of it. That's not my impression of how a rig works. And I think I must have heard gunshots just before that helicopter came out. I wasn't sure, it was too faint, but I think so now."

~

Harris and Mermaid wait until they hear the helicopter lift off and fly away from the rig. It is only then that Kathy comes out from hiding. They do not want to risk being shot down from the air.

The helicopter can still turn around. But there is no time to waste. They will have to risk it.

The rig is not going to blow up, they know that, but the fire will spread, warp some of the metal, collapse the sections perhaps. They need to get down to the docking port, which Sam's boat is approaching now, before the fire makes it inaccessible. That might happen in five minutes or five days. There's no way of knowing.

Mermaid has lost blood. He is doing his best to stay conscious. He cannot walk much.

"What happened to the girl?" Harris demands of no one in particular.

"What girl?" Kathy asks. She is applying a tourniquet to Mermaid.

"The girl who ran out of the laboratory."

"She fell overboard. That man jumped on her near the railings. They struggled and both fell into the water. I could see from up there."

"Damn," says Harris. Then he remembers the other woman, the human guinea pig, Dr. Yong. He runs into the laboratory, but all the cages are open and empty. Harris runs back to the vault-like door. He turns back to look at the laboratory once more. The machines and dials and screens glow and whirr and glare at him. He looks at them from the entrance. There is no one in the garishly lighted hall. The generators are still working. Harris unslings the automatic he had picked up and shoots at the machines until he runs out of bullets. There is a shower of glass and sparks all over the room. He tosses the weapon to the floor and finds Kathy standing next to him.

"That was unnecessary," she tells him with a smile. Their eyes catch for a second—it is the first time he has allowed himself to really look at her—and what washes into his soul, or heart, or brain, or liver, or stomach, or whatever it is, is a wave of joy. She takes out a plastic explosive with a timer. "I kept one for the lab," she says, and hands it to him. She presses a button on it: "This will give us fifteen minutes."

Harris re-enters the hall and puts the explosive next to the wall of computers that had so captivated the three dead scientists.

Then he runs out to join Kathy, who has hoisted Mermaid on to her shoulders and is moving towards the deck stairways leading down to the docking port. Sam is down there in the boat, a gun still pointed at the skipper they have shanghaied. He looks funny holding a gun.

In less than ten minutes, they are in the boat, and on their way out, full throttle. There is always a chance that the rig will explode. It all depends on what chemicals were left behind, and how much oil, from the time when it was active. They know that.

When they put some distance between themselves and the rig, Sam shakes his head,

"It won't be good for the environment if this sleeping beauty explodes," he says.

"None of these sleeping beauties are good for the environment," Harris replies. Then he says to Sam, "After I have slugged Mermaid, I am going to slug you one too, Sam."

"Honest to God, Harris," says Sam, "I did not know either."

"You'd better not die on us," Harris tells Mermaid, who is still conscious.

~

I hear a helicopter. Are they leaving, or are more reinforcements arriving? The fire is still bursting out of windows and doors here and there. How will they put it out?

But I do not have time to think much about such matters. I have run up and down this side of the rig, watching out for any sudden ball of fire, though there is nothing like what had chased me out. I am exhausted. I am bleeding from a dozen cuts and bruises. My hair smells burnt. My lovely hair, my hair that I have always worn natural despite Maman's injunctions to straighten it out. It is weird what extraneous thoughts cross one's mind! But I know I am not thinking clearly: I am exhausted and despairing, ready to lie down and die. I have scrambled up and down the spider deck on this side, looking for lifeboats. There is nothing. There is nothing.

The water is lapping just a few feet under me. It is blue green, frothed with white. The seagulls that had taken to the sky with the shots and blasts are returning to the rig. The men must have things under control up there. How long before Kurt or Mr. Watch come looking for me? Or perhaps the fire, which seems to be in the levels between us, will give me a few more hours.

Of what use the hours, if I cannot find a lifeboat? I cannot swim away from this place. There is nothing within swimming distance, and I would freeze to death in less than half an hour in the water. I grab a railing and sink down exhausted; I rock myself on my haunches again, moaning. This time I do not even have the strength to sing a nursery rhyme. It is over, I tell myself, it is over. I won't die here. No, you won't die here, gal, no, I tell myself. Better to die trying to swim out of this hell. Better to swim, and sink into the deep, stiff and frozen. Yes, I tell myself, getting up, yes, better that death than to die here… Then I see her. The word escapes my lips involuntarily, even as I know that I am wrong: Maman?

She is standing at top of one of the spiral staircases leading up from this level.

Of course, it is not Maman. It is the woman in the cage, I think. She has followed me! But then I see more clearly: this woman is taller, she is beautiful. Ah, her face! I can still remember it: it is the most beautiful face I have ever seen, a face full of the knowledge of suffering and strangely untouched by it. Like one of those Buddhas that they make! She is wearing a long, flowing dress. It is far too thin; she must be freezing, I think. But she shows no sign of discomfort. She raises a hand and beckons; I follow.

I never catch up with the woman. I never even see her walking. She is just there, at the head of the stairway, and then when I climb up, she is somewhere else, at a gap in a corridor, and then when I reach that, she is at another spot, always looking at me, sometimes beckoning. I follow her like that, never getting any closer to her, until she has led me through a maze, perhaps the only maze that is free of fire and melting debris and leaking gases, she has led me to another side of the rig. I would never have reached it on my own. Then I see it, hasped to one of the metal sides of the spider deck, a small lifeboat. There must have been more here when the rig was operational. I can see loose ropes hanging along the metal wall. They must have been removed when they stopped working this rig. All of them, except this small lifeboat. Maybe it was too small and worthless to bother with. Maybe someone forgot. But there it is. Just one.

I look around. The woman is nowhere to be seen.

~

When Mehmet killed the motor of the yacht, they were still about half a kilometer from the rig. They could see smoke from some of the middle levels. It was obvious there was a fire. But it was not an active rig, or it would be humming with activity. It seemed dead.

They were certain that they had heard a faint explosion just a few minutes back.

"Can't we get closer?" Jens Erik asked.

Mehmet shook his head. He did not want to risk taking his yacht closer. They had already radioed the coast guard, though the control room had replied that the rig was not being used. When Aslan pulled his rank, they reluctantly agreed to send a patrol boat out there. But, they had warned, it will take a couple of hours. Maybe more. Don't go in on your own. Don't get too close. At least one abandoned rig has been known to blow up. There is always gas and leftover oil, combustible chemicals.

Mehmet, Aslan, and Jens Erik looked at the smoking rig from a distance, sharing the binoculars between them. There were seagulls flying around it.

"It seems abandoned," Aslam said.

"Why is it smoking then?" Mehmet asked.

The sun started sinking into the sea. The water around them turned dark gray, but the clouds were touched with yellow and orange, and in the West the sea seemed to be on fire. The rig was still emitting wisps of smoke. As they had nothing else to do, they grilled the salmon. It was when they were washing it down with beer that Jens Erik pointed in a direction away from the rig.

"What is that?" he asked.

Aslan was holding the pair of binoculars. He turned them in that direction.

"There," Jens Erik pointed at a speck, three or four kilometers from the rig. "There."

"Jesus!" exclaimed Aslan, "It looks like a woman in a flimsy lifeboat."

EPILOGUE:

VIOLETS

STORIES never end. We just decide to tell other stories. Scientists recently identified stardust that's seven billion years old, tucked away in a meteorite, a massive rock that fell in Australia in 1969. It contains pre-solar grains, four billion years older than our sun. So, when we start telling the story of life on earth, how far back do we go: to the birth of farming 10,000 years ago; to the first Homo sapiens in Africa 300,000 years ago; to the Neanderthals who preceded us, and still linger in our genetic inheritance; to the first animal; to the first eukaryotes; to the first microbe; to the creational dance of amino acids on earth four billion years ago; to the birth of the sun and the planets from the solar nebula 4.6 billion years ago; to the Big Bang 13.8 billion years ago? And beyond that, beyond what we conveniently call "singularity", which is the point where human thoughts and equations stop? Or take this smaller and seemingly easier trail: Your human cells hold up to 25,000 genes. But there are at least twelve million other genes inside you too. They belong to the microbes in your body. Some microbes are useful to us; all, except a hundred or so, are harmless. Now, what story out of those 12 million and 25,000 possible stories do you want to tell me as your individual story?

Aslan Barzani always laughs at the story of Jens Erik, sometimes even to his face, for the two remain friends after the latter retires. They throw a party for him in a restaurant. Then they drive him back to his *parcelhus* in Hjortshoj. The guy is sozzled, of course. He has been saying more than humpf. For a change! He unlocks his front door, and out pops this naked bimbo. They had hired an escort. But drunk or not, Jens Erik brews her and himself a cup of coffee and then escorts her to the bus stop where she can catch a late night—early morning, actually—bus. He is too inebriated to drive, you see. The girl still laughs about it. "He doesn't so much as touch me," she says. He says, "Humpf," and then, after a pause, when he looks at me as if I was fully clothed, he asks: "Don't you want a cup of coffee too?" Then he enters his kitchen to start brewing the coffee.

In Greek mythology, the Chimera, is a flame-breathing monster resembling a lion in the forepart, a goat in the middle, and a dragon or snake behind. She is female, so, one assumes, she can give birth. The word is now used to denote a fantastic idea. The hydrogen hypothesis is a theory arguing that the eukaryotic cell, without which multicellular organisms would be impossible on earth, originated as a chimera between two different prokaryotic cells, in a metabolic symbiosis.

Pernille puts down the newspaper. Jens Erik and Aslan have been in the news. It is seldom that such things happen in Denmark or to Danes. This is not Nigeria, India, Brazil, Russia, America, no, not even the UK. "Danish Policemen on Vacation Unearth Organ Trade. Danish Cops Discover Secret Refugee Route. Foreign Mafia Gang War off Danish Coasts. Abandoned Rig Used for Organ Trade."

Every paper has its own take, but the story is in all of them. She looks at her father, who is sitting there, in her flat, sipping from the mug of tea that she has just brewed and handed him. He hates tea, so, she knows, he is making an effort for her. He has told her his story: how he had not been able to forget the body of that black man. He has made an effort and said "sort," not "nigger." She looks at him in a way that he pretends not to appreciate. Far, she says, So you do care about what happens to strangers. Humpf, replies Jens Erik, his face assuming that obstinate look she knows so well: "I care about what happens in my country."

Homo Sapiens is the only species on earth that produces junk. This is interesting, no? Not excrement, not waste; junk. Our planet fills with junk. We eat junk food. We even junk human beings: Parents, class-friends, ex-partners, Anti-nationals, Jews, Palestinians, Yazidis, Rohingya. It is a never-ending list. Our civilizations can be indexed against it. But, for a species drowning in junk, we think we are perfect. Little surprise that when we decoded our genes, we were expecting it all to be, ah, perfect. Except that it wasn't. Most of our DNAs were superfluous. It seemed that 98 per cent of the DNAs in a human cell are just freeloaders, bums, welfare queens, refugees, anti-nationals, discards, rejects, dole-recipients, aliens, retards, sitting around doing nothing, stuff that should not be there. Being who we are, Homo sapiens, we called them junk genes. Except that they were not; they are not. They have their roles, some immediate, some prospective. They are part of a dance we cannot see, because we can only see ourselves dancing. They are not junk. Nature, it appears, does not create junk. In that, we, *Homo junkiens*, are unnatural.

Mermaid returns to the organization he works for, or to some other. It hardly matters. They exist on the shadowy margins of government and corporation. They are all-powerful and totally ineffectual. Mermaid knows it. That is why he stays with them. To them, he is probably junk. To Harris, he is the Undead. He cannot manage to talk Harris into joining him. There will be other cases; I can use you again, he tells Harris and Kathy. Kathy shrugs. Harris says a clear no. You are free, Mermaid tells Harris, remember Doubinsky's shackles? But Harris is unmoved. Too much collateral damage, mutters Harris, and he thinks of the ravaged woman in the cage, of the woman who was once Dr. Julia Yong; he thinks of Elizabeth howling over the Professor's body. Too much collateral damage. But Mermaid is different. He will not be just one of the Undead. He knows there are more like him, in all kinds of places, in all kinds of positions, people who are not just the Undead. He knows a few of them, a brilliant scientist now in a mad house in England, a general in the shadows of the Pentagon, a philanthropist billionaire in Hong Kong. Others. It is up to them, he feels, to stop a murderous species from coming into further knowledge. For this is a species with the Midas-curse: it turns everything into lifeless gold. Progress for our species, Mermaid believes, is regress for life on earth. Until, unless … unless what? He whispers to himself, not realizing he is using Vijay Nair's words as reported by the murdered journalist, Jyoti Lankeshwar: Unless everyone has an equal share in the good.

Kilometers deep in the oceans, where water embraces the molten lava at earth's core in the darkness of another night and temperatures rise to a hundred times that of a warm summer in Spain, there are rose gardens. They extend across the thermal vents and the volcanic vaults, for as far as the eye can see, if the eye could see down there, these worms with the color of blossoms on them, these rose gardens filled with shrimps and fish and crabs, all blind, all living without light, all able to survive due to microbes that turn chemicals into energy for them. As the world above them, the world of oxygen and light, darkens every year, even as people like Mermaid fight to save it—and who can be certain that theirs is a righteous fight?—these rose gardens wait, teeming with another life, another chance at life.

Kathy and Harris are in a resort on the French Riviera. It is an expensive suite. The sea is visible from the windows. It reflects the morning sun. Kathy and Harris are still in bed. They are naked. Harris has his arms around Kathy. Kathy has her legs around Harris. But she is not squeezing. They are lying there, touched with perspiration, having made love all night. They have spent a week in this artificial paradise, this dream vacation spot, as it is advertised on TV. This will be their last night together. They share too many nightmares to be able to live in a dream. This is all they can manage. And it will suffice. This too, Harris thinks, is life. This moment which is just that: a moment.

If microbes were to be eliminated from the earth, many infectious diseases would disappear. But much of life would disappear too. Grazing animals need microbes to break down the fibres of plants. Insects need them. Fish, worms, shellfish need them. It would be over for most of them within days or weeks. Humans would survive a bit longer. Maybe even for a few years. But without microbes to produce the nitrogen that plants need, the Earth will be shorn of green plants within months. Our flocks of animals would be dead too. Slowly, we would perish. Painfully.

That girl Michelle comes out of the blue, back to Sunset Beach on St. Martin, with a stack of dollars—and not a word about where she got it from! Lips sealed. Doesn't even hear the questions, the little miss! The money is enough to enable her to start her own restaurant. First she rents it. It does well. She is a beautiful woman and a good cook. She turns out to be a clever businesswoman too, smart at making deals, bargaining, advertising. Fun to be with, but tough as nails. Her friends and family appreciate all that about her, despite her insistence on speaking like Jane Austen—yes, little miss does have hoity-toity ways, but she gives you a job when you need it, lends you money when you are short. No, they do not have any complaints about her, though God knows how she made the dough. I mean, wouldn't you wonder too in my place? What they really cannot understand is this: Why did she have to name her lovely restaurant, with a sea view, The Oil Rig? The Oil Rig? For Chrissake!

A hookah-smoking caterpillar sits on top of the most famous of all mushrooms and informs Alice, in Wonderland, that, "One side will make you grow taller, and the other side will make you grow smaller." For Alice, it turns out to be literally true, though, of course, Lewis Carroll might have been inspired by the known hallucinogenic properties of some mushrooms. Mushrooms are closer to animals than to plants. But they are also the visible tip of fungal networks—scientists call it the Wood Wide Web—that connects trees to trees, plants to plants in nature. Honey fungus—or Armillaria—are the biggest living organisms on earth. There is one in the state of Oregon, in the US, which sprawls across ten square kilometers and might be more than 5,000 years old. If one teased out all the mycelium found in a spoonful of soil, and laid them out linearly, it would stretch for kilometers. But not all mycelium need to sprout into mushrooms in order to propagate themselves. Some, like the truffles that cost thousands of pounds per kilo, mix a potent cocktail of microbes into such a pungent scent that animals, including humans, dig them up to eat them. They do not just make us see things; they can also make us do things.

Sometimes, Harris walks out to the pond, picks up a weed and looks at the dots attached to its underside. He has read of the girl those Danish police officers had rescued from the rig and is glad to know the beautiful Caribbean woman—he now knows she was from St. Martin—has survived. What happened to her, he wonders. He thinks of the policemen, and their determined quest—as one newspaper reported—for the killers of an unknown black body that had washed up years ago. That is what saved the girl, he knows. It makes him think of Mermaid, that being who can live in different media and not lose his tongue altogether. Is there hope after all? He shakes his head. No, he tells himself, that is a dangerous thought: it can lead to the atrocities committed by the original and the remarkable. He wraps his windbreaker firmly around himself, this copy he has made of himself, and shakes his head to clear it of the thought. He looks again at the dots on the seaweed. "Hydra," he mutters, and he thinks of Kathy.

We all grew up with the idea of cells containing a lot of haphazard bodies, like mitochondria, in some sort of amorphous goo, the cytoplasm. But now, it is clear that the cytoplasm is far more organized that the amorphous jelly we were told it was. As one scientist puts it, "the nature of this organization is elusive, but it is clear that the cytoplasm "streams" through the cell, and that many biochemical reactions are more carefully defined in space than had been assumed."

Sometimes, when Kathy wraps her legs around a man, or a woman, and squeezes, she thinks of Harris. Sometimes when it all gets too much for her, and she sedates herself with Crobe and hallucinates into a semblance of balance, she sees Harris. He comes to her in her stupor. But they do not even phone each other. They continue to write letters. It is not because they want to be secretive anymore: they are both convinced that nothing is a secret any longer, and everything is secret at the same time. It is just better this way.

We were told that the earth contains isolated bits of life, and we, human beings, are the only beings capable of communicating, and especially communicating across species. This idea was enlarged a bit by allowing space for some complex animals. But trees, shrubs, mushrooms, fungi, microbes? They were all islands stranded in time. It turns out now that many of them are far better at communicating than we are, and that they communicate between species too.

Sometimes when Pernille feels like ticking off her Far for some stubborn or xenophobic remark, she thinks of what Aslan had told her: Your dad could see the woman was shivering and frozen in that lifeboat, which was leaking. She had been bailing out the water with her hands. I called on the woman to grab the rope we had thrown her. But she could not hold it. Her hands were freezing. So, suddenly, there is a splash, and your stupid dad is in the freezing water swimming for the lifeboat…

We were told that we are individuals, we are unique. It turned out that we are teeming with organisms, inside us, on us, outside us, and that they affect us in ways that we are only beginning to figure out. We are not just part of an ecosystem. We are ourselves an ecosystem. Every individual self is a teeming ecosystem which relates to the larger ecosystem in which it thrives, survives, or perishes. The sages had said something like that ages ago. The scientists are saying it too now.

Sometimes when Aslan sits with his children (whose photos he never keeps on his office desk) at breakfast, his oldest is in college now, and the children recount some angry story of racism or prejudice—a word like "perker" in school, refugees allowed to drown in the Mediterranean, another piece of discriminatory legislation—Aslan starts talking about his trip in the North Sea with Jens Erik and how the man had turned out to be different from what Aslan had considered him. Aslan had not been entirely wrong about him, but he had not been right either. He had not understood all of the man he had worked with for years, and slotted away years ago as read. His children look blank; Far is rambling again, but Aslan hopes they will understand. There are many kinds of understanding. Not all is direct, not all visible, not all verbal. Understanding, not knowledge. He notices the sunshine slant in through the kitchen window and fall like a carpet on the floor. Is it too much to hope for?

Textbooks tell us that fungus are somewhere between plants and animals. They grow like plants and subsist on organic material like animals. Their cell walls are made of chitin, which they share with insects. And some, like the slime mold that we see as yellow mats on rotting wood, also move. If you put slime mold in the center of a maze, with food at its entry, it slowly moves and finds the shortest route to the food. It even remembers which turns are blind ends. How does it do so? It is just a large cell with many nuclei. A scientist, who often got lost in his local IKEA store, like most of us, built a maze based on the floor plan of the store. He placed his slime molds in it, and, without signs or even the ability to see, the slime molds found the shortest route to the exit. Japanese researchers used slime molds to replicate the transportation routes of Tokyo. They placed slime molds at a point representing the center of Tokyo and marked the principal neighborhoods with piles of food. Sure enough, the slime molds found the shortest routes to the food-neighborhoods, and the map they traced corresponded to the train network of Tokyo.

In the year 2032, the oil rig still stands. There is a controversy over all these abandoned rigs, and it appears that governments might use public money to dismantle or clean up some of them, as the powerful oil corporations refuse to do so. Until, and if, that day dawns, there stands in the gray-green waters of the North Sea, among other rigs, that particular oil rig from which bullet-holed bodies were recovered some months ago. Ammunition, guns, destroyed research facilities. Rooms which showed evidence of class, despite the fire that left them blackened and charred. Two bodies pulled up from its waters. Maybe more bodies rotting in the sea. Who knows? All this was news for a week or so, and there was much online speculation and some outrage about the source of the mysterious blasts and the fire that petered out after two days. That was a piece of luck, as ownership of the rig disappeared in a maze of shell companies, and no government wanted to bear the financial burden of dousing the fire. The rig stands like a spacecraft in the sea, something both prehistoric and futuristic. For a few months, it even became a kind of tourist attraction. Though forbidden by notices in five languages to board it, rich owners of yachts, always in search of a thrill, sailed around it and picnicked. Sometimes, late in the evenings, when the deceptive light throws shadows, they claimed on Twitter and Facebook to have seen a woman on the spider decks, a woman in a long dress. The photographs they posted showed nothing. They often claimed that the water around the rig smelled of violets, not seaweed or oil. They called it the haunted rig.

Acknowledgements

are due to Claire Chambers, Sharmilla Beezmohun, Seb Doubinsky, Michel Moushabeck, Udayan Mitra, Prerna Gill, David Klein, Jim Hicks, Isabelle Petiot, Samarpita Mukherjee Sharma, Jaya Bhattacharji Rose, Evelyn Johnson, Simon Frost, Rupa Bajwa, Pam Fontes-May, Matt Bialer, Naveen Kishore and Karthika VK. I cannot even begin to list the dozens of books of science, ecology, popular science, history of science, and history that enabled this novel about, ah, well, symbiosis.

About the Author

Born in 1966 and educated in Gaya, Bihar, Tabish Khair is the author of critically-acclaimed books, including the novels, *An Angel in Pyjamas, The Bus Stopped, Filming: A Love Story, The Thing About Thugs, How to Fight Islamist Terror from the Missionary Position, Just Another Jihadi Jane, Night of Happiness,* and the poetry collections, *Where Parallel Lines Meet* and *Man of Glass*. His studies include *The Gothic, Postcolonialism and Otherness* and *The New Xenophobia*. Winner of the All India Poetry Prize, his books have been shortlisted for more than a dozen prizes, including the Man Asian, the DSC Prize, the Hindu Prize, the Sahitya Academy Award, and the Encore. His novels have also been translated into a number of languages across the world. He recently published a poetry pamphlet, *Quarantined Sonnets* (Kitaab, Singapore), on the pandemic, with profits being donated to a migrant worker charity.

After working for the *Times of India*, Patna and Delhi, Khair moved to Denmark in the late 1990s. He did his PhD from Copenhagen University and a DPhil from Aarhus University, where he teaches. Khair continues to be an Indian citizen.